FADE
IN

M. Mabie

Fade In
Copyright © 2014 M. Mabie

Cover Design Copyright © 2014 by Arijana Karcic, Cover It! Designs
Formatting by Stacey Blake, Self Publishing Editing Services
Editing by Mickey Reed, Mickey Reed Editing

ISBN-10: 1496035151
ISBN-13: 978- 1496035158

For everyone throughout my life who told me I should be a writer and for the girl inside me who always thought it, too.

PROLOGUE

"WELL, HE'S COMING HOME. And that's all that matters. I have class tomorrow, but only until two, so I'll just see you there," I say as I half-look where I'm going and half-look backwards to wave at Charlotte. "See you later."

Then I'm flat on my ass on my way to the door of the waiting room. The cute girl who was here and left about fifteen minutes ago is back. Ass stinging a little from the fall, I sit on the hardwood floor where I landed and just watch as she's waving around like a maniac.

"Did you forget something?" I ask, but I can't stop watching her as she frantically looks around. It's a rhetorical question.

"My bag. I think it's… Yep, there it is." And she snatches the gray bag by the body and swings the loopy part over her head.

"Wow. How far did you have to run back here for that? You must have been halfway downtown." I'm still in her wake and totally distracted by her.

She's looking through the orphaned sack is as if someone may have stolen something out of it while it was tucked up against the chair in the patient sitting room. Then she abruptly stops like she's confirmed that everything she owns is still intact and accounted for inside that suitcase-sized bag she's lugging around.

"No. I was just waiting on a cab. I have to be at an interview in, like, twenty minutes and I didn't want to be all sweaty." She laughs at the thought of it, probably because she said it out loud. Following which, the real-life cartoon girl standing above me changes her voice into a deep, faux baritone. "Uh, yeah." She scratches her chest like she must think guys do. "I'm here for the

1

inner-view. Har-har." Then she laughs a little again—at herself—while pretending to fan her underarms for dramatic effect.

Just as suddenly, she's switching back to her normal speaking voice that is years younger than even her pretty face. She whispers almost to herself, looking at the ceiling. "Why am I still talking to you? I have to go. Get up. I have to get another cab." She acts like her knocking me down is somehow *her* biggest inconvenience.

It must have interrupted her act.

After she grabs one of my hands and almost yanks my arm clean off, she rushes past me, not saying another word. Before she gets all the way past me, I realize that, on the other side of her dress where her purse thing is holstered, it is bunched up on the side and back and her ass is showing from behind.

I reach out and miss her. She's fast.

She's out the door and weaving through the foot traffic on the sidewalk towards the street before I can make it to her to help.

Her underwear is funny. They say "The Days of the Week" across her butt. Not any one in particular. No. Not that kind. That's the funny part. These just say "The Days of the Week." I'm staring at her ass the whole time I'm chasing after her to tell her that they're on display.

I'm dodging pedestrians while she is wading through them to get to the road.

I know I'm supposed to be saying something before she goes any farther, communicating that she should stop, but now she's wagging her arms and the one-woman show still has me watching this bizarre creature in what must be her only and natural state—frenzied.

Her cute little blue dress is wrapped up and around her purse like a wind-whipped flag on a pole.

First, I sort of feel bad for her. Lots of bystanders have no doubt seen her ass cheek and her preference for comedic under-garments. Then, I think she just might deserve it, like the Universe gets as big of a trip as I do from watching her spectacle. The Universe knows she can handle it. It's almost too awesome to stop it at all.

But I'm still getting closer, and she sees me rushing through the people. I probably look a bit deranged with the shit-eating grin I'm bringing with me at Frogger speed, arms out like I want brains for lunch.

"What now?" she spits, shaking her head back and forth, raising her arms in wild animation. There are people watching across the street who should be hailing their own cabs, but they're just as caught up in her luminosity as I am.

She unconsciously begs for attention.

"What the fuck?" she fumes.

I know I don't want to draw more attention to the scene, for her sake, because she's doing a good enough job of it on her own, but instead of just coming out with it and saying, "Your dress is up," or something equally as direct, I grab at it and hastily try to fix it myself.

I am so damn stupid.

It's after I get my hands on it and start redirecting the errant fabric that she starts swinging.

"Who do you think you are?!" The untamed tornado slaps at me like she's riding a bike with her arms, blond hair swinging over her shoulders like a shampoo commercial.

I'm laughing and trying to tell her to stop. Covering my face and vital organs, I attempt to shield off this pretty lunatic's assault.

She tells me that she has mace.

My voice comes back. "No. Stop! Your dress. It was stuck. It was up!"

Her roll slows just a little, although she's still swatting at me every second or so. "What?" she huffs. Her cute forehead wrinkles. She looks down. Then up at me. "What did you say?" The hitting never completely abates. Though now it's just her one arm running into my arm in methodical repetition.

"I fixed your dress. It was wrapped up in your bag thing."

Her face shows her brain's recognition of what I've told her. "Shit."

I wave around her and get the attention of a cab driver. She still needs to get downtown, and she's lost her train of thought, realizing she just half-mooned lower Manhattan.

The cab pulls up and she steps over to it. Turning back to me, she confirms, "Is this for me or are you...?"

I shake my spinning head and gesture for her to take the cab. She's so fucking pretty and my instinct says, "Don't let her go." Instead, I settle for, "I'll get the next one."

"You'll get the next one. Okay." She opens the door, a light going off in her head, reminding her of the time, I suppose. She speedily says, "Okay. Yeah. Sorry about beating you up. Thanks." She keeps popping her head back towards me, punctuating her words. "Yeah. Sorry. You saw my butt. Oh my God."

She's a calamity.

Then she's back in the game again, yelling the address and building she's headed to, and just waves at me out the window.

When they pull away, she gives me one last look out the dirty cab's back glass. I see her smile wide and shake her head. She waves one more time and then smacks herself in the forehead.

I can't really think straight. I raise my arm first as a gesture of goodbye before I turn to hail a yellow ride of my own.

I've thought about that girl a lot in the last few years.

I only met her briefly on one occasion, but she left a pockmark in my mind. She was dynamite and she had an indefinitely long fuse that never stopped burning. Those around her never knew when she would blow up, not looking away because she was a mess who was fun to watch.

I hope she's still like that when my mind drifts back to her through the years that pass by.

Maybe I should have shared the cab. Got in with her. Stayed with her.

I don't know.

Who ever really knows that it is the first time the first time you meet? It's only the first time after there's a second time. Up until then, it's just an only. One moment to the next could alter everything.

Every decision pushes you or pulls you where you're going in life.

At times, after running into her, when I felt like I was pushing every day to do better, to get further, make a bigger difference, and like I was getting nowhere and I was just spinning my tires, I'd think of her.

She pulls life along. That girl was making life keep up with her.

And that's too special to forget.

CHAPTER
One

"DATE OF BIRTH?"

"Are you fucking kidding me, Charlotte? You know my date of birth. You just told me happy birthday when I walked in! I know you have to ask, but do you really have to ask? I've been coming here since I was a teenager. It's a little redundant. Don't you think?"

Charlotte is Dr. Meade's receptionist. She's about a hundred years old and wears "slacks," and a lovely parka could be fashioned from all the cat hair hanging from her blouse. She's my favorite brand of old lady. Don't tell anyone I said that.

"I'm sorry. I'm just anxious. I didn't mean to cuss you out for doing your job." That's me. I blow up and then apologize. I have no filter when I'm nervous. "Four, twenty, nineteen eighty-five."

"Thank you, Tatum. Dr. Meade is on schedule. It should only be a minute. Are you doing anything fun for your birthday? Is Kurt taking you anywhere?" She waves her hand in a big way to let me know I can sit.

"I think we are going to dinner with Winnie and Coop. They are picking me up here in a while. Any recommendations? I'm supposed to be deciding where to go. I hate that. Deciding where to eat. It's like—" And mid-sentence, on my way to the seat, that, mind you, I've sat in almost every time I've been here for years, I slam my shin into something. "Son of a bitch!"

I look down and see that I hit it hard enough to shove the coffee table back a foot or so.

"Charlotte, when did this piece of shit get moved here? Ouch."
Oh, yeah. I'm losing my sight. Seems cruel to move furniture on an
almost blind klutz, doesn't it?

I sit, and she comes around her desk to check on me. Moving
the offending table back to its rightful position, she picks up the
magazines that fell off.

"I'm sorry, dear. I put that there the other day. It was by the
window. Then the ficus was dying and—oh dear. I'm so sorry. I
should have said to mind the coffee table." Looking as guilty as the
cat that ate the canary, she stands before me, all apologies. Like it's
her fault I can't navigate around a four-foot-long inanimate object.

"It isn't your fault," I say, rubbing my battered leg. It isn't like
that is the only bruise I have earned myself. Today.

As if on cue, Dr. Meade walks through the door that leads
back to the patient rooms. "Tatum. Happy birthday. Did Charlotte
finally get sick of your potty mouth and kick you?"

Ha. Ha. They look between each other and have a nice chuckle
at my expense. No pity from him.

"No, Dr. Evil. I whacked my leg on that wretched table," I reply in an innocent singsong voice. "Real classy to shift around the
furnishings before your favorite handicapable patient arrives. Bra-
vo."

He comes to me and offers me a hand up. I accept and limp
my lame ass towards the door with him. His hand is warm and big.
He lets go so I can follow him down the hall to the examination
room towards which he is steering us.

He stops just short of exam room four and waves me past him.
He smells like rubbing alcohol and cologne. Strangely, it smells
good to me. It's familiar.

I have tried to figure out how old Dr. Meade is many times.
When I first met him, he seemed way too young to be my doctor. If
I had to guess, I would say late thirties or early forties.

I've always thought he was handsome. His dark hair is beginning to lighten around the edges, and his kind and easy smile has

left charming laugh lines around his eyes and mouth.

Of course, I get to look at him closely during my visits, and I have been his patient for a long time. I can see pretty well up close if I'm looking directly at something. That is the strange thing about my condition.

I have RP, or Retinitis Pigmentosa if you're fancy. Let me break it down for you. It started when I was a teenager. I had poor peripheral vision—not awful, but poor. I was diagnosed then with RP. It didn't seem like that big of a deal. Who needs peripheral vision?

It sort of stayed the same for a long time, and other than that, my vision was pretty good. I made it fine through college, sight in tow. I landed a great job. Bought and renovated a fabulous apartment on the Upper East Side, and everything was smooth sailing.

Then around the time I turned twenty-six, it started getting worse. I always came to see Dr. Meade on a regular basis to monitor the condition. He could tell, too. I suppose he'd be a pretty crappy eye doctor if he hadn't noticed.

Our plan was to just monitor it, and then he would let me know if treatment became available. So far, it's just a good dose of vitamin A. Seriously. That is all the remedy they have.

I can still see pretty well. Although, it is not as good as it was six months ago. Simply, it's like tunnel vision. For a long time, it has just been a fuzzy gray edge around my field of sight.

Then it got darker and the rim got wider. Now it is about thirty percent gone. So it's still better than it could be, but it's a lot like looking through a porthole on a ship, and my night vision is really starting to suck a big one.

"I like your haircut, Tatum. It looks nice for summer. I don't think I have ever seen you wear it this short."

"Thank you. You can't help but flirt, can you?" I wink, and he lets my flirting slide. He always does. "It is just easier to fix in the morning. We've been busy at the show, and it was just a pile on my head by the end of the day anyway. I had no use for it."

"Well, I'm glad you are cutting out the unnecessary. Simplifying." Dr. Meade smiles as if it were his idea to have Luis, our staff stylist, cut nearly a foot off my blond hair. He motions for me to sit in the chair and I do.

"You look pleased. Should I have my stylist send you the bill?" We laugh—him in earnest and me sarcastically.

"No. I'm just glad that you're making things easier for yourself."

I know he's just being honest, but I don't like it. It makes me uncomfortable being real about what's going on.

Sitting in his chair, he wheels towards me with his clipboard. "How have you been feeling? Any headaches?"

"Only when I smack it off something. Same goes for my toe aches and leg aches." That earns me a look. "No. I still haven't had many headaches."

"Good. Have you noticed your peripheral vision getting worse? Is your tunnel vision narrowing more? Are you more tired than normal?" He writes something and then lifts his head up. "Just answer, Tatum. I can't say anything to anyone. You can tell me."

"It is getting narrower, but not by a lot. I've been measuring it sort of. Like at work. I use to be able to see both of the cameras from offstage. Now it's like I'm looking right in between them. My night vision is almost nonexistent. If I wake up in the middle of the night and there isn't a light on, I can barely see to get to the bathroom without waking up Kurt by bumping around. It isn't like he wants to sleep with the light on. Who would?" I sigh, aware that I didn't really need to tell him all of that, but again, I'm nervous and can't help it.

"Well, we were expecting that. If the light is on, can you see better when you wake up?" he asks as though he is talking to a child.

"Yes, but it takes a minute for everything to focus. It comes back in a few seconds and everything is back to shitty-ass normal. Tell me the truth. Is this because of my adolescent masturbating? I

9

was told that leads to blindness."

"This again!? Would you quit with the masturbating!" he almost shouts.

"I wish I could. It's just that I'm so good at it." I know it's bad timing, and timing is supposed to be everything. It's just that sometimes my dirty mouth rescues me with a perverted life jacket and it's always just my size.

Why should I be the only one uncomfortable? If you can't beat me, I'll make you join me.

"You know what I mean. You need to talk to someone. Have you considered seeing a therapist that specializes in people who are visually impaired? Would you use a referral? You always do that, you know? This is serious."

"Do what?" I know I'm baiting him again to say something I can twist around into dirty word play and embarrass him into changing the subject, but it isn't as effective as it used to be. Have I desensitized my ophthalmologist?

"You know what. I think you could benefit from seeing someone who can help guide you through this transition. You should also consider going to a facility that can teach you practical ways to deal with how your life is going to be."

"Like a fat farm? No way. I'm not going to blind camp. Not going to happen."

This isn't the first time he has approached me with the idea of therapists and blind school. I'm not ready for that, and I don't mean to sound like a better-than-somebody snot either. I can hardly see myself keeping my mouth shut around other people who would probably benefit from me not being there.

He takes a few more notes as I continue."And I really hate therapists. How can they help me if I don't feel like myself when I'm talking to them? I wouldn't tell them the truth. I'd probably just mess with them. They're all quacks. Pill pushers."

"Don't totally dismiss the idea of getting help with this. I will try to think of some alternatives for you. You wouldn't last a day there anyway. They wouldn't be able to handle you." And there is my Dr. Meade. Swinging it right back at me.

"Great idea. Alternatives. You think on that. I will hire another assistant for my personal life and start interviewing housekeepers. See? This is compromise. You said to make life simpler. You do your thing and I'll do mine."

We finish up the standard exam with his agreeing that he can see more degeneration and suggesting we not wait as long in between visits.

After I make the appointment with sweet, old-ass Charlotte, I sit in the waiting room, eager to get the text from Winnie that says that they are outside. Winnie is my best friend, colleague, and soon-to-be sister-in-law.

Some say that if you let people go and you're meant to be with them, then they will come back. I say that if you have a smoking-hot college roommate you love, then hook her up with your adorable brother and you'll never have to worry about that leaving shit.

My brother Coop—Cooper if you are our Grandma—fell in love with Winnie the first time he saw her. But then again, in a way, I did too.

She is dramatic and wild. Her body totally matches her personality. And she has crazy curly brown hair, an ass that won't quit, and big brown eyes that make her irresistible. That's why she made a great actress with no training at all.

We are both writers. That's how we met in college. We had the same major, and admissions had paired us up as roommates.

Following graduation, we landed a couple of jobs as pages at one of the biggest television stations in the country, ABN. Don't ask me how that seriously lucky turn of events unfolded, because I will never tell. Neither will the two-pump chump Derek, the lead page at the time, who I ironically met on my birthday my senior year.

Then after slumming it for a year or so, we both were promoted to different floors in the building and on different shows. I was hired on as a junior writer for The Up Late Show, a late-night talk show, and Winnie was hired at a sketch comedy show to write and perform. We made friends with people, both of our shows came and went, and born was Just Kidding.

That is our show. Winnie and I would like to take credit for the entire thing, but it actually is a three-way—me, Winnie, and Wes Ruben. Winnie and Wes worked on the same comedy program before Just Kidding and had great on-camera chemistry.

If they were in a scene together, then it was gold. Their characters were always fan favorites, and that made them a hot-ticket commodity in the entertainment business. When they approached me as a writer for the spin-off of their canceled show, I was more than happy to say yes.

First of all, I was unemployed. So that was a no-brainer.

Second of all, I knew working with Winnie and Wes would be fun, profitable, and an opportunity that wouldn't ever come around again.

If I were a betting person, I'd bet that they will both be on the big screen in leading roles within the next five years. They are that good.

My phone buzzes with a text from Winnie.

Winnie: Birthday Slut, are you ready yet? We are 3 blocks away.

Me: I'm not Birthday Slut anymore. You can call me Birthday Bitch from here on out. I'm walking out the door.

Winnie: Oh, I bet Birthday Slut is in there somewhere.

How coy.

So, there was a time before Kurt and I got together that I might or might not have had some casual sex. I wasn't a whore or anything. I dated and had casual boyfriends. Nothing too serious. Dating within the business is like that. Here one minute and kiss my let's-be-friends ass the next. Every year on my birthday, if I were dating someone, I would break up with him and not look back.

Then Winnie and I would go out and Birthday Slut it up. Well, I would. She faked it by just going home with Coop and telling me that she'd called him by a different name. She has the best logic.

CHAPTER *Two*

I WALK OUT onto E. 63rd Street, and it is a miracle that Coop found a spot right outside the door. I'm instantly relieved. I love New York. It is my home, but at this time of day, it is a mass of commotion. Definitely a time of day when a person's peripheral vision would come in damn handy.

Looking straight ahead—like I have a choice—I see him opening the back passenger's side door of his brand new Porsche SUV. My big brother, the high roller.

Coop is in real estate. He's the guy on all those billboards that say, "Hi, I'm Cooper Elliot. Welcome to the Upper West Side," unless you are driving on the Upper East Side or any of the boroughs. He welcomes rich assholes home all over New York City.

He's smart and everyone loves him. He's made a great career by being honest and truly dedicated to finding buyers what they didn't know they needed and getting sellers the price they dreamed of. I am very proud.

We are not doing too badly for the two kids of vagabond hippies. You heard me. Our parents aren't really that bad, but they're not that far from it either. When we were kids, they were only marginally weird, but now they travel the country in a camper, or whatever, and "live free," as they say.

Coop leans in and gives me a kiss on my cheek. "Happy birthday, Tater. Hungry?"

I nod and get in the vehicle. Shutting the door, he smiles at Winnie while walking around the front and winks at her.

14

Cooper states, "We are going to Sear. Is that okay with you? Kurt called and said that it is close to his late meeting and he can just meet us there when he finishes up. Sound okay?" Coop knows that I would rather douche with battery acid than pick a restaurant, so he already knew to tell him that it would be fine.

"That sounds great actually. I could use some meat and a strong drink. Did he mention how long he would be? It's been a long day." I don't know if it is because Dr. Meade asked if I've been more tired lately or if I really am, but I'm really feeling run down right now.

"He didn't say a time, just that he'll be there when he wraps everything up." Coop looks at me through the rearview and gives a not-sure-what-to-tell-you look.

"I'll just text him after we have a table. I can't imagine those bankers working that late anyway." I check my phone and it's about five thirty. "We can get the last bit of happy hour."

We arrive at Sear, a posh steakhouse in Midtown, and belly up to the bar while waiting for our table.

"So I picked out your bridesmaid dress," Winnie blurts out like she's been holding it in. "It's beautiful so I just ordered it a size larger than what you wear. That way we can have it tailored perfectly. Your tits are going to look sinful and you'll love it." She looks like she is ready for me to take a swing at her, and I kind of am.

"You ordered it without me even seeing it? What the hell, Winnie? I thought we were going to shop for them together? I don't want you to have to do that shit on your own. When did you get it?"

"Just this afternoon. After you left. The show is almost entirely buttoned up for next week, so we all cut out early. I wanted to stop at this place Luis and Tilly told me about and I just went. I didn't see anything for me, but I think... No, I know you are going to love this dress," she says like it's an excuse for being so impulsive. "It really is stunning. Here, I have a picture on my phone.

You're going to be ravishing."

I grab the phone and prepare to rant, but when I get a look at the dress, I see that she's not wrong. It's fabulous.

"Fine then. I accept your birthday gift of the bridesmaid dress," I state, acting put out. "And I will also accept the birthday shoes to go with it. Just no more doing that stuff without me. I want to see you do all of it. Okay? I want to be there."

I know it doesn't seem selfish to want to help your best friend plan a wedding to your brother, but all I can think of is, *What if I don't get to experience one of my own?* Not that I don't think I'll ever marry. I just don't expect to see it.

Don't get me wrong. I am independent. I own my newly re-modeled and fan-fucking-tastic condo outright and alone. I don't require jewelry for special occasions, and I can have dinner by myself and not shed a tear.

I am the boss. Well, I'm at least one of them. And I am a damn good writer. I have three awards from this year alone that remind me of that every day on my mantle.

But then again, I've never had that thing that Winnie and Coop have. So this could be my only chance to literally see a wedding like that.

"Okay, no more," she concedes. "I won't take a wedding-shit unless you are holding my hand. Promise." She gets it. She knows me well.

"Okay. I love the dress anyway. But isn't your sister going to be a cow by then? How is she going to look in that dress?" Her sister Molly is bona fide pregnant. Winnie and Coop's wedding is later this summer, but by then her sister will be about six weeks from her explosion date.

"She's not wearing it. I've decided to go with different dresses. I will pick hers out too, if that makes you feel better. Hell, I'll even let you pick it out. You guys wouldn't have looked the same in any dress. So it just didn't make sense making one of you—or both of you—look like shit. It's going to be the best day of my life. I don't need you guys bitching about your dresses. Am I right?"

I look to Cooper for an ally, but he's idly messing with his phone on the other side of Winnie, totally zoned out for most of our conversation. He only peeked up when she mentioned that she'd bought my dress.

She's right. I thought that same thing a while back when Molly, Winnie, and I were at lunch a few weeks ago. Molly said that she wanted to find something long to hide her already growing tree trunks that were formerly her shapely ankles. And I thought about how I was one hundred percent sure I would get tangled in a longer gown and fall flat on my ass walking down the aisle.

"No. You're right. I like the shorter one for me, and she wants a longer one to hide her cankles. This works."

We are on our second drinks when I glance at my phone. Six twenty. I decide to text Kurt.

Me: We are here. Our table is about ready. Are you close?

I receive his response quicker than I expect. Still having my phone in front of me, I read his reply.

Kurt: Yeah, we are around the corner having a drink. Change the table to six. These guys are joining us.

Well, that's a little irritating. Not that I'm not a "the more the merrier" kind of girl, but it is my birthday. Am I out of line in thinking that he should have at least asked if that was cool? And would I have been out of line if I'd used the opportunity to say no?

I need more information from my boyfriend the socialite.

Me: Who is coming? Do I know them?

He promptly shoots back a response.

Kurt: I doubt you know them. They're clients of mine. Just change the table. We'll be there in 30.

That was that.

I'm pissed. No happy birthday. No flowers at work—not that I give a rat's ass. No nothing. What the hell?

"Coop, Kurt wants us to change the table to six. He's bringing some clients. Can you go do that? I'm going to the bathroom." I need a minute to fume in privacy.

"Are you serious? You're joking, right?" The irritation and utter shock is boldly written all over my big brother's face.

"Not joking. Totally not funny. I'll be right back."

I walk to the ladies' room, which I had scoped out before I even left the bar since it doesn't work well for me to wander these days. I need to stand here and just breathe for a few minutes.

Fuck him. Fuck those asshole dinner-crashers. I'm really upset.

Eying myself in the mirror, I see that I don't look remotely happy. My cheeks are flushed hot and my eyes look like blue flames. My blond hair, cut in the new shoulder-length bob, looks edgier than it did last week. My skin is tinted pink and my hands are fisted. My brows are pinched, and I have to think to release the tension in my forehead. I don't need wrinkles adding insult to my already prolific injury.

I'm going to take a stand. I take a few deep breaths and reach for my phone. My hands shake as I grab for it out of my clutch and it drops, sliding across the floor.

Gross. The worst place to drop a phone happens to be right here and just when I'm about to Mount St. Helens via text message.

I quickly bend down to take hold of it and miss on my first attempt. Turning to get a better notion of where it landed, I kneel down. Grasping the vile germ-soaked device from the floor, I pivot to stand back up in my three-inch heels. Save it. They're pretty. I don't want to hear about it.

Smack. And it's lights out. My head bounces off the counter and now I am the vile germ-soaked thing on the bathroom floor.

That is where Winnie finds me a few minutes later.

When I wake up, she has her purse under my head and there is an unfamiliar woman standing next to her, telling Winnie that they should call 911.

"No. She's waking up." Looking at me, Winnie says sweetly, "Hi there, Rocky. The counter took you out. Are you okay?" She has a wet paper towel pressed against the side of my throbbing head, and she looks worried but calm. "Tatum, are you okay?"

Remembering that I need to answer her, I shake my head yes. "Where is my phone?" She looks at me like she thinks I'm still out of it. But I'm not letting a mild concussion ruin this for me. My foot is coming down regardless.

"Your phone? It's right here. What do you need that for? Are you calling an ambulance? Are you hurt? Let me do that." She looks down, ready to make the call, and sees the message that was left open from Kurt.

She shakes her head and hands it to me.

I type out my message to him.

Me: Why don't you guys have dinner without us? I'm fine with Coop and Winnie. I'll see you later at the apartment.

Then I say to Winnie from my new low, "Can we just grab some takeout and go to my place? I'm covered in shit debris and piss splatter. I need a shower."

"Sure. Whatever you want. Let's get you up." Winnie waits for me to sit up on my own and quickly holds her hand out to block my second go-around with the countertop.

"Shit. Thanks, Winn. Fuck." I'm frustrated and embarrassed, but she pretends like it is no big thing and helps me to my feet.

Coop is standing in the hallway outside the ladies' room when we make our way out. He looks angry, but I know he's just upset that I'm hurt.

"How did you guys know I fell down in there?"

"The hostess went in there and saw you. She came running out to us, saying that you were on the floor and had blood on your head. She wanted to know if she should call an ambulance. Then Winnie ran in there and she followed," Coop explained.

"Yeah, you were out cold for only a few seconds more after that. Just long enough for me to put my purse, which you can re-place, under your head and take the paper towel that the girl hand-ed me. Must have clocked yourself pretty good."

I rub the goose-egg emerging from my forehead.

"Yeah, I dropped my phone and bend down to pick it up. I was mad. I am mad. Coop, I want takeout and a shower. Can we go? I don't want to eat with Kurt and those suits tonight. I told him we were leaving. I really want to get out of here."

Coop doesn't hesitate, only looking at me with caring eyes and a genuinely sympathetic smile. "Sure. You sit here. I will go pay the tab and we're out."

They come up to my place with me. I can smell the Mexican food they ordered from the place down the street while I wash the typhoid out of my hair. I feel a lot better after that, but the cut and bump I'm freshly sporting on the right side of my head looks worse.

Coming into my living room, I see that Winnie took it upon herself to make us margaritas and Coop set the table and opened up the food. There is enough to feed a small army.

We eat and they give me presents. Coop bought me the new Kate Spade purse I wanted and Winnie bought me a new iPod loaded with all our favorites from college. I love both of them and their gifts.

Against his will, Coop and Winnie leave. It's only about ten o'clock. He would rather just stay the night and see how this Kurt thing unfolds. I know that is why he has hung around, but she wants to get up early and go to yoga since we are wedding shopping in the morning.

She claims that she will have to do more than just downward dog to keep the south-of-the-border feast we just consumed off her ass.

Shortly after that—and after finishing the pitcher of margaritas on my own—I hear Kurt at the front door.

"Where's the birthday girl?" Brilliant. *Now* he wants to celebrate. "Tatum, I landed that deal. Sorry I missed dinner with you guys. You know how it is. How was Sear?"

I turn to look at him from where I'm sitting on the couch.

Waiting. Stewing. Seething.

"We just had a few drinks and then came back here. They were busy and changing our table made our wait longer. We had Jose's and margaritas."

The sight of him reignites my hostility from before the head trauma.

I try to begin calmly. "Listen, I am a little pissed about earlier. It was my birthday dinner, and I understand how juvenile that sounds, but I was looking forward to it. You didn't ask, you just told me that you invited clients. You didn't tell me happy birthday. You didn't ask how my doctor's visit went." My voice is ramping up to a volume close to yelling. "Now you're here for what can only be described as a birthday booty call? I'm not really sure how to take all of this. Why don't you help me understand what the fuck you think this relationship is to you? Okay?"

He just stands there. Handsome and a little drunk, Kurt is a classic white-collar man, just like his father and grandfather before him. Ivy League educated, entitled, and rightfully confident. To top it all off, he is striking to look at. That's the icing on the asshole cake standing before me.

Chiseled abs, perfectly sculpted dark brown hair, hazel eyes, perfect tan—which usually means he is easy to forgive most of the time, based on his exterior qualities alone.

Inside, he seems more greedy and selfish lately. Cold and distant at times, especially in the last couple of months.

I decided to accept his booty call after my brother and Winnie left. I'm not sure when I'll get my next lay, and it is better than just breaking it off over the phone. Right?

Maybe he needs closure on these kinds of things? I'm such a giver.

Now, as I look at him and realize that in a few short months I won't be able to see-see him, he suddenly doesn't look all that great. Soon, all I will be left with is this smug bastard who is always wondering what he's getting out of everything.

Okay, Tatum. Ass first, then 'kiss my ass' second. It's perfect.

I guess I do have a Birthday Slut left in me after all.

I can see the strategy working on his face. He's trying to contrive a plan that gets him to the sex part of our evening the quickest and with the least amount of bitching.

"I'm sorry, Tatum. I didn't realize dinner was that important. How about I take a shower and make it up to you?"

Yeah, see that? One sentence to apologize and straight into what he wants out of this negotiation.

"Make it quick."

He makes his way past the bar, dropping his keys and briefcase on the counter. Shrugging out of his designer sports coat and slinging it over a barstool, he makes short time of getting to my master bathroom.

Making a mental note that after tonight I won't have to straighten up his messes all over my condo anymore, I smile and head to my bedroom for my parting birthday gift.

What is supposed to be my apology screw turns into his victory blowjob after flying through a quick wash-up. *Happy birthday to me.*

I'm not trying to brag, but it is what it is. Fellatio is a talent of mine. I have always liked doing it, and men have always appreciated it. They appreciate them...quickly. See where I'm going with that? I'm a penis-sucking prodigy. I'm sure if they knew, my family would be very proud.

So I expect that this isn't going to take long. Besides that, I know what he likes, and I decide that this is as good a time as any to dump him. At least I have his attention.

I take the length of him in my mouth to the base and gently do my classic Tatum head shake, which always gets a reaction. Predictably, he moans the word *fuck* like a prayer.

Working my hand in my mouth's absence, I pull completely off him, asking, "Kurt, baby?" I want him to listen to me. "You are so hot." *That's true enough.*

"Yeah? You like that cock, don't you? Keep going, babe. I'm really close."

I oblige and take him deep again. "This...mmm...isn't working for...mmmm...me anymore." I punctuate every few words with my mouth all the way down the length of him. I even cup his balls for good measure. If I'm going to do something, I'm going to do it right—hummers included.

"Huh? Is your jaw sore or something? Just hang in there a few more seconds." What a sweet guy.

I quicken my pace and feel him working up to a pretty decent climax. His stomach tightens and he leans forward like he always does.

I pull away just before my big finish and whisper, "We are over," before waxing that dick for the last time. His hand taps my head—like usual—warning me of the explosion about to happen.

Some guys will only spooge a little. Not Kurt. His dick could be compared to the likes of a fire hydrant in Harlem in the summer after the neighbor kids rig it to spray them.

I know what's coming. It's about to be Kurt.

"What, Tatum? Oh, shit," he pants as his orgasm begins to rock him. The tapping is striking me funny tonight. It's like he is tapping out Morse code.

I'm a douche. Tap, tap, tap.

I'm an ass. Tap, tap, tap.

And at the exact moment I feel the first pump go off, I pull his cock from my mouth and aim the head of it right at his face.

"I said we are over, you selfish prick." Then I get up and walk towards my bathroom. Of course I ram my toe into the dresser on the way and quickly turn the light in the bathroom on.

"What the fuck, Tate? Are you out of your mind? God, get me a towel. Shit!" You could say that the message I sent him isn't well received.

"You heard me. I'm over this." I motion with both hands between where I am in the bathroom doorway and where he stands, naked and hunched over, swiping at the come all over his face and chest. "This isn't going anywhere and I'm really not that into you anymore. How about you go home?"

With that, I turn, grab the washcloth he annoyingly threw over the shower door, and fling it at his face.

"Clean up and get out, babe." I close my bathroom door and wait until I hear him leave.

Was I expecting pleading? I'm really not sure. You would have thought after years of dating and almost living together that he would have at least put up a small fight. He certainly could have asked why, right?

Nothing. Not. A. Word.

That probably bothers me the most. He doesn't want me anymore either. Now I'm wondering if he has been such an ass so that he didn't have to break up with the blind girl.

I suppose Kurt choosing to be an all-out asshat sort of hammered the final nail in our relationship's coffin. He's even too selfish to break up with me.

Now I sit here alone on my toilet with a banged-up toe, a contusion on my head and Birthday Slut didn't even get laid.

CHAPTER
Three

"THAT IS THE BEST fucking dump in history!" cackles Winnie the next morning while we're sitting at my table, drinking our coffee, and planning our day of shopping. Scaling down the enthusiasm a little, she asks, "Are you sure you feel up to doing this today? We can do something else, or I can leave if you just want to be alone for a while? Coop and I can bring dinner over tonight, or we could cook for you?"

I hold my hand up to put the brakes on my friend.

"Winnie, I'm fine. Actually, before I did it, I was thinking about how awesome it was going to be not having to clean up after his pretentious ass. I'm feeling a little relieved. Maybe I will be sad later, but I'm just right now."

And that was the truth.

"It's like I was finally sick of shuffling the expired milk around in the fridge and just dumped it. I knew that it was bad and kept working around it anyway. Why? Because having spoiled milk isn't exactly the same as no milk, Winnie. If anything, I can ironically still see my hindsight clearly."

Her pretty brown hair sways as she shakes her head at my stupid comparison. Since Winnie has a shit-ton of wedding things to get done and I'm such a good friend, we decide to skip the cry-fest and nurse my broken ego the mature way—with retail therapy.

"We're not getting much done. We at least have to work on the cake," she tells me as she pulls me into the bakery.

She's not too particular. We eat some cake, we like it, and

she's ready to order. After they confirm that they can deliver it to Martha's Vineyard in August for their wedding, she signs the contract and boom it's off the list.

She and I do a little more shopping and she finds some small gift things for people in the wedding party. We talk about my breakup a little more. It isn't a complete waste for her.

I cuss her out for agreeing with Dr. Know-It-All about his ideas of me getting a shrink. Honestly, I'm starting to think I'm crazier than blind by the way everyone's pushing it.

"I don't think you're crazy. I have a psychiatrist. Does that make me crazy?"

She's not going to win this game with me. I went to see a psychologist—or a therapist or a psychiatrist or whatever—right after I was diagnosed. It was dumb. She said that I was depressed and made me take so many fucking pills that I wasn't myself.

I think that depression is natural when there's something to be depressed about. I was fourteen and just told that it was very likely I'd lose my sight at a young age. So, yeah. I was a little bummed for a while.

The quack wrote me a prescription after my first visit and then I was basically a lump of a girl for a few months. I didn't go anywhere. I was always tired. I didn't give a shit.

My parents knew that the medicine wasn't the solution, and neither was that therapist. They took me out and didn't refill the prescription.

So that's my big shrink story. They're just not for me. I know that lots of people get what they need from them and it is possible that the one I saw when I was younger just wasn't that good. I can't discount a whole medical profession because of my shortcomings resulting from a single experience. Again, it's just not for me. But I can tease Winnie about it.

"Yes. You, my dear, are a lunatic. I'm surprised they let you wander freely."

We walk down the street to the store I've been waiting for—

the shoe store.

"You're a bitch. You should get help. Even your brother thinks so." She points at me with a pretty, red acrylic nail to articulate her crass. "Eat shit, Tatum."

I buy not one, but two pairs of Jimmy Choos and the wallet that matches my new Kate bag. So I'd call that a pretty fucking decent day.

Deciding to forgo the "Are you really okay?" conversation with Coop, I tell Winnie that I'm planning on a night of writing and suggest that they go out without me. Winnie can read me like the paper though, and I think she can see that I'm, even if just superficially, actually doing well with the whole thing.

I catch up on some ridiculous gossip magazines, watch some reality television, and read Page Six. Those three things alone can get my sarcastic writing voice to rear its ever lucrative head. Staying current on the un-news is a huge part of my job. If someone shows a tit on a carpet, I want to know. If someone gets drunk and does something unfortunate, we bring light to it in a silly way.

Our show also has original characters that we have developed over the past few years, and we are always trying new ones. It's the relevant segments that make the biggest splashes. Without being bullies, we like to think that we just point out that everyone is human. That is what makes it funny.

So for a few hours, I dive into that world. As I'm wrapping up for the night, I decide that I will hire a new personal assistant. Not a work PA, but a life PA.

Lots of people have them. Why not me? I quickly make a note in my phone to talk with Neil, my work assistant, and see if he can help sniff out where to find one.

My phone vibrates with an incoming text, and I'll be a son of a bitch if it isn't Kurt.

Kurt: Did you really break up with me?

I look at the clock on the corner of the screen. It is almost one thirty in the morning. I bet he's drunk-dialing.

Me: I did. I'm sorry. I'm just looking for something else.

That was the truth, and just because he is a major jerk from time to time doesn't mean we didn't have a few nice moments when I saw his personality underneath. So I feel like we are even, considering the hole self-bukake thing I did to him. We broke up. There's no need to argue about it now.

Kurt: I'm sorry, too. I was a prick.

Is this really happening? Has his phone been stolen by a...a man?

Me: Are you drunk? What's with the late night texts?

Kurt: No. I was just making sure that you were sticking by this thing. I thought maybe you were mad and that you would call me today after cooling off and then you didn't.

Now, I feel a touch bad. Just a touch though. Maybe he should have given more of a shit about it before. I'm a clean-break kind of girl. I won't go back.

Kurt: Have breakfast with me? To make up for your birthday.

I'm so surprised that I decide to go.

Me: Well, I do like breakfast. I can meet you around nine. You pick the place.

Kurt: I'll meet you at our place around the corner.

Our place? Okay. He's being weird. You know how sometimes people sound different in text messages? Without the inflection in their voice? You can't really understand if it's sarcasm or sincerity. Well, not without a smiley face or a winky face, which equally appall me. I won't be caught dead winking in a message. I don't wink at people normally. Why would I do it in a text? I'd prefer a middle finger emoticon, but those are hard to find.

Me: Okay, see you there in the morning.

Kurt: Okay. Love you.

I look at the screen for a long time. What in the fuck is this all about? Someone really has stolen his phone. This can't be the same Kurt.

My cell again buzzes.

Kurt: Shit. Sorry.

Me: Are you alright?

I feel a little more than sorry now, and I'm not sure for whom.

Kurt: Probably. I'm realizing some things is all. I'm really sorry for being such an ass. That isn't who I want to be. See you at nine. Goodnight, Tate.

Kurt has a conscience? Who would have known? I sort of like him more post breakup than I did before. However, I will stand by my decision. Maybe we will be friends. This could be interesting or really fucking weird.

CHAPTER
Four

THE NEXT MORNING, I shower and dress quickly. Around seven, I'm strapping on my new shoes and wearing a simple slip dress with my favorite scarf. I decide to take my tablet with me and people watch for a while out of the window in the little diner that Kurt thinks is ours.

I get there, find that the booth I want is open, and take it. I order coffee and watch out the impeccably clean window.

This is the time of day that I love the city most. Everything feels clean and new.

A couple walks past pushing a stroller and they drink back their coffees as fast as they can. I make up a little story in my head about how they haven't slept in days and the only way their baby stops crying is on walks.

I make up stories about lots of the passersby. Let's see. There's the nun with white earbuds in who's listening to erotica on her way to confession.

Oh and there's a pair of girls doing the walk of shame after their threesome with the musician they met at the bar last night.

I spend the next hour or so blissfully scandalizing strangers and probably martyring others. I take notes when worth it—funny things for the show or new characters.

Taking advantage of seeing it firsthand, I watch the sun start to make its way down the street and shops open up. Dog walkers triumphantly handle multiple breeds on webs of leashes.

It's like a long soak in a warm tub for my brain.

Then I watch a man walk across the street about a block down. His shoulders are slumped and he looks tired. Running a hand through his hair, he stops and looks behind him like he's changing his mind about something. He just stands there for a minute with people walking by him. I can see him take a few large breaths. As if filling his lungs with just the something he needs to put his feet back into motion, he starts this way again.

Shit. It's Kurt, and he looks bad. I wasn't expecting this. Walking into the diner and scanning the room for me, he taps his hand on the side of his leg. Maybe his tapping is a nervous tick and not just his silent gesture for "I'm going to come."

He smiles and walks to the booth we will share for maybe the last time. Leaning over, he kisses my cheek before taking his seat across from me.

"Happy late birthday. You look great," he says to me before turning to the waitress, who's come to get his drink preference. "I'll have coffee, black. Thanks." His posture is different.

"Do you feel all right, Kurt? You don't look like yourself."

"I feel fine. I'm just tired and…I don't know. Shit, sad?" I can tell he's being truthful. This tiny conversation is more than either of us have openly committed to for over a year.

"I didn't expect you to be so upset about this. Honestly, it seemed like you weren't really invested in us."

"Me?" He looks down at his hands, which are playing with the paper that once held the napkin around the silverware. He's wrapping it around alternating fingers. "You know, that's probably true, but I wasn't the only one like that."

"What? When did I ever—"

"Tatum, all I heard was, 'I don't need you for this,' and 'I'm doing this.' At first, it was nice. You're a knockout"—he lowers his head—"great in bed, and you're successful. It wasn't like you needed me showering you with things, because you can just buy whatever the hell you want. I think it was after the first year that I just got settled into that role. The guy you spend time with on the weekends, go to events with, and fuck."

I'm speechless. It takes everything in me to blink.

"I'm sorry, Tatum. I have been thinking about this since I left your apartment the other night. I was a complete jerk. I deserved what you did. I'm sorry that I didn't talk to you in the beginning when it started. Instead, I took advantage of the situation and rode it out. It made me an asshole. I turned into a fucking asshole!" He lets out a long breath. "I don't want to be like that. I want someone who needs me. I want to feel like the other person would be crushed without me. You look fine. Hell, you look fucking hot!"

On one hand, I'm pissed that he's blaming me for his behavior, and on the other hand, I see where I am at the very least an accomplice to the murder of our relationship.

He's right though. In the last few years, I didn't notice right away when he didn't show up. I didn't care that his focus was on his career and not me. He started acting like *I* was acting. Now that I have been a little more—fuck—needy lately, I've been angry at him for doing what I didn't even give a shit about before.

I am a bitch. A selfish bitch.

I am the bigger asshole in the booth by the window.

"I'm sorry. Kurt, I don't really know what to say. I didn't mean to do that to you. I just… I don't know what to say." And for the first time in ages, there is no punch line. I have no clever quip, no retort to what he's said to me.

Kurt grabs my hand in his and rubs his thumb across my knuckles. "It's okay. You don't have to say anything. I just wanted to let you know that I feel bad about this and I do love you, even if I was a terrible boyfriend."

I feel conflicted but still set in my decision.

We spend a few minutes sipping our coffees and ordering our breakfasts. It's almost comfortable.

"So how was your appointment with Dr. Meade yesterday?"

His concern shocks me. Was this the guy I could have been dating if I hadn't been such a fucking do-it-myself control freak? It is just like me to push someone away and then blame them for it later. I almost want to cry. Almost.

"It went well. He didn't like my masturbation joke...again." I smile and wait for him to return one. When he does, I keep going. "I thought it was growing on him. He told me to start taking this blind stuff seriously." I try to make my answer sound playful and jovial, but he sidesteps it.

"That might not be a bad idea." When he says this, he grimaces like he knows I won't take well to the advice.

Is it possible to choke on humble pie? I'm overwhelmed. I'm frustrated and ashamed.

"I know you're independent. Shit, everyone knows you're independent. But asking for a little help might do you good."

I have to let that sink in. I watch him intently, looking for a recount on his suggestion, but one doesn't come. He reads my silence correctly and goes for a different angle.

"Are Coop and Winnie ready to bash my teeth in?"

Good boy. Change the subject. I'm granted a reprieve.

"No, not at all. Winnie is so wrapped up in the show and wedding plans and Coop has been really busy at work. They have bigger fish to fry. And I'm sure they will love this right here. Maybe I will tell them you stood me up," I say, smiling but only half kidding. It isn't a bad idea.

Kurt shrugs his shoulders and offers me an apologetic grin. "It would be easy enough to believe."

We're given our food and eat while we chat about things. It is the best date we've had in months. It's too bad that it's likely our last.

After he pays for our breakfast, instead of sliding back into his side of the booth, he slides in next to me. Scooting back against the window, I shift sideways to face him. He's turned in towards me, too.

His handsome face is earnest. The color in his hazel eyes looks bluer with their red, tired rims.

"Tatum, if you ever need anything, please call me. Will you?"

I nod my head yes, still a little shocked at his closeness.

He continues. "I'm sorry that I didn't try harder to fix this before it all blew up. I'm sorry that I hurt your feelings on more than one occasion. Yet again, now that I'm thinking back on it, you should know you hurt me, too. I'm not saying this to hurt you. It is probably for the best." He pauses and clears the audible lump in his throat. "I really want you to be happy. And after thinking about this for way too long in my apartment this weekend, I realized I want to be someone's man and not just their date." Smiling, he cups my cheeks in his hands and leans in to kiss me.

His lips are sugary and taste like maple syrup. It's a sweet kiss.

His hands tighten on my face, and he pulls away just enough to talk and look at me. "And until I find her, whenever you get horny, you call me. Got that?" He's joking. Well, he's also totally serious, but it makes me feel a little better anyway.

"Deal." I smile, and he kisses me quickly once more before he slides out.

"Anyway, maybe we could be friends? With benefits? Yes?" He looks for approval, but not long enough for it to show. "No? Either way, call if you need anything from me. Now that would be fucking weird, huh?" Ours eyes meet and I can tell that he's not sure if he wants to go. Maybe he thinks I'll stop him.

But I won't.

He walks off and turns back to say, "See you, Tatum."

"See you, Kurt."

With that, he leaves our diner with some of his confidence and swagger back.

CHAPTER
Five

I CALL WINNIE WHEN I get home and consider asking her to come over and help me lick my wounded ego, but that doesn't really appeal to me. I tell her about meeting Kurt, and she thinks it was good but a little weird. I know she never really liked him. She tolerated him though, because that's what best friends do.

Cooper calls that evening and asks if I need anything. He says that he has an evening showing in my neighborhood and wants to stop by afterward. At about seven thirty, he knocks on my door.

"Hey, Tater. I brought you some ice cream. Winnie told me about breakfast. How are you dealing with it?"

I take the bag from his hand and walk towards my kitchen. Pulling the Karamel Sutra-flavored Ben & Jerry's out of the bag and setting it on my marble counter, I shrug my shoulders at him.

For some reason, I've always felt small or really young around Cooper. Sure, he's older than I am, but not by a lot. It's only a difference of a little over three years. Always my protector and, next to Winnie, my best friend, he looks at me with brown eyes full of sympathy.

Finally, I answer him. "I don't know. What do you think about it? I mean, is it all my fault? Did I create that whole thing? Am I really that awful?" After I rattle off my self-deprecating list of questions, I turn to the drawer and pull out a fork.

"No. You're not awful. You're my kid sister and, therefore, awesome by association alone." He playfully messes my hair and tells me, "I did see it happening, but I thought that was how you both liked it. I mean, it really didn't register for you until lately? You know he was just playing the role you gave him. It wasn't his fault that your role changed."

What the hell is up with this day? Did I miss the RSVP to 'Tatum is a Dickhead' Day?

"I know!" I snap and quickly rein in my aggressiveness. "I feel so cold and mean. I didn't consider that I was acting like that. I suppose I can be that bad."

I put a bite of the over-the-counter, sugary medication into my mouth and let it melt.

"He gave me an open invitation to hook up until he finds a new girlfriend. Sounds bad, but I might take him up on it."

Cooper looks genuinely offended. "Don't. You deserve better than that. Maybe this is just something that needed to happen for you to see that things are changing. Even if you don't realize how much, you're changing, too. Tater, you sort of have to."

I again rake my fork through the half-frozen, half-melted ice cream, poking around for a good bit, and shake my head.

My eyes start to burn, but I fight back almost escaping tears. "I don't want to. I like my life, you know? My job. My apartment." The thoughts of it all vanishing begin to steal my composure. "I love my independence, Cooper. And up until lately, I loved my fine-as-fuck boyfriend. What is the next thing to go? Huh?" I look at my big brother and pray that he has the answers like he always did when I was small.

"Oh, come here." Cooper opens his arms and comes to me. His embrace is warm and strong, just like him. I set the cardboard container down and hug him back. He says into my hair, "This is going to be okay. We'll figure it out." He kisses my head before letting me go. "What did Meade say? Is it getting worse? You don't really talk about it much. Talk to me."

He's gathering data for our offense.

"It's getting worse a little at a time. Shit, have you seen my legs and my head?" I point to both. "It's like there are booby traps everywhere. Only, I'm the one who set them up. He says that I need to simplify and get prepared, but I don't want to. I don't want to, Cooper. This is my life." My voice is desperate.

He shakes his head. "Well, simplifying doesn't sound so bad. Right? And getting prepared will help you stay in control. Not lose it. We need to get ready for this. I know that it fucking sucks. Shit, I would be mad at the world."

"I'm not mad. I'm frustrated." I'm annoyed that I can't do things like I once could. Frustrated that when I need help I'm too damn proud to ask for it and then furious at myself when I fuck everything up with no one to share my blame.

"Okay, well let's make a plan."

"What kind of plan?"

Cooper states, "We will get organized. Prioritize." This is why I love him. He knows what I need to keep moving.

In college, I once failed a test I'd studied so hard for. I swear on Matt Lauer—whom I will forever have a crush on—that that motherfucking professor had it out for me. I just knew he did, but Cooper maintained that at least we knew what I didn't know.

So he gathered all of my returned assignments and papers and helped me study for that Pap smear of a final. He suggested only working on the stuff I hadn't done well on and not the stuff that I had.

He helped.

He pointed out the necessary things I needed to focus on. Yet he has never once offered to fix something for me. Cooper never hesitates to help me do it on my own.

I hug him again really hard, knocking the wind from him. "I love you, Coopie pants."

He lovingly pushes me off him.

"Back up. I know." He smiles. "Now, let's get your shit to-gether. I'm gonna need a piece of paper, a pen, and a spoon. I never understood why you eat your ice cream with a Goddammed fork. You are such a weirdo."

Cooper and I sit there at the bar in my kitchen until we've eaten all of that tub and the partial tub I had in the freezer. My assignments for the next week are to find the following people to hire: a personal assistant, a cleaning company, and a car service.

He can help with the driver. Cooper knows of a good one who he uses when showing properties to people who don't really know New York that well yet. He offers to forward the contact information in the morning. He advises, "Ask for Ray Dabney. He's good."

CHAPTER
Six

I'M STILL A LITTLE rattled by the weekend, but I fell asleep last night feeling like it was going to be alright—comfortably with the lights on.

This morning, I gather all of my weekend's work out of my home office. I put on my favorite blue wrap dress, pairing it with my peep toes, and feel ready to kick this week's ass.

In the cab on the way to the studio, I answer a few emails I received about the never-ending bounty of drama that Hollywood's biggest train wreck, Chelsea Royce, supplies us with. The typical childhood sweetheart actress, she put out a terrible record, dated an awesome young man, broke up with him for a bad boy, and did an amazing job in a movie only to follow it up with a leaked homemade porno and a stint in rehab. All too common in twentysomething Hollywood, but people can't help but beg for more of it.

This will be an easy week.

Entering the downtown building among all the energy of the city, I wave the badge hanging on my briefcase at the security guard and take the elevator to the thirtieth floor, which is home to the offices for the show.

"Good morning, Tatum. Here are your messages. Did you have a nice birthday?" inquires Cynthia, our receptionist.

Cynthia is a sweet, almost naïve girl. Her stick-straight brown hair is most often pulled into a half-up, half-down 'do that is very neat in the morning and slightly askew by late afternoon. I like to think she's from the country or some similarly Podunk place, but she most likely comes from upstate.

Always quick to be polite and helpful, she usually wears a smile that is very genuine and only shakes her head at me when I say something off-color in her presence, which is usually about three times a day. Nevertheless, she comes in early each morning—I guess before everyone else—and stops at my office each evening before heading out to inquire if there is anything else she can do for me.

I like her a lot. The devil in me can't wait for the night when we go get a drink and she gets piss drunk while letting me into that seemingly innocent mind.

Lying to her about my birthday, I tell her, "I did, thank you." Then I ask, "Is Winnie in yet?"

"She is. She, Tilly, and Wes are in the writers' room, and I think Neil just left to get your coffees."

"Great. Thanks." I walk around the pit, which is a round pool of desks and cubicles where most of the show's staff resides, and into my office at the end.

My office is sleek, but not cold. I guess it's a lot like my condo—decorated in dark browns, creams, and silver. I know I'm boring in the decorating department, but clean and simple always make me feel calm. And clutter, again, is my enemy. So call me a minimalist. I don't care. You break a knee cap once a week on a piece of furniture and have tabletop shit flying everywhere and then you can judge my strategies.

Settling into my morning and lining out the day, I set into some of the tasks I chose for myself. I received the driving company's contact information from Coop, I forward it to Neil, my work assistant, so he can call and inquire about their services.

Then, grabbing my things to head into the writers' room, I run smack into Neil coming through my door.

"Shit, Tate. Are you okay? Geez, I'm glad I already put the coffee down. You'd be soaked." Neil is what I like to call "metro-gay." He's flamboyant in a posh way and more ladylike than most women I've met. He's classically queer.

"Dammit, Neil. Can you get me a few possible contacts for a new personal assistant?" I blurt while checking to make sure I have all of my weekend's notes still in my hands.

He freezes. I take in his perfectly pressed gray trousers that he's coupled with suspenders. This morning, Neil is sporting lime green glasses. He looks adorable.

"I like the glasses," I tell him.

"Tatum, I'm sorry. I didn't mean to rush in here like that. Are you firing me?"

Now I can see the worry that my request gave him. I didn't even think about how that sounded. You can make another tick mark under the heading 'Tatum is an Asshat.'

"Fuck no! You're mine forever, Neil. I need a personal assistant for outside of work. I need to..." Waving my hand around my head, I sing, "Simplify."

His cheeks puff out like a blowfish as he exhales his relief. "Oh, thank God. I almost shit my pants. Sure, of course. When do you want to interview them? Should I set up a time for them to come here, or I could help you do it at your place?"

"I'm not sure what the week looks like yet. Just get some information about PAs who might, I don't know, live around my area, have experience with, uh, all of this." Waving again like a crazed lunatic, I'm forever talking with my hands. "Someone who is young, even though you can't say that. Just say energetic. And available to start next week." I stand there while he absorbs my plight.

"Got it. You need me in there?"

"Nah. It's going to be a simple week. You can set up in my office if you want. Oh, and do you want to grab lunch after the morning meeting? We can talk about what you find out and I'll tell you about breaking up with Kurt." If my last unintentional bomb didn't nut check him, then that will.

His eyes almost fall out of his head. "You can't do that! Ahh, this is going to be the longest morning! Damn you, Tatum Elliot. You're a wicked bitch."

I nod in agreement. "Yeah, I learned that too this weekend," I tell him as I start around the pool of desks floating in the pit. "Do some work."

The writers' room, which is fundamentally just a conference room that has everyone's shit in it—everything from laptops to the most current tabloid covers taped to the back wall to the three televisions we have hanging on the wall above the windows—is the nucleus of our show.

When I walk in and see everyone already hard at it, I'm pleased. Wes and Winnie are the main attractions, but this show is my baby. Yeah, I'm the momma.

"Okay, guys, this should be an easy week. Chel-Ro went batshit crazy at a strip mall in Santa Monica. Then she wrecked her lawyer's car." I point to the screen that is conveniently reporting about the whole situation as I speak. When the segment is over, I say, "See? So I'm thinking we play up the mall thing and the car committing suicide from not wanting to be seen with her driving it. What have you guys got?"

They laugh a little and agree she's a hot mess that we can't pass up.

Wes leans over the table to say, "Wow, someone is on a mission." He sits in the lead chair at the head of the long, smoke-tinted glass top table wearing his signature lame graphic t-shirt, sports jacket, and jeans. Then he adds, "Winnie said you dumped pencil dick. You doing okay?"

I somehow maintain my cool. "His dick resembles nothing even close to a pencil. That could be slander. He has a great dick," I retort, pointing my pen at his quizzing expression. "Actually, I'm doing great, and so is he. We had breakfast yesterday like adults and it's fine. So mind your own fucking business and let's get this week lined out. I have shit to do."

"Ha! Look out!" bellows Tilly, Winnie's assistant. "That girl is on fire!" She's singing and laughing at my obvious take-charge attitude about my breakup.

"Well, if you're all ready, then let's do this. Over the weekend, I took home some of the segs that the junior writers have been working on and there are some really great ones. There is one about a mock award show for retired models—so funny and kind of sad." I laugh thinking about it. "There was a good one with a fictional metal band called Death Face but needs a little working on. There was bit about the bearded duck hunter show. A parody thing that the Devons are working on and it's killer. I think we probably have a good show with those."

"The duck guys skit is hilarious! We should open with it. I love everything about it," adds Winnie. "I heard them talking about it Friday from my office before I left. That one will be huge."

"Good. And the leftovers from last week are still current and we can fill in with the digitals that the Devons did over spring break," I say.

Winnie has a soft spot in her heart for the pair of Devons that work with us. I think they remind her of us from a few years ago. She states very matter-of-factly to the whole room, "Those Devons are rocking it right now. We should think about giving them their own office though. They really get into their stuff." Making a case for her favorite duo, she continues. "They work great together, and they are coming up with stellar scenes. What do you guys think about that?" She looks to both Wes and me like a child asking her parents for money for the carnival.

"I don't want to stifle them by saying, 'Dudes, shut the fuck up. Everyone else is working, too,' but they are a distraction for the others in the pit. That office by reception would work great and they deserve it." Winnie sounds like she is pleading with a jury.

She adores those guys, but she is right. When they are playing with ideas, it turns into office improv, and I am even guilty of hurrying through calls to go out and watch.

Last week, big Devon was holding little Devon upside down,

trying to shake out his pocket change for the vending machine. I almost pissed myself.

The rest of the morning meeting goes well. The week is already shaping up to run smoothly, and I figure I can probably do the interviews from home any day I want to.

That's the beauty of working with some of the most talented people in the business. Everyone wants on the air. Everyone wants to do their work, and if you don't watch it, then they'll do yours, too. And if you're really unlucky, then they'll do it better.

CHAPTER
Seven

I'M GRACED WITH the good fortune of telling the Devons that they can move into the office across from reception. I can have some fun with this opportunity.

Back in my office, I think now is as good a time as any. "Neil, please go get the Devons for me."

Neil's face screams injustice. He looks so guilty all of a sudden. Everyone one loves the two Devons, but they can be a handful. Let's just say that Wes, Winnie, and I have all had our little chats with them.

He tells me, "It wasn't really piss, you know? They just put food coloring in the water thing. They feel really bad about it."

"It isn't about that. Besides, if anyone actually drank that, then it's their own fault. Who the fuck would drink piss then bitch about it?" He hesitates and cocks his head to the side. "You are paranoid today. Are you getting a man period or something? Just go get them."

I'm well aware of just how unprofessional and misogynistic I am. You can kiss my ass though. Neil loves me and would be crushed if I didn't give him the attention that I do. Plus, he adorably blushes when I insinuate his femininity. I have to give my people what they want. Remember, I'm a giver.

I watch through the glass wall that frames my door as Neil saunters over to their side of the pit and leans over the half-wall. I see one fat head and one skinny head poke up and look directly at my office. They catch me staring that way. So I raise my hand, wave them here, and mouth, "Now."

I wait until they are in earshot and shout, "Come on! Pick it up, guys! I don't have all day!" My phone rings. I can see it's Winnie. I grab it quickly. "Yeah."

"Did you hear about the pot plant the janitor found on the roof?" Winnie whisper-shouts into the receiver. I can see straight into her office from mine. She's mimicking puffing on a joint and passing it to me.

"A pot plant?" I can't help myself.

"Yeah, you know, like weed, the chronic, dope..." She could go on forever, and I don't have enough time for her to recite every slang term for cannabis right now.

I cut her off. "I know what the fuck weed is, you moron. Never mind that. Keep going."

"Right." She giggles. "Okay. I heard the Devons talking about it. Let them think they are in trouble and leave me on speakerphone. I'll call you if I think of anything else. This is gonna be so fun!"

You've guessed it. Winnie is just as big of a troublemaker as I am.

"Okay. Shut up. You're on," I say to Winnie and twist my most serious face on tight. "Shut the door, little Devon. Guys, take a seat." Then I sit back and just stare at them for a good minute.

They look back at me, waiting, and then look at each other. To add to the drama, I begin clicking my pen in and out.

Click-click. I look at big Devon.

Click-click. I turn my head to the skinny one.

"So, fellas... Winnie, Wes, and I had a little talk about you this morning. They brought some interesting things to light that I wasn't aware of. Care to tell me firsthand?"

They are sweating.

Keep it together, Tatum. Don't crack.

"Uh, is this about the water cooler? We can explain. We bet Cynthia that Devon here" —little Devon gestures to Big-D—

"could drink a whole water jug by lunch. We put a bucket under our desks and he poured the water into it. She didn't even ask what she'd have to do if she lost." He looks to his partner-in-crime with wide eyes and then back to me. "She might be gullible, but she was pretty sure that he couldn't do it. So he emptied the cooler a cup at a time." The poor man's leg is pumping up and down nervously. "We knew she'd take the bet on Wednesday, so we hid a jug and colored it to look like piss the night before."

It's killing me. I want to laugh so bad that my eye is beginning to twitch.

The big Devon offers the excuse of, "We don't get out much." Then he punctuates it with, "Fuck."

Little Devon runs his fingers up and down his pants like he's trying to start a fire and burn the office down. "The idea was to make her think that Devon filled it back up...with his piss...and that her losing wage was that she'd have to drink it or empty it out or move it or whatever. She just had to get rid of it. Of course she said no and was really stressed about it being there."

"Yeah she was," the bigger Devon confirms, more elated than remorseful. "We told a couple of the other guys what we were doing and they decided to play along, too."

Watching him tell this is almost funnier than the story itself. His fat ass is up on the edge of his seat.

"You should have seen her face when Charley from editing turned his head and talked to her the whole time he filled up his cup. It was priceless. Then she got up and tried to stop him. Apparently she couldn't even get the words out!" That fat bastard can barely keep from losing his shit. His smile is so wide and his ninety-degree bent arms are holding tightened fists on both sides, joy and vigor radiating off of him. He doesn't care that it's quite possible they are in deep trouble.

Keep it together, Tatum.

I look to my phone and notice that Winnie has already hung up. Amateur.

Big Devon carries on. "This is where it got bad. Charley takes a drink and tells her it's a little warm, but it tastes really good to-day!" He howls. "It was so perfect!" His laughter echoes through the office.

A few people seated close to my door even turn to see what's happening in here.

Big Devon is laughing and trying to keep his part of the story going through what is morphing into hilarious sobs. "She turned, like, fucking green and shit. I think her eyes rolled in the back of her head! Then she started to fall. Like pass the hell out."

"Don't worry, Tatum. I caught her," the small one hurriedly adds. "She didn't even hit the floor. So really I saved her. If you think about it."

Little Devon is on the edge of his seat now too. That's the per-formers in them shining. They can't just tell a story. They have to live it.

"Yeah! Who knew bird legs over here was so nimble? He caught her and laid her down and she was only out for like a sec-ond." He looks to his friend perceptively. "Then she woke up and I thought they were going to make love right there on the Berber. I think that chick has Stockholm syndrome or something," says the bigger Devon.

"No, she doesn't. It wasn't like that," little Devon says to his partner-in-crime. Then he turns to say to me, "She was a little out of it, so I drove her home after work. I felt bad. Shit! She passed the fuck out...from comedy. That's serious."

My leg is shaking. It makes me miss being in the cubicles back at The Up Late Show. I don't know how I'm still holding it together.

"So then what?" I question.

"What, like after we got to her place? Uh, we watched Dexter and ordered a pizza. She's actually pretty cool."

"Did you apologize?"

"Yes."

"Yes." Big Devon makes sure that I hear that he did, too.

"Well, this isn't about that? Anything else you want to tell me about?" I say towards big Devon to see if he has anything to offer as confession.

"There was a pot plant found on the roof," says the bigger half.

"And?"

"And what? My pot is at home. That's it. Not ours."

"That's it? Not yours?"

"Not ours. Is that what you wanted to talk to us about? I mean, we are really busy and it's about lunchtime. You know how crazy I get before lunch. I gotta eat. I'm a big guy." The lardass grabs his stomach with both hands and shakes it at me. Like, literally shakes his belly. It's both totally disturbing and funny.

"Well, since you claim the pot isn't yours and you apologized to Cynthia, then my opinion of you two hasn't really changed from when I asked you in here." I sit back in my chair, cracking my pretend boss-like performance. "I don't give a shit about what you guys do as long as your work keeps being top notch like it is right now.

"Winnie, Wes, and I decided to give you two the office on the corner by reception. You guys are loud and out of control sometimes. No one has ever complained, but it only makes sense since you're getting your segs on and you work great together. So, after lunch, if you are all caught up, then you can start moving the random show shit out of there and your stuff in. We all think you guys are doing a great job."

I finally smile at them, and their reaction is so worth all this torture.

Their faces are priceless. Not much beats your boss telling you that, since you've mastered fucking off at work, your reward is a corner office. I can remember my first real move up, and it was like snapping that rogue puzzle piece into place. It felt like all that flipping and changing angles had paid off and that somehow I had just fit in. It's a gut-check moment.

Their guts are checked. Well, big Devon's is probably triple-checked. Big Devon's arm rises into the victory V, but little Devon stays board-still.

"Are you messing with us? Like we did Cynthia?" the tinier one asks. That's a valid inquiry.

"No. It is real. Just don't make us regret it. Really, do me a solid and don't do anything too crazy in there, huh? No running hos. No porn making. No major renovations. Just move your desks in there and work."

"Okay, what about a foosball table?" asked big Devon.

"If it fits, sure." I can appreciate the talking things out that playing a game like that offers. Hell with it. I am buying that '#1 Boss' mug I saw on Amazon.

"Okay, can we have a refrigerator?" Big Devon really has some big ideas for his new work environment.

I start to shuffle my papers around, faking their importance—and mine. I really just want them to get the hell out so I can go to lunch, too.

I break it down. "As long as you're not drunk on our clock, okay. Guys, really? Nut up. If you think it will get you into trouble, then don't do it. If you are too stupid and need reassurance of that stupidity, then just go ask Winnie. You are her favorite dummies. Go! Go to lunch."

I watch them walk out the door with a new bounce in their steps. Not more than five paces outside my office, the bigger Devon picks up the smaller one under his arms and holds him high in the air, showing him to the pit like that old monkey does in The Lion King to baby Simba.

"We get our own office everyone! We will drink all the beers after work. Little Devon here is buying!"

The pit erupts in shouts and claps. The pair struts back to their cubbies, Big-D kicking his trash can over like it's too vile for his kinglike presence.

CHAPTER
Eight

A FEW MINUTES LATER, I'm staring off into the large open office in front of me, reminiscing, when Neil comes in to gather me for lunch. "You ready? I want sushi."

"Yeah, that sounds good. Let's get out of here." I grab only the necessary things and let him lead me out.

Winnie meets up with us at the elevator. It turns out that Neil went into her office and also listened to the beginning of the Devon action on Winnie's phone. After my dear friend couldn't hold her gumption together, he invited her to lunch.

"So, Ms. Elliot, I'm dying over here. Tell me about this breakup." We aren't even to the ground floor—or even in the privacy of our own company. With no less than four other riders, he asked like it was everyone's business.

"Just a minute." I pinch his arm to shush him.

"Ouch! No. I've been waiting too long for this to happen. I have to know now. Did you catch him bumping it with his secretary, er...administrative assistant?" He corrects his faux pas and states, "They don't want to be called secretaries anymore. Did you know that?"

Taking the temporary way out of his first topic of conversation, I offer, "It sounds demeaning and debasing. There are many male admin assistants and they probably aren't fond of that dated term. You of all people should understand labels, Neil."

"What are you getting at?" The elevator doors open up to the lobby and we start for the doors that lead to the bustling New York streets. "Am I gay? Yes. Am I a personal assistant? Yes. But if I were a garbage man, I wouldn't insist we queer-up the title. What would that be exactly?" He looks at me like I know the answer.

Winnie chimes in with, "Can packer. Dumpster Diva. Sanitation Queen."

We continue laughing at ourselves and making up silly names for homosexual garbage men all the way to the restaurant.

We love this place. It's a hip little sushi bar named The Best Bite, and we come here all the time. The walls are lined with the pictures you'd expect—fish and vegetables with large Japanese words on them. It never smells awful like the sushi place on 32nd and the line moves fast. Plus, they have the best plum iced teas.

After getting our orders, we find a table that's tucked out of sight for Winnie's sake. She signs everything and then never gets to eat. That bitch deserves lunch, too.

We make small talk about this week's show, and I decide to get the other business talk out of the way about the assistant I need to interview. "So did you find me any babysitters?"

"Yes, actually. I did. When can you see them? Some have current positions. We might need to start in the afternoon one day this week and continue into the evening so the ones who have jobs can make it, too?" he says and asks at the same time.

"Cooper told me about your list. I personally think it's genius! I want a PA. If Neil finds you a good one, I'm gonna have him do me next," Winnie says to me and winks at Neil, clapping her hands.

"I'd like to get it moving. Tomorrow works." I know that, for work purposes, having a show crisis at the beginning of the week is way more manageable than at the end. At least this will be out of the way in the event that the Devons really do slack off.

He accepts with, "Okay. So we'll take off tomorrow. I'll be there about eleven to help you prepare. I have five, possibly six, applicants that I think sound like people I wouldn't want to kill."

Winnie resurfaces the other subject of interest in the current events of my life. "Why don't you go ahead and tell Neil how you broke up with Kurt on your birthday?"

"You didn't? Birthday Slut?" Neil bounces up and down in his seat. A fan comes over for a signature, Neil locks his mouth up, rushes Winnie through her autograph. Then he dismisses the fan-girl quickly with his 'shoo-fly' flapping wrist as to get us right back into our conversation.

Winnie and the girl exchange smiles and she's gone. Neil is about to chew through the side of his cheek that he's biting. His bony elbows land on the table. He brushes his meal out of the way and motions for me to spill it.

"Well, not exactly. It was the new and improved Birthday Slut, I guess." I prepare myself for the story with one more spicy tuna bite and a deep breath."Okay, so Kurt was being sort of a dick on Friday. He went out with work people after he got off and sort of ruined my birthday dinner."

Neil's face scrunches as he looks to Winnie for confirmation. When she nods her head with a disappointed expression, he turns back to me with a pout.

I wave off his sympathy. "Anyway, he came by after he was finished and well..." There wasn't a delicate way to tell the story. "I was giving him my special job—you know, the *real* special job—and then I just"—I mime the actions of what I did with Kurt's penis—"aimed it back to his face and let him shoot himself with, um, himself while I told him to get out and that we were over."

I slump forward, breathless after rambling to get the last part out. I won't have to tell this story again. Thank God.

Smacking the table and sucking in air like a ninety-five-year-old asthmatic, he squeals in delight. "That is. The best. Breakup. Ever! Oh my God. It's brilliant. What did he do? Was he pissed?" I should have waited for Christmas to give Neil a gift like this story.

I look at Winnie warily, because she knows the rest of the story from breakfast Sunday morning, and keep that part minimal. Neil knows of my condition, but I don't need his pity. Better to let him think I'm a badass than the mess I am inside.

I vaguely go over the talk we had and that we parted as friends. Winnie's favorite part is still the booty-call loophole good-bye. In all honesty, I kind of like that part, too.

My phone buzzes from inside my new bag, and I reach in, looking at the screen that reads Dr. Evil. *Dr. Meade's office.* I let it go to voicemail, and the three of us keep talking and laughing over amazing sushi.

Neil apparently went on a date over the weekend, and the guy was nice, but he called him sugary. I have suspicions that Neil likes the bear variety of homosexual. He always dismisses the "too sweet" or the "icky nice" men.

Winnie updates the both of us on the guest favors she ordered online and how Coop about shit a brick when he saw the total. It wasn't that much, but other than the fancy-schmansy car he drives, Coop is pretty frugal. She is under the impression that money is meant to be spent. My thinking lies somewhere in between.

"I called the driving services and asked for Ray like you said in the email, too," he tells me as we start our walk back to the studio. "Cooper already called them, so they knew we were going to call. They sound pretty good. That Ray guy is their most popular driver." He wags his eyebrows suggestively. "Do you want to use them a few times before making a commitment? They can start on Wednesday." Neil asks, getting us back to my self-inflicted tasks of the week.

"Yeah, line it up. I doubt it will matter all that much. It's just a car service."

Winnie can't hide her small twinge of jealousy, "Dammit, now I want a car. Okay, I've got it. What if we share? I mean, I can foot some of the bill and we can share your new PA, too. You're too boring to need one all to yourself." She walks ahead of us and stops us with two hands to consider her idea.

"No," I deadpan and push past her, grabbing her arm so she doesn't fall behind. "Whoever I hire will be too busy to mess around with a bitch like you." I lay my head on her shoulder as we walk back into the building.

"Fine, but if their workload gets low, just tell me. I have errands all over the city with the wedding and it would be nice to have someone to do my bidding." I think she's probably serious. She'd love someone doing all of her dirty work.

"Yeah, okay. I'll just say, 'Excuse me, assistant? Do you mind picking up some things for my best friend, Bridezilla?'" I say in the bitchiest voice I can find. It's a little too close to normal, and I laugh at myself before continuing. "Who do you think I am? An assistant pimp? Get your own." And she could, too. She banks more than I do, getting star credit, writing, and performing at the show. Recently, she's even been approached for endorsements.

We finish out the day by sitting in my office, making fun of Chel-Ro, and thinking up costumes for the Southern duck hunters seg—you know, being professionals.

I listen to Dr. Meade's message. He just wanted to let me know that he'd emailed me some recommendations for a therapist. I delete it before it is all the way finished.

One step at a time.

CHAPTER *Nine*

TRUE TO HIS WORD, Neil shows up the next day just before eleven, kissing my cheek as he walks in with his hands full.

"You look ridiculous. It's almost eleven, Tatum. Pajamas still? Really?" He unloads his arms putting their contents onto the counter. "I brought you coffee, bagels, and schmear. You're welcome."

God, I love the schmear. First of all, it's just plain old fun to say. And secondly, there's not much better than a lightly toasted cheese bagel with veggie schmear for breakfast.

Well, there's dick. Dick would be nice, but I probably won't be enjoying that for breakfast anytime soon—if ever again.

Goodbye, morning sex.

"So, I have everything organized and I have some of the questions that I thought may interest you in a questionnaire, if you will," Neil tells me, sounding quite involved.

"I'm sure you do, Neil. I would expect nothing less. So who's our first victim?"

"Ah, yes. Victim number one hails from NYU and is trying to get a leg into personal relations. She is smart and organized, and my friend at the agency said she was, and I quote, 'classic Type A.'" He looks like he's a bit scared. I don't know if it's for her or me.

"Doesn't Type A stand for type asshole? What time is she supposed to be here?"

"In about thirty minutes. Eat up and get changed unless you plan on doing these interviews with a nod to 1999 slumber-party casual."

We finish our breakfast, and I do as I was told, dressing out of my pink sweats and 'Eat Me' t-shirt and into a pair of skinny jeans and a flowing chevron-print top. Since I'm not going out, I just slip on a pair of flats and call it good enough. My hair is much easier to whip into shape with the new short 'do I have going on.

Good move, Tatum.

Ms. Type A is punctual and basically reciting her answers like a pro. She says all the right things and very politely lets us know that she thinks of this job as a leg up in the industry. Even though she isn't going to be assisting me in my professional life, she knows that the events I attend would be very beneficial to her Rolodex.

Her personality is also about as dry as a popcorn fart and she sort of gets on my nerves. She's dressed in a gray tweed business ensemble, and worst of all, she wore dark hose. Not my thing. Type A earns a maybe-we-will-see sort of score.

Neil preps me for the next batter up, who is more of a free spirit. What Jamie lacks in organizational skills, she makes up for in fashion and her own connections. Turns out her family lives on the Upper East Side and she's quite the debutante. Her motivation for employment is more to make her family happy and less about beginning a career.

Her pros are knowing my area like the back of her hand and that I could definitely send her out for clothes. She wore a darling cowl-neck top and an asymmetric mini with this season's Louboutins.

Mama like.

Jamie's perky and easy to talk to, but my life can be a bit chaotic and I'm not sure I want Business Barbie handling my day-to-day affairs.

The next interview is fine, but the back-to-business stay-at-home mom doesn't really clinch my attention. Though the scrunchie was a nice touch, the vomit on her shoulder indicates that she'll be a mess.

We have the majority of them out of the way and it is almost three. Neil and I only have one more who could make it and that's this evening. With a few hours to burn, and since by now I'm in serious need of a stiff cocktail, I suggest one. But Neil negotiates me down to mere iced teas and sandwiches from the corner deli.

He's only been gone for about five minutes and I hear a knock at the door.

Earlier I alerted the door man, Phil, that we were holding interviews today. So he made sure that when my perspective assistants arrived he showed them the way up to my condo.

He knows Neil and never really bothers to buzz for him anymore. So it's odd that someone is knocking with more than three hours before our next potential PA is supposed to show up. Besides, Neil can't possibly be back this fast. The deli is more than three blocks away.

"Did you forget your wallet, dumbass?" I ask as I open the door. I barely look up. I fling the door open and turn to walk back into my kitchen, where I have my laptop open so I can watch last week's show again.

"No. I have my wallet," says a man I don't know. I look back towards my oversized mahogany front door and there stands a vision of pure...well, man. He is wearing dark gray slacks, a fitted black shirt, and a smile that has something wicked in it. His green eyes sweep over me like he's assessing me, too. But he doesn't look at me like I'm a stranger. It's weird having people recognize you when you don't know them.

Sure, a female personal assistant would be a little more comfortable, but this tall, blond Adonis would be so rewarding to look at every day.

"Oh, excuse me. You must be early. Or maybe Neil got the time wrong. My other assistant just ran out for sandwiches."

"Oh, well I suppose I'm late then." There's a fleck of sarcasm dotting his words.

"Late? I beg your pardon?" In this moment, I feel dumbstruck. What time is it? Who is this guy? Why does he think he's late? How in the hell do I get his shirt off?

"Yes. I was going to grab a bite to eat before I came here and decided better of it. I suppose if I were a little earlier, I could have sent an order with your assistant."

"Now wouldn't that be a great first impression?" I laugh in earnest. "Showing up to a job interview for a personal assistant's position and ordering a turkey on rye." It is kind of funny. And then again, he also seems presumptuous. And confident. And playful. And hot as fuck.

"How are the interviews going then? Sorry, I didn't mean to surprise you." His face shows something that I can't put my finger on. Something about the way he squinted when he reached for the word interviews catches me off kilter.

"I like surprises. Don't worry about it. Do you want to come in or are you going to stand in my doorway the whole time?" I slowly walk back in his direction. Slowly, for one, to make sure I don't run into anything that I obviously am not paying attention to—because I can't break his laser gaze. And slowly, two, because as weird as this strange man in my threshold is, I don't want to scare him away.

His curious green eyes look from side to side before he takes the few measured steps the rest of the way in. In witnessing only about three sentences and two strides from him, I find myself fascinated by this guy. He's so graceful and calm.

"Thank you. So how are they?" His eyebrow arches and he grins. "Have you found who you're looking for?"

Was there ever a more loaded fucking question? Well, as far as personal assistants go, not so much; but as far as a contender for later tonight's fantasy finger friend, I have a clear dead ringer—this man with the dark blond hair and verde eyes.

I walk back to the kitchen and he slowly follows behind. "Neil, my other assistant, has certainly found some great possibili-

ties, but I probably won't know until I have interviewed everyone."
I tap my fingers across the work surface of the counter—pinky to
index, index to pinky—as I talk to him. "Hiring a personal personal assistant is different. I always thought that having one would be
pretentious, but I don't really have a great alternative plan right
now. So I suppose it's going well."

I'm rambling, but he's engaged and doesn't seem to mind.

"Have you done this sort of work before? Of course, you don't
have to answer that if you'd rather just wait for Neil and we can go
through your interview a bit more formally."

"No need to wait for him," he chimes in as he takes a seat at
the bar across from where I'm standing. "I don't mind answering
your questions. No, I've never been a personal assistant, but I have
a lot of experience with helping people. So it couldn't be much
more complicated than that, right?"

"Yeah, I guess. But my life is a bit unorthodox. I work about
sixty hours a week from the office, sometimes more from home.
Occasionally, I have multiple social events and meetings to attend
in a week's time, often with little notice." I think about how that
was true at one time, but not so much lately. "I have an active social life and like to be out and about. Well, I did. That may all be
slowing down in the near future."

"Sounds fascinating. What kind of work do you do?" He listens, and I can tell he's paying close attention just by the way he
looks at my eyes as I speak.

"Oh, I thought you knew. I write for and produce Just Kidding." Feeling pride and a sense of confidence, I hold my head a
bit higher, summon my business posture, and say, "I'm Tatum Elliot."

He stands, walks around the island, and extends a hand to me.
This simple gesture, one that I do nearly on a daily basis, all of a
sudden seems foreign. I stand, looking at him, lost in my own
thoughts for a minute at the possibility of touching this smoking-
hot guy.

The air between us gifts me with a lungful of leather and sandalwood. It's like I have an infinite capacity for oxygen, and I inhale for what seems like minutes, never wanting to stop.

"Tatum, I'm Ben Harris. It's a pleasure to meet you."

As these words float in the delicious air around me, I somehow find my bearings and raise my right arm waist high. Just like that, his fingers wrap almost completely around my offered hand. His pinky bridges across the back of all four of my fingers and his thumb settles on my wrist.

I know I have miniature hands, but his huge hand swallows mine, and it suddenly feels like the handshake has lasted just a beat too long.

"You too, Ben. The pleasure is all mine." This kind of tunnel vision is unlike what I'm used to. I'm hoping that it's from the heady feeling I'm getting from being around him and not one of those possible dizzy spells Dr. Meade mentioned.

His calmness makes my mind feel like it's floating away. I haven't experienced anything like it before.

I withdraw my hand, and he returns to the seat he left for our formal introduction.

I shake my reverie back and try hospitality on. "Can I offer you something to drink? As I mentioned, we were going to have a bite to eat before your interview. You're quite early. I wonder if there was a miscommunication with the time? Do you have anything that you need to do? Then perhaps come back at five? Or you could just hang around here until Neil returns and we could go through everything then?" I'm rambling again.

"I would love a glass of water. No, I don't have anywhere to be. Is it necessary that Neil is here for the interview?" he asks, and it's a fair question.

I open the cabinet door, take a glass out for Ben, and then fill it from the dispenser in the refrigerator. I narrowly miss bouncing my noggin off the still-open cabinet door before handing him the drink. Thank God I didn't though.

"No. I suppose not. I just hadn't prepared to do this alone. But you are here and I am here, so I don't really see why not. Excuse me. I'll just go get my notes and things. We can do it in here."

"That works for me." I walk into the dining room, where we've been seeing the other applicants, and grab my legal pad and one of the question sheets Neil printed out. I hear him ask, "What is it that you are looking for in a personal assistant?"

There are many ways I can answer that question, but for some reason I answer more candidly than I did when Ms. Type A had asked the same one just hours before. "Well, Ben?"

"Ben," he offers.

"Ben, then. I am losing my sight. There isn't any way to avoid it or predict when it will be gone. The only thing I know is that it is inevitable, and my sight is getting worse at a faster pace than it was. My doctor suggested going to a blind camp or something like that and to simplify. So, in lieu of the whole blind camp suggestion, I decided to take the latter part of his advice and simplify. I thought that having a personal assistant would be a good idea. You know, run some of my errands, help me stay organized and on schedules. I'm also hiring driving and cleaning services. See? Simplify."

"Sounds like you have it all figured out." I can still see something else in his eyes. The man looks like he's humoring me.

"Yes, Ben. I would like to think that I do have it figured out. I believe that, with some assistance in those areas of my life, the blindness will have a smaller impact. Therefore, it will be more manageable easing into."

"You are planning to ease into blindness?" He is without a doubt humoring me. And he isn't even making an attempt to hide it.

"Do you see an issue with that? I'm sorry, I thought you were here to be interviewed, not me. Why exactly do you want this position? You seem amused by all of this." Irritation begins to grow within me, but I'm curious about what he is thinking.

"I am not really sure how to answer that. I think that I could certainly be helpful to you. I suppose I've been looking for something a little more"—he pauses as if thinking of the right word—"challenging."

I look up at the microwave and notice that Neil's been gone for longer than normal. He should be walking in at any minute. I could use him right now. He wouldn't let this interview derail like I clearly am. "Excuse me."

"Of course."

I reach around where Ben is sitting and grab my purse. It takes two swipes to hook the strap, and I think he notices that my aim is a bit off. I take my phone out and see that I have missed calls from Winnie and Cooper. Plus, I have a text from Neil.

Neil: That place was packed. Are late lunches the new black? After waiting I got pissed. Went down to the other deli on 82nd street. I'll be back in 30.

I reply with a short and sweet 'hurry up' message and set the phone down. "It seems that Neil will be a bit longer. How about we talk about your credentials? Where did you go to school? Do you have a degree?"

Again, thoughtfully taking his time with his answers, he replies, "Yes, I have a few degrees actually. I went to school at Georgetown. I also have a lot of experience with blindness. I have relatives who are blind. So that might be of some use to your situation." He looks to his hands and then directly back to my eyes. "I love your condo. Do you live here alone?"

"I do. I had it remodeled after I bought it. Thank you. Do you live nearby? That would be convenient for both of us." As crazy as this interview began, he's actually pretty ideal for the job.

"Yeah. I live about twelve blocks from here. What are the hours for this position? Is it full time or part time?" He still looks relaxed, confidently leaning back in the barstool with his arm hanging over the back. He's perfectly comfortable. Surprisingly, I kind of am too.

"That's a good question." I stop to think and bite my lip. Finally, I say, "I've never had a personal assistant like this, so I can't really say just yet. I would guess that, for the time, it would be minimal. Mostly mornings or afternoons." I study his face to see any resistance, but it's not there. "I will have a better handle on it after I find someone and we naturally find a schedule that accommodates both of us. When would you be available to start? If hired, that is?"

Am I going to hire him? It's starting to feel like I've already offered him the position and he's deciding whether or not to accept.

"I could start immediately. Tomorrow if you'd like." There is a smile in his eyes that's brighter than the one bending his mouth. "I think this will be a wonderful working relationship."

Now I know that he assumes the position is his. "Well, hold up just a minute. I, uh… Wait." I shuffle my papers, trying to find the other questions I know I am supposed to pose, but before I land on any, I ask, "Aren't you interested in knowing about benefits or salary?"

"No, not really. I'm sure the package you'll provide will be adequate. Why don't we just start on a trial basis?"

"Did you just hire yourself?" I inquire, half laughing and half serious.

"Well, I certainly was able to assist you in doing that. So at very least, that should say something about how well we will work together." And then he gives me a radiant, full smile. I can't keep my own from sprouting on my face, and for the first time today, I know that he is the person I want to see every day.

Shit. Maybe I should have him sign a non-disclosure or at least a waiver of harassment.

"Ben, I work in an industry where press can be tricky. I don't get a lot of it, but my close friends do. I would require you to be very tight lipped when it comes to my private life and theirs. And since you will be wading through my private life on a daily basis, I would require your discretion." Most of that feels like it could have been left unsaid, but I want him to know that I won't tolerate it.

"Furthermore, I am really inappropriate most of the time. It is part of why I do what I do and how I do it well. I don't filter myself much and you may not like that. Do not be mistaken—I am usually a lady when I'm in public. But in private, I can be downright vulgar and I swear like a sailor. If you are, oh, I don't know…super religious or easily offended, then you may want to fuck off right now." Ah, here's my mouth. If he wants this job, he has to be cool with me. I wait for his reaction to my favorite four-letter word to seal our deal.

"Tatum, you can trust me to protect your privacy and I fucking love sassy women." He chuckles a bit, saying, "As long as you understand that I may tell you things that you don't want to hear from time to time, with regards to my job, I will have your best interest in mind at all times." He's all business again by the end of his sentence.

He's a sexy-as-hell, sassy-liking businessman. I smile at him, and his reappears.

"I can live with that." For the next few minutes, we discuss a schedule for the next week that we both can live with. I offer him a healthy wage and tell him that I'll pay him cash for our trial period. We exchange phone numbers and that's that.

I have a new fire-ass-hot personal assistant.

"Well, I guess that's all we need to discuss today. Thank you for coming, and I'll talk to you tomorrow," I say to Ben as I walk him to the door.

When we get to the entryway, he offers his hand to me again, and this time I don't feel as hesitant to take it. This time it feels natural to put my hand in his. So I do, and once again, his masculine hand swaddles mine.

"Thank you, Tatum. Please don't hesitate to call or text me if you think of anything else you'd like to know. I'll see you tomorrow morning."

I open the door, and here comes Neil with his arms full of paper bags and a drink carrier. He walks up with a confused look on his face. "Sorry that took so long, Tatum," he says to me before he turns to measure up Ben. "Hello. I don't think we know each other."

I grab the food from his hands, seeing what he brought me, and I'm instantly famished.

"Hello. It is nice to meet you. I am Ben Harris, Tatum's new PA. I'll be seeing you. I'll let you guys get to your late lunch. Goodbye, Tatum." And like that, he breezes past us and walks straight down the hall and around the corner.

"W—w-what the hell did he just say? He's your new PA? What the fuck did I miss? Who was that?" His face is painted with questions and his cute little eye brows cinch together.

"I don't know. I thought you knew him. I thought it was just a misunderstanding about the time. He's qualified and very nice. I like him. He's laid back and chill. I could use that. I wonder if the agency slipped him in last minute or something?"

"Yeah, I guess that is probably what happened. You hired him? Really? Is it because he looks like he stepped out of GQ? Not that I'm complaining. I will love seeing him on a regular basis." Neil's looks confused and also like he knows something I don't. I can only imagine what he is thinking about the whole ordeal.

"You're right. I should probably start saving money for my sexual harassment defense fund now, huh? Come on. I am as hungry as a hostage." I am, and I want to tell Neil all about the mysterious Ben Harris, Personal Assistant at large.

CHAPTER
Ten

I GOT A TEXT from Ben a few minutes ago asking if there was anything he could grab for me on his way over and I all too eagerly told him about my coffee preference. There isn't much use in being coy.

I dressed up this morning a little more than I would have on a normal Wednesday. There is no point in pretending that he isn't hot. I know I'm his boss, but I can't have him showing me up on the first day. He wore some nice clothes yesterday, and I need to be prepared.

My yellow jumper dress and blue heels will give him a run for his money. I even gave myself a blow-out.

Just as I thought. Ben arrives wearing dark brown pants and a fitted ivory button-up. I almost want to tell him he is fired and attack him.

I must suffer from major morning horniness and a very potent version of female morning wood.

I need to get use to this.

"I have a list of things that I need done, including: finding a cleaning service, some scheduling things that I need you to rearrange so I can spend more time with Winnie on wedding stuff, and picking up my dry cleaning and a few groceries. Are you sure you really want to do all of this?" I ask, wondering if this is as stupid as it feels.

He's so hot for Pete's sake. Why in the hell would he want to do this?

As I explain the tasks I need him to take care of for me, he only listens intently and smiles. "Relax, Tatum. You don't have to worry about this stuff today. I've got this. Just go to work and do your thing. I'll be here, well, I guess…doing your other things. Really, this is under control."

His simple words make me feel like it really might be fine.

I give him a key to the door, and he offers to walk me down to continue our conversation. I tell him how to contact my new car service and I ask him to contact Neil about synchronizing our schedules.

None of the tasks seem that difficult or time consuming. I let him know that, if he doesn't have any issue with it, after he finishes he can leave for the day.

"If you have any questions, don't feel weird about calling me at work. If I can answer, then I will. If I can't, then I will call or text you back."

"Got it."

He ushers me out the revolving doors in the lobby of my building with his great big man hand in the middle of my back. It isn't exactly sexual though, being a little too high to be the small of my back, but I like it. It's nice and comforting having his capable hands guiding me.

Capable. I bet they are. *Focus, Tatum.*

"I'll forward you all of the changes I make to your agenda and I will update you when necessary. Have a good day today. Is this your car?"

"Good morning, Ms. Elliot? I'm Ray, your driver. It's very nice to meet you," says the giant of a man walking towards us. He looks like a linebacker. He's good-looking but way too beefy for my tastes.

"Hello, Ray. This is Ben, my assistant. Thank you for starting so soon. I've never had a driver before. It feels a bit weird."

"Don't worry about that. You'll get use to it." His big, warm smile is easy to like. "Nice to meet you too, Ben." Then Ray goes back around to the driver's side, seeing that Ben is already making a play for my door.

"You too," Ben says, giving Ray a friendly smile. "I'm sure we will be seeing each other." He lifts handle of the black town car and opens it for me.

I brush my hair behind me ear, running my hand over the tender bruise that is starting to fade. "Thank you, Ben. See ya later."

"You're welcome, Tatum." He smiles at me kindly and then his face sours when he sees my bruise. He looks at it for a second before his eyes soften again. I sit and swing my legs into the car.

He shuts the door and gives the top a few taps to notify Ray that I'm all in. It is a different experience, but one that I can definitely get used to.

Looking behind the car, I see him standing there. I watch him as we pull away, overwhelmed by all of the new things I've experienced this morning. Standing on the side of the street, he looks so strong and confident.

As I watch him get smaller and smaller, the urge inside me to call in sick, just to learn more about him, gets bigger and bigger. There's something special about him.

This is going to be a mess.

———— • ————

Today goes on and on, but without incident. All the plans we laid out on Monday are falling perfectly into place and it's a bit unnerving. You know that feeling when everything seems to be working the way you plan, only to be blindsided by an unexpected catastrophe? It sort of feels like that.

My phone goes off and I'm pleased to see it is my new personal assistant. I get a rush of adrenaline as I read his message.

Ben: Sorry to bother you, but do you use a fork to eat ice cream? And would you like me to get you more at the market?

He sure doesn't miss much.

Me: Yes, I eat it with a fork. I don't know why. I never turn down ice cream.

Ben: Same flavor? Do you mind if I do some organizing in your kitchen?

Me: Same flavor is fine. Organize away. Is it really that bad? I left the fork in the carton. Right?

Ben: Bingo.

Bingo?

My imagination vaults into overdrive. What if he's going through my whole house looking for things to organize? He found my ice cream fork. What else is he finding? What if he goes into my bedroom?

I type to him, hoping I isn't too late.

Me: Just organize the kitchen.

Ben: Your sock drawer is a mess.

Oh. Shit. My sock drawer, the quiet upstairs neighbor to Mr. Right. In case you are wondering, Mr. Right is my vibrator. No use in getting all bent out of shape about it. It isn't like you don't have one hidden somewhere, too.

He finally sends another message.

Ben: Just kidding.

I quickly fire off a reply.

Me: We need some rules. Rule 1: My bedroom and bathroom are holy. Thou shall NOT pass.

I shouldn't have been that blunt though. It makes it seem like I have something to hide even more.

Ben: Religious? I was just teasing.

Me: Hardly. I'm just certain I need no personal assisting in there.

Good thing my dress is sleeveless or I'd have pit stains. My phone vibrates in my hand while I'm still looking at it and waiting for something back from him.

Ben: No assistance in the bedroom. LOL. Noted.

I'll let it end there. I'm trying not to flirt with him. It's a challenge. He is so sexy. But it's not like I'm going to start our working relationship off like that, and it's not like he gave me the impression it would even be welcome.

He is my employee. I am his boss. Isn't that the premise of a porno? Yeah, I've seen that one—Naughty Boss-Woman and the Off-Limits Assistant. My juvenile thoughts litter my mind. I can't help myself.

The rest of the day moves about like a well-oiled machine. I go through all of the motions effortlessly. I nail down the week's segments and send some emails. I'm functioning stress free.

Maybe there is something to this simplifying thing.

Around five thirty, I check out and head home. On my way, I have Ray stop for me at the market so I can grab a six-pack and all the newest gossip mags. I didn't ask Ben to by my alcohol on the first day. It felt too soon.

Ray doesn't even shake his head when I emerge from the store with an armload of scandalous reading material and beer.

I know. I know. Wild life.

I walk though my door and Ben is still here. And he's singing—not well, but singing nonetheless. The song is familiar, but really old. Otis Redding maybe?

He likes the oldies. That's hot.

There are boxes and tools on the counter in my kitchen, and it smells like heaven. Where am I?

"Um, hello?" I round the wall to see the rest of my kitchen. "Whoa, you are quite the overachiever. What's all of this?"

"No 'Honey, I'm home'?" Ben asks, wiping his forehead with a that hand that also holds a screwdriver. So much for getting to know each other. Here I am, worried about flirting, and I walk in to a modern-day version of I Love Lucy or the Twilight Zone—I can't decide.

Should I mention that his ivory shirt from this morning is balled up on the floor next to him? Because it is, and his undershirt fits like a second skin. Ben's tall, lean frame is mouthwatering.

He probably notices that I'm not chiming in on the domestic banter and clarifies, "I'm just making some adjustments."

"Like what? Those are brand new." I put my beer and literature—okay, beer and celebrity trash—on my cluttered counter. "I don't remember my contractor explaining the need for yearly 'adjustments' to my cabinets." I actually did air quotes to recite "adjustments" back to him sarcastically.

"I changed the hinges. These close on their own if they're left open." He opens a cabinet door and looks at me like I'm not getting it. "After a few seconds, if you don't close them, then they close themselves. Voila. No bumping into open cabinets." He is quite proud of himself.

Initially, I'm taken aback that someone thought to do this for me. I'm also embarrassed. When did I bump into something around him? I just met the guy. I haven't tripped over the bastard barstool left out too far yet or missed the cupboard shelf with a glass in front of him. Am I that obviously awkward and clumsy?

"Why? Why did you do this?" I'm totally confused about what to think about it. It's nice and practical. It's also a little pathetic.

"It's helpful," he points out, demonstrating how they work.

"Yes. I understand that, but it is your first day. Did it seem that urgent or something?"

Pride. I've whacked my head against every one of those cabinets. It never hurt as much my as my pride does right now.

Ben looks at me empathetically, seeing that I'm upset.

I'm not an actress. I can't believably hide my emotions. Like, at all. I'm lousy at poker, and don't bother telling me a secret you don't want told. It's in my nature to tell...everyone.

He has to go. I'm not sure if just for the night or permanently.

"Maybe it's time for you to call it a day, Bob Vila. I can clean up. I'm still getting use to all of this," I say, standing in front of him, feeling like a fool.

"I'm sorry, Tatum."

I notice the apology in his expression when I hurriedly glance by it. Then I quickly scan around for anything else to look at. Something to distract me from the infiltrating stare he's giving me.

"I wasn't trying to imply..." Ben says, looking down and blowing out a fat breath. He stands up to his full height first before he leans down to me so that we're eye to eye in my kitchen.

He's not letting me avoid him like I want.

"Look... This is new. To both of us. You're used to not relying on someone else to recognize something you need because you're capable of doing things yourself. And I'm a man who doesn't hesitate to attend to something that needs attention. Maybe I moved too quickly, and I'm sorry that you're offended, but the truth of it is"— I follow his eyes over to my goose egg peeks out from under my bangs—"you hit your head. I can see that. I just want to make sure that you don't do it again."

As much as I want to scream, I want to cry. I want to lunge at him, but I'm still not sure if its to smack him or shove my tongue down his throat.

He sees me as a defenseless weakling. He thinks I'm more broken that I do.

"Oh, this?" I brush back my bangs. I'll show him. I'm not weak. Sweeping my hair back and tilting my head as if proud of my wound, I volunteer my best faux laugh. "No, silly. This is from my, uh, headboard. You're not the only man I know who gets carried away." I laugh again, pretending to do so at him. "This was no accident, just a little rough...you know. And you should wait to make adjustments to *my* home until I ask for them. I'll call you tomorrow."

His jade eyes are blank of emotion. He doesn't even react. It was a bitchy thing for me to say. Though, I can't see an ounce of rebuttal. Did I speak or not?

Without a hint of chiding in his calm low voice, he says, "There's chili on the stove, and your revised schedule is ready to sync to your phone." Ben leans down to pick his shirt up and his head is right in front of me. Like, the lower me.

He doesn't move. He just hangs there for a second. I can't look down. I know he's down there, and without moving my head quite visibly, he is out of my sight.

I feel his finger lightly touch my leg. His thumb actually. It has to be his thumb, because his other four fingers wrap around the top of my calf muscle while his thumb rubs a tender spot on my leg.

The hairs on my legs threaten to shoot out as feel a shiver coming on. My spine is like a jump rope that's been whipped on one end and the ripple races all the way up the back of my neck.

A breath escapes my mouth like I am trying to fog up a window to write my name on it. Too soon—or not soon enough—he's back up and leaning over to grab his keys from the counter, only millimeters from my ear.

I'm frozen.

Ben whispers like he's telling me a secret, "That must have been some show. Did you get those bruises on your legs from the headboard too?"

The only thing I can think to say is, "Bingo."

CHAPTER
Eleven

"BINGO? WHO THE FUCK says bingo?" Winnie shrieks over the phone when I call her to get her take on the matter about five minutes after Ben left. "I think it was nice. Why'd you have to be such an ass?"

"Because! He just took it upon himself to make 'adjustments' to my house! Why didn't he ask first? Don't you think that it was a tad presumptuous? I said to organize! Who does that?"

I'm tidying up the mess left in my kitchen, unable to sort the anger from the gratitude in my head. I really want her to be as annoyed with him as I am, but I've totally under-calculated her temper.

"All I'm saying is maybe he wasn't even going to tell you. You told him you usually work late and he was probably going to have it all cleaned up and done before you ever noticed. For real, Tatum. If you hadn't caught him doing it, you'd probably think they always did that! He's either a really perceptive PA or that man has the hots for you."

"He was overqualified!" I don't even know how that applies to my argument, but I shout it nonetheless.

"Oh for crying out fucking loud. Drop it. He wasn't being a jerk. How is your head anyway? I saw it today and it looked a little better. Hell, is still looks painful." Winnie knows I won't complain about or mention it unless she asks.

"It's sore, but better. Think I should call him?" I rub the sore spot and finally feel the bump receding some.

"No. Talk to him tomorrow. You just want to argue anyway."

This girl and I are cut from the same cloth. I do want to argue. I've only known this guy for a hot minute and he is already so far under my skin that I can't think straight.

I sigh in defeat. "You're right. What's Cooper doing?" I ask as I finish cleaning up the last of the small renovation mess and help myself to a bowl of the chili Ben left warming on my stove.

"Hi, Tate. I'm right here."

My eyes roll on their own free will at the knowledge of him listening this whole time. "Shit. What do you think about all that? And you two twats should tell me when I'm on speakerphone." What I did I tell you? There is absolutely no confidentiality between either of those two and me.

"Can I be honest?" And he waits for the answer to his stupid question.

"No," I deny, facetiousness getting the best of me.

"I thought about doing that a while back. I was showing a house that had them a few weeks ago and I think they're cool. Winnie's right though. He's either a super assistant or he likes you."

Typical.

"He's a stupid jerk." I chuckle, sounding so childish.

My mouth takes a bite of chili and moans. It. Is. Amazing.

Winnie hears me. Hell, my next-door neighbor probably thinks I have a cow in my condo with the noises are coming from my body. "What's that? Are you moaning?"

Talking with a mouthful of heaven, I sputter, "Ben made me chili."

In unison, they say, "He's likes you." That suits me just fine in this moment. His chili almost makes up for my bruised ego. It is first class.

———— • ————

After I finish the bowl—okay, two bowls—of chili and go over some wedding stuff with them, I lie in bed watching entertainment news. While flipping through countless tabloids and taking a few notes for the show, I notice that I'm looking at my phone. A lot.

I want to call him. I can just call and thank him for the chili. That won't be weird, right? Dinner is a nice gesture, and it'll let him know that I *can* be appreciative.

Picking up my cell and putting it down a half dozen times, finally I just do it.

"Hello." Ben's voice sounds gravelly like he's been sleeping.

"It's Tatum. I'm sorry. Were you sleeping?" Pulling the phone out, I look at the time. Shit, it is eleven thirty. *Real smooth.*

"Yeah, but that's okay. I fell asleep reading. Is everything all right?" I can hear him shifting around and further waking up as he yawns. "What time is it anyway?"

"Oh, not that late. Anyway, I was just calling to thank you for the dinner. It was delicious." I am derailing quickly. *Short and sweet, Tatum.* Why did I think was a good idea?

"You're welcome. But you could have thanked me tomorrow. It is nearly midnight. Why aren't you sleeping?" Busted.

"I know. Listen, I'm sorry for waking you up. I didn't realize it was this late. I was watching TV and lost track of time. You're right. I need to get to sleep."

"No. No, it's fine. You surprised me is all."

"Touché." Talking to him, my softens. I don't want to argue at all. I'm pulled more towards apologizing. "I sort of overreacted earlier about the cabinets. I do appreciate it. I'm just... I don't know." I click off the television and lie there in the dark on the phone with Ben on the other end of the line.

"No. I should've asked you if I could do that. It was rude and insensitive of me." There is sincerity in his low, sleep-cloaked voice. "That's my Moo-Moo's, or rather, my grandmother's recipe."

"What?"

"The chili. She taught me how to make it when I was a kid. I love it."

"It was wonderful. You have to let me repay you for it. You're not my cook or whatever. You don't have to do all of that."

"I wanted to. Besides, you had most of the ingredients. I only had to grab a few things when I was out on the way back from the hardware store."

My hand absentmindedly picks and fiddles with the fuzzy knots that adorn a nearby throw pillow. "Well, it was thoughtful. Let me buy you lunch tomorrow. I'm not used to all of this, I don't know...?"

"Assistance?" he offers, and we laugh.

"Yeah, I guess." I stupidly nod, though he can't see me. "It's weird having someone in my space who I don't know, you know? It is intrusive." Here I go again. "Not that you're an intruder or anything, Ben. I'm not making any sense."

"I get what you're saying and I understand. It's awkward getting used to new people, but we have time."

"Are you always like this? So insightful? What are you, some kind of life coach? You're very Yoda-like."

He laughs loudly, and it's music to my ears. Some people love the sound of babies cooing or the ocean. I love the sound of a laugh that I've earned. "Yoda-like? That's a new one. I've just spend a lot of time examining people. Sometimes I don't realize that I'm doing it."

"Hmmm, well you'll have plenty of time to examine me. I guess." Shit. I'm almost flirting again. Why do I always want to flirt with him? Oh, that's right. Because he's fucking hot as sin.

"Trust me, I know. I'm looking forward to it." Is he flirting back? Because it sounds like he is.

We talk for over an hour about our favorite places to go in the city and college. He's easy to talk to and even easier to listen to. As it gets later, his voice gets even lower and quieter, making me pay even more attention than I normally would. It's grainy and smooth at the same time. I think about recording him and side with my peek-a-boo sanity not to.

"Well, I've kept you up long enough. Your boss will be upset if you're late," I joke, trying to get off of the phone before this call turns down a road I'm not sure I can handle facing in the morning.

"Well, what if it was sort of her fault I was *up* all night." His voice takes on a sensual tone, and my body reacts when he says "up."

Maybe it's the few beers I finished while we've been talking creeping up on me, but my head is swimming and I'm glad I'm already lying down. My thoughts turn to what part of him I'd like to see up.

I facepalm myself in the forehead and wince as I hit my injury. That's what I get.

"She wouldn't do that. She's very professional." I say.

"Pro-fess-ion-al," he repeats back to me slowly.

"Yes. Professional. She takes her business very seriously and she doesn't like to be kept waiting." Shit. That one was all me. I hear a hitch in his breath, and I know this is having the same effect on him.

"I wouldn't want to keep her waiting, now would I? That would be frustrating."

"Ben?"

"Tatum." Hearing my name cross his lips in that sultry voice is more of a turn-on than I could have ever imagined and I need to shut it down. "You looked really pretty this morning."

"I did?"

"Yep. And I bet you look even better right now in bed."

My pulse races. How does he know I'm in bed?

He yawns and I yawn, too, even though now I'm wide awake.

"Thanks. You weren't that bad to look at yourself. What makes you think I'm in bed?"

"I don't know. I was just guessing. It is the middle of the

night." He pauses before adding, "And that's where I've been picturing you."

My cheeks are hot. My everything is hot. "You're picturing me? What am I wearing?" I laugh to myself, thinking that the cliché question is suppose to be "What are *you* wearing?" But we're in his imagination and I'm eager to know what he keeps there.

He makes a humming sound that vibrates all the way through me. "You really want to know?"

"Yes." My one-word answer comes out slowly and wavers in and out, sounding more like a question.

I hear the air hiss through his teeth before he says, "It isn't much. Sleep well. I'll see you in the morning." Then he's gone before I even say goodnight or get the chance to talk him into a pay-by-the-minute type of conversation.

I won't bore you with the details, but my faithful device, Mr. Right, just didn't cut it tonight. Maybe it's time for a new one.

Or new lots of things.

CHAPTER
Twelve

I WOKE UP this morning feeling amazing, even with the little sleep I got. Showering, I thought about lastnight's chat with Ben. I'm glad it stopped where it did. I know where it could have gone, but thankfully it didn't. I'm ready to take on the day and whatever it might bring, as long as it isn't a late-night telephone call with a smoking-hot employee of mine. That is just begging for trouble.

As I fill my coffee mug, I hear him unlock my door. Pausing in my tracks, I'm excited by the thought of seeing him. It doesn't hurt that I dressed up a little extra again today.

"Good morning, Ben. Coffee?" His face looks a little tired, but offers the sweetest of smiles. He's dressed well, but more casual than yesterday or the day before.

"I'd love some. Thanks. Did you have time to review your schedule?"

"I did. I think that it looks great. I have a few things that need to go to the cleaners. And I'd really like to have a cleaning service hired in the next week. So you can look more into that if you want. Ugh, *and* I need to start on plans for Winnie's bridal shower." I know it's a long shot, as he is clearly a man and probably won't want to be bothered with things like that, but I most definitely need assistance with it.

"Sure. I can help with that. We'll just need to discuss what you're looking for and I can get the ball rolling."

I hand him a mug, saying that it's only black but I have cream and sugar if he wants it. I suppose that's silly because apparently he's already very familiar with my kitchen.

"I'm gonna go now. No need to walk me down. In fact, relax and wake up. You look a little tired." I offer an apologetic smile. I can't stop myself.

His hazel eyes look at me with kind acknowledgment and he huffs a short laugh. "I'm plenty rested, thank you. You look very *professional* this morning." His full smile takes my breath away. Damn. Tired Ben Harris is hot in the morning.

"Yes, and oddly not the least bit frustrated."

He's amused, and he shakes his head at me a little. We lock eyes right before I close the door behind me. I smile back at him and wink. I suppose I am a winker in real life.

Once in the car, I send him a text.

Me: I still owe you lunch. Eleven. You pick the place.

Ben: I'll pick you up.

About ten minutes later, I'm strutting into my office and predictably met with a very perky Cynthia.

"Good morning, Tatum. You only have one message and you have flowers in your office." Her face looks like the cat that ate the canary. Then she peeks into the corner office that now belongs to the Devons and I observe that little Devon's desk is strategically in view of hers...still. Cynthia blushes, and I tell her, "Thank you," before turning to walk back towards my office.

When I reach my door, I'm not exactly sure what I'll find. My first thoughts go to Kurt. Maybe he is sorry and wants me back. They could be from a friend or a thank-you, but deep down I secretly hope they are from Ben.

They are. The beautiful rectangle pot hosts two huge, dark plum orchids. They're stunning. I see a note attached at the bottom and round my desk to read it.

I can't help but cackle out loud as the delicate card contains a recipe titled, "My MooMoo's Chili." Ben is funny. I'm in deep shit.

But then I turn it around and read another little note.

Tatum,

I was right. You looked beautiful this morning, too.
Ben

I call up to Cynthia to find out how long the flowers have been here. She tells me that the delivery man walked in with her over an hour ago. Warmth surrounds me as I realize that he probably sent them before he even saw me this morning. Ben is sweet. I'm in the deepest shit.

Winnie enters, giving me a knowing expression that says, 'I told you so.' "Those are sweet. Are they an apology?"

"Nope." I quickly put the card down and pretend as if the flowers aren't even there. "Is everything ready for the morning hoedown? I want to go down to the set and make sure everything is shaping up for air tonight."

"Yeah, everyone is here. Tatum. Who are the flowers from? They're not from Kurt, are they?" Now she's backpedaling. She is so fun to play with.

I maintain my nonchalance about the gift. "Nope. Are the digitals edited yet? We should watch them this morning, too."

"Tatum! Where did the Goddamned flowers come from?" It's driving her crazy. I can almost see her curly hair grow tighter as her blood pressure rises.

"Ben," I say, as if it's totally normal for a boss to receive flowers from an employee after his first day on the job.

"What does the card say?"

"Oh, it's delicious. Probably the most mouthwatering thing I've ever read."

"I knew it! He wants to bend you over! I have to see this guy. You have to fire him. When can I meet him? Neil says he's a God. Ahhh! Gimmie. Let me read it. They're so pretty."

I hand her the card and just wait for it.

"What is this? His MooMoo's chili recipe? What in the fuck!? How did he know you liked...?" The proverbial light bulb above her head flickers on. "You called him. What did you say?"

I tell her to shut the door. Then I make her swear on her Prada pumps. You see, we need something sacred. I tell her what happened last night and about what could have but didn't.

On my way downstairs at about ten before eleven, I swing into the Devons' lair to see what they're up to. They are debating the pros and cons of pubic hair. Thoroughly, I might add. They have a list on their whiteboard, and big Devon has his glasses on. It's all business in here.

"How's it going, fellas?"

"She can tell us," big Devon gestures at me. "Do women like it when a man has hardwood flooring or a manly shag quaff? I myself like the way my rig looks sans merkin."

"Merkin? What's a merkin?" I ask. Do I even want to know?

"You know, it's a dick wig. It's peni-flage. I guess it could also be vagi-flage, depending on gender. But in this case, it's a dick wig," explains big Devon.

I love it here.

"Well, there are pros and cons to both varieties I suppose. A well-groomed rig, as you call it, says 'I'm aware of how this operates and I pay attention to detail.' However, a wild downstairs dick-do says 'I'm up for just about anything,'" I deadpan. "See you after lunch. Get your shit ready for tonight. I'll see you on set at one."

Like I knew he would be, Ben is waiting for me in the lobby. He looks so naturally attractive. His jeans fit him in all the right places, and his gray v-neck shirt rests just above his belt. Is this a swoon? Am I thirteen again?

He seems to be much more awake than he did just a few hours earlier, and I'll admit that now I'm sort of dragging.

"Do you like Greek food?" is the first thing he says.

"Yes. And it's close. Greek sounds perfect."

He leads me out of the building, and I can feel him watching me closely.

"Do you go to lunch alone much?"

"No, usually I go with Winnie or Neil. You've met him. Or we have something brought up. Why?" I ask as we walk out into the beautiful day. Horns honk and people wait for lights to change. Only, 'red light, green light' isn't as much fun when you're older and you're standing with total strangers and not your friends.

"Just curious. How's the show coming along? I watched a bit of it last week. Very funny."

"It's going really well, truthfully. This week was sort of a cakewalk. We had most of the segments lined up on Monday and it has just been polishing work the last few days. You can come watch it at the set any time you'd like."

Our show tapes live in front of a studio audience. Well, it is time-delayed for obvious reasons, but it's as live as live is these days. Thanks to the boob plop heard around the world a few years back.

"I'd come to the show. Sounds like fun."

He walks so close that our arms brush against each other every few feet and I like it. I enjoy it so much that I manage to 'accidentally' do it on purpose when his arm misses mine too many times in a row.

"So have you lived in New York long? Does your family live here?" I curiously ask. I want to know more about this man. To Ben, life is sort of an open book and I don't know very much about him at all.

"No. I stayed in D.C. after school for a while. I just recently came back. I have a few relatives who live in the city, but most of my family lives up the island in Amagansett."

"I've been through there a few times on our way to the Hamptons. That town is beautiful. It's like a postcard. Did you grow up there?"

He leans his shoulder into mine as we round the corner and walk up to the door of the restaurant. The smell of cooked lamb is strong, and it makes my stomach growl.

"Yes. I'm a small-town boy. How about you?"

"We've always lived in a borough somewhere around here.

Yonkers when we were young. My brother, Cooper, and I are Shore kids."

We stand in line at the counter and look at the menu board, waiting to place our lunch orders. Ben moves his arm around my shoulder and it surprises me. I look up into his face to see what the sudden contact is about. He nods over my right side and says, "Excuse us."

I turn my head completely so that I can see what's just out of my peripheral. A man stands there, brooding with his hands full and looking quite put out that I am in his way. "Sorry. Excuse me," I whisper, and I step closer to Ben.

The guy huffs, "I guess so," rushing past.

I didn't even notice he was there. It's just another reminder that my world is getting smaller around me.

"Don't worry about that, Tatum. What looks good?" Ben brushes it off like it's no big deal that I plainly didn't see the guy standing right next to me and somehow keeps me moving forward.

After we order and receive our food, we grab a small table on the sidewalk and eat in a somewhat comfortable silence. That is, until he clears his throat and begins talking.

"It was fun talking to you last night."

"Yeah, it was. You flirted with me." I smile, teasing him to see what will happen. I'm a girl who pokes wild animals with sticks.

"No, I don't remember that. I think you were flirting with me." His eyes lift up from where he's just about to take a bite of his gyro. "Do we need to talk about that?"

"I don't think so. Especially not while you're working. That would be inappropriate." I can't help it. I feel my face warming.

He smiles. "I'm on my lunch break."

"A little flirting is only natural, Ben. Last night's phone call between two single... Single?" I question, and he responds silently with a long blink and bowing head. "Single adults was just that. The gentleman was clearly just too attracted to the woman to help himself. Happens all the time."

"Happens all the time." His head bobs and he puckers his mouth. His eyes look up in the air as if to confirm that he feels the same way. "All right. I'll buy that. Are you always so honest?"

I think about it. It seems like such an easy question to answer, being that I just totally owned up to my almost wanton behavior from last night. But I don't know what to say. Saying yes feels like a lie.

"I don't know. I suppose it depends on who is asking."

"So that happens all the time, huh? You casually call men you've just met in the middle of the night."

"Not just men." He chokes on a laugh through a mouthful. "I'm an equal opportunity conversationalist." I laugh, too. This is fun. This is easy. He's so fine.

"Clearly. I'm sure your phone rings off the hook." His features are so much more youthful today.

I all-out giggle now as my cell goes off. We look at each other and both of our mouths fall open in surprise. Perfect timing. I couldn't have scripted it better if I tried.

I reach into the pocket of my trousers and see that it's Winnie.

"Excuse me," I say to Ben as I answer. "Hello?"

"Did you fire him?" I hear the excitement in her voice.

I turn and lower my voice a little so that it isn't obvious that we are talking about Ben as he sits there looking at me. "Of course not. I'll be back in a while. Do you need something?"

"No, Cooper brought me lunch. But we think you should bring your new personal assistant up when you get back so we can meet him."

Shit. "I'm sure that he is busy. We can arrange that some other time. We have the show to get ready and this afternoon is going to be busy, Gwendolyn." That's right. She got full first-named.

"It will only take a second, and we are part of your personal life, and you said he was going to be helping you with your maid of honor duties. We'd like to meet him. Ask him." She puts me on the spot.

I cover up the speaking end of the phone and ask in a not-too-enthusiastic way, "Ben, would you like to come up and meet Cooper, my brother, and my asshole best friend Winnie?"

"I would. We're done here. We can leave now so we don't push back your afternoon." He puts his thumb in his mouth, licking off the dressing he found there. I almost lose my train of thought.

"We'll be right there." I hang up on her.

Ben picks up our garbage, darts around to the trash can, and returns to my side for our walk back. "You don't want me to meet them or something?"

"No. It isn't that. It's just that it is only your second day. It seems rushed. Don't you think?" I don't know what my problem is. I almost feel like Ben is mine, and if he's exposed to them, he'll be one of them. I'm batshit crazy.

"I don't know. Rushed seems to be working all right for us. Considering how yesterday almost escalated." Damn, he's cheeky today.

"Fine. Just none of that shit when we get up there. It's my office and my family. Put your damn game face on and wipe off that shit-eating grin."

"Yes, ma'am."

As instructed, Ben exudes nothing except polite professionalism. I introduce him to Cynthia as my new personal assistant and walk him past the pit, pointing out the faces that are visible on the walk to Winnie's office.

I knock once and open the door. No doubt awaiting our arrival are Neil, Winnie, Tilly, Wes, and Cooper.

"Jesus." I stop and get a load of them all hanging out as if it were just a normal day at the office in Winnie's ten-foot-by-ten-foot space. Her office is the smallest one on our floor. She likes it because it's easier to keep clean.

My head falls to the side on its own accord and my eyes roll as we're met with five wide smiles.

Cooper stands up walking over to Ben, offering a hand to shake. "Ben, is it? I'm Tater's big brother, Cooper Elliot. It's nice to meet you. I hope she's treating you well."

Ben's face lights up at the mention of my brother's nickname for me. I meet his gaze and scowl.

"She is. It's nice to meet you, too. Tater has said so many nice things about you. I'm sure she's taking them all back right now." Everyone laughs. Strangely, this pleases me.

They take turns introducing themselves—all but Neil, whom Ben says is nice to see again. Tilly, Wes, and Neil leave us four in the room and Winnie goes on to say, "Ben, if you're not busy later, we could all go get drinks after wrapping up the show? It would be fun if you'd join us. We are interested in getting to know you since you'll be working so closely with our girl here."

I butt in. "Oh, I don't know, guys. I was thinking about skipping that tonight. I'm a little tired." Immediately, I want to retract that last statement. Winnie and Ben lock eyes and the bitch winks at him, making it obvious that she knows more.

Cooper chimes in. "Oh, just one drink. You'll be home by ten thirty. Suck it up." He just wants an opportunity to get to know Ben more at the bar.

"Well, if Tatum feels up for it after the show, I'd be happy to join you guys for a drink."

It's settled. We're all having drinks after the show.

Winnie happily mentions, "Great. You can either meet us at Matty's down the street after the show wraps at about nine or come by the twenty-eighth floor around seven and watch the taping."

I glance at Ben to see what he decides. I don't expect him to look at me for acceptance, but he does.

"I guess I will see you at seven?" It is more of a question in my general direction, but Winnie and Cooper take it as a confirmation. I stand there like a freaking dummy.

"Yeah, sounds good. First round is on me," I say, aware that I've been railroaded by the three of them.

By six, we are going through the dress rehearsal and everything is on. The punch lines hit their marks, the cast—including Wes and Winnie—is in great spirits, and there is a cool buzz in the atmosphere. It's almost my favorite time—showtime.

I'm perched up on my chair, talking to the guys in the booth with my headset, when I see Ben walk in around a quarter before seven. He's changed his clothes. He looks divine in jeans and a black fitted t-shirt, but he's added a tan jacket since it's still slightly brisk at night, even for almost May.

I don't realize how long I'm staring when Wes saddles up next to me in his chair. He only has two scenes tonight—one in the opener and one towards the end of our hour.

"So what's the deal? He's your personal assistant and you're looking at him like he's dinner. You're going to get into trouble." Wes's tone is warning, but he's just teasing me like usual.

I snap out of it and turn directly to face him. "Whatever. He's only been my PA for two days. He's just so fucking handsome," I admit. "I'll get use to it in a month or so. Or a year."

I've known Wes for years. We even fooled around a few times way back when, but nothing ever came of it and we are much better suited as friends. There isn't any reason to hide my blatant attraction, especially when I've been caught staring so hard.

"Mmm-hmmm. You gonna fuck him?" He's a straight shooter, just like me. He stands in front of me pretending like he's leafing through his script one more time.

"Probably not. That isn't really conducive to an employer-employee relationship. But I can still fantasize about it. You know, now that you've mentioned it, I've always had a fantasy where you and I and some other guy have hot sex in my office. What are you doing later?" I make kissy lips at him.

He coughs through his laugh. "You're such a dude. Just watch out, Tatum. You don't know that guy. He has access to all of your shit. It isn't smart to shit where you eat." His face turns serious before he parts with, "Think about it."

Now, there's a thought. Wes has a good point. I don't know much about Ben. I don't even know how he knew about the interview. When Neil called the agency to cancel the rest of the applicants' appointments, they didn't have anyone named Ben even considering the position.

It's possible that he just heard about it from a friend who was though. Neil called a reference on the resume Ben emailed him since he hadn't brought it to the interview. They said positive things about him, so who knows?

What if he's a stalker? Like, a real one. I'm both turned on and intrigued by this mysterious employee of mine. Maybe I'll just have to have enough cocktails to get to the bottom of how he knew about the job opening tonight.

The show is smooth like butter. Time runs perfectly. Nobody fucks up, except big Devon, but who cares? It's more fun to watch when the actor is just as affected by the joke. The audience eats it up when they crack just a little.

Everyone says their "great shows." The crew begins tearing down a few of the bigger sets to make tomorrow morning a little easier on themselves, while the cast gets out of wardrobe. I wander over to where Ben is patiently waiting. He rises as I approach.

"So what did you think? Looks different from back here, huh?" I ask him.

The first time I was behind the camera watching a show taping, it was like seeing behind the curtain at Oz. I know everyone doesn't get their jollies like I do, but I'm always interested to hear what people who are out of the business think of the whole thing.

"You're fun to watch working." He pockets his hands and shifts towards me a little, rocking on his heels. "You're good at your job."

"Thanks, but I meant the show. Did you like it? Big Devon is a riot. Well, actually both Devons are, but the fat one gets me every time."

"Big Devon? Does he know you call him big and fat?" He

feigns offense to my rude pet name. "Can't you get into trouble for speaking to him like that?"

"Not as much trouble as he's gonna be in if he doesn't lay off the shit he eats. Seriously, it's their shtick. Big Devon and little Devon. They are best friends and writing partners. It's totally his preference to be big Devon. I've seen pictures of him in high school when he was just tall, average Devon. He got the name after they met in college."

"Oh, well, all right. They play well off each other. They're hilarious." Ben scans the set that is already almost vacant. "Are you almost ready to go? Do you want to grab a jacket or something?"

"I don't need one. I'll just forget it at the bar. I have a few there already if I need one when we leave. True story." We go to Matty's every Thursday night when the show is in season. Even before we were Thursday-night regulars, Winnie and I were there a few times a week since we worked in the same building.

I send a quick text to Cooper saying that I'm heading down the street with Ben and that we'll see them there.

Ben and I talk about the show, and he is interested in all the ins and outs. I promise him that he can come whenever he wants, and he says that he will.

When we get to Matty's, Ben holds the door for me, and as I walk through, he runs his warm hand down my back. He leaves his fingers spread at the top of my hip as he follows me in, and we make our way to the bar. My body naturally goes where he steers me.

The moment is broken when I stiffen, seeing Kurt sitting at the bar where we all normally congregate. This should be interesting.

Ben must sense the change in my body language, because he tightens his fingers into me. I remove his hand and quickly pull Ben with it back outside. I nearly trip on the uneven doorstep and Ben steadies me, clutching my elbow.

I say, "Wait a minute." Because I'm trying to figure out how to play this one out.

"If you're really tired, I can take you home, Tatum." He thinks that I'm tired and he wants to take me home. Wants to take me home. He wants to... Ahh!

Shoving the impulsive thought of letting him do just that and mount me on the counter, I say, "No, I'm fine. There's someone in there that I know."

"Right. Everyone from the show is coming. Someone you don't like? What?" He's totally lost, and his brow creases.

"No. My ex-boyfriend, Kurt, is in there. He sometimes meets all of us here after the show and he's here now. But we are broken up." Fuck. Where in the hell are Winnie and Cooper?

"So what? You've both probably moved on from it. Just say hi and play it off. It's fine."

"You don't get it. We broke up on Friday. Last Friday. On my birthday." Finally, recognition spreads across his handsome face that I'm telling him our breakup is still in its infancy.

"Oooh. Well, do you want to stay? Or go somewhere else or something?"

I don't know what to do. I hear Winnie's laugh coming down the street and I swing all the way around to see if Cooper is with her. Miraculously, he is.

I whisper-scream, "COOOOOOPER!!" and stomp my foot. "Kurt. Is. Here."

"No fucking way? Let's go in! You can introduce him to Ben." Cooper smiles and his eyes sparkle like this is fascinating. Winnie playfully smacks his arm and gives me the 'he's your brother' look. Apparently, Cooper loves drama more than fourteen-year-old girls.

"Are you serious? This is too messed up. I think I might just go. I don't want it to be awkward. Ahhh... This is going to be a train wreck." I can't decide. If I stay, it could get uncomfortable. If I go, I might end up fucking my new employee on his second day.

I look at Ben, who is only feeding off of Cooper's reaction, and he smiles like I'm overreacting. That damn smile.

I choose the train wreck.

CHAPTER
Thirteen

"COOPER!" KURT YELLS as soon as he sees him walk in with Winnie on his arm. "Where's Tate? I wanna talk to her." It sounds like Kurt has been saving our seat for a few hours now by the slur in his voice.

"She's right here, bud. Are you cool though? We are all here to have a good time. Right?" Cooper sees that this isn't the situation he thought he was walking into and squares his shoulders to make his point clear.

"Yeeeeah, we are all friends here. Me and you are friends. Me and Winnolyn are friends. You and Winnolyn are friends. Everysbodies friends."

Cooper looks to Nick, the bartender who is typically working when we come in, with wide eyes. Poor Nick shakes his head and raises his shoulders in an apology.

My brother faces me, deciding if leaving would be a better idea.

"Who is that? Is that my friend Tatum? Tay-Tum!! You're my friend, Tatum. See all friends, Coopie."

As funny as it is, it's not. Cooper seems a little pissed, and Winnie isn't saying anything. She's watching and waiting for the second our other colleagues come in so she can run away from this whole situation.

I can't even look at Ben. I'm embarrassed, but mostly for Kurt. I told them about how he took it and all about our breakfast, but they didn't see it firsthand. They were mostly just witness to his dicky behavior towards the end of our relationship. I need to say something.

"Come here, Kurt." And I move in to hug him. It will only be more uncomfortable if I pretend it isn't happening, but it is happening and I know best how to handle him. Kurt isn't a raging alcoholic by any stretch of the imagination, but I can tell that he isn't himself. I'm a little worried. "When did you get here? You should have come by the show."

"I came here earlier. I was going to leave before you got here. I was, Tatum. Then I just wanted to see you. You're so fucking hot right now. You look so good." His hands wrap around me, and I'm okay with it. It hasn't even been a week since I broke up with him mid-blowjob. I can't play the 'I have physical boundaries' card.

"Come on. Let's go sit over here for a minute. Then we'll get you a cab. Hmm?" I decide that if he wants to talk to me, I can handle it. What's five minutes with a drunken ex-boyfriend in the broad scheme of things?

Quickly, I sneak a glance at Ben. His eyes are narrowly pinned on Kurt. But I tell myself that he's just my assistant, not my boyfriend.

With my right arm wrapped around Kurt's waist and my left arm straight out as counter balance, I try to wade us through the small crowd that has filled Matty's. He is really plowed and not walking that great. He's sharing more weight than I can confidently manage.

Just as we get close to an empty booth on the other side of the bar, I hear this *pop* and feel a sharp pain that shoots right through my side. The breath whooshes out of my lungs. Literally blindsided, I freeze.

"Oh, shit. I'm sorry, Tatum." It's one of the sound guys from the show, Pete.

He shoved a pool cue during his break into my ribs. I think he broke one. He's in my face apologizing and I can't grab the air to breathe. What's with me and getting hurt at the fucking bar?

In an instant, Cooper shoves a stumbling Kurt out of the way and Ben is by my side. "Tatum, are you hurt? I saw that jab." He's squares my hunched-over shoulders to face him, and I feel tears burning my eyes. I don't know if I can inhale yet and I'm light-headed. Still bent over a little, I don't want to move. "Tatum. Say something. Are you okay?"

Then he's lowering himself and putting an arm behind my knees. His other wraps around to my right under arm and he picks me up. Finally, I take a breath and it's what I imagine being stabbed feels like.

I yelp. The sharpness of the ache on my side is severe. My breaths are shallow and I can't inhale fully.

Ben shouts at Cooper, "Hey, I'm taking her to the hospital!"

I try to say no, that I want to go home, but only, "Home," comes out.

Ben's face is angry, and he says, "Hospital."

I gather up enough air to say, "Please." I know I've won out when he huffs, "Fine."

Before I know it, Winnie has hailed a cab and Ben is getting in without even putting me down. He simply slips in the door Winnie is holding and I hear her say, "We'll get the next cab when Cooper gets out here. We're right behind you. Can you stay with her until we get there?"

"I'm not leaving her. I'm taking her home. She doesn't want to go to the hospital. If I change my mind and take her, I'll call you from her phone on the way," he says.

Winnie acknowledges his plan with a quick, "Okay." Then she shuts the door.

I feel every bump and turn the vehicle makes and as we come to a stop outside my building Ben wriggles his wallet out from under him and tosses money at the driver. "Thanks. You can keep it." Opening the back door, he lifts me out with him. He hasn't set me down or loosened his hold on my body in what feels like twenty minutes.

The pain coming from my ribs is barely tolerable. Every breath is torture.

"Tatum, are you breathing okay? I think he just knocked the air out of you. You might have a broken rib or two. He hit you pretty hard." Ben's face is inches from mine as he carefully navigates the door and stops at the security desk.

"Tatum?" I hear Phil say. "Sir, is she all right? Should I call for an ambulance?"

"She's fine. I work for her. I'm Ben."

"Okay. Do you need some help? What can I do?" Phil sounds worried, but Ben's tone doesn't leave the topic up for debate.

"If you can grab an elevator for us, that would be great." Ben walks towards the lifts. He's not short of breath like I am, yet he's been carting me around this whole time.

I can only manage to pull in tiny breaths, and my head is now leans on his hard chest. I'm not crying too hard because I think that would be even more painful, but my eyes keep overflowing with hot tears.

Pete got me good. I bet he feels awful.

Finally at my door, Ben somehow has his key ready. When did he have time to fish for it? He leans down slightly to the right and unlocks the door. We are in my apartment in short order.

Walking me straight to my room, he sets me down gently on my bed. All I can say through my tears is, "I. Didn't. See. Him." Every word is punctuated with a short breath.

"I know you didn't. I saw it." His voice is soothing and calm.

I'm sitting on the edge of my bed and Ben is on his knees in front of me. With one hand on my leg, his other swipes at the steady stream of tears I haven't been able to impede.

"Can you raise your arm? Go slow."

Something about his voice has my battered body doing his will. I slowly begin to lift my arm and the pain is blinding. I almost feel like I'm going to pass out.

"Here. Lie down on your other side." He lifts my legs onto the bed and I roll away from him. "I'm going to untuck your shirt. I want to lift it up and see, okay?"

"Oh. Kay." I rotate my arm in front of me and close my eyes. While his right hand is pulling at the bottom of my button-up shirt, his left hand is sweetly rubbing my hip. It is such a small but caring gesture.

Why is he doing all of this? And again, where in the hell are Winnie and Cooper?

I feel the cool air hit my side and his hand runs from the top of my pants up to where it hurts so badly. I can't help but flinch when he nears the spot.

"It feels like he broke it, Tatum. You need to go to the hospital. Are you breathing any easier?" He releases an exasperated groan, not waiting for me to respond. "I'm so sorry I didn't get over there fast enough. God, you didn't even want to stay." The regret in his voice is evident. "I should have just brought you home. Shit. I shouldn't have insisted on going out earlier."

Since he is still kneeling on the floor behind me, I can't see what his face looks like, but if it is half as sorry as his voice, I don't want to see it.

"It's. Not. Your. Fault. I'm. A. Big. Girl. Can. You. Call. Cooper?" Yeah, this big girl wants her brother.

"Sure. I'll get your phone." He is up and back before I know it. "Here it is, Tatum."

I grabbed the phone and dialed.

Finally, Winnie answers. "Hey, is she all right?"

"It's me."

"God, Tate. Sorry we aren't there yet. Shit. The cops are here. Kurt might be getting arrested. He sort of got into a fight? That's what's taking us so long. Cooper got in the middle." There's a lot of commotion in the background and it's hard to hear her.

I take as big of a breath as I can. "Yeah, my side…hurts like hell. Kurt got in…a fight?" It's a little easier to talk, even though my eyes are still watering from the tenderness. I really just want them to get here.

"Yeah, he hit Pete...with the pool stick. Pete is okay and says he isn't going to press charges, but someone called the cops and they're here now. We'll get there as soon as this is all worked out. Cooper's talking to the cops. We'll be right there. Gotta go." She hangs up and I drop the phone on the bed.

"I should have let...you bring me home...earlier," I wheeze. "We could have...been in here...having fun." I try to hold the laugh back from my terrible joke.

He comes around the other side of the bed and sits in front of me. "There you are." He looks relieved. Ben leans down so that his head is lying on the pillow facing mine and brushes my hair out of my face. "Are you sure you won't go to the hospital? It looks pretty nasty," he insists.

"They won't do anything...for a broken rib...except wrap it...and send me home. If it even is broken...I'm probably...just a pussy."

The little bit of blue that swims around in his green eyes lights up at the naughty word that tripped out of my mouth. He gives up. "Do you have an ace bandage?"

"Of course I do. I'm a blind klutz. They are in the...bathroom closet." I move my arm to point the way and it kills. "Ouch!"

"I'll get you some ice and some pain killers too. Just lie there. Don't move around."

When Ben returns, he has a tray of supplies.

He warns, "This might hurt."

"I've heard that before." I seriously need to learn how to shut the hell up. "I mean, okay. I can take it."

"Yeah and I've heard that before, too." He smirks.

"Touché, Casanova. Can you help me up?"

Coming closer, he sits the tray on the mattress. I roll back over to my other side, and I'll be dammed if I can't sit up on my own.

"Hey, just a second. I don't want to pull on your arms. Let me help you."

He gets so close that his face fits beside mine like a puzzle piece. Ben slides his arms under me to wrap his arms around my back, crisscrossing them up to my shoulder blades. He's favoring the sore side.

"Are you ready?" he says in my ear, and with those words, I grow feverish. "Just hold on to me. I'll go slow." Either everything he says is laced with innuendo or I'm just really hard up.

He lifts and it hurts, but I relax when it isn't as bad as I imagined it would be. Once I'm up, he lets go and I don't like it. My arms are still around his neck, and when he grabs my wrist from behind his head to move them away, it feels like a rejection. I know I'm hurt, but I thought we were having a moment. Maybe it was only in my head, like everything else.

"Hey now. What's all this?" His thumb rubs my brow out. "What's in that head? Spit it out." His intent face begs for me to share my thoughts.

"I don't want to. Can we just get this over with? I'm tired and really sore." He nods like he's waiting for the joke. It doesn't come. "For real," I add.

"All right then. Your shirt has to come off. I'll wrap you up and then I'll let Ben & Jerry take it from there."

My top is a button-down, so I move my hands to the top one. I'm not a modest girl. I'm comfortable in my skin. It is just that, in this moment, I'm feeling vulnerable. It's foreign and I don't know what to do with myself.

"Ben, will you turn around? Please." Without hesitation, he does as I ask. My fingers make light work of the buttons, and I slide my good side out and then let it fall off the other. "Just another second." I turn around on the bed slowly, because I'm so sore. I don't want to watch him look at me. "Okay. I'm ready." My head is bowed and I'm slumped forward. I hate having someone help me.

One of his hands lands on my shoulder and then another matches the other side. It shocks me at first, and then he begins working them into my tight muscles. It's healing. As he gently massages me, every muscle in my neck and back start to relax. I can feel the tension leave my person, but not my mind.

He moves both hands to my right side and works them in time to a beat that lulls me. Fairly, he moves to the left. His long fingers flex on me and run up the back and side of my neck and into my hair. My body involuntarily shivers. I've never been touched like this. If he weren't doing this to make me feel better, it would seem erotic.

"You're cold, aren't you? I just don't want to wrap you up while you're tense. You'll be uncomfortable," he says like an excuse. "Your skin is so lovely." He keeps working, massaging away the stress that I've most likely been carrying around for months. "This is going to sound bad, but I think your bra has to come off, too."

I reach around to fumble for the clasp as pain shoots across my ribcage. I make a sound that's almost a whine.

"Shhh, I'll get that."

My breath stalls altogether.

He undoes my bra and runs his hands up my back. Then he slips his fingers under the straps on either side. My bra falls loose in front of me and I instinctively hug myself to hide my breasts.

Then he tenderly kisses the top of my head and softly says, "I'm so sorry."

He's sorry? I am mortified. He probably has much better things to do than take care of an baby like me. *Pity, party of one.*

"You'll need to raise your arms so I can get the bandage around you correctly. Can you do that?"

"Yes." I lift, and before I know it, he's got me wrapped up like a mummy. It's tight and it feels really good, like it's holding me together.

"Better?"

I nod.

"Can I get you some PJs or something? I can help you lift them over your head."

"Thank you. There are some tank tops and sweatpants in the closet on the shelf. Anything will work. And socks too?" I realize he must have taken my shoes off at some point, because my feet are cold.

"Anything you need, Tatum. That's what I'm here for."

I think, *Yeah right. Anything. How about a time machine so I can go back and watch where the fuck I'm going?*

This is all so messed up. If he's smart, he'll resign tomorrow.

"You know you don't have to do all of this. I will pay you for working so late. I'm sorry you've wasted your whole night, Ben. Really. This is pretty embarrassing."

He walks back into my room frowning. "What part is embarrassing?" He lists, "Getting your rib broken while trying to help a drunk friend get his shit together? Um, not complaining about the plate-size bruise you already have forming on your beautiful skin? Nothing about how you're acting is embarrassing." His gaze lowers to the floor as he steps back to me. "I think you're graceful."

"Are you high? I'm the least graceful person on planet Earth!" I'm still holding my boobies in my hands so now isn't the best time to pretend I don't like compliments. "Thanks for saying that, but you don't have to. Can you just put that over my head so I can put these down already?"

This makes him grin. Ben opens the top of the shirt and slides it down around me, and I let my arms come through.

I take my pants off and kick them across the floor, hoping that by tomorrow I'll be able to at least bend over and pick them up. I pull the sweats up slowly, and I'm dressed. *Ta-da.*

"Look. They will be here in a few minutes. And like you said, Ben & Jerry can handle it from here. You can get on with your night," I say, coming off a bit short.

He shifts his stance and plants his foot. "Did I upset you or something? Because I have apologized for not listening to what you needed today. Or are you just frustrated and irritated that your sight is unmistakably getting worse? Because if that's it, I can take it. But if I did something wrong, you need to let me fix it."

"Whoa. I have known you for two days, mister. Where do you get off?" I am mad. It's none of his business.

"I told you that I could take your mouth if you'd be able to take mine. Now here it is. You're cramming all that fear and pride down inside yourself and it's going to explode soon, Tatum. I've only known you for what, like, forty-eight hours? Hell, I can see it. You tell it like it is to everyone but yourself." He turns around in a circle like he's trying to cool off, his hands laced together behind his neck as he faces the door leading out.

"You don't even know me," I retort.

He spins back. "We'll see about that."

"How did you know about the job opening?" I blurt. "Because Neil's friend at the employment place didn't send anyone named Ben."

"I just happened to hear about it. Are you firing me?" he challenges.

"No. But don't go pointing your judgy finger in my face about being all honest with myself. There is something weird about you just showing up. If you weren't so hot, I would have told you to leave." My hands are on my hips. I mean business.

His face softens for a split second then resets back into a handsome glower. "Don't try to flatter me when I'm being serious."

"I'm not. You're hot. You're so fucking hot. Hands-down the hottest personal assistant I have." In my head and out my mouth. I need a muzzle.

"Well, your other assistant isn't that bad." He raises an eyebrow and cracks a mischievous half grin.

"Do you want his number? Because Neil thinks you're hotter than I do. He would be more than happy to hear from you." I like arguing with him more than I like pleasantly speaking to most people. It's fun now that I can tell real spat has passed. My specialty—bait-and-switch.

"No. I'm not interested."

"Good. I'd hate to have to fire you both."

"Is this how we're going to be?" Ben asks with both palms outstretched towards me. "Boss and employee by day and...I don't know? Flirty and argumentative by night?"

"We could just fuck and get it over with already," I declare, but when I hear the words, they sound ugly off my tongue.

He moves lightning fast and it startles me. In two strides, our personal space is shared. His eyes are unyielding and they peer straight into me. "Tatum, if it comes to something like that"—he motions between our barely separate bodies"—in the future with us, then it won't be just fucking. And, doll, you won't ever want it *over already*." He exhales noisily. "I think you're feeling better. I'm going home."

I just stand here.

Two nights in a row that motherfucker has bested me.

Two nights in a row he's left me horny as hell.

Two nights in a row I have to make a valiant effort to not beg him for more.

When he gets to my front door I hear, "Call me if you need anything. Tatum. Anything,"

Then he's gone.

Thank God Cooper and Winnie show up about half an hour later and distract me from calling him. Not that I was going to.

CHAPTER
Fourteen

THE LOVEBIRDS STAY the night in my spare bedroom. They insist that they want to be here if I need to go the hospital, but I know I won't.

Cooper calls me stubborn mule-bitch, but I don't have a defense. He's right.

I am taking today off. There's no way in hell I can get out of bed in any efficient capacity. Looking at my side, you would think I was hit by a Mack truck going at least forty.

Winnie makes me breakfast and coffee, hangs around, and then goes on to work. I tell her that she has to go so Pete doesn't jump off a building. I call into the office around eight and talk to him, letting him know it wasn't his fault. I tell him that I honestly didn't see him and I should have been paying more attention. He admonishes my self-placed blame and offers to pay for any medical bills.

He also notifies me that my boyfriend—ex-boyfriend, I correct him—grabbed a pool stick off the wall after Cooper let him go and whacked him a few good times in the back. He said that if Kurt would have been sober and had a better aim—because he only really connected with him a few times—that he'd probably be worse off than I am.

After talking to him, I look through seeing that I have texts.

Kurt: That was bad. I'm sorry. Call me.

Delete.

Ben: I'll be there in an hour. Do you want me to pick anything up for you?

I don't reply to that one either. Instead, I make plans for a quick bath before the overachieving assistant gets here. The hot soak is just what I need. I turn on my music, dim the lights, add some bubbles, and bam. I'm good to go.

Then I think, *I should text Ben to go get some stuff so I can buy myself some more time.* I send him a message, asking him to go by a bookstore and get me the memoir I want to read about a female comedian I've loved since childhood and some wine. He tells me that he will and to let him know if I think of anything else.

I soak in the tub for a bit longer than I should and am more raisin-like than pruney when I get out. It takes me some time, but I manage to get the ace bandage back on after inspecting the purple bulge on my side. It isn't as tight as when Ben did it, but it will just have to do.

Slipping on a fresh pair of yoga pants—which I have never done yoga in—and my NYU sweatshirt, I'm ready to relax and possibly get some things done—comfortably—from home.

I didn't hear him come in, but as I make my way to the kitchen, I overhear Ben talking on the phone. He is holding his cell to his face with his shoulder and putting away a few groceries that he must have picked up on his way here, too.

"No. I think she's fine," Ben says, and then he listens to whoever is on the other end for a few seconds. "I know, but I don't want to. Not yet."

I'm not sure if he is talking about me or someone else. I don't want to get busted eavesdropping so I make my way to where he can see me and smile.

"Hey, I'm gonna let you go. I'm at work. I'll call you later," Ben says, looking straight at me. "Yeah, that sounds good. All right, bye." He sets the phone down on the island and lays both of his hands down flat, assessing me.

"Good morning, Ben," I announce, setting forth our typical beginning-of-the-day banter.

"How do you feel this morning?" He appraises me up and down, looking for any sign of discomfort.

"I feel much better. Thank you for helping me last night. That sucked." It did suck. And it still hurts like a bitch, but I don't want him thinking about it. I don't need him assuming he has to be a freaking nurse on top of everything else.

I see that, in addition to the groceries, he brought a few bottles of wine and a backpack.

"I thought that since you were going to be here all day we could start on the plans you want to make for Winnie's shower. If you're feeling up to it," Ben adds at the end, showing that he's not too sure about how I'm feeling with the questioning look on his face.

"I think that's a great idea. We can do that and then I think I'll lounge around. Maybe read, maybe a movie?" Then I think to myself that I hope the planning takes a while because I don't fancy being alone. I know that Winnie and Cooper wouldn't mind coming over and hanging out this evening, but I'd like to avoid being a third wheel again.

Maybe I'll call Kurt later. I should probably call him either way. We didn't get to talk, and he clearly needs to get some things off his chest.

"A movie sounds great. I'll help you with the shower thing and then we can veg out and I'll make us dinner. How does shrimp Alfredo sound?"

"You really like to cook, huh?" I'm interested in this. Where does that come from? Do guys like cooking? I'm going to be asking lots of questions today. There's so much more that I'd like to know about him.

"I do. I cooked a lot at home growing up and I've always enjoyed doing it. Do you cook?"

"No. I mean, here and there, but not ever really *cook* cook. You know? I'd like to, but I never had a reason. There isn't much point in cooking for one." God, I sound pathetic.

Ben busies himself with stocking my cupboards with things he's brought, and I take a seat at the island.

"You never cooked for Kurt?"

"No. Our relationship wasn't ever like that. I mean, we ordered food in a lot and we spent time together, but it wasn't something that we did together."

As I listen to myself speak, I'm reminded about what Kurt said and how I didn't encourage or initiate those types of things with him in our time together.

"What kind of relationship was it then?" Ben asks and stops to pay attention to my answer.

I shrug. "It was just different. We spent time together. We took trips together. We went to events and social things with each other. I don't know. Now that I think about it, I suppose it was mostly superficial in the end." Saying this out loud sort of brings it home. Makes it real. Kurt and I didn't actually get to know each other. I kept him at arm's length. He was here, but I never really let him in.

"That's too bad. How long were you two together?" His questions aren't meddling. They just flow, and I'm comfortable answering.

"That's the strangest part. Two years. What about you? You're single, as I gathered from lunch, but what's your story? Crazy ex-girlfriends? Cheaters? Anything juicy?" I try to make it sound like I'm joking, but I really want to know. I maneuver the conversation, shifting it to dig up some dirt on him.

"No. None to speak of. I've never really been in a serious relationship. I mean, I've had girlfriends, just nothing for too long. Either I moved away or they did or things didn't work out. My dating history is pretty boring, honestly." He's relaxed and doesn't seem bothered by my query.

"Good. So what did you do before this? You never said." Now I'm getting somewhere.

"I worked in Washington for the government——the military

actually." He says this quietly and gets back to arranging the items.

"That's interesting. Were you in the military? What branch?" That must be how he got that body. That taut, lean body.

"Not exactly. It was more of a consulting position. That's why I moved back here. I needed a change. I needed to get away from it." He reaches his arm up around and behind his neck and rubs at it. He's uncomfortable. "We should make some calls and see if we can't book a place for this shower. Get it all out of the way."

I don't pry further. I'd rather him tell me things in his own time.

I agree, and we set up in my office and plan our asses off. Instead of a traditional bridal shower, we opt for a more contemporary couple's shower at The Yard, a great restaurant that has a wonderful outdoor area. It's perfect for a cocktail party.

We hammer out a guest list and email it to Cooper and Winnie making sure we haven't missed anyone, and both of them reply saying that it looks great. We book the place and even settle on a menu.

Ben is shockingly helpful. He gives me a few great choices, which are usually both perfect, and he offers his opinions when I ask for them. In a few short hours, we have the location, the food, the drinks, and we've even contacted a few musicians to perform at the party. It's shaping up to be fantastic.

Since all of the major details are lined out and set, Ben tells me that he will order invitations and have them ready to mail by next Tuesday, giving three weeks for the guests to RSVP. Even though he wasn't a personal assistant before, this dude is an excellent one.

True to his word, he cooks us dinner. We drink wine and laugh. I help by making the salad and keeping our glasses full.

I learn that his love of the oldies also comes from his Moo-Moo, who is his grandmother on his dad's side. We talk about his first car, which was a Chevelle, and we tell embarrassing college stories. I tell him about Winnie and Cooper and confess that I selfishly set them up. He asks about the famous people I've met and why I became a writer. It feels so good being with him.

We do our little flirt thing that comes so naturally and sitting down and watch a movie, I choose Monty Python's The Holy Grail. We sit next to each other on the couch as if we'd done it thousands of times before.

I forget that he's my assistant when we're like this. It naturally feels like he's something else. Then it hits me. It feels like a date.

I'm liking him. A lot.

He's sexy in the most casual way. I'm obsessed with his hands. I keep staring at them and picturing them touching me. I'm a lusty ho.

I think about just being honest and telling him that I like him. Then I shut it down. I've only known him for a few days, and Wes's words of not shitting where I eat keep ringing in my head.

Deciding that I won't say or do anything about it, I keep my mouth shut. But if he makes even the smallest move, I'm going to let him.

Good help is hard to find.

It's a real pain in the ass having poor side vision when you're watching a movie and you want to be sneaky and peek at the hot guy next to you. I have to invent different reasons for moving around to get my fix of his face. I have an itch. I have a wedgie. I reach for a drink. It's all very subtle, I'm sure.

After we finished off two bottles of wine and mocked lines from the movie we know by heart, I'm not feeling too much pain from the rib and I'm genuinely happy.

Ben turns the television off, and as we are looking at each other, he says, "I know I don't work tomorrow and you're probably busy... Wait. No, you're not, I know your schedule. Isn't that convenient?" He smiles through his tomfoolery. "I still want to see you."

Yawning, I start to stretch and wince when I pull at my tender side muscles. "You're going to get sick of me. You'll see."

Ben's brow furrows, and he does this funny head tilt move that I've come to learn is really his body language for, "Shut up, Tatum."

"I'm fine. Really. You don't have to babysit me."

Ignoring the jab I take at both of us, he states, "Your rib will probably still be sore as hell, but I thought we could take a drive. I want to take you somewhere."

I bite my tongue so that the rebound to that comment doesn't actually come out. I'd let him take me anywhere. The bedroom. The tub. This couch—right now. If he could read my thoughts, he would surely take me to an asylum.

I'm a little buzzed. That wine was good.

The only safe thing I can say is, "Where?"

"Just somewhere I think you'll like." Does this man ever all-the-way answer a question?

"Well, I'm not going unless you tell me." That ought to up the ante.

His green eyes flare at my resistance and he sucks the corner of his bottom lip into his mouth to think. "What can I do to convince you to go? Without telling you." He flirts just as much as I do.

My need to know more about him is driving me nuts, so compromising with myself, I counter with, "Tell me five things about yourself that no one else knows and I'll think about it."

"Five things? You want to know five things about my life that no one else knows?" Ben is stalling, tapping his deft fingers on his bottom lip in contemplation. He needs to leave that lip alone or I'm going to jump him. His head bobs. I think he is counting them off in his head.

"Well, it's that or I'm staying here and you're taking the day to yourself." I am a stubborn mule-bitch.

"All right, all right." His hands come up in surrender. My threats are actually doing their job. "I don't like fudge. I've tried. I just can't do it."

"Fudge? That's what you're giving me? You're ridiculous."

"Hey, that's useful information." He thinks about the next thing and smiles. "I lost my virginity in my bedroom while my parents were home and I got caught. By them." He laughs at the memory.

I'm laughing too. "Jesus, how old were you?"

"Does that count as one of my things?"

"It might if no one knew, and considering your parents knew about your romantic getaway for two in their house, that one really shouldn't count either. You know rules are rules."

He considers this. "I was nineteen."

"Wow. Late bloomer? Were you ugly back then? Have an aversion to deodorant? That seems a little old." We both laugh.

"It's not that old. We lived in a smaller town. I was a good boy." He holds his head up, defending himself. "I waited."

"Until?"

"Until I found a girl I didn't find to be absolutely crazy. And one I thought was interesting."

"Okay. I'll accept that. Was *she* ugly?" I tease.

"Hideous." He's playing me. "She had big teeth and stringy hair. She farted when she coughed. All the good stuff."

We're both trying not to laugh, but I can't help myself when he says that she had congestion-related gas. I laugh so hard my rid throbs, but it is so worth it. I think quickly about how I could use that in a bit at work.

Ben gets up and walks over to my mantle, where I've put some framed pictures. He studies each one, picking one up, smiling, and setting it back down for another.

"I like your smile in this one. What's going on in this picture?"

I stand to see which one it is. It's my favorite photograph of Winnie and me. "That is the day that Winnie and I graduated from college. We were out to have drinks with family. I think Cooper took it. I can't remember. Winnie gave it to me as a condo-warming present, saying that I should have a picture of her in my home."

"You look beautiful." He places it back where it belongs and points to one of me, my brother, and our parents.

"Those are The Hippies. Pat and Cola Elliot." He's sure to find this entertaining.

"They're hippies?" he asks.

"Cooper and I always joke about them being hippies. I don't know if they are official hippies, like if they've gotten memberships to the hippie club or anything."

His expression is cute. He eyes me skeptically and patiently waits for me to go on.

"They are all vegan. They make soap. They live in an RV now and travel all year long. The Hippies are minimalists and we suspect nudists when we aren't around," I say, only half joking. It wouldn't surprise me in the least if they were.

"That must have been a fun childhood. What did they do for jobs?"

"My father was a librarian and novelist and my mom was a photographer for a magazine. They were pretty successful. They are both retired from 'the real world,' as they call it. Now, my mom freelances for state parks and museums. You know, pamphlet stuff. My dad still writes from the road." I'm actually pretty proud of them.

"They sound really great." His admonishing tone suggests that I need to ease up on teasing them.

"They are," I confess shyly, "in small doses. Don't get me wrong. I wouldn't trade them in or anything, but they can be flighty. However, they love each other and that was nice to be around growing up. Winnies' parents divorced when we were at NYU and it was vicious. I love my mom and dad, but they are hippies."

He almost gets away without finishing our terms for his secret road trip.

"You're doing well at distracting me from your five things.

Care to share number three?" I put my hands on my hips, not leaving room for argument.

"I don't like storms. No, let me be clear. I'm a pussy when it comes to storms. Tornadoes. Typhoons," he lists. In a smaller voice, he adds, "Thunderstorms."

"You are scared of storms?! That's priceless. What do you do when it storms out then?" I pretend to be sympathetic and place my hand on his arm. "Do you cry?"

"No. I don't cry. I usually put my earbuds in and go to bed. I've never liked them. I was in a tornado once when I was a kid at camp. It scared the shit out of me. I haven't been right since." Ben's smile shows his embarrassment. It's endearing and my favorite secret so far.

"What else? Two more. You're almost there. I'm almost totally yours for the day."

Ben's eyes catch fire at the mention of me being his but it's fleeting. "Just for one day, huh?" His face sobers, and I realize that my hand is still touching his bicep. I look at it and feel it flex under my grip. Something in the way he says his last words changes the air around us.

"You know what I mean." I retract my hand and steadily say, "I'll go with you tomorrow. No questions. Two more."

He steps up to me. "I left Washington because my best friend, Keith, committed suicide and I couldn't stay. I couldn't be there anymore."

I don't know how to react to that one. I've never felt maternal or nurturing. I've never had reasons to. But hearing him actually tell me something like that almost knocks the wind out of me. My heart feels pained for him.

"I'm sorry. I'll go with you tomorrow. You don't have to tell me anything else. It was a stupid game." I move to start cleaning up the wine glasses and straighten up the couch pillows.

I feel almost trapped. I want to comfort him and haven't the slightest inkling about how. So I do the Tatum thing and get out of the situation.

When I reach the kitchen, Ben's still standing in front of my mantle, both of his large hands bracing himself and his head bowed. He's breathing so heavily that I observe the rise and fall of his shoulders from here.

He collects himself and joins me in the kitchen, gathering his things and acting like he's about to pull the ripcord on our evening and bolt. It is a bit relieving, honestly. I never know what to say in times like this.

"Ben, I'll walk you to the elevator," I offer, needing to at least make some sort of gesture that says I care. I actually care.

He nods. His mood is sullen. I hate feeling like I'm prodding for information. I was just trying to be playful while getting details on this man who has my life on view in front of him on a daily basis. I should tell him that.

It's quiet on the way to the elevators. Getting there, he pushes the down button and I begin my plight. "Benny, I apologize for prying. I simply want to know you better and thought it was a good way to pull at your particulars." *Benny? Where did that come from?* I fidget with my fingers. "I would have gone with you anyway. I trust you. I know it will be fun."

He smiles, and the acid I felt in the pit of my stomach drains away. "Don't feel like that. I'm sorry I slipped off like that." He leans in and quickly kisses my cheek. "I would have answered ten."

The door to the elevator rings its arrival, and I step back as he moves forward. "You only answered four."

Looking back at me, his grin still spread unashamedly across his beautiful face, he confesses, "Number five. I like you calling me Benny."

The door closes.

My phone vibrates a few minutes later with a text while I'm getting ready for bed.

Ben: Be ready at 9. Bring a jacket and wear reasonable shoes.

I'll be Benny's tomorrow.

CHAPTER
Fifteen

FEELING MUCH BETTER than the day before, I wake up and make myself coffee. I'm happy because have a few hours before Ben will pick me up.

I take my time showering and dressing for our day, opting for a pair of skinny jeans and a silk tank top. The weather is supposed to be warm, and with a jacket in tow, I'll be safe for anything. I finish the look off with a pair of suede flats. They are the most sensible footwear I have except for my running shoes. And those are not happening.

I drink my coffee and surf the net while listening to morning television. I reply to a few emails for work and finalize some things for Winnie and Cooper's party, approving the proof of the invitation we got back from the printers.

At a quarter until nine, my phone rings. It's Cooper and I answer. "What's up?"

"Good morning. What are you doing today?"

"I'm going with Ben somewhere."

"Somewhere? That sounds vague. Where are you going?"

I don't need to tell him that I don't know, but I sort of want to get his take on it. "I don't know where I'm going, only that I'm leaving at nine, I need a jacket, and it was recommended that I wear sensible—his words, not mine—shoes."

"Oh, sounds fun. How's the rib?"

I expected a bit more pestering from him. "It's much better. I took it pretty easy yesterday." My wayward thoughts revert back to what I said. "You're not worried that I'm unknowingly going somewhere with a man I've only known for merely a week?" I question, reviewing his best big brother card.

"No. Not really. I like Ben," he says rather plainly.

"You like him? You've only met him once."

"You don't like him? I don't get where you're going with this."

Men! And this one in particular is confusing the hell out of me.

"I just thought that you'd have more to say about it is all. He's a great P.A."

"And you like him." This is the badgering ass I was missing? I need to learn to pick my battles more wisely.

"I like him enough to employ him." He's going to see right through me. I rinse out my coffee cup and place it in the dishwasher.

"What else do you like him enough for?" I hear the telltale smooching sound of Winnie in the background.

"Is Winnie there?"

He moves the phone away from his mouth to talk to her. "Win, she likes Ben and she is wearing sensible shoes."

"I don't like him. I mean, I like him. I—" And my other line rings through. "I have to go. Ben's calling on the other line. I'll call you guys later or tomorrow or never again."

I hang up, not worried about offending them and answer Ben's call. "Hi."

"Good morning. Are you ready?" Am I ready? Every minute I spend with this enigma of a man, I become more and more ready for something, but I just don't know what.

"Yeah, I'll be right down. Do I need to bring anything?" I look around for something that I'm forgetting.

"Nope. Did you dress like I said? Comfy shoes?" he nags.

"Yes, sir. But for the record, all of my shoes are comfy. These shoes are comfy and sensible, I think. They're flats. That's what you meant right?"

"Right. Just get down here. I have coffee and a bagel for you."

Making it down to the lobby in record time and without any clumsy bumps or tumbles, I wave at Phil as I walk out the doors. I find Ben leaning on a jet-black Jeep with tinted windows. The man is wearing loosely fitting jeans and a Muse t-shirt.

"You like Muse?" I ask, inwardly delighted that he has great taste in music. Bad music can really sour a car ride.

"Oh yeah. Do you?" A megawatt beam shoots at me.

"Oooh yeah."

He opens the door for me, and do a quick bounce to lift myself into the vehicle. Ben stands close behind, waiting to see if I need help. When I don't, he closes my door and strides around to his side.

"Is this your Jeep?" I wonder out loud. I've never asked what he drives or if he even has a car.

"It's mine. I don't get to drive it much here in the city. It's just as easy to walk or take the subway as it is to find a place to park. I love it though." He flexes his right arm and pumps his fist low. "Tough, huh?"

"Very tough. So where are we going?" I can't even wait until the damn Jeep is in motion to ask.

"Pennsylvania. That's all you're getting from me."

"What the hell is in Pennsylvania?" I'm puzzled. "Philly?"

"Nope. Just sit there and enjoy the ride. Your coffee is hot, you have a bagel and schmear in the bag by your feet, and my iPod is ready to go. Relax and enjoy."

"Okay." I look him straight in the eye, handing over control to him. What am I in for?

He starts driving, so I open the bag, and damn, he got the good stuff. My favorite bagel. I like him.

Wait. I think I pay him to know that.

"I hope you saved the receipt for the breakfast and all that stuff yesterday, too. You don't need to be buying my meals," I say with a mouth that's half full.

Contrary to his earlier remarks on parking, he quickly pulls the Jeep into a lot and smoothly parks in an available space. He turns the engine off and shifts to face me.

"Okay. We need to get a few things straight for today, Tatum." Emerald eyes look at me with utmost determination. "Today, I'm not working. Neither are you. Today we are Ben and Tatum, out and about, having a good time. Think of it like a date."

"A date?" Is this a date? Hold up. When did I agree to a date? Then again, what could it hurt? It's one day-date.

"A date. I'm paying. I'm driving. I'm in control. Do you agree or disagree to this arrangement?"

"No one has ever asked me to go on a date while I'm already on the date." I can't help but smile and be a little excited that he wants to be on a date with me—and he didn't mind telling me so either.

"Will this date interfere with our working relationship?" That's the responsible question that needed asked.

He shakes his head no.

"Is this like a friends-buddies kind of date?" My eyebrows rise and I lean forward, trying to gauge where he's at in this whole thing.

"Not for me, but I can't answer that for you. You don't even have to think about that right now. Just relax and let me show you a good time. Deal?" He says this with such confidence that I'm speechless.

And *not for him?* He doesn't want to be my friend or buddy? Then the little dinger-bell goes off in my head with the answer.

Ding. He likes me.

I'm in. "Deal."

We drive west out of the city. He opts for county highways as opposed to the major thoroughfare. He looks strong and peaceful while driving. The radio has been turned down so far, and now that my bagel is gone and my coffee buzz has set in, I plan to test our musical compatibility. You can learn a lot about someone from the music they listen to, and I am about to see what Benny is into.

"May I see your iPod, please?" I ask rhetorically as I grab it from the perch it sits on. I scroll through the artists first. He does like the oldies. He's got everything from Sam Cooke to Alice in Chains. I'm very pleased.

I ask, "Wanna hear anything? I'm taking requests."

"Surprise me."

I make it my mission. I run across a familiar band, browsing by artist, but I can't remember what song by them that was so popular. Playing it, the tune comes back to me. "Got You Where I Want You" by The Flys.

The single guitar riff begins and I turn it up.

"Great song." Ben taps his fingers on the steering wheel to the steady beat. Both of our heads bob in time to the music. Just as the chorus begins to bellow from the speakers, we both start a second too early with, "Ooooooooh, got you where I want you" and laugh in concert, picking up the lyrics on time the second go-around.

The song ends and he does a 'gimme' gesture with his hand. He takes the player and pulls over onto the side of the road. He jumps out of his door and asks me. "Do you mind if we pull the top off? It's a good day for a topless ride." He wags his eyebrows.

Facetious bastard. "By all means, the top has to go." I know this double entendre well. It sounds like something I would have said. Reaching down to grab my sunglasses and lip gloss, I'm brought back to reality with the thump of my head off the oh-shit handle on the console in front of me.

Before I can bring my hand into contact with the smarting spot on my head, he's there by me with an 'ouch' face, gently rubbing the spot back and forth. I'm busted and busted.

"Yeah. My bad," I confess, biting my lip as a distraction from my newest injury. "At least it's out of the way now. I do that about once a day. I'm a klutz." I know that sweeping this under the rug won't work, but it comes as second nature for me to play it off that way.

"Got you good, didn't it?" Ben's mouth closes in on my fore-head and I fossilize in my seat. His lips are warm and soft as they affix to my thumping skull.

These kinds of kisses really are magic. They're "all-better kisses." I think the healing powers come from endorphins that kick in from the sheer knowledge of someone's pure affection for you. I try to memorize the feeling. My close-paid attention individually registers first his top lip pulling away while his lower lips stays stuck to my bruised skin for just a few seconds longer.

With the pads of his longest fingers, he touches under my chin to lift my eyes to his. "Better?"

I can only nod my head. This is an official swoon. I'm not sure if it's the mild concussion I might have given myself or the tidal wave of emotions dizzying me.

Ben gets into the driver's seat after stowing the Jeep's soft top. We set forward and he hands me the player again. "Just hit play," he instructs. I hit the center button and let song after song soothe my confused mind.

As we drive, I see more and more primitive-looking buildings and vehicles. We pass a real-life horse and buggy at one point be-cause the traffic formed a long line behind us.

Finally, he turns us down a long lane that hosts trees on both sides. It is a beautiful sight. Straight in front of us and going on for at least a half-mile, the trees are in bloom, and I can smell the sweet blossoms with every deep breath.

"Where are we? Is this it? It's so pretty, Ben." I look back and forth from him to the way and back again.

"We're almost there. Just around this corner." Ben alternates between watching me and the road. He sighs, "There's that smile." Ben puts his hand on my leg and runs his thumb back and forth as we round the last curve into a parking lot.

He's so affectionate, and I'm not used to this. Any of this. I might go into shock.

We walk up to a white building with a long wraparound porch covered in rocking chairs. I read the signs and realize where we're at.

"Welcome to No Diamond Cave," a round little man says from around the counter. "What can I do for you two today?" He smiles, lifting his arms like he'd gladly give us the whole wide world.

"We'd like to see the cave," Ben answers. "Is it open?"

"Well, the cave is actually without power right now. I have a service man here to fix it, but he had to run to town to get some things. If you'd like to wait a bit, I'm sure he'll sort it out."

Ben looks to me to see what I think, and I shrug a noncommittal whatever. Ben tells him that we're fine waiting and asks if there's still a little restaurant.

After being pointed in the right direction, we are seated in a tiny little diner near a window that overlooks a beautiful valley.

"It's so pretty here. Thanks for bringing me."

"I'm glad you like it. I think you'll like the cave too. I came here as a kid once, and for some reason it just sounded like a good drive."

"Well, Mr. Harris, this date"—I drag out the word so he knows that I know what we're doing—"is very original. No one has ever taken me out of the city on a date. I like it."

Pleased because I am, Ben leans towards me in the seat and whispers, "I prefer Benny to Mr. Harris."

"Really? I'll make a note of that. So you were little when you came here, huh? Is it the same?"

"I think so. I was only about five or six when my Moo...grandma and grandpa brought me." He catches himself, but not soon enough.

"Again, Moo-Moo? I like her already. Tell me where is this Moo-Moo you speak so fondly of?" Instantly, I'm praying that she's still alive. I shouldn't have been such a dope. It's very likely that grandparents of grandchildren our age aren't still above dirt.

"She lives in a retirement home north of the city. She loves it there. She's pretty happy I think. I try to visit when I can."

"That's nice. Do your parents visit her, too?"

"They do. It's just not as easy for them. Sometimes we go together." It probably would be hard seeing your mother getting older and having to think about a loved one's mortality.

"It sounds like you spent a lot of time with her when you were growing up. She must be great." My mouth stops just before I say something that I need to keep to myself. Something exactly like, *I'd love to meet her sometime.*

"I did. My grandparents were always very close by when I was little." The tension in his face leaves almost completely when he's speaking about his Moo-Moo. It's irresistible.

"Do you have brothers or sisters?"

"A brother. Eight years older. I guess they knew they could do better," he kids.

He's so different today. Forthright and open. I really like this side of Ben Harris.

After his last comment, he pretends arrogance as he grandly stretches his arms out on the back of his bench seat. Spread out like that, he looks huge. I take my time cataloging every infinitesimal detail. The definition of his pecks and the spattering of reddish-blond hair that's peeking out from his jeans. The long ridge that symmetrically runs along the bicep on each arm. It's the perfect time of day, and the light through the window makes his skin glow. It's quite the sight.

One I hope to never forget.

CHAPTER
Sixteen

WE ORDER SANDWICHES and fries. We're in no hurry or rush. He's thoughtful and asks me about everything. It isn't so much the things he wants to know that grab my attention. It's more the way he listens.

I really think he likes me.

"I hope we get to go inside the cave. I've never been in one before," I admit. This is mostly true. Honestly, if anyone would have suggested I go to a cave before, I would have thanked them to fuck off. I'm nearly blind. A cave isn't really the safest place for me. But being with Ben makes it seem different. It doesn't seem so daunting. It feels like an adventure. I'm not scared.

"We will. If they don't get the power on, I'll see if we can take lanterns in. I kind of hope that the power says off." Ben's face beams with excitement.

I look at him like he's insane. "Are you sure that's safe? I mean, if the lanterns went out, we'd be in complete darkness. We should wait." Okay, now I'm a little apprehensive.

"Don't you trust me? I'm a guy. My sense of direction is unparalleled. You'll be safe. Promise." I know he's already decided that we're going in, so there isn't any use in protesting.

"I trust you. I think." I try to smile, but I'm certain it looks more like I'm going number two.

"I'm going to go see how it's going with the power and see if we can go in anyway. I'll be right back." Slapping the table top, Ben gets up in search of the jolly round man.

I hit the ladies' room before we trek into the cave in the dark. It'd be a shame to piss my pants on our first date.

———•———

Ben somehow convinces the guy to let us go in. We sign a waiver releasing him from liability or whatever. That was a big flag for me, but Ben just rubbed his hands together like a madman, laughing at my nervousness.

Before I know it, we're walking into a dark cave with only a lantern to light the way. Immediately, I feel a little apprehensive. The temperature is drastically cooler than outside no more than a few feet from the entrance. It's quiet and still, and it smells earthy.

I follow behind him as he walks us into the main entrance, and he stops before the path turns to stairs for a rapid descent into God only knows what.

"Are there bats in here, Ben?" I should have worn a turtle neck. Something about knowing that they could be lurking around in the shadows gives me the creeps.

"I'm sure there are, but I don't think they'll bother us. We're too big. They can see us." I can only see a little ahead of him where the light from the lantern washes the ground. "Tatum, are you honestly scared?"

"I don't know. It's just really dark now that we're in here. I don't know if I want to go without the power on." I can feel my heart beginning to race and my senses go on high alert.

"What are you feeling?" He never bullshits.

"Nervous, I guess."

"What is making you nervous? Is it the bats?"

"I don't know. I think it's because I can't see where I'm going."

"Neither can I. Here, hold my hand. We're on equal footing in here. I can't see much either." His protective hand is a small comfort, and my fingers lace with his as he pulls me a little closer.

When he sets the lantern down at our feet, our bodies make a shadow on the cave's wall behind him. It looks romantic—a man and a woman holding hands and looking at each other. Ben's other hand frames my face.

"It's dark in here, but nothing in here will hurt us. We just have to relax and use our senses. Our bodies are made to make up for what we can't see. What can you hear?"

This is a lesson. I'm so stupid. He doesn't like me—he wants to train me. What a foolish girl I am.

My carefree mood is soured. I say, being short with him, "I hear water." Then I think, *To hell with that. I'll tell him what I think about it.* "I thought this was a date. I'm not that scared anymore. Let's just get this over with."

I make to pick up the lantern. He can hear the annoyance that I didn't try to hide. And I feel his hand squeeze mine.

"Don't do that. This is a date, but it's also a chance for you to open your eyes, too."

"Is that supposed to be funny? You take an almost blind girl to a dark cave on a date? What the fuck, Ben? I thought it was just an adventure, but you just made this fun, spontaneous trip feel clinical. You made it about my sight, not about me. It feels like therapy. Is that what you're trying to do?"

"No. That's not what this is. You're being defensive." His voice isn't patronizing, but he speaks calmly even though I'm almost shouting at him.

"That's awfully easy for you to say. I'm the one being schooled here, right? I'm the one who needs to open her eyes, right? This was a use-your-senses field trip, right? I think I'm going to go wait in the Jeep."

My hand tries to rid itself of his, but he won't let go.

"Dammit. Stop." He shakes our linked hands.

"This was a mistake. You work for me."

"I said stop it, Tatum!" The authority in his voice demands my attention. His volume echoes off the walls.

My ears are so tuned in. With the shock of his shout, it feels like they've opened and now I hear his breathing, too.

Ben inhales and exhales slowly, calming his approach. "I wanted this to be fun. The power is out. So yeah, that changed the game a bit. But don't assume that I didn't want this to be a date. I didn't have ulterior motives. Can you please just take a walk with me in here for a little while? Hold my hand. We'll talk, probably argue. I'll say that you look beautiful and you'll ask me out on our second date." His volume recedes the more he speaks. "I don't want to upset you. I just wanted you to see that even if it's a little scary in here, even if it's dark, I'm here. I won't let anything happen. That's what I meant."

Why does he always have to say stuff like this? It's so confusing. One moment he's all analytical and the next he's sweet and caring. I can hardly make heads from tales with him. I did hear one thing loud and clear though. He wants to go out with me again.

"But no more blind crap. Got it? It's like I'm on a date with my ophthalmologist. That's not fun, Benny."

He picks up the lantern, and hand in hand, we start down the steps that lead us to a dirt path.

"Oh, come on. Mark's not so bad," Ben says.

I laugh, but then I think, *Mark? Dr. Meade?*

"Mark Meade? My doctor? You're on a first-name basis with my eye doctor? Do you know him?"

How would he know him? I asked him to call and confirm next week's appointment the other day, but he wouldn't have spoken to Dr. Meade himself. Charlotte would have answered, and she never calls him Mark.

He tenses for a second like he forgot something and then asks, "Isn't that his name?"

"Yeah, but—"

"Hey," he interrupts as if something just hit him. "You called me Benny."

"You said you liked it."

"I do. A lot." Good thing it's dark, because I feel myself flush red hot.

The farther we walk into the cave, the cooler it gets. Ben stops us at few different places where there are nameplates and information about the most popular spots in the cave. There are allegedly rocks and formations that resemble animals and objects. Ben says that he can see the formations in just about every place we pause. I see pointy rocks, but it is a good time.

After an hour of strolling around, we stop in a large room. I can tell it's big because our voices carry in the space and the light from the lantern doesn't make it to the ceiling. He washes the light around the chamber and finds that there is a bench close to where we are.

"Want to sit for a minute before we head back? I think this is the turnaround point." He walks to the built-in seat that's made from the same type of rock that lines the walls and floors. Brushing off room for both of us, he sits and pats for me to join.

"Thanks for taking me out today." I know he wasn't trying to piss me off earlier. I think he meant what he said about not trying to upset me, too. I get so emotional around him. Okay, I'm just emotional.

"You're welcome. You're fun to be with. Nothing like my slave-driving boss." He bumps his shoulder into mine, telling me that he's just kidding. This is another Ben Harris signature mannerism.

I nudge him back, playing along. "That's good to hear. You do bring up a good point though. I'm your boss. What is this going to be like tomorrow?" This has been sitting in the back of my mind all day. "I mean, how does this work?"

"That I don't know, Tatum. But what I do know is that you're my boss and intend on maintaining a professional relationship with you when I'm working. I also know that you've just got out of a relationship. Plus, I know that you're a busy woman." He adds to the inventory of his finding, "The last thing I know is that, even though you hate to admit it, you're dealing with a lot of changes right now. You see, I know all of these things."

"All true. But...?"

"But I haven't been able to stop thinking about you. You're unlike anyone I've ever met, Tatum. You're funny and sexy. I'm crazy attracted to you. I just want you."

Relief and something close to excitement roll through my body. I wanted to hear those words. I'm crazy attracted to him, too. But everything else he said is also true. Only a week or so ago, I was in a long-term relationship with Kurt. And all of the other points he made were just as valid.

"So what does all that mean? What do you want me to say? That you're right about all of that?" We sit here for a few more seconds, and everything in my body screams to say more.

"You don't have to say anything. Don't think that this is an offer that will expire. It won't. When you're ready for me, I'll still be here. I'm a patient man, baby."

I don't have a chance to think about what he just said, because the lights flicker on, then off, and then on again.

All at once, the walls above and around where we couldn't see with just the lantern are ablaze. It is breathtaking.

The ceiling is probably a hundred feet high or even more. All around us are glittering flecks—millions of perfectly cut diamonds adhere to the walls—and they were here this whole time, just beyond our sight.

I'm on my feet, head lifted towards the epicenter of the grand, shimmering kaleidoscope above us. I can't tear my eyes away. It is mesmerizing. Every color in the rainbow is shining like I've never seen before. It's breathtaking.

Finally, after having my fill, I can sense Ben's warm body behind mine. I pivot all the way around to find him gazing upward like I just was. Then, without thinking at all, I wrap my arms around him tightly. I cling to him like ink to paper. It's not a decision. I need to touch him. Even though I can't say what I'm feeling, I can show him with my body, and I hold on tighter than I ever have before.

Without hesitation, his return embrace wraps me like a blanket.

"Thank you," I say into his chest, overwhelmed.

"Tatum, just because something is in the dark doesn't mean it won't shine."

CHAPTER
Seventeen

BEN DIDN'T KISS ME after our date. I mean, I don't know if I was really expecting him to or not, but I guess we agreed that it was best we keep things professional—at least for now. He did tell me that I have to ask him out for our next date and that he'll go wherever, whenever, I chose.

I have to think about that.

He comes every morning with breakfast and coffee, and he rides with me to work most days for us to the discuss things that need done. The shower is coming along great and is fast approaching this weekend. The past three weeks have gone by so fast.

With network sweeps week and the Just Kidding finale fast on our heels, and so too our hiatus for the summer, things at work are busier than ever. The Devons consistently bring their A-games. Even Winnie, with her wedding just around the corner, is ever present and focused.

To our surprise, Chel-Ro's people call Wes and she wants to be a part of the show's finale. We say yes, of course. It will be a great flip for her to publicly bust us for poking fun at her recent proclivities. Honestly, we don't care where the laughs come from, as long as they show up. We are fine with the joke being on us.

I visited Dr. Meade the week after our trip to No Diamond and told him about what we saw. He was really interested in the changes I made in such a short time and was pleased to hear of my getting more help. Of course, he asked a lot of questions about Ben since I mentioned him in every other sentence. Dr. Meade dropped his retinoscope when I told him that Ben had called him Mark. He thought it was funny.

He noticed more degeneration, but it was small and the difference only minimally noticeable to me.

It was a good appointment.

He wasn't particularly happy to hear that I hadn't gone to the hospital when I hurt my ribs, but he affirmed they wouldn't have done much anyway.

See? I know what I'm talking about after all. My ribs, although at times still tender, are doing much better and I've been feeling great.

Luckily, I've managed to avoid any major accidents lately, and I can only hope it means that either getting better at this whole blind thing or Ben has secretly been moving all of my furniture a centimeter a day into safer positions.

Either way, I am cool with it. Ben's so helpful. And kind. And handsome. And every day I'm with him, I like him more.

Sure, he's sexy. He's always been sexy, but now it's like as much as I am attracted to his body, I'm attracted to his personality. The way he licks his thumb when he's cooking drives me insane. The way he tries to be subtle when he tells me that he doesn't have any plans on the weekend compels me to scribble our names together with hearts, like I'm back in junior high. The way he leaves Post-it Notes all over my condo with reminders makes me feel treasured.

My favorites are, "You look so 'professional' in the blue dress," and the one he left last night—"Remember that time you called me to thank me for the chili? You should thank me for the chicken I left in the oven tonight."

Don't be mistaken. I've almost dialed his number at night with the sole intention of letting him talk me into a climax like he almost did only a month ago, but what if it gets messy? Not my orgasm, but our working relationship? I'm comfortable the way things are. He has his place in my life and I have mine in his.

Boss and employee.

Employee and horny-as-hell, needs-to-get-laid boss. That's a bit more accurate.

I haven't called Kurt to take him up on the offer of the one last shag for old time's sake, but I'm not too proud to do it if I don't figure something out.

Then again, here I am at work, thinking about Ben. Sitting at my desk, having a minute to myself. Daydreaming about his gorgeous hands. Thinking about having them roam all over my body.

In the shower. Yeah. Oh, God.

Or maybe he bends me over my counter, works my dress up to my waste, and fucks me right there in the kitchen.

"Tatum! Shit. Hello?!" Winnie shouts even though she's standing right in front of me.

I've done it again. I'm in fantasy land and totally zoned out.

She startles me and I jump, knocking my phone's handset off the receiver. Catching it, I think I need to lock my door more often. That bitch walks in at the worst moments.

"What? What!"

She tries to hide her laugh with her hand but fails. "Hey, are you sleeping with your eyes open? You look freaky when you do that. You need to get some lovin'. You're all washed up." She's right. I'm edgy and tense, wound tighter than Richard Simmons's perm.

"Shut the fuck up and mind your own damn business for once. Please, Gwendolyn. Damn!" I grunt like a grumpy cavewoman. I'm also sensitive about my lack of orgasmic activity, I guess.

Winnie sits in the chair in front of my desk and makes her know-it-all ass comfortable. "Hey, is Ben coming to the couples shower party thing this weekend?"

That's a good question. I don't think we've ever talked about it. I mean, I might need him. I'm not sure what for, because the whole thing is pretty much taken care of. The fantastic little band that Ben finally talked me into has been paid and he's called to confirm everything down to the decorators. It's pretty much on autopilot from here on out.

"I don't know. Did you invite him?" I ask her in response as I right the shit I misplaced when she bitchslapped me out of my naughty thoughts. Let's see how she plays this.

"Well, actually that's what I'm in here about. Cooper and I would love to invite him if you're not bringing him. We really like him, and he's going to be around for a while. Most of the people from the office and Cooper's work will be there. We'd love for him to come. So are you going to ask him or do you want us to?" She raises her eyebrow, and I know she's not going to let up. Shit. I knew she would turn this around on me somehow. She's tricky, that one.

I play it off. "Yeah, I'll ask him. No big deal." No big shit. Who cares?

Oh, no. Now Winnie has that look. The face of 'can we chit-chat and decide what's best for one of us?' twists into her brow. Even worse, she gets up and shuts my door. Here we go. She resettles herself in her chair.

"Tate, what the hell are you doing?" I can tell she's concerned and not just being nosy. She's my best friend, but the truth is that I have not a fucking clue what I'm doing.

"What are you talking about? I'm working. Something you should do. Don't you have, like, five scenes tomorrow?"

That pisses her off. I know because her tongue goes straight behind her bottom lip and paces back and forth while she nods, a classic 'pissed Winnie' move.

Good. Maybe she'll go away.

She says nothing and just keeps staring. Her perfectly sculpted brows rise, and I think the left one is twitching just a bit.

"What, Winnie? What? Spit it out."

"What's going on with you? Why haven't you asked Ben out? You said that he told you he wasn't going to ask you out again, that you had to ask him. So what's the dealio, Emilio? He's hot. He's into you. He's hot!"

I count off on one hand. "He works for me. I just got out of a relationship. I barely know the guy outside of the fact that he is great at time management and he has impeccable phone skills." That last bit made me blush. Almost-phone-sex talk aside, he really is quite proficient and well spoken in a professional capacity, and that's what I meant. Okay, well I meant it both ways. "It's so messy."

"Who cares! He's amazing. You are constantly in here having fantasy fellatio hour with him in your under-sexed mind. Don't think I don't know how twisted you are, Ms. Elliot." She's goading me well. "I can see right through you. You check your messages more than ever. You answer ALL of his calls."

I blow up. "He works for me!" I look around and out my window to make sure no one heard me. "Okay, he's great. He's made my life so easy lately. But what would I do if we *did* start seeing each other and it didn't work out? Huh? What about that!? What would I do then, if you know so much?" I can't control my hands. They are flailing about like Michael Flatley, Lord of the Dance's feet. "How would I do this without him? He knows what I need before I tell him. Hell, before I even know I need it! Where will I be if I screw this up?"

If she didn't know how seriously I was into him ten minutes ago, she does now. I haven't gone crazy like this since 'N Sync broke up. I try to catch my breath after I lose my shit, and I tone it down a notch while Winnie just looks at me.

I whisper, "What if I just push him away, too? What if I become a burden? What if he just feels sorry for me?"

"Is that what you think? You think he just feels sorry for you?" Winnie comes around my desk and sits on my lap. "Oh, baby girl. You're so fucking blind!"

I smack her arm rather roughly. "Fuck you, asshole."

"Ouch! Hey! Sorry, I didn't mean it like that. I meant, you have to at least give it a shot. Yeah, he is your personal assistant, but has he been weird or awkward since your last date?"

"No. Not really."

"Well what makes you think that it wouldn't just be okay?"

"It would be weird to pay someone I'm dating to do my shit, Winnie."

She snorts a laugh. "Yeah, that would be weird, but don't get ahead of yourself. Go out on a few dates. Bring him to the shower. As your date. Let him hump your brains out! Tatum, I'm really about to do you. If you don't go out with Ben, I'm going to break it off with Cooper and make you my lesbian hostage."

"You're batshit crazy. Get off me." I shove her.

"You'll do it? You're going to ask him out?"

She is so annoying, but I know she's a little right. Just a little. "Yes. I'll ask him."

"When? You're going to chicken out. I know it. Call him and do it right now. While I'm in here. I want to hear you do it."

She has a good point. I probably would chicken out. I'd probably text him something un-sweet like, "Hey, want to go the thing with me?"

I've never been like this.

I effectively push her fat ass off me. All right, it's not fat. I'm just bothered about how she's uncharacteristically correct today, in terms of my behavior.

"Okay," I give in. With her here, I can't puss out if this. And honestly, I don't want to. I like him so much.

She picks up my work phone and waits for me to dial. I hit number three on the speed dial and see the look of recognition on her face. Three on my speed dial is major.

She walks back over to the chair in front of my desk, giving me some much-needed space.

It rings once.

Twice.

"Hey," he answers. No, "Hello." No, "This is Ben." Just, "Hey." Like, "It's you."

"Hey, how are things going? Did all of the deliveries arrive at The Yard today?" I'm not really sure how to break the ice, but party talk seems like a good way to lead into it.

"You know it. I'm just leaving there now. It's going to be great. No worries, remember? I've got it taken care of. Is Winnie excited?" Who wouldn't like this guy? He isn't just dicking me. He really wants to know if they're looking forward to it.

"Yeah, actually they both are." My pest of a best friend is doing the international sign for "get there" by wafting her hand in front of her black Donna Karan number she's rocking today. By the way, I should borrow that.

Focus, Tatum!

"So, actually I was calling for personal reasons, not professional. Um—"

He cuts in. "Are you all right?"

"No. No. I'm fine, really. I was calling to see if you wanted to go with me to Winnie and Cooper's party on Saturday?" God, not my smoothest moment, but I got it out, so that counts for something. Even though I sound like a pimply sixteen-year-old virgin asking the football star to the Sadie Hawkins. Sound? Hell, I feel like that girl too.

"Tatum?"

"Ben?"

Winnie's eyes are about to bug out. The way her ass is barely touching the chair now is almost comical, and she's giving me the 'oh shit' face, teeth bared and all.

"Do you remember what I told you?" His voice changes into the authoritative, seductive one I crave. I'm just worried that this time it's to tell me no.

"What? Do you have plans or something? That's fine. I just… I didn't want to be rude and not invite you. You've been working so hard on it and all. Oh, shit, never mind. I'll just talk to you later." I'm about to hang up. My blood feels like it's all being pumped to my face.

"Tatum, wait. I want to go with you. You said personally though, right? Not professionally?"

Winnie's sweet ass finally makes contact with the wingback and I see relief wash over her face.

"Right." What the hell? What does he want me to say?

"Call me Benny and ask me again."

"Are you serious?"

"As a heart attack. Ask me again, like you're not asking me to put your dog to sleep and call me Bennnnnyyy." He says it slowly, and his voice puts me into that Ben-trance I'm becoming all too familiar with. He's going to make me jump through hoops, eh? I probably deserve it for waiting this long to ask him out.

It's getting a little too intimate with Winnie sitting here. But she's all settled in now and eating this up like an inmate's last supper. There's only one way to keep this from getting embarrassing for real.

Ham it up. I can play his game. I invented this game.

"Oh, Benny." I put a little needy pant in my voice. "Benny? Please. Please, go with me on Saturday. Please, Benny?"

"Fuck, Tatum." He clears his throat. "I'm trying to walk down the street here."

Winnie taps out. With both hands on her head, she walks towards the door to leave, but first she does a very classy and mature table hump, mouthing the words "Fuck. Him. Already."

"Tatum, are you still there?" his voice sure and deep asks across the line.

"Yes. I'm here. Seriously, though. If you're busy, I will be fine going by myself. You shouldn't feel obligated."

"I don't. What time do I pick you up?"

"Pick me up? Uh…" Shit, this is a date. This is a real freaking date.

No sensible shoes.

No pretending.

He's serious.

"Yes. You've asked me to take you on a date. Right? You did just ask me out, or am I mistaken?"

He's so intense when it comes to stuff like this. I never know what to think or say. "I did, but—"

"But nothing. Do you want me to go with you?" How many different ways and times is he going to make me say it?

"Yes," I huff. "I want you to pick me up at six. I should be there a little early. I hope you don't mind."

"Nope. I don't mind at all." Then he's quiet for a few seconds. "Why are you asking me out now?"

He's so maddening. "I'm not sure what you're asking me." Is this an ego trip? As crazy as he makes me, when he behaves like this, it's such a turn-on. He's never easy.

"Tell me why, Tatum? What made you call me and ask me right now?"

"I just thought of it and I wanted to know if you'd like to go."

"And?" Fucking fishing bastard.

"And I want to go with you."

"As your...?"

"As my date, all right!? I want you to go with me. To a party. As my date. With me. On a date. Ben. Please?"

"Great. Call me Benny again." I can hear his smile, and mine cracks my tempered face.

"No."

"Please?"

I'm regretting this already. "Nope. You don't deserve it. You have to earn it from here on out. Now that I know how much you like it, I don't want to waste it. You have to work for it."

"Fair enough. Listen, I was going to call you. I need a few days off."

My gut reaction is to say no. To ask why. To know where he's going and what he'll be doing. But it isn't my business, so I say the only thing I can. "Of course. When?"

"I'll need to be out of town tomorrow and I'll be back either late Friday or early Saturday morning. Everything is set for the party and I'll still be over in the morning. I have some things I need to do. Will that be all right?"

Again, I have to fight my curiosity and just agree. What choice do I have?

"Sure. I'm sure I can manage a few days. I hope everything is okay."

His evasive excuse has my mind thinking all sorts of crazy scenarios in my head. We've yet to discuss at length how he knew about the position or exactly what he did before working for me. I only know that it was in Washington and for the military, but not in it. Maybe I'll dig up more information on our date?

Hell, he could be some undercover spy for all I know. He'd actually be a brilliant spy now that I think of it, and then it flies right out of my mouth.

"Ben, are you a secret agent or something?"

He laughs. And then he laughs some more. If it weren't one of the best sounds, then I'd chide him for laughing too long at my not-joke. It morphed about twenty seconds ago from one of the laugh-*with*-me kinds into the *at*-me variety. But it still sounds perfect to my ears.

"Answer the question," I insist.

"Nope. I guess you'll have to earn that bit of information. Ms. Elliot, that's classified." Then the smartass laughs even harder.

"I have to go, Double-O Dickhead. I'll see you later."

About an hour later, a delivery man walks past Cynthia, and in equal measure, I hope that the package is for someone else and for me at the same time. As he rounds the pit, I know—it's for me.

He knocks almost knocks, but I get it to the door first.

"Ms. Elliot? A package from Agent Benjamin."

I can't help myself. Laughing, I sign and thank the delivery man.

When I open the package, first I see the note.

Tatum,

Since I'll be gone tomorrow and you'll likely be bored with no one to torment, here are two tickets to the Monty Python show on Broadway. Take Winnie. I owe her one.
Enjoy,
Agent Benjamin

CHAPTER
Eighteen

BEN ARRIVES FIRST THING in the morning. I sent him a text last night after I got home to thank him for the tickets. Of course, he made me re-text "Thank you, Benny." But he deserved it. I really want to see that show and he got us fantastic seats.

He comes in and I'm surprised that he isn't wearing his usual casual Ben attire. Not today. Today he's in a suit. He looks so good that I want to put my schmear on him and lick him up for breakfast.

"Good morning, Tatum." He smiles at me on his way into the kitchen. Grabbing a bottle of water, Ben stands across from me at the bar.

"Good morning, Ben. You look very nice," I say in my most innocent voice.

"So do you. Are you ladies ready for tonight's show? You wrap for the season next week, right?" He's right. We have one more show—the Big Show—and then it's adios for a few months. I'm so looking forward to it. This summer I'm helping a few screenwriters with edits, which won't be much, and that's it. I would be nice to take a vacation, but who knows. I guess I'll have to see what comes down the line.

"Yep. One more and then we're out until probably late July or early August. I am totally ready for a break, too. What are your plans for the summer? Any big trips? Secret rendezvous? Any covert operations?"

"Not that I can think of or speak of," he replies on a wink. My stomach does a little whoosh.

Check yourself, Tatum.

"So you'll be back in time for Saturday night then? It won't be rushing you?"

"I already told you. I'll pick you up at six. Quit trying to back out. You clearly want to go out with me. So drop it." He takes a long drink of his water to camouflage his glib grin.

"You're so arrogant in the morning, Ben. I'm not trying to back out. I want you to go." There. See? I can be a grown up. "I'm really looking forward to it. I think we've planned a great party."

"Are your parents going to be there?"

I'm surprised that their attendance is only now coming up. "No, they couldn't attend. Prior engagement. But you'll meet them at the wedding I'm sure." Even as I'm speaking that sentence, I'm regretting it. The wedding isn't for another month and a half, and here I am, making assumptions that he'll be going.

"I'd like to meet them. From what you've told me, they sound really cool."

"Oh, they're cool all right. I hope you like patchouli, and you should probably brush up on your celestial easy-listening music." Hell, they'll probably share a joint if they like him enough.

"I'll have to remember that. What are you going to do after the show tonight?" This is the question I've been asked every Thursday morning since Pete sticked me.

"I think that Cooper, Winnie, and I are going to go get some dinner and then I'll most likely come back here. Don't worry about it. Ben, that was a freak accident and totally my fault."

"It wasn't your fault. Accidents don't have fault. I was just asking." He seems a little sensitive about it, but I don't care. I'm a grown-ass woman. He can't babysit me all the time.

"Seriously, I've lived in New York my whole life. I can make it a few days without you baby-proofing ahead of me."

"That wasn't what I meant and you know that," he says sternly.

"Okay, fine. I'll wear a helmet. I've been wanting to get one anyway. I've been thinking about a Kevlar vest, too. That would have come in handy at the bar. Seriously, I'm not a child." As I hear myself say the words, I actually feel like a child throwing a tantrum. However, I commit to my arguments and give him a death stare for good measure. Benny can deal with it.

"I know." Ben's arms shoot in surrender. "Look, I just want to make sure that you're safe. That's all. I'm not trying to get into your business. I care about you."

Such simple words. I care about you.

I care about you.

He cares about me.

"Thank you. That's sweet." Before I get all goo-goo eyed, it's time for me to head downstairs. "Are you riding with me to the studio today?" I ask as I grab my bag and briefcase.

"No, I can't. I brought the Jeep and I need to head out. I just wanted to stop in and make sure there weren't any last-minute things you needed me to do first."

I'm not sure why I'm this disappointed, but I am. He is only leaving for two days and we've only been on one kind-of date. However, we've spend the better part of the month together and I'll genuinely miss him.

"I'll walk you down though."

He smiles sweetly in consolation. Offering me a hand to hold, he takes my briefcase with the other and we head down. Together.

"I'll have my phone on me all of the time. So feel free to call if you need anything or..." He trails off, and this is when I notice the back and forth of his thumb over my knuckle.

We step into the elevator and the air is thicker, pregnant with what he was about to say.

"Or what?"

"Or you could just call me if you want to. I'd like that." How can the most basic of sentences say so much?

They *mean* so much.

"Okay. Maybe I'll call you tonight when I get home."

His grin is as wide as Bow Bridge in Central Park when I offer. "Maybe I'd really like that."

"Maybe it's settled then. I'll call you later and you'll have a nice trip."

"And you'll have a great show."

"Peaches." I smile too. Stepping off the elevator I feel lighter than when we stepped on it.

The car is waiting, and Ben leads me right to the back passenger's door, saying good morning to Ray. Ray is quiet and polite to a fault. That man is more punctual than a Rolex and makes the NYC traffic his bitch.

I love having a driver.

"Okay, I'll see you on Saturday. Six o'clock sharp," Ben tells me, leaning in so that I can smell is cinnamon breath.

Nose to nose, we just look at each other.

"I'll talk to you tonight?" he says like a question, and I nod my compliance. "Okay then."

At the same time we kiss each other on opposite cheeks and hold the touch a beat longer than one would classify as platonic.

"I'll miss you, Benny," I say into his ear.

The man hummed. Literally hummed.

That warm feeling stays with me all day long and through one of our best shows to date. Might I add, three people told me I looked really good today? The kicker is that I feel really good.

———— • ————

The show ends flawlessly. Winnie and Cooper decide to call it an early night and go on home, which is fine with me. I'm tired, and the weekend is going to be a busy one. So instead of going out with the rest of the cast and crew, I head home too.

Neil called Ray to pick me up soon, so I go down with him a

few minutes early to wait in the warm night air.

When we hit the ground floor, I see Kurt before he sees me, which, let's be honest, doesn't happen for me that often. He's pacing in the lobby.

Neil, having ridden down with me, notices him too. "Do you want me to stick around, Tate?" Concern is obvious on his perfect-pored face. *I need a facial.*

"No, I'll be fine. I'll just tell him I'm going home. Don't worry. It's just Kurt, Neil. He's not a bad guy."

"I know. It's just weird that he's here. Do you guys still talk?"

"No, not really." As we approach Kurt's earshot, I whisper reassurance. "It's fine. Seriously."

"All right, girl. Goodnight. Good show. Are you coming in tomorrow?"

"Yeah, I'll probably come in early. Get a good jump on the Big Show for next week."

"Okay, I'll be here at eight." Neil winks and waves a civil hello to Kurt in passing.

I wait until Neil is out of the doors before saying anything, stopping in front of my ex-boyfriend. "Hey, Kurt. Whatcha need?" I politely smile. I don't have any bad feelings towards him, but Neil's right. It is a bit strange that he's here.

I never texted him back after the bar fiasco, and he's called a few times since then. I never know what to say, so I don't answer.

"Can we talk?" He looks all right, and I've never been afraid of him. What could it hurt?

"Sure, but I've just got a second. I'm meeting someone." I figure that's vague enough to get me out of any long, drawn-out heart-to-heart that, at the moment, I don't have the heart for.

"Who are you meeting? Winnie and Cooper? They can meet us. Are you going to Matty's?" Whoa, that's a lot of questions.

"No, actually. I'm meeting someone at home." I read his instant reaction to my statement, realizing it was a giant mistake. Why don't I know when to shut the fuck up?

"Is it *that guy* you were with the other night?" He starts to slightly bounce like he's getting hyped up. He isn't acting at all like the Kurt I know. I gather that he didn't like my answer and all, but *that guy* isn't really any of his business.

"Listen, I'm not upset about Matty's if that's what you're worried about. Everyone drinks a little too much every once and a while. Pete isn't even pissed about it. So let's just drop it." I feel my cell buzz, and I desperately want to see if it's Ben.

I put my hand in my pocket and reach for my phone. I see that it's Ray, and I'm instantly relieved. I don't think that Kurt will do anything messed up, but I also didn't ever picture him swinging at a guy with a pool stick. So what do I know?

Ray: Everything, okay? I'm waiting in the car in front of the doors.

I say, "Excuse me," to Kurt and quickly text Ray back.

Me: I'm fine. Be right out.

"Is that him? Who is he anyway? Do you really already have a boyfriend?"

"No. That's enough! I don't already have a *boyfriend* and I don't see where it's any of your business, Kurt. Actually, I really don't appreciate you showing up at my job after a show like this either. What do you want? And make it quick. I have to go."

Kurt moves to grab my phone. I feel him grab for it before I see him do it. Looking down to our hands that are now joined, I yank my arm back.

"I think we're done here. I'm going home."

"Don't be a bitch, Tatum," he venomously spits. "A bitch?" This is the Kurt that I was sort of expecting when we were dating. Funny that he was just waiting to show up after we went to Splitsville. What a piece of shit. I can't believe that I felt bad for the prick.

"Listen. We broke up. End of fucking story. I suggest you leave and don't come back here. You hear me? I don't want to see you again. Ever!"

I start to walk away, but he grabs my arm. It isn't even seconds before I see Ray walking through the double doors, and he looks murderous. His huge chest is puffed up bigger than I've ever seen and his dark brown eyes look black. When he gets closer, I see a throbbing vein laces up Ray's forehead and across his bald scalp. We meet eyes and I silently ask for help.

"Hey, buddy. Why don't you let her go and back up?" Ray's growl echoes from across the lobby as he gains speed, heading towards Kurt and me.

"And who the fuck is this guy, Tatum? Are you so God-damned blind you can't tell who you're fucking anymore?" I'm frozen. It's the cruelest thing anyone has ever said to me. "Did she suck your dick yet, pal? She's at her best when she's on her knees."

Kurt laughs and I feel sick. My stomach knots, and I don't know what to do. I don't know where to go. But I do know one thing and that is that Ray looks like he's going to beat the shit out of Kurt.

"Let her arm go. Now!" Ray approaches Kurt and doesn't look like he's going to stop. He might plow over him. Ray is a huge dude, and he's much thicker than Kurt. Right now I'd say Kurt is in deep shit. I'm just thankful that Ray's here.

"I'll let her go. I'll sure as fuck let her go! She's a fucking bitch and you can have her."

That's all Kurt gets out before Ray's hand is around his throat. Kurt struggles for a second and then realizes he isn't going to win this fight.

"Ms. Elliot, do you want to call security or the police? I think you should," Ray says so calmly, while holding Kurt's neck in his grip. Kurt's face is bright red, and I'm sure he's going to pass out soon if Ray doesn't let go.

"Ray, you're going to kill him. He can't breathe." I'm not as worried about Kurt as I am Ray. I don't need this guy going to jail. We've only just had our first full conversation. And right now he is pretty much my favorite person to speak of.

"No, he'll pass out first. Police?" Ray's expression says, "Make the call."

I don't know what to do. I don't want Kurt bothering me, but I don't want him to go to jail. Maybe this will scare him off.

Then I think, *Fuck him,* and dial 911.

After I tell the dispatch lady what my emergency is—and that it's currently not really an emergency anymore thanks to Ray—she tells me that a squad car is enroute and asks if we can hold him there until the police show up?

Seconds later, the building's security guards bail out of the elevators and come straight for Ray and Kurt. Ray must have let up some, because Kurt is still conscious.

"Ms. Elliot, are you all right? We just got back to the watch room when we saw the end of this," says a security man I recognize but don't know by name.

"Yeah, I think I'm fine. He just grabbed my arm. Ray, my driver, saw what was happening and came in." By the time I get the words out, the other two officers have Kurt on the ground and handcuffed.

"We'll give the police a copy of the video. We got everything."

"Is he going to jail?" Why is that my concern? It isn't, I guess. But for some reason, I feel awful anyway. What happened to make him so crazy?

Is he drunk? He doesn't smell drunk.

"Probably. At least for questioning. You'll have to ask the police officers. They might want you to go down to the station, too."

This sucks. I just wanted to go home and call my hot personal assistant, and now I've been manhandled, verbally assaulted, and a witness to a near death by choking. And I have to go down to the motherfucking police station?

Bullshit. Complete bullshit.

Thankfully, the police take my statement right there in the lobby after they put Kurt in a cop car. Turns out that he is going to jail whether I like it or not. The tape looks like an attempted robbery, and even if I dispute it, they maintain that he was trying to take my phone and he got physical.

Way to fuck yourself, Kurt. You did this one all on your own.

Ray gets his own line of questioning and is released on the spot. Apparently, he comes from a family of cops and they pretty much thank him for stepping in when he did.

On the way home, Ray insists that I sit up front instead of way in the back by myself. I do and it's kind of nice. We talk for the twenty minutes it takes us to get across town in the night's traffic. Ray is divorced with two little boys. They're cute. He shows me pictures, and they look like little versions of him.

When we reach my building, he asks me again if I'm okay, and I tell him again that I am. I'm also hoping that it's true. I mean, I wasn't actually hurt. It all happened so fast. What's in fact bothering me are the things that Kurt said.

He was so callous. He was trying to hurt me, and unfortunately, he kind of did.

It is after ten thirty when I finally walk through my door and I go straight for the shower. After taking my shirt off, I notice the mark that Kurt's grip left on my arm. Charming. That will look great with the pretty dress I was planning on wearing to Winnie and Cooper's couples shower.

On my second date with Ben.

I want to talk to him. I shower fast. Breakneck speed.

It's lovely that I'm so used to my bathroom that I don't have to worry about bumping and knocking into things in there. That's when you're most vulnerable, and naked and klutzy don't mix well. Trust me.

After drying off, I don a long t-shirt, hop into bed, and dial Ben. He picks up on the first ring.

"God, Tatum, are you all right? Ray said Kurt is in jail. How's your arm? Why didn't you call?" He's almost frantic. His voice is loud, and it startles me at first.

"Shhh. I'm fine. I'm fine. Calm down. I just got home and out of the shower. Ray was there and I'm okay. I swear." I try to sound soothing, but I nearly fail. There is something anomalous about how desperate Ben sounds. He almost sounds injured himself.

"Are you really okay? Did he hurt you? Ah! I wish I were there with you." He's upset, and I can't bear to hear one more person yell.

"Stop. Please. Just don't scream." I hear my voice crack and take a breath to tamp down the emotions that waited until now to surface. "I'm fine. Can you please just talk to me? Please. Let's talk about something else and this later. Okay? Please?"

"Okay, I'm sorry. I'm not mad at you. I didn't mean to shout, baby." His voice is instantly more gentle. It's the second time he's called me that, but it's the first time I let it sink all the way in.

There is something that is so singularly romantic about a man calling you baby that it makes all of the shitty things of the day a little less shitty. It's nurturing and gentle. It's exactly what I need to hear.

Considering that he told me that he likes it when I call him Benny, maybe I should tell him that I like it when he calls me baby. Isn't turnabout fair play?

"I like it when you call me that." My voice sounds modest. It is hard for me to say stuff like this. Vulnerability isn't my forte.

"Baby?" he asks.

"Yeah. Maybe not all the time, but sometimes it's nice." His simple honesty is contagious, it seems.

"I like it when you tell me what you like." His voice has tamed and returned to the calming sound that soothes me.

"All right. I liked it this morning when you held my hand and rubbed it with your thumb. I thought that was only in romance novels."

"Really? That's easy. What else?" he cajoles.

Now *this* is how I wanted my day to end. This is what I craved. Just simple conversation. Me and Ben talking.

"I don't know. You tell me one."

"I like it when you lick cream cheese off of your lips. It gets me every time." I remember this voice. It's the same one I talked to the first night on the phone. This voice could convince me to do anything.

"I liked when your shirt rode up your belly at the diner and I could see your happy trail. A lot." I giggle, and he laughs with me.

"Mmmm, feel free to lift my shirt any time. I like the way your skin feels under my hands. It's the smoothest thing I've ever felt."

"I like that one, too."

We fall silent for a while with that thought, and I'm pretty sure both of us are deciding how far we want to take this. My phone beeps in my ear. I flip it in front of me and it's my brother.

"Hey, Benny?"

"Yes." Chuckling, he adds, "Yes to anything."

"My brother is on the other line. I hate to let you go, but he's probably heard what happened and is worried. I need to take it." I don't want to rush him, and I know Cooper will call back as soon as it goes to voicemail, because he's a madman who hates leaving a message.

"That's fine. I'm glad you called me and I'm glad you told me those things. Sleep well, okay? If you need anything just call me, all right?"

He really *does* care about me.

"I will. I'll see you in a few days. We have a date on Saturday."

"I might come back early tomorrow if I can. I'll let you know. Goodnight."

"Goodnight."

I quickly switch the line over to Cooper's third consecutive call in a row.

"Cooper, I'm fine. Ray, my driver, was there. I'm all right." I state very matter-of-factly, not wanting him to know if I'm upset or not. Hell if I even know right now.

"What did that motherfucker do, Tatum? I've been pretty cool about that douchebag, and now I'm ready to beat his ass. What happened?" Panic and fury color his voice.

"What is with guys yelling tonight? Take it down a notch, *capisce?*" I draw a long breath in an attempt to give the cliff's notes in one fell swoop. "Kurt was downstairs when I came down with Neil. Neil went home because I'd told him it was okay. Kurt's never been aggressive or anything like that with me ever, Cooper. I would have told you if he was. I wasn't expecting him to get so angry. I told him I was going home to meet someone and he got mad and said a bunch of stuff and called me some names. Ray texted me from out front when he saw what was going on. Kurt thought that it was Ben—or as he calls him, *that guy*—and tried to grab for my phone. Ray came in about the time that Kurt grabbed my arm. Blah, blah, blah. Ray choked him. Kurt went to jail and I came home. That's it." Well, I almost got it out in one breath.

"What an ass. What did they arrest him for?"

"Well, the security cameras showed him trying to get my phone, so they charged him with attempted robbery and assault. But, Cooper, I'm fine. He only grabbed my arm."

I can hear his angry huffs of breath and I know he's livid.

"Did you press charges?"

"I called the police and it doesn't really seem like it matters whether I do or not. It's all on tape. So he pretty much fucked himself."

"I'm calling the police station in the morning. If that prick makes bail—and he will—we're going to have a talk. Did you tell your door guy?"

"Oh. No. I should do that though. I'll call down there when I hang up. I doubt he will come over, but I should tell them that he's not welcome here."

I don't want him to come back. He acted so strange.

After I hear him finish repeating the story to Winnie, I say,

"Cooper, he went nuts." Every time I rehash the story, his venomous words somehow cut just a little deeper. "He said some stuff that was really mean. Just really, really mean. Ugh. That's probably the worst of it. How did you find out?" I ask, figuring it was Tilly and Luis, since I saw them coming out when I was talking to the cops.

"Luis called Winnie to see if you were okay. Why didn't you call us? We could have come right back there. Shit. If Ray hadn't been there, what would have happened, Tate?" He sounds so sad. My poor big brother.

"The security guys were coming down to help. They saw it on the cameras. I would have been fine."

"I need to tip Ray. See? I told you he's good?"

"Shut up. I already thanked him and I'll be the one to give him an appreciation gift. Not you. Got that?" I should get Ray something. He didn't have to do any of that. I'm really lucky he was there.

"What did Ben say?" inquires Snoopy Coopie.

"He's pretty angry about it. He's out of town for a few days, so he feels frustrated that he isn't here to help. Even though he may not have even went to the taping. Who knows?"

"Hey, I get it. You and Winnie are my girls. I don't want anyone messing with you guys. I bet he'll be having words with ol' Kurt soon, too."

"I doubt that. There is no point. I don't want Ben—or you—getting Kurt all riled up. I don't ever want to see him again. Ever."

His words hit my memory again. *"Are you so Goddamned blind you can't tell who you're fucking anymore?"*

The worst part is that I haven't been fucking anyone! And I really could use a good pounding.

"Well, don't worry about that. I think you should get an order of protection. He's already gotten physical the last two times he's been around. There's no need to have a third time." He demands, "Say you will."

"I will." And I honestly do agree. I don't want that psycho anywhere near me. "Cooper, I'm tired. I'm going to bed. Want to have lunch with me and Winnie tomorrow?"

"Yeah. I'll come up and get you guys about eleven. Call me if you need me. I love you."

"I love you, too. Goodnight."

I switch the light off and roll over, thinking about everything. The sting from what Kurt said replays over and over in my head. I have to know if he was right.

Grabbing my phone again, I text Ben.

Me: Are you still up?

A few seconds later, he replies.

Ben: Yeah. Talk to Cooper?

Me: Yeah, he's pissed. Hey do you think we should wait a while?

Ben: For what?

Me: For this. Dating? I mean, Kurt and I did just break up.

Ben: I don't, but you have to feel like it's right. I'm not going to pressure you for anything.

Me: I know. I'm just thinking.

Ben: If it's about something that jackass said, then stop. He's wrong.

Me: I know.

Ben: No, you don't. You're letting his crazy shit get to you. Don't. Now if you feel like it's too soon, then we're good. I told you. I'm patient. If this happens, then it's at your speed.

Me: Okay. Let's take our time.

Ben: I've got time.

Me: I've got time, too.

Ben: You're thinking too much. Go to bed, baby.

Me: Too soon.

Ben: Ha. You like it.

Me: Guilty. Goodnight.

Ben: Goodnight, who?

Me: Goodnight, Benny.
Ben: That's right. I'll call you in the morning.
Me: Good.
I really like him.

CHAPTER
Nineteen

TURNS OUT THAT I won't have to worry about Kurt coming to my condo. After I got off of the phone with Ben last night, he called Phil to make sure it is known to the building manager that he isn't allowed on the property. Besides, Cooper paid Kurt a visit this morning, after learning of his release sometime in the night.

I didn't ask all of the details, but I'm no fool. I know my brother, and I'm certain that he threatened him within an inch of his life. Cooper only told me that he's sure that they, and I quote, "got some things straight."

This morning sucks. My coffee doesn't taste as good as when Ben makes it. I'm hungry and I didn't allow myself enough time for breakfast. My hair is weird and I'm...off.

It's probably the turmoil from yesterday getting to me and I'm pretty anxious about party. I know for a fact it'll go well, but I want Cooper and Winnie to have the best time.

It's their wedding shower. Sure, it'll be a bit unorthodox in terms of showers, but it suits them. Cocktails and eveningwear definitely suit my best friend. And if she's happy, he's happy. They'll love it. I hope.

As I ride to work in the front seat—again—with Ray, I'm determined to get something that has been pacing through my mind figured out.

"Hey, Ray?" I begin. We don't talk much. Sure, last night altered our professional relationship a bit, but it isn't like we're going to paint each other's toenails or wax poetic about our favorite hot-ties. He's my driver.

He doesn't speak, but looks my direction as he slows down at a red light ahead.

"Why did you call my personal assistant last night and tell him what happened?" I didn't want to offer much information, but I'm sure he sees us. He knows that we're, umm...whatever we are. He must have witnessed our goodbye yesterday morning.

"Ben asked me to call him if anything happened or if your safety was a concern."

That's sweet, but it is also a little fucked up. I'm their boss.

I need to think that through and let it sink in.

By the time we pull up to ABN, I have scripted and re-scripted exactly how and what I want to say. That's a writer's occupational hazard for sure. Typically, my mouth just barks out any old thing it wants to, but when it counts, I analyze the shit out of myself.

As we come to a complete stop, I stay put, not reaching for the door or my bag. I want him to see that this is important.

"Ray, first, I appreciate everything you did last night. It was above and beyond your responsibilities as my driver. Thank you. I'd like you to pick a few ball games to take your boys to this summer, or whatever you like, and let me know the dates. My treat." I give a sincerely grateful smile.

"Ms. Elliot, you don't have to do that—"

I interrupt and my hand deflects his rebuttal. "I'm not finished." I turn so that we are face to face. "Ben is my employee, like you are. He also has gone above and beyond his duties, and for that, I am grateful and very happy to have him. That said, you work for me. I pay you to be discreet, punctual, and a good driver. I pay him to *discreetly* assist me with errands, schedulings, and things of that nature. Am I making sense?"

The rock of a man clears his throat and stutters a little confirming, "I-I think so." His posture loosens like I've really hit home.

I state firmly, "If it doesn't have to do with scheduling your services, I don't really see the need for you two to chat about my personal life. Ben is wonderful and so are you. I can't stop you two from becoming friends or whatever the hell guys do. You've been easy to work with, and I'd love for our working partnership to continue. But I want to remind you—you work for me. And my privacy is something I take seriously. If you're calling Ben this time, maybe you'll call someone else next time. I don't think that is what this situation is about and I don't think you meant any harm. Please, let me be the one to tell other people, whom I socialize or work, with my business."

I know how cold I sound. But truly, it rubs me the wrong way to know that Ben gave orders to call him, like Ray is some sort of fill-in keeper.

"I apologize, Ms. Elliot. I completely understand. I should have mentioned it to you and let you know that he'd want to be informed. That was your decision to make and not mine. You're absolutely right. I was out of line." The look on his big scruffy face is genuine, and I cave a little, smiling at him after his apology.

"Okay, then. You get some ideas about what you'd like to do with your little fellas and we don't have to talk about this again." It's easy not being too upset with Ray. You know? Considering he damn near squeezed Kurt's head off for me.

"I will. Please have someone call later when you're ready. I'll be here."

"Thank you, Ray."

After my diva moment in the car, and after consuming about two pots of office coffee entirely by myself, I start lining-out the Big Show. The Devons run lines by me for a funny skit where they are twins and no one can tell them apart. I love those kinds of skits. There are no punch lines to misdeliver. It's all about body language and reaction. And they do it so well.

I watch throughout the morning as little Devon finds excuse after excuse to walk up to Cynthia's desk and chat her up. Those two are adorable. Both a little awkward. Both a little nerdy.

They're so perfect for each other.

I cancel on Cooper and Winnie, citing that I have too much going on, which is almost true if you count my greediness for what I pray is nerd-love.

I end up calling Cynthia to see if she wants anything from the Chinese place I'm ordering from for lunch. I'm hoping she will extinguish my burning need to pry into what might be a budding office romance. She accepts, and before I know it, it's lunchtime and we've got box after box of Mr. Woo's spread all over the small meeting table in my office.

"So, Cynthia what do you think of litt... uh, Devon Janke? Seems like you guys are becoming pretty good friends." *That's it, Tatum. Nice and slow.*

"We are. I think. He's really funny and surprisingly sweet." I see her blush drain all the way down her neck and onto her creamy chest. I know she's into him.

"Sweet, huh? Like how?" I pry.

"Oh, I don't know. He is always asking me what I'm doing on the weekend. We text when Dexter is on. He brings me tea, because he knows I don't like coffee. Just friend stuff." She's either never had a guy crushing on her or she's just waiting for him to make a move.

I know that he's invited to the party tomorrow, so I ask, "Are you going to Winnie and Cooper's thing tomorrow?"

"Um, no I wasn't planning on it. I haven't been here that long and I don't really know Winnie or your brother that well."

"I see."

As I start cleaning up my lunch mess, we chat about what our plans are for over break. Meanwhile, little lover boy walks past my closed office door. Twice.

He is so fucking into her.

I'm taking off early to go home and shower before my date with my best girl. But first I need to have a big chat with little Devon. I call him into my office, since his is so close to reception, and try to find out for myself just how into her he is and if I can pull the Love Train out of Friend Station. I'm so fucking cheesy.

"Hey, Devon," I say as he comes in with a notebook in his hands. Oh, I may have told him to come in here so I could give him some pointers. I'm a jerk sometimes.

"Hi, Tatum. The Big Show is going to be huge! Did you know that Chelsea Royce is coming? She's either clueless or brilliant. And she's got great tits, so it really doesn't matter." He smiles while trying to break the ice. Devon Janke and I have rarely had a one-on-one—the two Devons usually come as a unit. They're a package deal.

"Yeah, next week will be stellar." I quickly rush through pleasantries since I don't have time to dick around the bush. "Hey, are you coming tomorrow to the shower thing for Winnie? It'll be a lot of fun."

"Yeah, I don't know. I thought I might, but Big-D has a family thing outside the city and I think I'll probably skip."

"That's ridiculous. You're a grown man, Devon. Why not ask a lady friend to go with you? It would be perfect for a date. Think about it. Free food, free drinks, music, dancing. It could work out pretty nice." I nod, trying to put off a bro vibe, but judging by his face, I'm not that convincing. I hit a different angle. "Ask a girl, Devon. Bring a date. You'll have more fun because there will be lots of couples there. Trust me."

"I don't know? It's kind of last minute now." His thin face looks like he's already thought about—and talked himself out of—it.

"Right, so you better hurry. Who are you thinking of asking?" Now I'm getting somewhere.

"Are we girlfriends now? Shit. I don't know... Maybe Cynthia. I don't know." Devon looks at his hands, and I can tell I've made him pretty uncomfortable. He'll manage. For a guy who acts professionally, he isn't hiding much.

"I don't know. She said something about maybe having a

date," I say, hoping that this will either cause a major reaction or not.

Forget not. His instant reaction proves that I'm right and he's crazy about her. By the way he immediately turns in his chair to look at her sitting at the reception desk, like her possible date is happening right here, right now, I know he's more than just into her.

"She did? Did she say with who?" He does a good job at keeping his mild panic attack at bay, but his small frame is completely tense now and he's breathing much harder than necessary for casual conversation. Tiny beads of sweat form on his forehead.

"No, just that she might have plans tomorrow night, but she wasn't sure yet." Nudge, nudge, nudge.

"So she hasn't decided yet. I wonder if it's Paul, that fucker in the mail room. He's always talking to her when he comes up here with the mail in the morning. *'Hi, Cynthia. You look nice today. You look nice every day,'* he mocks in a fan-fucking-tastic creeper voice.

I make a note to insist that we add that to one of his characters. My note just says "Lil Creeper." I'll know what I mean. Don't worry.

"Well, if you care so much who she's going out with, then maybe you should just ask her out. You guys seem to get along really well, and I think she likes you."

His head snaps back to me. "What? Did she say that?" Priceless.

"No, but I've seen you guys. I don't know. It isn't any of my business." Except that I've meddled into it so deep that the bullshit is waist high right now.

"No, don't worry about that. Do you think she'd want to go with me?" His face is coated with hope and insecurity.

"I think she'd love to go. Ask her. And quick, before she has other plans. Hell, she may have other plans already."

No "Goodbye." No "Talk to you later." No "Did we need to

talk about anything work related?" That scrawny ass is up and out of my office on a mission.

Immediately, I dial Winnie's extension. "Hey, whore. Watch reception." And I hang up.

I don't know what they're saying, but their body language is so sweet. He leans over the counter that comes midway up his chest. As suddenly as he shot out of my office, I predicted he'd look more rattled, but this little Devon looks hell-bent on claiming Cynthia for his own. After leaning in and asking her, I guess, he grabs the counter with both hands and leans back. I see the contemplation on her face.

Cynthia's adorable pink cheeks and smile light up the room, and it's visible all the way back here. Then, her head gestures yes. Devon's shoulders sink as he exhales and relief runs off his body. He slaps the countertop and then his hands and walks back to his shared office with one hundred percent more swagger than I've ever seen him exude. Hotshot Devon looks over his shoulder as he grabs the doorframe and gives her another quick smile before heading in and closing the door.

Seconds later, a victorious, "Wooo!" is heard throughout the office and Cynthia covers her happy laugh at her desk.

Tatum Elliot, matchmaker, strikes again.

CHAPTER
Twenty

SINCE WINNIE AND I are catching the late show, we're making a night of it—complete with dinner and drinks. Even though I see her all the time at work and we talk on the phone constantly, it's clear that our alone time, sans Cooper and outside the workplace, is now scarce.

I'm putting my long silver earrings on and hear my phone chirp, notifying me of a new text. I play it cool, even if only for myself. There is no reason to go all junior high and run to the phone every time someone tries to contact me. So, I calmly put the back on my new Ippolitas like my heart isn't pounding through my chest.

Casually, I walk past my Blackberry, take a sip of my wine, and then nonchalantly pick it up to read the message.

Ben: Have fun tonight. Send me a picture.

I do a little bounce and shake, happy to see it was from him. I'm such a girl.

Me: I will have fun tonight. I'm going on a date. A picture of what?

My face? Does he want a tit shot? That isn't happening.

Ben: A pic of you. I want to see you.

Me: My face?

Ben: Sure. Whatever. Just send me a damn picture, Tatum. Please?

I've never been a fan of selfies. I turn the phone around after opening the camera app, take a quick one with my head tilted to the side, flashing a faux smile, and turn to view it. Fail.

I take three more. Fail. Worse fail. Fail. My eyes look weird and my smile looks like someone who is suffering from constipation. That's the thing with pictures. The best ones are when you're really smiling. You know?

Ben: I'm waiting.

Me: I'm trying. I suck at this.

Ben: Let me judge.

Me: No, they all look weird.

Then my phone vibrates, and it's a picture. I open it to full viewing size and there's Ben. Not really smiling—more like grinning. The photo is pretty close to his face, so unfortunately I can't see where he is or what he's wearing. Another reason to hate the ever popular selfie.

Me: You look good.

Ben: I really need to see you. Please just send anything. I miss you.

And just the thought of him missing me, wanting to see me, provokes a real cheek-to-cheek smile. I hurry to take the picture while I'm still thinking about his last text and send it without giving it the typical examination.

Ben: There you are.

Ben: I needed that. You look so good.

Me: Agent Ben, you're making me blush.

Ben: Let me see.

I snap another, again not stopping to criticize, and I send it right away.

Ben: Now we're getting somewhere.

Me: Winnie's going to pick me up in a few minutes. What are you doing?

Ben: Sitting in my hotel room. I should have driven back today.

Me: Are you having fun? Good trip?

Ben: Not exactly, but it's about over.

Hoping it'll lift his mood a bit, I send him this response:

Me: Oh. Well, I'll be busy tomorrow. I have a hot date.

Ben: You do? What's the lucky guy like?

Me: He's a pain in the ass, but he's handsome. So, I can over look the rest.

Ben: He's not good enough for you.

Me: Au contraire, mon fraire. He'll be sick of me sooner than later.

Ben: Pfft.

Me: Did you just pfft me?

Ben: Yep. Send me another picture. Your legs.

Now that's insightful. He's a leg man. Good thing my pins are two of my best assets.

I walk into my bedroom, where I can stand in front of my full-length mirror and orchestrate the perfect leg shot. If he's had a bad day and my legs will help, I'd be a real bitch not to give the man his simple request.

Slipping on my heels, I lift my dress a little higher and pose. I take the shot, hiding my face and the camera in the mirror. I place my left hand on my thigh and make like I'm clawing myself. I don't know where it comes from, but it just feels right. They look pretty fucking good if I do say so myself.

Ben: Damn.

I take that as a good sign and finish getting my things together for my night with my best friend.

Winnie calls, letting me know that she's downstairs in a cab, and I grab my clutch and head down.

We eat at Mazios, an amazing Italian restaurant between my place and the theater, and walk up the street to The Lounge for a few more drinks before showtime.

Winnie asks me about three drinks in, "Are you going to kiss him tomorrow?" We sound like high-schoolers, but it's fun. We never talked like this when Kurt and I were dating. That fever pitch of excitement was missing. No wonder it wasn't too difficult to blow out a barely there flame.

"I don't know. I'm still not really sure if it is the wisest thing to do with him working for me. I don't want it to get awkward." With the aid of a few vodka cranberries, my resistance to the honest truth has been weakened and I could care less. "But he's so..." I get hung up. So *what*? Hot? Sexy? Fuckable? Fun? There is a voice in my ear saying, *To hell with this assistant bullshit and just mount the guy.* That's what I want. I think.

"Perfect?" she offers. "I think you need to just do it. If he's a bad lay, then put the kibosh on the dirty business and use the work thing as an out, but if he's good, make him find a new job. He's not going to find another you."

"Aw, the wine reveals all! Is that why you're marrying my brother? Because you're secretly in love with me and this is the only way you can stay close? Is he your beard? Winnie, I'm flattered." We giggle.

"I'm serious. It's an assistant job. From what you've said, he had a big-time job in Washington before. He'll find other work, you bullheaded bitch. Quit worrying about it." Her face is heated, and the drinks are hitting me the same.

"Thanks, Win. But there's also that other thing—the mystery of him knowing about the job. It drives me nuts."

She maturely sticks her tongue out at me and blows a raspberry into the air. "Did you flat-out ask him about it?" she asks, sloshing a little wine out of her full glass as she animatedly talks with her hands while they're busy keeping her blood alcohol level on the rise.

"Yes. I did. He gave me a vague answer and changed the subject. I'd just feel better knowing, is all. I doubt it would change anything. I just want to know." I clean up the spill, not wanting it to get all over the split sleeve of my pretty pale blue minidress.

"You could always ask him post-coitus. I've gotten lots of things out of Cooper by springing it on him right after climax."

She nods for effect, giving me her best 'I'm totally serious' face. "It's easy. You fuck his brains out like it's the last time you'll ever have an orgasm. Then wait about three minutes for the fuck-fog to lift, and while he's still in pooty-land, ask him."

I look at her, half disgusted that she would manipulate my brother like that and half in awe of her cunning woman powers.

"Kurt made me feel so awful the other night. It really made me think about whether this is all too soon. Is it too early to date?"

"Uh, no." Her curls shake side to side. She looks me straight in the eyes and rants, "You broke up with him. You could have gone out that night. That guy is a bona fide whack-job, Tate. Don't even think about him. Coop said that after he got to the police station they found coke in his jacket pocket. Cocaine! That's fucked up. Who does coke anymore? It's not 1985. Are you going to listen to a coked-out lunatic or me?" That's pretty logical talk after three red wines. She's a keeper.

"I hear what you're saying, but he said other stuff too. You weren't there. It gets stuck on repeat in my head." I check my phone for the time. "It's almost nine. We need to get down to the theater. I'm not going to miss Monty Python to sit here and bitch about my fucked-up sex life."

"Let's haul ass. Curtains are in fifteen." She slugs back the last of her drink.

The show is killer. I laugh so hard my sides hurt. At intermission, the lines to the ladies' are terribly long, but since Winnie has a friend in the crew, we are let backstage to use the talent washroom. *Bonus.*

The whole night is fantastic.

After the show, I call Ray, hoping that he's still available, and he is. We ask him to meet us in an hour out in front of the bar across the street from where we saw the show.

These bars are my favorite. The sunken bars. They remind me of little rabbit holes. Like if we're below the street, no one can find us.

But they do find us—or Winnie, rather. She is bombarded as soon as we walk down the steps and into The Mez. We should have guessed though. The type of people who go to see The Book of Mormon make up her fan base.

She smiles and takes pictures with fans, signing some of their playbills. It isn't all for nothing. We do get a few free drinks. As if we really needed them. I text Ray to come in and escort us out—it's that crazy. It makes me nervous as hell, but Winnie —always the performer—loves every second.

We drop her off at her building and Cooper meets her outside. He asks to see where Kurt grabbed my arm, but I brush him off. It's over and done. Winnie's right. I'm not going to let that ass-hat make me feel bad or pitied.

At home, I get ready for bed feeling happy and truly excited. I'm going to let whatever is meant to happen with me and Ben happen.

He knows I want to keep things at a slow pace and I trust that he will, but on the off chance that he does try to make his move, I'm going to be prepared.

Eyes wide open.

CHAPTER
Twenty-One

I'LL TREAT MYSELF to a little pampering this morning. Waking up early, I call my favorite salon for the works and the heavens are smiling down on me, because they have an opening. Peaches.

With my iPod in tow, I arrive at the salon and let them do their worst. In a matter of hours, I'm massaged, I've had a facial, a pedicure, a manicure, and my hair has been rewashed, trimmed, and styled. I feel divine and my body is rejuvenated.

There isn't anything like having your body in the shop for a few hours that can as thoroughly make you feel like a new woman. I can accomplish anything feeling like this. I'm ready for anything.

Ready for Ben.

It isn't until about two o'clock that I hear anything out of him. I'm glad to learn that my naughty leg picture didn't kill the poor man or send him running for the hills. He texted asking how my day is going and if I still want him to pick me up at six. I tell him about my full-body maintenance regime and that I'll have bells on.

Opting to conceal the mark left by Kurt, in hopes of the whole topic not coming up, I choose a backless black silk dress that has full sleeves. My favorite part of the dress is the jeweled pendant that hangs about halfway down my back. Functionally, it holds the shoulders up, but it looks so pretty. It's back jewelry.

The sleeves work in my favor, because the day turns out to be a bit on the dreary side and cool for May. Plus, paired with my out-of-this-world red Viviers and the sultry eyes I was masked with at the salon, I look like a temptress.

At about five thirty, I receive a text from my date—not my assistant.

Ben: I'm a little early. May I come up?

Me: I'm not all the way ready, but you can come up.

Liar, liar, pants on fire. I was ready at five. Like *ready* ready. Clutch packed. Lips glossed. Schpritzed from top to toe.

Ben: I'm on my way up.

Minutes later, I hear the knocker at my door, which is funny to me because Ben has a key. But I humor him and go to the door anyway.

"Why are you knocking?" I ask through the door before pressing on the oversized door latch.

"Tatum, this is a date. A man doesn't just walk in on a woman. He knocks. So..." His voice fades off, inquiring as to whether I will play along and open up.

"That's silly. We know each other and you have a key. Come in whenever you want. It's unlocked."

I'm walking back to the great room when I hear him open the door. I fully look over my shoulder to see his face. He stunned and stunning at the same time. Jaw open, he bends at the waist, his hand catching his weight on his thigh. I see him whisper, "Whoa."

"Hi," Is all I manage to say.

Hearing his voice on the phone and on the other side of the door didn't ring home just how much I missed this man in only two short days, but seeing him here in my foyer audibly catching his breath is too much. Like a magnet, I turn to him, flipping the polarity in the room so that the attraction is front and center.

"That dress is dangerous," I hear him say—to me or to himself, I can't tell.

The temperature rises tens of degrees and I sway side to side, feeling the pendant run like a pendulum across my radiating skin.

"Are you going to come in?" I ask.

"Are you wearing that to the party, Tatum?"

He moves his long arm to shut the door behind him, not breaking our gaze. He's dressed in a tailored black suit with a skinny charcoal tie and a tight white dress shirt. He looks delicious. His hair is tamed down to the side, and he has just enough stubble to outline his strong jaw.

Who am I trying to kid? I want this man.

"Yes. Is there something wrong with the dress? I like it." I look down at the mid-thigh cut and lift my arms to check if it's ripped or still donning a tag.

"No. You look sensational, but damn, baby. Whoa," he breathes and begins my way.

There is a second that I rethink my choice of attire, but I can't help but swim in the hungry pools of lust evident in his eyes. I made the right choice.

"Thank you. You look good. So good that I'm rethinking your work uniform, in fact. I could definitely get used to seeing you in a suit."

In five long strides, he's in front of me, and even though I'm fully clothed, I feel naked in front of him. His beautiful eyes sweep across my chest and body.

"I'm glad you're back." I whisper.

"I'm glad that I'm back, too." Ben's hand runs up the length of my arm and slowly retreats back down to my fingers. He comes closer still and presses the softest kiss on my neck. His warm lips part and I feel his tongue lightly stripe up my throat. "You smell incredible. You look like a siren," he quietly states, so close that I feel the air of each syllable breeze into my ear.

I swallow and try to bring myself out of the heady trance Ben has led me into. He alone has the ability to make my body purr, and I know we need to get out of here before this gets out of my control.

"I'm ready when you are. We should go." I loath leaving, but I can't see how we'll make it out of here if we stay like this for any measure of time. I'm already ready to strip off this dress and do his bidding.

I'm in so much trouble.

"Good idea. I need a drink." Ben takes a step back and runs his hand down his face. It's like he's tempted to do the things my mind is screaming at him to do to me. Can he hear my thoughts?

Can Agent Ben read minds? That would explain a lot.

Ray drives us to The Yard, and as expected, everything looks magical. It rained this morning, but not enough to steer the party inside. Instead, the light shower left everything looking crisp and clean.

The tables are covered in deep red linens and they look lovely with white candles in all different heights staggered atop them. The trees that outline the outdoor area are dimly lit with different sizes of glowing round orbs that sway in the light wind.

The band is on one side and they are finishing with their fine tuning and setup as we arrive. The dance floor area is big, but it's small enough that it keeps the feeling intimate. We arranged for a portable bar closer to the dancing area and to line it's perimeter with pub tables without chairs, all adorning white linens and blood-red lanterns. Along one side of the building, there are tables for gifts and the thank-you bags that Ben and I put together, which include gourmet chocolates, a card for the car service reserved for guests to use upon leaving, and a personal thank-you from the couple.

Everything is perfect.

"It looks great. Doesn't it?" Ben asks as he looks around at our work. Well, our planning, anyway.

"It does. It's much more romantic than I pictured. Winnie is going to love it." As if on cue, I hear her gasp from behind me.

"Oh my God, you guys! It's gorgeous! Wow!"

Ben and I greet the pair and easily see the gratitude and pleasure in their expressions. Cooper offers Ben his hand and gives him a bro hug. My heart stretches. My brother's a softy when it comes to putting that kind of smile on his fiancée's face. Cooper hugs me.

Hard. My still-mending ribs strain to stay together and I tap his back so he'll let up.

"Tater, you guys have out done yourselves. This is awesome."

Winnie joins the hug. I'm sandwiched between my brother and my best friend. They rock me side to side, and I see Ben's megawatt smile. He's obviously thrilled, too.

"Okay, okay. Stop. Ben did most of the work. Just have fun tonight. And remember we already have cars arranged to get you home, so bottoms up. Enjoy."

They spin off, looking at all the tables, which also have pictures of them from throughout their relationship we had copied and framed. We did a great job.

Ben's shoulder nudges mine in recognition of our awesome party-planning skills.

I look at him. He's relaxed, and his eyes are alight with excitement.

"Now, pretty girl, what would you like to drink?" he asks as he leads me to the table next to Cooper and Winnie's designated one. I put my purse down and tap my pointer finger to my lip in contemplation.

"I think I want champagne. What do you want?"

"Well, of course I'm drinking what all secret agents drink."

And we say at the same time, "Dry martini. Shaken, not stirred." He kisses my forehead, and with his hand on the naked small of my back, he walks me to the bar.

The night's like a dream. Cooper and Winnie are laughing or smiling the entire time and the band is phenomenal. They do a mixture of classic standards and contemporary songs with an unusually cool loungey twist. They're lots of fun, and just about everyone dances all night.

Especially little Devon and Cynthia. They dance almost every song. I leave to use the ladies' room and see him, with her, up against the wall behind some trees. That little fella has some macking skills if he gets a little nudge.

Cynthia looks pretty tonight. Her normally half-up hair is all down and curled. She is wearing a hot little dress, and I couldn't believe it was her at first. I know that's rude, but she really looked different.

Janke cleans up too, by the way. He is sporting slim gray dress pants and a fitted black dress shirt. He looks sophisticated and sharp in black, square-framed glasses. That kid has his game face on. I couldn't be happier for them. They're so, ah, right for each other. I silently give myself a congratulatory pat on the back on the way into the bathroom.

Ben's been a perfect gentleman. My glass is never empty, and when I stand to leave the table, he stands and offers to go. When I introduce him, he shakes hands and kisses cheeks like a seasoned politician. He listens and engages in conversations, and everyone likes him.

I really like him.

Leaving the ladies' room and walking towards the entrance of our party area, I see Ben waiting for me outside the glass doors. With his hands clasped behind his back, he sways in time to a song I can't hear from where I am. I take a minute and appreciate all of him.

He's such a beautiful man. His shoulders are strong and proud. His stance is one of a man who is confident and in charge. But even though he looks so big and masculine standing there, it's his mind and heart that are his most dangerous weapons. Piece by piece, they are breaking through my self-preserving will to keep everyone at arm's length.

Then he looks behind himself and catches me staring. He smiles and lifts his hand, gesturing in a 'come here' motion for me to go to him. Without hesitation, I do.

He opens the door and meets me, saying, "Dance with me."

I smile. Right now, I'll follow him wherever he leads.

Just as we get to our spot on the dance floor, the soulful voice of the singer croons "These Arms of Mine." Everything goes even more blurry than I'm used to, and I'm thankful that I don't have to worry about falling. Well, on the ground at least. Ben's already got me in his grasp, and I've never been safer.

His arms surround me completely, and he presses my body so close. Our shared space is only separated by a thin piece of silk and the most heavenly smelling Armani on the planet.

His hips rock and pull me with him, my body fitting with his just so. Ben's fingers run slowly up my back, right under the jewel swinging to and fro from the neck of my dress. Once he reaches my shoulders, his warm fingertips press into me firmly. Chest to chest, our bodies synchronize in perfect time to the magical song that surrounds us.

For minutes upon minutes, forever it seems, I cling to him and forget all my worries and doubts. How could this be the wrong thing to do when it is the only thing that's ever felt this right?

His steady breathing and the way he softly sings along when the band does "You've Really Got a Hold on Me" lulls me, and I instinctively squeeze him, telling him with my embrace how good he makes me feel. We dance and dance until my feet start their end-of-the-night routine of surrendering to my shoes.

By about midnight, everyone is gone. We generously tip and thank the staff of The Yard and Ben texts Ray to pick us up. I wonder to myself what Ray does when he isn't waiting around for us to call. It's kind of funny to me in that moment and I deliriously laugh. Partly from sheer exhaustion and partly because it's so strange to think about.

"Are you drunk, baby?" Ben asks, standing behind me with his arms dangling over the front of my shoulders. His fingers are pointing and poking at my cheeks.

"No. Well…maybe a little buzzed. I'm not drunk. I was just thinking about what it is that Ray does in between running me all over the place. Like, is there a club where drivers go to wait for their passengers?" I laugh again at the absurd and hilarious idea.

"Ha! That's a good question. I never thought about it. I suppose I thought they were driving other people around in the meantime like cabbies. That isn't right either though. Is it?" The way his belly jiggles the jewel on my back when he laughs tickles, and I laugh more.

"No. Or maybe it is, and when we call, he kicks them out and hightails it back to me. He's like Batman and I run the Batphone." I continue to crack up.

"You should ask him when he gets here. I bet he'll tell you." His poking has ceased, and one of his hands rests across my collarbone and lightly traces it.

"I don't know if I want to know. Ignorance is bliss and all that. I think I'll maintain my stupidity."

"Have it your way," he says. "Hey, I think I'm going to have Ray drop me off after he lets you out if that's all right with you?"

Is this a trick question? Is he trying to coax me into asking him to stay? Or maybe he really did get sick of me?

"Yeah, sure. I'm tired. You have all of tomorrow off, too. So I will just see you Monday morning." I can't hide the sudden turn of emotion I have in my gut. I shrug out of his arms and go to stand closer to the curb. I'm instantly cooler, both inside and out.

I'm so stupid.

At this moment, the car pulls up to the curb, and without waiting for Ray, I open the door and scoot all the way over to the opposite side. Ben and Ray exchange pleasantries over the roof of the town car and I wait. Impatiently. I'm ready to be home.

How the winds can change. When did my feelings get this sensitive?

Toughen up, Tatum.

"Are we going or not?" I say with a little more venom than I intended, but my ego is hurt. Both men get in and off we go. I lean forward to talk to Ray. "Hey, Ray. Thanks for picking us up so late. You're the best. Do you mind dropping Ben off on the way?" I sit back in the cool leather of the bench seat and wait for his answer.

"Sure, I can take him, but your place is actually closer. Should I take you home first?"

"No, we'll drop him off first." My foot is down.

I glance in Ben's direction and find him sitting comfortably. There isn't a worry on his face. This only makes me even sourer. As we ride through the streets that are still bustling at this time of night, I watch the people we pass out my window and think about the party. Regardless of how it's ending, it was incredible.

I smile despite myself and hear Ben say from across the wide seat, "That's a better color on you."

"Excuse me?" This time I'm not as bitter sounding as I am tired. Feelings are exhausting.

"You are upset, but just now you're smiling. I like that better. You misunderstood me, by the way, and then overreacted. I wish you wouldn't have." I think he knows he's walking a thin line and his words are cautious.

Did I? "I'm not following. I'm fine." *Deny. Deny. Deny.*

"Tatum, look at me." His hand reaches for mine and I look at his fingers stretched open for me to hold on to. Again, my body can't resist him, even if I am rubbed the wrong way. "You told me on the phone that you want to take this slow. I'm fine with it. This is our second date. What do you want me to do?"

Oh, yeah. I did say that. I suppose slow, in this context, needs a little definition. Like any other woman, I meant 'slow until I want it faster.' I thought he would know it's really more like 'let's take it slow until I change my mind and then follow my lead.' That's what that means. *Men.*

"All right. I admit that I said that, but it wasn't like I asked you up for anal and some light bondage. I didn't even ask you up. You didn't give me a chance to." I can't believe I just said that. Yes I can.

"You don't *still* have a chance?" He smiles. "Light bondage?" He smiles bigger.

"Well—"

"No, instead, you got bent out of shape and threw a tantrum."

"Hey, I didn't throw anything, Ben." What can I say? Is he right? Did I blow up over nothing? God, this man is an irritating, thought-reading bastard.

Pulling my hand closer, Ben reels me into him. I go hesitantly at first and then cave, curling into his side. "Do you want me to come up, Tatum?" he asks in a low voice so that Ray can't hear him.

"I don't know. I mean yes. Wait. No. You were right." I look up at him apologetically. "I'm sorry. I don't think I know what I want. But I want you to want to come up. Does that make any sense?"

"Yes," he says and lifts my chin towards his. Our lips are so close that I can feel how warm his mouth would be to touch. So close that even not pressing them together feels like a kiss. My eyes close instinctively and I wait.

And I wait.

And I wait some more.

"You're so beautiful when you stop fighting." The kiss moment vanishes, but something else replaces it. I leave my eyes closed in fear that he'll see more than I'm willing to show.

The things he says and how good he is to me are more than I deserve. This isn't fair to him. No matter how badly I want this little fantasy he's painting of an us, it just isn't right.

I'm too stubborn. Too selfish. He should be with a woman who gives more than she takes from him. The sad thing is this was—almost—just the beginning. I can't imagine how much taking I'll do in my dark future.

Ben's thumb traces both my brows and then tenderly skates over my eyelids, down my nose, and across my cheeks. So faint are his touches that they almost tickle and leave nothing but calmness in their wake. A finger traces first my upper lip and, in turn, my bottom one.

He knows I'm not glass. I don't shatter when dropped. So why does he insist on handling me like this, with such care?

"Fighting who?" I finally ask on a whisper.

"Fighting yourself. Fighting me. Fighting the truth."

Ben doesn't kiss me, but I want him to. So I don't call him Benny as a quiet punishment. I'm such a rebel.

He gifts me the customary forehead peck when we drop him off first, per my request. He says that he's had a wonderful night. Before he shuts the car door, he leans in and tells me that he'll ask me out again and that he won't be waiting as long as I did to do it.

CHAPTER
Twenty-Two

THE DAYS AND WEEKS fly by after Winnie and Cooper's party, and soon it is almost the end of June. I received thank-yous from many guests, saying it was the best shower they'd ever been invited to. I believe them, because it was the best shower I've been to also.

The last week of the show's season was turbulent to say the least. Chel-Ro was a no-show, which fucked with our whole lineup. Luckily, Winnie, Wes, and I were able to wrangle up a few old friends and rising stars to make appearances. It worked, but it felt a little half-assed.

The Devons' skits were funny and they did amazing. They did one of the planned Chel-Ro skits with a cardboard cutout of her likeness and it was funnier than if she would have been there. After wrapping that Thursday, I skipped the after-show party that was hosted by our network, saying I didn't feel that well, and went home.

I just felt so tired, and my mind and heart were at odds with everything.

I can't stop thinking about Ben and how he deserves more than what I can offer. Seriously, I'm a pain in the ass as is. Add my hectic life, a crazier-by-the-day ex-boyfriend and then, for good measure, top it off with a good old-fashioned case of vision impairment. Peaches.

After the night when Kurt lost his shit in the ABN lobby, he called so much I had to change my number. He's sent flowers with rambling apologies. He's even started calling Winnie to find out how I'm doing.

I got a formal order of protection, and Cooper went a step further and spoke to his family. They assured him that they'll do whatever they can to help. I try keeping it played down in front of Ben, but I'm glad it's finally ended. He sent one more flower arrangement and it just said "Goodbye."

Then there's the whole sight thing. I hate to admit it, but it's making me depressed. I can tell that my moods are all over the place. Nothing is funny. I'm having a hard time writing anything for next season, which has never happened. I don't want to go anywhere unless I have to. I know the wedding is coming up, and I'm mentally preparing myself for it. But I'm laying low until I get out of this funk.

I avoid Ben to the point of getting up early and going down to my building's gym and walking on the treadmill in the mornings when he arrives. Sometimes I sit in the coffee shop if he's dropping things off.

It seems unfair to have all these feelings for him. I can't figure out a way in my mind to make it work out for either of us. If I give in to what I want, then he's stuck with me. Good for him.

What happens when I'm completely blind to our relationship, if there is one? He'll be stuck taking care of me like a child. He can do so much better.

What if he wants marriage and children? How does that work out for a blind chick? You use your cane to smack all the ankles of the guests as you walk down the aisle?

Our working relationship continues being totally beneficial to me, but the week after the show closed for the season, I told him that he could just work Mondays and Thursdays, thinking that I'll be a lot less busy. And I am.

Mostly my time is spent editing and reading projects for other people I know. I'm actually really into one by a screenwriter in L.A. that I met while working on Up Late.

It's about a band that breaks up and reunites after the loss of a member years later. I love the story, and I've been asked in to add ideas where comedic scenes are concerned.

They are quite good already, so I'm basically just making notes for timing and delivery. Mostly, I am wrapped up in the love story within it. And it makes me want one of my own.

Ben asked me to go out with him the Friday after the last show, but I used the same excuse as I had to get out of the wrap party. It wasn't a total lie. I'm having more frequent headaches and I'm too nervous—or scared—to admit that there is a major deficit in my sight. My vision's peripheral now blurs into where it, just weeks ago, was unclouded.

Even though I'm staying clear of Ben and cooling it with the flirting, he consistently asks me out all the time. I make up excuses, but the last time I just smiled and shook my head.

He simply replied, "You will."

Today, I'm sitting in Dr. Meade's office, where he's telling me that my condition is more rapidly sliding into a territory that we both knew was coming.

"What do I do, Dr. Meade? Are you sure that there isn't anything available? Treatments that are in trial? Anything?" The quicker this is happening, the more I am desperate to find a fucking loophole.

There has to be some experimental monkey piss treatment or a treatment where I only eat raisins and goat's milk. A treatment where I have to sleep in one of those hyperbaric oxygen chambers and listen to The Cure for six hours each day. Something.

I just can't accept that this is it. And at the rate that the fog framing my sight is swallowing up my vision, Dr. Meade and I both estimate that it will be only months until it is mostly gone.

My heart is breaking. I feel isolated and scared. I'm angry and irrational. Not only is my sight fading away, but the glimmer of hope that I'll have anything normal in my future is vanishing too.

"I'm sorry, Tatum. I think you need to see a psychiatrist. For real. Someone you can talk to about this. Someone who is educated about the stress and anxiety you are and, most likely, will continue to feel for a while until this stabilizes. I can't say if you'll be totally blind when it does, but that is usually the way this disease works." He sighs and offers me a kind smile. "On a hopeful yet atypical note, it could slow down again. It could stop getting worse altogether and remain like it is. There is no way of knowing, but at the rate it's deteriorating now, the chances of that aren't all that good."

I bite my bottom lip to not start crying right here in Dr. Meade's office, releasing it only when the taste of blood is potent enough to distract me from my bigger problems.

What am I going to do? How am I going to work? Function? Anything? This feels like a death sentence.

Dr. Meade recommends—again—that I start using a walking cane. I tell him I'll, at least, get one and see how fucking stupid I feel using it. He is winning.

I'm definitely losing.

I dial Ben from the car on my way home since I need some blind girl supplies and figure I might as well go big or go home. Remembering that he knows people who are visually impaired, I assume he can offer guidance and insight. If I'm succumbing to the idea of trying the cane, I might as well try out whatever else is in my future and attempt to get used to it.

"Hey, Tatum." Ben answered quickly, probably because I was leaving the doctor's and curious to see how it went. "What did Dr. Meade say?"

"He said I'm going to need help going fucking blind, Ben." I can't help sounding so bitchy. If I am trying to hide my emotions from him, I am doing a piss-poor job.

And the Academy Award for worst-ever acting goes to that bitch, Tatum Elliot.

"What can I do?" This is where I never know if he's saying that because he cares or because I pay him to.

"Nothing. Why don't you take the rest of the day off? I'm going to lie around and I don't want to see you buzzing around my place being productive." What's worse when you're feeling awful than watching someone else be perfectly fine? I wouldn't fucking know. "But Dr. Dickhead gave me a list of things I might find useful. So I'll need to either go get them or have you find them for me if that's okay. But I can worry about that tomorrow, and if I don't, then you can worry about them next time you come over." My words taste bitter, but I can't stop.

"If that's what you want. I have to be back in your area this evening. Do you want me to bring over some food? I can be there around six?" Here we go again.

"Ben, I said you could have the rest of the day off. I'm an asshole today. I think I'd rather just be alone." And that is the biggest lie of all. Here it is—my biggest fear—and I keep on asking for it. I'm sure there is a far more intellectual name for that condition other than being a fucking idiot, but I'm at a loss for the words among everything else.

"I wasn't asking if you needed anything like that. I meant it as in, would you like some terrible Chinese food and a side of company? I'd like to come over to see you. Not work for you."

"Not tonight, Ben. I don't think that is a good idea. Why don't you go have fun?" I want to say that he should find a girl who isn't his boss, isn't a batshit crazy freak, isn't going blind, and isn't so complicated.

Not about to bother him with all this today, I'm feebly attempting to follow through with the decision I made after the wedding shower. It isn't fair to be telling him one thing and then putting signals off for another. It's not fair to give him a false sense of relationship, that no matter how bad I want, will only make me feel like a pity fuck.

That and I still can't get the things Kurt said out of my head. I can't shake the fact that I don't know where the hell Ben even came from and that he has no problem dodging the question at every pass.

It's too much. Everything is too much.

I feel empty. A new low.

But when he says, "I'd rather have fun with you," I want to take back the abuse I caused my lip earlier. Then I could resort to using the same lip-biting method to hold back the tears that fall from hearing his words. I want to be the girl he has fun with, too.

———— • ————

I need out of this funk. I need a good cry. And judging by the number of times I've either almost cried today and the times I actually cried, I need a massive fucking blubber-fest.

I do what any normal girl would—plan a day of drinking and watching sad movies. Ray stops at the store so I can get needed supplies. I need a box of wine, a few pints of ice cream, a bag of peanut M&Ms, and Kleenex. Too bad they were all out of maturity pills. I would have bought a case. It doesn't matter though. I am determined on beating my shitty mood to death, giving myself an emotional cleanse.

The thought of calling Winnie springs into my head, but I can't. Same with Neil. I just can't put them through it. And Ben is off-limits. Even if Ben is the one I want, I can't risk confusing him. Staying professional for both of our sakes is the right thing to do. The strange part of it is he's my assistant and knows everything about my life right now, down to putting away my laundry and buying me tampons.

Yeah, he does that. When I questioned why I had a ridiculous supply in my bathroom cabinet, he just shrugged and said that I'd been low. Awkward.

My problem lies in keeping my personal thoughts and feelings to myself. Because he is all up in my life. He does all of my shopping now, too. He runs every errand I can think of. He hired the cleaning service himself and I've only ran into the lady once. I still have a hard time remembering her name. I know it ends with an 'andy.' Sandy? Brandy? Mandy? Candy? Fuck. It's something like that.

He basically does it all. Which is helpful, I have to say, but it's also smothering at times. In one moment, I feel like it's badass having someone doing all my shit work and in the next I feel a little sad because it'll soon be nearly impossible for me to do any of those things. Lately, I desperately want to do them all myself.

I know. I'm a Goddamned conundrum. Typical female, right? Wanting only what she can't have. Maybe that isn't just females. Look at Kurt's fucked-up ass. If he would have shown that much interest during our relationship, instead of afterwards, then we'd probably still be together.

Wait. Scratch that. That's bullshit.

But here I am now, with a man who seems to be interested in me—flaws and all—and I revert back to this mentality of: This is my space. I'm the boss. I won't let you in so quit trying.

I can't tell who I'm trying to protect. Him or me? But, hey. That's Tatum fucking Elliot, the emotionally constipated.

So tonight I've showered and put on my prettiest pajamas. Pretty things make me feel better because they remind me I don't mess everything up. I have some things going for me. I have pretty fucking pajamas.

With the first movie in, a box of Kleenex beside me on the table, and a full glass of wine, I start the Great Feeling Purge of 2012. The first movie gets me, but only at the end when she reads all of his letters in her car. There was too much love and it only served as a reminder that I'm no Allie and Ben's not Noah. I'll probably go to hell for thinking it, but I'd take some Alzheimer's right now.

The second one has me crying from just about start to finish since I know that Julia Roberts is going to die the whole time. And the third just about fucking kills me. If there is a woman out there who hasn't lost three pounds of water weight watching Beaches, I'll shake her hand. That movie rips my heart out every time.

It's still pretty early considering that I started watching chick flicks at one in the afternoon. I take the chipped polish off my toes. Even the best pedicurist can't paint these babies Tatum-proof. Brooding, I choose to repaint them black like my mood, but I can't find the damn polish. I know I have some somewhere, and I'll lay money that it's in my closet where I store all things dated and unused.

I'm still here, a few hours later—sitting on the floor in my closet. I'm piss drunk, I have a big, ugly scarf wrapped loosely around my neck, and there are dozens of shoes scattered everywhere.

Not a single one remains in its box. I take them out and study each one. I look at every stitch and color. I look inside them, and yeah, I smell them too, filing each one in my mind under 'My Gorgeous Shoe Collection That I Won't Get to See Anymore.'

I feel like everything is disappearing. My brother and Winnie are more wrapped up in each other than ever before. Don't get me wrong. That is what's supposed to happen. I'm over-the-moon happy for them, but maybe I wasn't thinking clearly when I hooked them up.

Refilling my glass from the classy boxed beverage I packed with me into the closet after three trips to the refrigerator, I look at the clothes and mementos lying around me with rapt attention.

As shallow and materialistic as it sounds, I'm going to miss my stuff. That is a tough pill to swallow. I've never counted myself a person who sets such value on possessions, but I have. I don't have very many things, and what I do have, I love. They're mine.

There's the dress I wore to my first award show, the hat I wore to the polo match when Wes was dating the equestrian chick, the Jimmy Choo that's missing a heel from the night Coop and Winnie got engaged, my college graduation gown. What good is all of this shit if I won't be able to see any of it in a few months?

The only thing I get out of them now is looking at them.

I'm so fucked.

What a boring world this will be when I can't see someone's expression or smile. I'm going to lose smiles?! How fucking crazy depressing is that?

I take the lid off the next shoebox and I know that the contents aren't shoes. This is the someday box. Some girls have hope chests where they keep a bunch of shit for their future. They harbor old hand-me-down wedding dresses and dead ladies' jewelry.

Not me.

I have trips and random things I want to do. It isn't exactly a bucket list, because I never intended on the box being that or my time to do them so short. I thought that my sight would just stay the same sucky way it was.

I was wrong. So, with the rush that my life has been in up until recently, instead of pulling from the box every so often, I added to it another rain check to myself.

Some of these are funny. I'm trying to read them, but my drunken state has added a convenient extra haze to my already crappy view.

I cry harder. I cry for my beautiful things. I cry for all of the things I'll never get to see firsthand. I just cry.

Through my sobs, I hear the board in my bedroom floor creak and know it's him. I can feel him before I can see him. Maybe my blind superpowers are kicking in.

"Tatum, are you in here?" Ben asks in a knowing voice. He probably sees the light on in my walk-in and heads this way.

"Please go away, Ben." I can't stand for him to see me so pathetic. As I try to hide the tears in my voice and wipe at them the best I can, I learn that my request isn't taken seriously.

"Hey, are you all right?" He's standing next to my closet door and isn't looking in. Maybe he thinks I'm naked or something. It makes me smile a little to think that he's being a gentleman by not invading my space.

Then another realization hits. In a few months, I won't know the difference. And the tears are back in full force.

"Mmmm hmmm. I'm just looking at some old things. I'm fine." I hiccup from crying.

"Can I come in there? Are you, you know, decent?"

"I've never been accused of being decent with or without my clothes. You can come in here if you want to, but I'm warning you. I am a hot mess." I inhale through my nose most unattractively to clear the snot that's accumulated through my hours of sobbing.

Slowly, his head peeks around, and I immediately see the worry on his face. The normally calm and rational Ben is gone. I'm looking right into pity and I hate it.

"Don't look at me like that," I implore. Bowing my head, I turn so he can't look me straight in the eyes.

"What is all this? Did you fall or something? Your things are everywhere. What are you looking for? I can help," he rattles off. Maybe it isn't pity. Maybe it's something else.

Ben comes and sits cross-legged like a fifth-grader ready to read me a book. He seems to be approaching me like I'm a child and he's mirroring that in his body language.

"No. I just wanted to look at my things. With wine." I look up into his face to see understanding there.

"A box of wine?" his voice asks.

I nod my head up and down, signaling that his observation is truly as unrefined as it looks.

"Okay, and you wanted to see them all at the same time?" he smiles, trying to make a little joke at my expense. I allow it because I'm looking like a poster child for mental instability right now.

"I'm safer with cardboard. And I don't know. I just sort of started pulling things out and one thing led to another. You know? I guess I'm just..." And I can't finish. The words choke me. I'm about to emotionally barf all over this beautiful man and he won't ever look at me the same again.

His beautiful green eyes find mine and I look into them. I look for an answer. Look for a question. Look for comfort. My lower lip quivers as I feel myself try to look away, but I don't.

I can't.

Ben scoots closer, draws one of his legs up, and plants his foot on the floor next to my knee so that he can get as close as possible. I can smell him so strongly that it's making me a bit high. Already a hostage to my thoughts, I find that the few slivers of control I had leftover are escaping me.

When his thumb moves to my bottom lip, his fingers curl under my chin. His eyes are still locked on mine. "Tell me," he pleads. "Tell me what you're thinking. No. Tell me what you're feeling. No jokes. Just the truth."

I inhale his simple request and exhale the truth. "I'm so sad and I'm really, really scared, Ben. I hate this. I'm angry. I feel stupid and foolish and I'm afraid I'm going to be so lonely in the dark." I break. There isn't a second to think of how I sound or what he thinks of me. I'm too overwhelmed by just saying it out loud.

With the softest voice I have ever heard from his lips, he says, "I won't tell you to stop being sad. That's useless. You are sad. And you should be scared, too. You can own those feelings. They are yours alone. But, Tatum, don't think for a second you are foolish or stupid. You're as sharp as a tack. Your mind won't ever be questioned by anyone whose opinion matters." He sighs heavily. "As for lonely, I can't really say. I know this though. If you let your sadness and your fear bleach the color from your life, you'll end up that way. On your own account. No one you love will leave you because of this. I promise. They'll all be right here. I'm right here. I'm not going anywhere."

"You're getting paid to be here."

"Fine. I quit." His voice is sure and without doubt.

"No, you can't quit. I need you too much." I worry my lip, afraid that I'll successfully run him off.

"You need me?" That's when I see his weakness. Hidden underneath his confident exoskeleton lies a hairline fault. His vulnerability. His burden.

"Of course I need you. I'd be lost if you weren't here. Look at me. I'm half drunk and crying in my closet. I couldn't need you more if you were a psychiatrist."

Ben's face appears almost haunted. "Don't say that. They don't know everything."

I'm just buzzed enough that I feel like telling him more. I feel like getting that smile to shine on me.

"Remember that first night on the phone?" It feels peculiar to talk about that after all this time, but here we are in my closet and suddenly I'm weighing the pros and cons of just putting it out there. "You called me pretty?"

For a long minute, we just stare. His eyes are fixed on mine, and it's like were having a conversation but we don't utter a word. I'm only too sure that my face looks like a punching bag and I can't be all that attractive. Regardless, he looks around that and straight into me.

I want to kiss him. No. I want him to kiss me. I want to know what it feels like to be his. I crave the comfort that his affection provides.

I just nod my head yes. There wasn't a question, but yes is my answer with tears veining my cheeks. I will his lips to find mine.

He hears it somehow, because the emotion grows in his features. His tolerance for my resistance is as low as mine.

Ben inches closer and closer, saying, "Baby, just be honest. Please, just say you feel this. Tell me you feel it for real, not just for some fling. Not just to scratch an itch. I want you so badly that I'm losing my mind, baby. But I won't stop after you say go. Tatum, give us this."

My eyelids flutter to the precious sounds of a man who wants me. "Kiss me. Please. Just kiss me already."

I watch thick sheets of relief wash his face. Like he's been wearing a steel mask and I just lifted it. His hand goes around my neck and into my hair. His other strong arm rounds my waist and pulls me near. My head naturally tilts and I continue to wait. If he wanted my full attention, then he has it.

"Please really want this, baby," he breathes into my open mouth. "Don't give me this—you—and then take it away. I won't take just a piece, Tatum. I want it all."

My heartbeat is trying to reach out to him through my chest, but I cannot speak. I don't know if I can make that promise. But, oh, how I want to.

"I want this mouth." He preys on me, licks a kiss over my bottom lip, and then he moans. His mouth skims across my jaw to my ear. "I want to say all the things I've been thinking into these ears." The sound of his amorous breath that close makes my back arch into him.

He's not flirting. This is pure intention.

Moving down over my neck, he whispers, "I want to feel your pulse race against me." And he kisses my neck. His mouth is hungry and passionate. Pulling back just as I'm about to beg him for more, he promises, "But I won't take all of this until you're willing to give me more. You can be as afraid of it as you like, baby, but you have to let me in—everywhere. Otherwise this means nothing. And dammit, this means a lot more than that to me, because it's you." There's no joke in his tone. Not a laugh in his eyes. He means business.

I find my shaky voice. "I want you. I want you so badly. Don't you think I want that? Don't you think I want a fairytale? I do! I just don't want to be someone's burden. Someone's job! I'm afraid that you'll lose sight of me. Make me believe this. I want to believe this."

"I'll make you believe it. You don't ever have to doubt me, Tatum." Shifting his attention to the box of wine next to us on the floor, he asks, "How much have you had to drink?"

Am I drunk? Of course I am.

"I don't know. I've been drunker. Why?" Drunk Tatum has never had a problem getting laid before, but she rarely thinks in third person either. So, okay. I may or may not be very drunk.

Moving his mouth back to my desperate skin, he pulls in a long breath. My arms wrap around his waist to get closer.

Between kisses, he admits, "I told you I want all of you, Tatum. That means your mind, too, baby. I don't want us like this." But his kisses say that he does.

"What? You've never fucked a drunk girl?" I tease.

"Fucking is child's play compared to what I'm going to do to your body with mine. You deserve better than that." Then something that looks like a light bulb goes off over his head. "I'm not going to have our first time be on the floor of a closet, after you've been drinking and upset either, but..."

Yes! A but! But what? But what?! The heavens part. Angels sing. My body is tuned and ready to be played. I'm worked up and signing up for whatever he offers me.

"I'm listening," I say.

"I'm enjoying how honest you're being and how you're telling me what you're feeling. So how about we play a little game?" If his smile wasn't so damning, I wouldn't agree, but I will do anything to make it permanent.

"What's in it for me?" Our faces are inches apart now, our eyes locked. I squint in hesitation. "I agree to nothing."

"Oh you'll not only agree—loudly—but it'll be your new favorite game. We're playing Show and Tell."

I adore playful Ben. He could probably talk me into dancing naked on public-access television if he would promise to keep looking at me like this.

"I have lots of show things all right here. What do you want to know about first?" I barter.

"That's not how we're playing it this time," he says with a wicked smile. He fingers the bottom of a black chemise hanging on the lower rack next to us. "That said, I would like to know more about this sometime, please."

"I'll see what I can do. How do we play this game of yours, and what am I going to win?" My foul mood is abandoned.

"It isn't a complex game. We will sort of wager or bet on things. One of us gets to ask a question and the other person will tell what it's worth."

Ben stands and lifts me up with him. Grabbing both my hands in his and walking backwards, he pulls me into my bedroom. He looks like the devil himself.

CHAPTER
Twenty-Three

"HOW DO WE FIGURE out who's going first? And what are we wagering? Maybe you should go first," I advise, not knowing what I'm getting myself into.

Ben leads us through my room but doesn't stop where I guessed he would. Instead of leading me to the bed, which I was secretly praying for, he steers us to the raised sitting area off to the side. Stopping me in front of one chair and walking himself to the one across from me, he says, "Stay there."

I think he did it so we can't touch. Only just getting skin-on-skin contact from this gorgeous specimen after all this time, I'm not that impressed by the arrangement. After finally letting him touch me, all I want is more.

Ben stands board-straight, wearing jeans and a gray v-neck. I'm less sure of what's going on here, so I slouch with unsure posture in my long nightgown, the granny sweater I added earlier in the evening, and the scarf. I sway as I wait for him to instruct, still feeling the effects of my cheap drunk.

"Okay. I'll ask you a question. You can either answer it and choose what I show or you can pick a mulligan of sorts and I get to tell you what I want to see. You only get one mulligan for every three questions answered. Does that make sense, Betty Ford?" he explains, eyebrows raised in challenge.

I laugh wholeheartedly through my embarrassment. "Yes, Ben. I get it. Be gentle," I say, hoping that I don't have to use my mulligoonie or whatever right out of the gate.

"Why are you a writer?" he asks, and the easiness of the question relaxes me instantly.

I release a long chestful of air in relief and think about the question. Then my wandering mind gets caught up in what I'm going to choose for him to show me.

I consider telling him I want to see his whole naked body, but where is the fun in that?

"Yoohoo, over here." He waves his hand in the air. "Time is up. Answer the question."

"I was always a goof-off in school. I didn't really like science and I was terrible at math. I liked reading and thought it would be fun. I loved drama class and writing skits for talent shows. It just came natural to me. Easy. There. Now what?" I'm smiling and pretending to be innocent.

"Okay, now you get to tell me what to show."

He's so confident, as if whatever I say won't affect him. Perhaps he only gave me the easy question so that I would go easy on him when it came to my reward. He even kicks his shoes off and does this shoulder shimmy like he's telling me to bring it.

Just as I start to open my mouth, I see a hand go up in a 'just a second' gesture. "Mulligans count for either thing. You can mulligan out of a show, too. Just saying. Now proceed." He smiles brightly. I know he just thought of that rule, but I let it slide.

"Take your shirt off," I tell him, throwing my chin with my words like a dominatrix.

He doesn't lift from the bottom like a normal man would. He doesn't even do the arms-cross-in-front grab. Ben lifts his right arm, shakes it out like he's about to pitch the last out in the World Series, and the fucker blows on his fingers. Cocky is Ben in this moment. He takes just one arm and reaches it behind his head, all the while every muscle in his biceps damn near bust the stitching on his short sleeve. I don't get the chance to watch that for long, because my old friend makes an appearance. And, oh, how I've missed that spot.

The same blond dusting of hair that I remember from our lunch at the cave is here and visible in my bedroom. I give him a good work-up with my eyes, not allowing myself to overlook a single centimeter. He has a scar on his collarbone and a thin spread of hair just across his chest. His muscles are well defined in his upper body, but his waist is lean. He's just the right mix of muscle and man, and I hate that there is a table between us.

Smart is Ben.

"See? This is easy. Now you ask me a question."

I'm still in a trance, trying to soak up all of the new physical information coming my way, downloading and backing up every frame into my memory. I know that my sight failing has something to do with how I look at things lately, with more attention on the details, but I can't help but wonder if I'm about to see a naked man for the last time in my life. I feel both excited and incredibly robbed.

Hell, today was probably the last time I'll see that hot rainy, wet kiss in The Notebook. My life sucks.

"Just give me a second. I'm memorizing you," I say before I can stop myself.

Thanks, box o' wine. When my eyes finally climb to his, I see a look that I've not seen there before.

"What?" I ask.

"Nothing. Just what you said. Are you trying to memorize everything you see, Tatum?"

"Hey," I bark like a fool, attempting to keep the mood playful. "This isn't your turn, or did I get skipped?" Receiving a look I'm more familiar with, I don't push for an argument. "Where did you get the scar?"

Ben looks down to find the scar I'm talking about, and he runs a finger along the four or five inches that parallel the length of his clavicle.

"Remember how I don't like storms? Well, when I was a kid, I was at my parents' house and the power went out. It was storming. I knew my parents would be fine, so I ran to my grandparents' house.

"When I was running, I slipped in the wet grass and cut it on one of those wire things they use in a garden for tomatoes. I didn't know it was that bad until the power came on a few hours later and my grandma almost had a heart attack when she saw my shirt covered in blood.

"I knew I scraped it really bad and it hurt, but the blood mixed with it being wet made it look so much worse." His eyes glaze over as he walks himself through the memory.

"It was funny. My grandma was freaking out and my grandpa thought it was cool. I was, oh, maybe ten or eleven. He went with me into the bathroom and helped me clean it up. Joking that MooMoo was probably calling an ambulance. They were complete opposites." He smiles and I see the memory leave his focus. "And I think it makes me look tough. Don't you?" Grinning, he does a muscle-man pose and resumes his back-to-the-game stance in one long, fluid motion.

I giggle a little because he is so damn cute. "So tough. Okay. What do I have to do?"

"I'll be nice. This time." That's disappointing. "As lovely as they are, the scarf and sweater have to go."

Refusing to bring light to the fact that he's chosen two items and I'm only wearing three, I simply comply. I'm not anything close to graceful as I unwind the long knit scarf from around my shoulders and let the sweater fall off my arms. Here I stand in nothing more than my long peignoir, my hair a total mess.

"That wasn't so bad," I offer.

"If you knew what I was thinking, you wouldn't agree." I hear the lust in his voice.

I'm not wearing a bra, which is plainly obvious. And the neckline of this nightgown is very low in the front and the back. With only thin straps to hold it up, the long, light pink fabric almost touches the floor.

"Baby, will you turn around for me? Please?"

I do, and I hear him say, "Jesus Christ," to himself. I've found another good reason to wear pretty pajamas.

"You're up," I say a little shyly but think to myself, *I bet he's up all right.*

It's weird, standing with this scrap of distance between us. It's such a tease to see him so close yet far enough away that I could reach out and touch him. It's taking control I don't think I'll have for much longer.

"You said you were scared of being blind earlier. What's the scariest part for you?"

Damn. One question in. My knee-jerk reaction is to do one of those Gilligan things and take something else off. But I've only got one thing left. And he's got jeans and underwear.

I choose the hard route and take my chances. If I were soberer, I'd probably pass, but I can't see what it will hurt at this point. He's already been so sweet tonight. And I know I'm going to start getting some answers, too. We can both play this game to our advantage.

I start with a calm breath and speak slowly to steel my composure. "I'm afraid that I'll lose my independence and I won't be fun, for starters. I'm afraid that everyone will pity me and that I'll pity myself eventually. I'm afraid I won't be able to work. I'm afraid that I'll be lonely. But I already told you a lot of that."

"Yeah, but saying it helps. The more you say those things out loud, the better you'll feel about them. I promise." He smiles at me, aware that this is difficult. "What else?"

"I'm afraid I won't remember everything and I'll forg..." I stop mid-sentence at hearing the shakiness in my voice. "It makes me sad. Is that enough for that question? I'll take a googley thing if you want." I bow my head and try to rein in my emotions.

"You answered it." I hear his warm words and they relieve me a little. "I don't want to you be sad. I just want to know how I can help. If I know what the worst parts are for you, baby, I can work on those first." There is sympathy in his voice, and I know he wants to make it all better. I just don't know if he can.

The wine catches up to me, and I'm heading into the sleepy phase of my binge. I say through a yawn, "Take your pants off. That question was rough. You owe me." I attempt at not staring this time around, but he turns completely around.

His toned back facing me, he asks, "Are you sure?"

"Yeah, I'm sure. Drop 'em. I almost started crying again, Ben. The pants go."

I hear the telltale sound of a zipper and then I'm gobsmacked.

Ben's not wearing underwear. Ben's naked. Ben only has socks on. Shit. Yes. Shit.

"Uh, where are your underwear?!"

"Where are your underwear?!" he shouts back, holding his hands out like 'what the fuck?' So that answers whether or not he could tell that there were no panties beneath my gown.

"I didn't know anyone was coming over! Wait," I correct. "I didn't know anyone was coming over to play strip twenty-questions without *their* underwear on!"

His muscular shoulders lift in defense of my teasing scold. "It was a spur-of-the-moment thing. I wanted to cheer you up. You were upset. I don't know. I wanted you to talk and I also wanted to see you with the sweater off. I thought it was a good idea."

This situation is so absurd that I can help but laugh. I'm half drunk, half naked. He's fully sober and totally nude. It is the things that sitcoms are made of.

"So why didn't you wear underwear?"

"I was at the gym down the street. That's why I was close. I forgot a clean pair so I just didn't wear any after I took a shower. I sort of forgot. I didn't know!" He's laughing now too and peeking at me over his left side.

Using his line and tweaking it for good measure, I ask, "Will you turn around for me, Benny?" I am by no means sobered up.

Let's be clear. But I'm not yawning anymore.

The muscles in his back are almost are just as lean and defined as his front. Ben's butt is white like it's never seen the sun in its existence. Two perfectly white cheeks flex as he thinks about his next move. I clearly have the upper hand.

"If I turn around, then we go one more round. That's only fair. You can't quit. Deal?" he wagers.

"Deal."

He slowly turns around and he has his hands covering himself. Both hands. Inside, my mind is screaming, *Jump this fine motherfucker!* Somehow, even through my tipsy state, I remain cool and calm. It's so funny how, in just a few seconds, if you add a naked man to the equation, this game is fun again.

"Okay. Ask your question," he says, looking anywhere but at me. I want to toy with him, but I'm having a hard time thinking about what to do.

"Ben, I'm over here."

"I know where you are, Tatum. I just can't look at you or this will get a lot more awkward."

Then it hits me. He's trying not to seem like a major pervert. And for no good reason, too. I would have had sex with him on the floor in the closet. Still, I can't resist messing with him.

"Benny. Look at me," I say in a softer voice, fully aware of what I'm about to get myself into. Or at least I'm trying like hell to get myself into.

"All right, but you've still got to go one more round. Remember?" His voice gains its weight back, and he's not the only one aroused.

"I remember." My brain stalls. There are so many things I want to ask him, but now I can't think of any of them. All I can think about is his hands on my body and touching him.

"What's your question, Tatum?" I can see that his self-control is dangling like a carrot in front of him, and if I push him even the tiniest bit, he'll lose it. That's exactly what I want.

His hands still cradle the only surprise he has left. He's reading my face and knows I'm not going to back down. It's like a sexual Mexican standoff in my bedroom.

I want him. I go for broke.

"Do you want to know what I taste like?"

He swallows and his jaw flexes before he says, "Yes." Determination flares in his eyes and his body tenses.

His hands drop.

My eyes follow.

"Are you sure you're ready for this? When I come over there, no more shutting me out. No more hiding from me. We're in this together," he states, offering me one last chance to back down.

I thought we were just going to have sex. He's hard as a rock and dead serious. I've never met a man who wanted some form, even the smallest, of commitment before getting it on.

Still, I can't deny that it's what I want too. I nod my agreement.

Before I can process what I've just gotten myself into, he's here. Standing directly in front of me.

"Are you going to ask me what your show is?" Ben asks me in a breathy voice. He skirts around my neck, never touching me, but I can feel him so close.

"Do you want me to take this off?" I pull away so I can see his face.

"No. I'm going to enjoy taking it off of you myself."

He walks me backwards to my dresser that sits against the wall. It hits me on the ass and I stop, unable to go any farther. He dips down low to his knees and moves both hands under the pink gown, bringing it up with him as he slides his hands up my smooth legs.

He looks up at me with hooded eyes and smiles. "Sit up there, baby."

Climbing onto the chest, I sit back just enough so that my feet dangle, not touching the floor. He kisses one leg up to my knee and then the other, taking his time to play fair with them, all the while stroking and caressing my tempered skin, higher and higher.

He hasn't even touched my center and I feel like I'm going to detonate the second he does. It's been a while, and it was never like this. I can't think of a time in my life when a lover took this much tender care of me.

I lean back on my hands to steady myself and lay my back against the mirror. Every light kiss Ben places on my body ramps up my excitement. Trying to remain quiet, I press my lips together so that I don't make a fool out of myself. A needy moan still makes it past my throat, but it only encourages him.

"Relaxed up there?"

"Yes." I open my eyes, not realizing that I closed them, and look down to see something that I hope stays ingrained in my memory for the rest of my life—Ben's face between my legs, smiling up at me.

He's worked the skirt of my pajamas all the way up to my waist, and it is now wadded up on my lap. Ben stands for only a second and lifts me with one arm, pulling the pink silk out from under my ass. Working both sides, he raises it over my head and throws it across the room. His mouth hits mine, and I finally let out the sounds I've been poorly trying to stifle.

He moves his hands to my breasts and cups them, adding only more urgency to our kiss, and my entire body is on fire. I can feel a pulsing between my legs, and I know it will only abate one way.

He moves his mouth lower and takes a tight nipple inside, lightly playing with it between his teeth. The sensational mix of almost discomfort and pure pleasure has my fingernails raking the dresser's wood top.

Letting my breast fall away from his hot mouth, he whispers, "You like that, don't you?"

I hum my compliance.

I'm torn between watching this man's head as he kisses and worships my body all the way down and just laying my head back and dedicating this moment to only the feeling. I steal a glance down and he's looking me over like a map. He stretches my legs wider and opens drawers on either side, placing a foot up high in each one. With me spread like this before him, I feel so at peace knowing that he'll take care of everything.

"Baby, you're so wet. I haven't even touched you." He runs his thumb up the crease of me before he sticks it in his mouth for his taste. He doesn't say anything. Moving towards me, he runs his tongue the same route as his thumb did only seconds before.

I can feel my thighs beginning to shake from having my feet held steady in their places. Leaning back so that I don't need my arms for support, I move my hands to his head.

"Tell me what you like, Tatum," he says between long laps at my sex. "I want to know your secrets, baby. Tell me."

"Lick my..." And he's already there, making the most heavenly circles on my clit with his firm tongue. "Yeah," I breathe.

I run my fingers through his hair, encouraging the pressure that I crave. My legs finally do twitch, and my stomach is following suit. I'm getting closer when one long finger slides into me.

He doesn't fumble around, looking for the spot. He just gets there. Ben's mouth works at a master's pace. I feel one talented finger become two and I come.

"Ben. Ben. Ben." I chant his name so many times that I sound like a scratched CD. He doesn't stop, only slowing until I catch my breath. My body withers onto the hard walnut furniture I am perched on.

Ben stands, his fingers never completely leaving me, pulling every last ounce from me. He erotically purrs into my ear, "I don't know what's sweeter, baby. The way you taste or hearing you say my name when you come. I've been waiting so long for both. Stand up," he croons.

I inch myself closer to the edge of the dresser and stretch my toes out to find stable footing. He seizes me to him in a tight hold.

"Turn around."

I oblige, and between his arms, which are caging me in close to the dresser, I turn to face myself and him in the mirror. I'm flushed and rosy. Ben looks so collected, but I can feel how much he's affected with how close he's standing to me.

"Look at you, Tatum." I meet his eyes in the reflection before us. "Not at me. At you." His hand turns my chin ever so slightly, and then I'm face to face with a girl who looks like me.

She's familiar.

She looks alive.

Ben crosses his hands across my chest and takes one breast in each hand. He works them in every direction and lifts them a little in his grasp.

"Look at your face. Your cheeks are red. Your lips are swollen." My head looks away from the mirror and rolls onto his chest. The feeling of his naked body and mine pressed together warms me from the inside out. "I see you in there." He places light kisses on my neck.

"I have a game we can play. It's called We're Both Naked So Let's Be Quiet." My request is met with a happy laugh from behind me. When he smiles, I feel his cheek move against my hair.

"You're so mouthy."

"Will you stay?" Behind my smartass comments is always something more. I don't want him to leave.

"Yeah. I'll stay."

He fetches my pretty pajamas, and I watch him tend to me in the mirror. He attentively opens the pink fabric so that he can easily slip it over my head in one clean motion.

We lie in my bed together talking for hours. We talk about things and places we want to visit, and I confide in him that I'm afraid I will miss out.

He softly runs a light hand up and down my back. "There's time, baby. We'll make time," he says as he kisses my neck just before I fall into the most restful sleep wrapped up in a perfect man.

CHAPTER
Twenty-Four

I WAKE TO THE SMELL of coffee and bacon. I stretch, feeling really great. I pad sock-less towards the kitchen, listening to the sizzle coming from the pan and some a cappella singing.

Ben's still shirtless, and his day-two jeans ride low, dragging on the floor under his bare feet as he cooks. His earbuds run down his back to his phone, which is tucked into his back pocket. The tempo must be building in the song because he taps the fork he's using to flip the meat against the rim of the pan.

He's jamming.

I wait to hear something familiar and that's when he belts, "Ooh, forgot my woman, lost my friends. Things I'd done and where I've been." I know it's Alice and I smile.

I examine everything, not wanting to miss a single element, and catalogue it away for another day. The aroma of food. The sight of him in my kitchen making breakfast, my presence unknown. He's in his own world.

I watch the sinew and pull of each of the muscles in his back flex as he shakes his ass and dances quietly, his hair messy and sticking up all over the place.

It's perfection. It's a dream come true. How did I not know about this? Where did I irresponsibly pass the exit sign that read "Sexy, dancing, shirtless man making breakfast"? I've had years and years to find and experience this feeling. It's ironic that now I realize how lovely it is to open my eyes and appreciate what's in front of them.

The Ben Show goes on and on. I slide down to sit, my back against the hallway wall, and pull my knees into myself. It's too good to interrupt.

He gets two mugs from the cabinet and pours them full. He doctors them carefully and turns the burners off, plating the food. I am aware that my PG-rated peep show is coming to an end. A little saddened by that, I know that the coming interaction will be a nice Band-Aid.

I don't want to startle him when his hands are full, so I walk up to him and kiss the center of his back. He takes a long breath and pulls the buds from his ears.

I hear the smile in his voice when he says, "Hi there. I was trying to be quiet."

"You were. I woke up on my own." I keep kissing him, each one landing on freckles that I make a mental note to map them out later. He smells delicious, and I would rather just have him for breakfast.

"What are your plans for the day?" he asks. "I have an idea."

My lips are reluctant to stop pecking his flesh.

"I like this. Let's do this today." I rain kisses on him, hoping I'll get my way.

"Mmmm. That sounds nice, but I have a better idea. Let's eat." He's up to something.

We eat at the breakfast bar, and I patiently wait for the announcement of our big plans.

"Last night you said something and I've been thinking about it every since." His face brightens. "Let's go. Let's go on a trip. We can drive, we can fly, or we can take a train. I don't really care. Let's map it out. Pick a few places and just leave."

I wasn't expecting this. My thoughts were a lot more in line with hiding out here all day and playing What Can I Put Here and What Goes In There.

He's ambitious, this one.

"Like where? For how long?"

"I don't know and what does it matter? What do you have go-ing on in the next few weeks?" His head cocks to one side and waits for the answer he already knows.

"Nothing really. The only thing I have to be here for is Win-nie's bachelorette party, but that isn't for a few weeks. You already know all that." The idea of running off sounds too good to be true.

"Where is one place you want to go? First reaction. Go."

"New Orleans." I'm not sure why that pops out. I've never been and have always wanted to go, but it doesn't seem like a first-choice type of place.

Smiling, Ben says, "Yeah, I like that." He gets up and runs to the office, returning with paper and pen. "Where else?"

"The Keys. I guess." His enthusiasm sweeps me along for a minute before a practical inner voice tells me to hold up. "This is crazy. We can't go to all of these places."

"Why the fuck not, Tatum? What are we waiting for? We have plenty of time. We have plenty of money. We just have to go. So what are you waiting for? Now, where else?" He's insane, but it sounds so fun. "Just give me two more," he says, scribbling notes, already planning things to see.

"Are you serious? This is crazy, Ben"

"I'm dead serious. Let's do it. We can leave in the morning for wherever. We'll be back in plenty of time to get everything lined out for Winnie, and when we get back, we'll do all of the stuff your doctor said. But first, we do this. Now." He aims the end of the pen at my face. "No waiting."

I think about it. It's spontaneous. My heart races. I haven't felt like this for years.

Free.

Alive.

"Where do you want to go?" I ask Ben. "It's your trip too. Oh, wait. You have work. You should probably suck up to your boss so she'll let you off. You don't want to get fired."

"I'll work on her in a little while." He taps the pen against his lips. "I've always wanted to go to Seattle, the Northwest. See the big trees in Northern California. Go to the Goonies house." He laughs.

"I want to do that too. That's on the list."

"Where else? One more." He looks like a younger, less serious version of himself, and I'm loving the change. He's always been fun and easy to be with, but this feels different. This feels honest. This is right.

"No. That's all. That's what I want to do."

"Okay. Let's talk about a few things." This is the Ben I'm use to. Rules-and-parameters Ben. If I'm being honest, I'll take him either way.

"You're such a buzzkill." I crunch down on the last piece of bacon that's on Ben's plate and wait to hear the guidelines for our adventure.

"All right. First, no boss-employee stuff." Ben looks to me for approval and to see if I'm on board with the idea.

"I like it," I quickly agree, deciding to put my own stamp on the rules. "I have one."

Ben wasn't expecting that, so I have his attention. Wide-eyed, he looks at me. I know he may not exactly like what I'm about to ask of him.

I request, "I want you to relax and just be you. I'll just be me."

"Deal. You have to tell me what you want the whole time. No matter what it is. Any time, anywhere. If you want something, just say it. If you want to leave, if you want to go somewhere else, just say so. This is your trip."

As much as I like the idea of a trip just for me, I feel a little guilty. I want him to think of it as his trip, too. "Deal, as long as you do the same thing. We share the trip." It's compromise.

"What do you mean?" he asks, like he's the most oblivious person on the planet.

"You have to live by your rules. If you want me to tell you

stuff, then you have to tell me too."

"That's fair enough." He smiles, and I can see the excitement in his pretty green eyes.

"Shit. I need to pack. You said we're leaving tomorrow morning? Where are we going first?"

"Get your laptop. Where do you want to go first?" he asks, and I know he doesn't care one way or another.

I retrieve my computer and open it up, forgetting that I was surfing some less than PG sites the other night. I blush. "Shut up. It's totally normal."

He just shakes his head and takes possession of it. "You said New Orleans." His lightning-fast fingers type, and within minutes, he says, "That works. We could fly there and then fly into San Francisco, drive up the coast, see the trees, and then check out Seattle for a few days. We can fly from there to the Keys and stay a while before we come back home." He faces me after unleashing his loose agenda for approval with eager eyes.

"God. How in the fuck were you not a personal assistant? Were you a travel agent in a former life?" I nudge his shoulder and chuckle. "I'm cool with all of that. I trust you. Ah! I can't believe we're going to do this. I seriously need to pack."

"Yeah, me too. I might run home and get my stuff ready. Do you want to come with me?"

I never realized that I haven't been to Ben's place. Now that I've been invited, I can't wait to see what it looks like.

"Yes. Let me get dressed. I can take a cab back in a while and get ready. This is fun." I loudly clap my hands together and rub them against one another like a crazed villain, wagging my eyebrows. "I'll get to see all your stuff."

"Well, you'll see the stuff I have there at least. It isn't much. Most of my stuff is still in D.C. I just brought the essentials. You know. TV. Clothes. Books. Music. Bed. Chair. That stuff." He sends a few pages to my printer in the office and I hear it beeping that it's finished.

I have to ask. "Does this feel weird to you? Us?" I know that I've thought about this for months and wanted to attack him since the moment I saw him, but it doesn't feel as strange as I imagined it would in my head.

"No. Not really," he tells me and stands to come close. He wraps me up and lifts me so that we are eye to eye. "I've wanted this. I want you. I just had to wait. Does this feel weird to you?" I see a hint of insecurity behind his gaze when he knits together his brows.

"Honestly, I thought it would. But it doesn't." I'm not a shy girl. I hardly make time for my brain to register what my mouth is saying before I'm spitting out obscenities. Then there are times like these when I'm not sure what to say. So I go against my best judgment and try this tell-him-my-feelings shit that he's been insisting on. "I wanted this too. Thanks for waiting on me." I kiss his nose.

"You're worth it. I would have waited longer." I feel my face warm with his sincere words. He kisses my nose and sets me back on my feet. "Get dressed. Let's go. I'm staying here tonight."

My face must say what my libido is thinking.

"It will be easier to get up and to the airport if we're at the same place," he says, but he looks like he's calling me a filthy-minded hussy. Which I am. So I'm okay with it.

I throw on a pair of jean shorts and a t-shirt. I really need to think about what I should bring. I need a list. Ben's been doing all of my stuff lately, and I, for the first time, realize how much I want to prepare for this trip. By myself.

I'm looking forward to packing. Probably because I'm looking forward to time away. Time with Ben.

I don't let my constantly negative thoughts pollute my mind with lasts. Rather, I choose to focus on the firsts that I'm getting.

We don't call Ray for a ride. Instead, we walk out to the street and Ben flags us a cab. I get in first and look at him as he stands there holding the door open with a huge grin.

"What? Aren't you getting in with me?" I ask.

"I should have a long time ago."

I think, *Yeah, like, thirty seconds ago, but whatever.*

He gets into the back seat next to me, he kisses me fiercely. He holds my hand the whole time. *Note to self, Ben likes cabs.*

I really need to text or call Winnie and Cooper, but I think better of it, keeping his hand in mine. It feels so good.

His building looks a little run down. But I know from Cooper that turning these old warehouses into modern living spaces is a really big business for real estate. I bet it's cool.

He walks me up a ramp that leads us to a big metal door. Taking his keys out, Ben unlocks the latch and swings the iron gate-like door open. Then he takes a different key and unlocks a latch in the center of the solid iron door. When he does, the center splits, half going up and the other half going down. An elevator. It's unique. I smile, watching him go through motions that are all new to me.

"Why haven't you ever asked me over before?"

"I don't know. I thought about it. You never asked me about it or, so I didn't say anything." He pulls a canvas rope and the two doors pair back up in the middle. There are two ropes on the side, and he pulls one down, the elevator jerks, and we move up, up, and up. I look skyward and there's no ceiling. I've never been in one like this.

"You like my elevator?" Ben laughs. "It's cool, huh? I liked it too the first time I rode in it. My brother owns the building, so it works out nice." He looks relaxed and more content that I've ever seen him.

"It's so old. Is it safe?" I could live without the jerking.

He laughs. "It's safe."

Soon, we're at the top and he opens the same type of door on the other side. Stepping out, I see that his place is big. The ceilings are very tall, and there are exposed pipes running in all different directions across the open overhead space. The multi-paned windows are huge—some clear, some frosted, some amber, and some a light green color. The floor is polished concrete.

He has a leather couch and chair next to a small coffee table against the far wall under the long bank of windows. His kitchen is on the right. The room is probably sixty by sixty, and he only uses about ten square feet of it.

"This is it. Like I said. I don't really have much here." He walks ahead, pointing out the major areas. "Living room. Kitchen. The first door down that hall is the second bath and the others are the other three bedrooms."

"Wow. This place is huge." I wouldn't have to worry about bumping into anything.

"It is. Come on. Help me." What a turn. He's asking me to help.

My face is splitting, and I take the hand he holds out to me. He likes touching me, and for the first time ever, I like being touched too.

In his bedroom, there are books in stacks dozens high along one side. It's like a book wall. He has a lamp sitting atop one of the taller piles.

"You read a lot."

"Yeah. It's sort of an addiction."

A man with a reading addiction? I've never met a creature like him.

"That's hot." I lick my lip thinking about a naked Ben reading in bed. In this bed. *Dear Lord.*

"It's hot? So that's what you're into? If I would have known that, I would have been reading on the job all the time. We can take a few if you want. I mean, I'm taking a few and I'll read them to you if you want. Since you're into that kind of thing." He winks at me and pretends to be seductive. All the while, he's being so sexy I can hardly breathe.

"Yes, please."

I plop down on his bed, and it's firmer than I was thinking it would be. Ben pulls shirts, shorts, and jeans from his closet. I fold them so they'll fit nicely into his luggage. He takes a suit out and gives me a questioning look.

"I don't know. Maybe if we go out or something? Maybe in Seattle or New Orleans? I'll pack a few dresses too. It never hurts to over-pack," I say like it's a creed of mine.

"All right." He easily gives in to the idea of going out somewhere nice.

"Don't forget swimming trunks." I'm looking forward to the whole trip, but I have to admit that I'm really excited for the Keys. I've never been, and I can only imagine how beautiful the views will be, including a half-naked Ben all day. "Maybe a few of those. I guess we can buy things we forget or don't have room for."

"When we get back to your apartment, we need to get a few details lined out. A rental car for the West Coast, and we should see if there are any places along the way we want to stay that require reservations. I really want to stay in a cabin in King's Canyon," he tells me as he continues to pile undershirts and socks onto his bed.

"Where is that? I've never stayed in a cabin before. Sounds dirty." When I agreed to this road trip, I wasn't exactly thinking camping. He must see the worry on my face. He comes to sit next to me.

"Don't think of it like that. You'll like it. I promise. Think mountains, a fire…" He nuzzles my neck and whispers, "No one around for miles."

Enough said. I'm easy. "You win. Cabin is on the list."

"I thought you'd see it my way." Ben leans in and puts his mouth to mine.

We finish packing his things and call Ray since we have all of his stuff. We swing by a drug store to buy toiletries we'll need before going back to my place to make our itinerary and get my shit together.

Why did I wait so long for this?

CHAPTER
Twenty-Five

WE CAUGHT AN EARLY flight into New Orleans. Stepping out of the airport before noon in the middle of June in the bayou is a lot like walking into a sauna. The smells and sounds of the city hit me instantly, and any ideas I had about this being a bad idea were left somewhere miles over the East Coast as we flew south.

Ben and I made a few decisions about our adventure last night, but only the necessary ones to make sure everything worked the way we wanted. We are going to spend two days in New Orleans, fly to San Francisco, and then road-trip all the way to Seattle.

He found a cabin that was open close to Sequoia National Park and King's Canyon. We reserved it for two nights and the Four Seasons in Seattle for another two days later, giving us plenty of time to drive and stop if we want.

The Keys are a different story. I had definite plans about what I was expecting. We found a secluded bungalow on the ocean in The Moorings Village and rented it for a week. We'll fly back home from Florida.

I want the typical secluded beach vacation. Walking shore-lines, watching sunsets. Of course I didn't say that shit, but I think he got the hints I was giving when we scrolled the websites. Before I fell asleep on his shoulder as we made reservations and mapped out our journey, he called me a closet romantic.

I've been called worse.

Ben checks us into our hotel as I look around. We've picked

one of the older hotels in the French Quarter. The ceilings are high, the colors on the walls are bright. I hear the music just outside of the grand doors that stay propped open.

"So what do you want to do first?" I question him, not able to keep my excitement at bay when we get to our suite. It is lovely, too, but I want to explore. This city has a wild buzz in the air, and I want to let it do its worst on us.

"I'm up for whatever. Where do you want to go?" he asks, looking out the window down the street.

"I think we should just roam. See what's happening." I've heard that that's the best way to do New Orleans.

Roaming lands us only a few blocks away at a bar. We sit out-side in the sunshine, drinking beers and eating shrimp and oysters. Laughing.

"So you just look at people and make up their stories," Ben says with a smug grin that cries bullshit.

"Yeah. Like what they're doing, thinking. It's fun. Try it." I'm leaning back in my chair and have commandeered another to put my feet on.

"Seriously?" He pulls the tail off his fifty-fifth shrimp, stops everything, and makes the same face he has with every poor crus-tacean he's already devoured. It's a food-induced O-face, and I love it every single time. Then, like it never happened, he's back. "Just whatever?" He laughs, thinking that my game is silly.

He's right, but it's fun.

"Yep. The next person who walks past the gate. Just say what they're thinking about."

Our first victim walks by.

He's an older person, probably late sixties. He has a cool hat on and carries only his paper and a coffee. He looks like a very practical, normal man. I look pointedly at Ben and shake my finger in the general direction of Mr. Cool Hat, insisting he goes.

"Okay. Um, this coffee is too hot." He winces.

I whisper-shout, "No! Like something personal. Make something up. Where is he going?"

He thinks for a second. Then he offers in a low, old man's voice, "I wish those two dummies over there would stop staring at me."

"Not bad." I laugh. At least, it's original. "You'll do better next time." I resign, figuring that maybe I'm the only one who does this.

He does do a little better on his second shot. His voices are terrible, but that's what make them so classic. I do a few more and he chokes on his beer when I make up one about an older lady who has nipple rings.

After we eat way too much and drink a little more than cool for lunch, we walk. It's pretty hot, and I'm thankful for only wearing a tank top and skirt. My flip-flops make their signature sounds in our wake all over the French Quarter.

Ben walks with his arm around my shoulder, which seems to be his preference. I can always tell when he's going in for it. He takes my right hand with his and then lifts it over my head. It feels like a choreographed dance move. I'm walking with the most romantic thing in New Orleans.

I send a picture of us in front of St. Louis Cathedral, which we asked a perfect stranger to take, to Winnie and Cooper. They were a little shocked when I told them yesterday that I was leaving town with Ben on a half-a-month-long adventure, but by the end of the call, Cooper was telling Winnie places for us to go and looking up fun things along our drive for us to see.

They made me promise to have a good time, and then Winnie ruined our adult conversation with questions about Ben's anatomy. I didn't tell her anything about what happened the other night, but it wouldn't be hard to assume things since we are on a vacation together.

I told her to fuck off and feed Cooper while I'm gone.

While walking the streets, our buzzes mostly worn off, we stop and watch street performers. Together, we stroll through shops and parks until the sun is about to go down over the Mississippi.

Turns out that New Orleans is pretty liberal when it comes to libations. I know. I was shocked too. We buy the biggest Hurricanes I've ever seen poured and take them with us to an overlook where the river heads to the ocean.

Here I sit with a man I'm coming to care for more than I realized even before today. I'm in a beautiful place that, if it weren't for him, I probably would have never seen. I drink from the long straw and soak up everything.

It might be the orange-and-red-painted sunset fading away that makes me eager for the darkness tonight. Or maybe it's the brazen hand that writes words on my thigh that I quit trying to read hours ago. I wouldn't know.

But I am ready. I want him. I have no doubt that he wants me. Even if I did have a moment of doubt, Ben would be quick to erase it. It's a foreign feeling to have. For the first time in my life, I don't wonder if the other person wants me as much as I do them. I'm certain. He's certain. It's a powerful thing to feel.

There has been a shift on our bench. Watching him, listening to him talk about his life, the fun and trouble he and his friend Keith used to get into. He doesn't say anything more about Keith's suicide, only talking about good memories. I don't push, only accepting what he tells me about it, though I know I has to be painful.

Instead of walking back to our hotel, we cab it. Proving my theory about Ben and cabs, his mouth is on me when the meter begins.

Before today, our relationship was like a blank coloring page with only the thick black borders. Carefully, we fill each empty space with pigment. We're learning where the boundaries are, only brave enough to wander out when worth it.

Who didn't draw in their own white puffy clouds in coloring books or color the grass green all the way to the bottom of the page as a child? There are no lines defining them, open for us to decide when to stop.

Tonight, I want the custom puffy clouds in the cyan sky. Tonight, I want the hand-drawn yellow sun with spiky-armed outlaw rays breaking the rules on my page. Tonight, I'm searching for the boundaries with Ben and hoping to make some as we go.

On the elevator, I follow one of his rules. "I want you tonight," I confess without shame. It's liberating. He wants me to tell him what I am thinking. So I do.

He squeezes the hand he has on my hips as we rise up to our floor, not saying a word. He only presses me forward when the doors open for us to exit. His silence makes my heart pound harder and faster. Anticipation sits low in my stomach.

I stand still, my back to him, as he unlocks our door around me. We walk through the threshold and I'm suddenly in the air. My legs swept out from under me, flip-flops falling off, and I'm carried to the bed and placed directly in the center.

He motions for me to stay put with an open hand in the air and I obey. Still silent.

Ben stands at the end of the bed and takes off one shoe at a time. I hear one thud then the second. Off goes his shirt. The shorts follow, and in less than a minute's time, he's standing there in his boxer briefs, looking at me.

"Say it again," he commands.

I can't take my eyes off of him. He ignores his modesty—if he has any—pulls off his underwear, and leans a knee onto the bed. He grabs one of my legs and slides my body down to where he is, my skirt sliding up and exposing what's underneath.

My voice is much smaller than the first time I said it, but I repeat, "I want you tonight." This time, it sounds more like a plea. I lie there, one leg on either side of him, as he climbs all the way up onto the four-poster bed between my legs.

He strips off my shirt and pulls the skirt over my head too. He gathers me up into his arms, my greedy hands buying brief purchase of his skin. My bra comes off, he diligently tosses it to the floor, and he returns me to the bed, laying me on my back. Wide, firm hands rove down and over my breasts, skimming their way to the elastic of my thong and pulling one side down a bit, then the other, until they stop around my spread thighs.

Ben guides my legs, and removing the panties, he kisses each before wrapping them back around him. I watch desire intensify in his covetous eyes. He bends to kiss my stomach, moving up my body, my gratified skin heating under his lips. Holding his weight with his hands, he finally brings his mouth to mine.

"One more time."

Amid the exquisite sensation of him against my hip, I'd gladly recite the Declaration of Independence if it would charm him inside me.

One adroit hand slips between is as he leans to the opposite side. He cups me and runs a finger through the wetness gathered between my legs. A moan rumbles through his chest at his find.

"I want you right fucking now." But this time, I add, "Benny," and he slips two fingers in me as his lips crash to mine.

"I love it when you call me that," he pants.

"I love it when you touch me there. Ah." The palm of his hand rubs my clit as his fingers work me over. "I need you."

I, too, reach between us to find him, desperate to explore. He's long and hot. The ridge of his swollen head is sensitive to my touch. His breaths are timed now with every knead my hand provides. When I firmly tighten my grip as far as my finger can reach around him, he lunges into my grasp and exhales a swear.

His working me and my working him only stand to heighten my desire as opposed to pacifying it.

Leaving my body rocking to the motion that was just about to make me come, he sways, freeing himself from my hand, and moves to my core. As he readies us, he looks at me. My breaths are short and fast, my breasts falling slightly to the sides.

Ben lingers, catching his own breath. Slipping his erection

through my begging flesh, he watches me with tender eyes as he presses into me for the first time. Like a key in a lock, my body welcomes him home.

With measured strokes, he runs through me at an almost teasing pace, his eyes never leaving my face. His hips roll every so often, emitting friction at a frustrating level, reducing my head to sink into the bed.

He steadily accelerates us, pushing deeper. His body melding with mine compels my arms to his back, and I hold tight to him as everything gets lost. My fingers bear down hungrily into him with my body wrapping around him in every way possible.

"You're so close, baby," he says, returning his motions to a torturous grind, burying himself to the hilt within me. "Just go. Come for me. I want to feel you." Ben's sex-filled voice rings in my ears as my body gives in to itself and him. I cry his name until I hear mine pour from his lips.

With his forehead pressed against mine, he releases into me with a hot rush, and I almost come again from the sensation.

When our bodies begin to recover, Ben rolls me onto his stomach, still embedded inside me, and plays with my hair until I fall asleep right there on top of him while listening to his praise.

I love New Orleans.

CHAPTER
Twenty-Six

WE DIDN'T END UP seeing much more of Louisiana's pride and joy, resorting to room service and the hotel bar for its proximity to our room.

I learn a thing or two about Benny. He doesn't like waking up in the morning unless I'm playing with his morning wood and investigating his balls. He says that I'm welcome to check him out every morning—if I don't mind. He confirms an appointment for tomorrow, citing this as his preferred style of wake-up call. I tell him that I'll see what I can do.

When we shower on our second day, I find out that his hips are ticklish if I squeeze in just the right spots. Also, he is a very thorough bath-time friend. Ben takes his time washing my hair and every satisfied inch of my body—depending on the part, sometimes twice. The man is very detail oriented. Just ask my squeaky clean nipples and vagina.

I like to think of it as an education, and I plan on having a degree in Ben's anatomy by the end of this trip, memorizing every detail I can. The surprised look on his face when he's just about to come, the incredible length he can stretch to, from toe to top, when he readies his muscles to wake up in the morning, and the endearing *rawr* that accompanies such moves.

I continue my study of the freckles peppering his back, telling him I'd like to get a pen out sometime and see if I can connect them into something cool.

When we fly into San Francisco, we pick up Ben's arranged four-wheel-drive rental for our road trip since we we're stopping in the middle of the mountains amongst the famous giant trees.

We only drive down by the Bay for a quick lunch and to see the Golden Gate Bridge before heading north towards our wilderness retreat. All the while, I hope there won't be bears. Or snakes. Or spiders. Or anything creepy or slimy. Or birds. I really hate birds.

"Bears and snakes I get, Tatum. But spiders aren't really anything to be afraid of, and almost everything you mention being afraid of doesn't want anything to do with you," he playfully admonishes.

"What if they do? What if they're hostile about me being in their environment?"

"I don't think that'll happen," he tells me as he looks at the road signs ahead. "Do you want to stop somewhere tonight or just keep driving? We have the place tonight if we get there. They said it is empty and the keys are in the lockbox on the porch." His face has his choice written all over it.

"Maybe we should stay in a city one more night. You know, take a shower and rest up. It's probably going to get a little rough out there," I say, hoping it will buy me a night away from the forest and its creatures. I realize I'm a wuss when faced with sleeping in the wild.

His hearty laugh rings out. "How many times do I have to explain? This place is nice. It will have showers, complete with indoor plumbing."

It's raining, and the longer we drive, the road grows narrower and towns become few and farther between.

"Are you sure? Those pictures can be deceiving." My apprehension is firm.

"It has a hot tub. And honestly, after sitting on a plane and driving, that sounds pretty nice." I forgot that he mentioned that before.

Hmmm. Hot tub. Ben.

Fuck the creepy crawlies and freaky birds with vendettas against me.

"Okay. Let's go straight there."

I fall asleep shortly after that conversation, and before I know it, Ben's at my side with my car door open. He whispers, and at first, I'm too sleepy to hear what he's saying. I only hear his voice.

Consciousness floats to the surface of my mind and I make out, "Come on, baby. I don't want the beasts to get you." My eyes open and find him smiling at me. He knew that would get my attention.

"What?" The sleep in my voice sounds like an eighty-year-old menthol smoker. I clear my throat after hearing its roughness. Not sexy.

"We're here. I've already unlocked and carried in our stuff. Let's go."

I shake my daze away and blink, trying to clear the cloudiness.

When he moves, the house comes into view. It's dark but lit up. It isn't what I pictured at all. It's a full-on house. A pretty big one too. The drive pulls up to the three-car garage we're parked in front of. The backside of the house butts right up against a huge drop, and I can see that a large porch wraps its way around that side. The front is stone and there's a porch swing by the door. The cabin is picturesque.

"I told you," he says, pleased by my surprised face.

Inside the massive greatroom, there's a huge fireplace in the center. All four sides are open, like four windows opening below the giant stone chimney that rises up and out of the ceiling. Walking around it, I notice the expansive windows that I'm sure give host to a beautiful view in the daytime. But it's dark and all I can see is the deck.

The kitchen looks new and well laid-out. Nice appliances. Nice design. This place is fantastic. Mindlessly, I roam from room to room, looking in cubbies and at the furniture. There are board games in the closets along with extra towels and linens. It's so inviting.

Every room of this hideaway smells like cedar and eucalyptus. Each bedroom has its own en suite bathroom and view. I walk up the stairs that lead to the back of the house. At the top, there is a lookout and you can see everything in the living room below.

There's only one door in the hall and it's for the master suite. Behind the door is a room fit for a king. Huge dark, wooden furniture flank the walls. Doors leading outside in the far corner cut the wall at an angle and open to a private balcony.

Flipping the light switch and turning the dimmer up to engage the outdoor lights, I see the hot tub. A small roof covers the area, and I take note of a mini-bar built into the wall that meets it on one side. I may never leave this place.

My bags are by the bathroom opposite the door to the terrace. Ben put them there. He thinks of everything. Finding my toothbrush, I freshen up from the long car ride with one thing on my mind.

I want in that hot tub.

Naked, I run a fresh washcloth under cold water then across my face. Ben was right. Nothing sounds better than sitting in the bubbles and relaxing after a day of traveling.

I leave the bathroom, still not hearing or seeing Ben, but I head to the doors that lead to my ultimate goal anyway. The air is cooler here, but the cool summer night feels perfect as I lift the cover to the tub in nothing but my birthday suit.

My feet tiptoe around to find the steps I need to get in. I climb up and into the hot water, first slowly to acclimate myself with the heat.

It's a little warmer than I'd prefer, but it doesn't take long for it to be comfortable. I take the long way around the tub to familiarize the footing and stop at the farthest edge that looks out to the wild. At this height, I can see through a little clearing in the trees, and the moon is peeking brightly through. The sight is serene.

I don't know how long I'm standing there stargazing before I hear him walk up behind me. I'm in such a moon trance that I just stay still, not caring that most of my ass is above the water and I'm totally bare standing with my back to him.

I look over my shoulder, trying to see where he is, but he's just out of my sight.

"Don't you dare move, Tatum. Let me watch you there. You look pretty damn perfect."

I let him look, staying in place. His eyes heat my back and my skin welcomes the light breeze that passes by and awakens every pore. My nipples pebble and firm up at the thought of him watching me.

I hear his pants hit the floor, and soon, the sound of breaking water behind me alerts me of his nearness. My obedient body stays where it was told. From behind, I feel two hands skirt my sides and hold me in place.

His mouth connects with my backside and a heated tongue licks my cheek. Ben's hands close in on my ass and squeeze. "So, so perfect, baby." He bites at me, and the sensation is something I've never felt. It isn't hard enough to do any damage, but it's enough to steal my breath.

"Put your hands on the sides. Can you do that for me?"

I oblige, and he runs his warm hands up the center of my back. Reflexively, I arch into his expert touch. From behind, he wraps his arms around and stands to envelope me, his hard chest sliding up my backside, and his mouth swaths me in wet kisses from shoulder to shoulder.

His masterful hand snakes around and finds me slippery and ready for him under the water. I part my legs to offer better access and he whispers, "There you go." My ass nudges against him like a cat begging for a pet.

"Thank you, Ben." I'm not sure why I need to express my gratitude now, but it overwhelms me. My head rolls back to rest on his strong chest. His unused hand guides my face to meet his for a needy kiss.

"No, sweetheart. Thank you." Who knows what he has to thank me for. "You looked so beautiful standing here. Your body against the moonlight. Sexy." Hot lips connect with my exposed neck. "So peaceful and calm. Waiting for me."

Our bodies are on autopilot. My mind absorbs the sincere words he offers. This delicious man slides into me from behind, showing me with a slow, seductive rhythm just how thankful he is. Turning me to face him, as if I'm weightless, Ben sets me on the edge of the tub and holds me in place as he drives into me with an intensity that makes my pruney toes curl.

Though the sound of his laughter ranks high on my favorite sounds list, the sound of him growling my name when he comes is alongside it at the top. I know he's getting close as my repeated name gets louder and louder until it's replaced with a feral groan that almost sounds pained.

When we come down from our post-coital cloud, we lounge in the bubbling water. I find a chilled bottle of Lambrusco in the handy refrigerator and we share the whole thing, taking turns drinking from the bottle.

With so many things changing in my life—and as piss-poor as I handle it all—in this moment, I feel content and cared for.

"I wonder what time it is." Now relaxed, I feel the weight of the day's activities making my lids heavy again. Hell, I must have slept for a few hours in the car, so he has to be exhausted.

"It's probably about three. It was just after midnight when we got here. Are you getting sleepy?"

We sit face to face—I'm straddling his lap—for a long time. Well, the length of time that it takes to drink a full bottle of wine anyway.

With his soggy hands, he clears the hair out of my face from both sides to get a good look at me.

"A little," I answer.

"We've been going at a pretty fast pace, huh, baby? You'd tell me if you want to slow down, wouldn't you? We don't have to—"

I shush him with my finger. "Don't slow down. Please." I re-place my finger with my lips. "This feels too good. You're too good."

"Well, thank you, but I meant the traveling." Green eyes shine with adoration back at me. "We can slow down if you want," he corrects, kissing my nose. "If I weren't so afraid of underwhelming you right now after that compliment, I'd be tempted to make you come again right here." I know he would, because I feel the start of a promising situation firming between us.

What is it about sex that does that? When we don't want sex, we use sleep as an excuse. And when we want it, if an opportunity turns up, we're suddenly wide awake.

"I actually feel great. Better than I have in a long time. Now get me out of here and take me to bed, Benny."

In minutes, my head is lying on Ben's chest, listening to the inner workings of this wonderful man. The steady breaths and his heart beating sound like two metronomes synchronized in time with each other.

I dream of things that I'll hardly let myself process. A life with him. A wedding of my own. Children with his green eyes who call me "Mommy."

We hike the next day, and after only a little stubborn argument from me, I get an impromptu lesson in canes with a stick in the woods.

There's nothing to it, really. Just tapping and swinging, but it really does make me feel a little surer on my feet knowing how to feel an obstacle with my hands before it becomes a danger to my path.

Ben even jokes about how hot it is watching with the stick, of-fering to misbehave so I could practice a stronger swing. I'm more at ease, seeing how comfortable he is with everything.

Maybe that's why I'm falling and falling deeper and more en-tirely into him every day. I don't have to pretend or conceal what

I'm going through. Not even from myself.

Basically, I have a full-fucking-circle moment while walking back from the woods when I realize that I'm falling in love with my assistant. Maybe that's around the same time I try to accept that Ben will be around, even if he doesn't work for me.

I go back and forth about that a lot in these precious days of our trip. I have so many things to worry and—shit you not—dread coming at me. But being with him is just the opposite.

He fills a lonely hole in me that I alone created. He deserves my honesty. He deserves my best.

That's why, on our last night in the cabin, I don't hesitate to tell him a secret—while riding him, mind you.

"I want all of you," I say on a sigh in his ear as I sink onto him and we both come apart.

Baby steps, right? First, sexual truths. Then full-on mature adult relationship. Right? Also, in my defense, it was one of the best orgasms of my life. I also almost barked. Clearly, you can see what I was dealing with. Is that temporary sanity?

It's his perfectly sweet reply that I question.

"I'm figuring it out, Tatum. I promise."

CHAPTER
Twenty-Seven

WE DRIVE THROUGH the towns along the beautiful coast of Oregon on our way to what is home to the Goonies. Talk about a man losing his shit. When we walk through the Oregon Film Museum, Ben goes back in time.

All of the quotes he remembers come spewing from his reminiscent face. He even looks younger. It's a pleasure seeing how happy it makes him.

I tell him to quit being such a fan-boy as he suggests that we buy matching Goonie hoodies. Don't get me wrong. I love the Goonies as much as the next girl, but Ben knows weird facts about the whole movie. He knows more about some of the stuff we see than the twenty-five-year-old guide who keeps asking us if we are finding everything and if we've been here before.

So when he practically begs me to be shirt buddies with him and buys me the exact same one just smaller, I simply can't resist. He says, "We'll be shirt buddies!" right in front of the cashier. It's priceless. His face is a cross between a Christmas tree, a grand-prize winner, and that expression girls get right before they start the speed-clapping for joy. Everyone's done it. Even Ben it seems.

"Now that we've been to the mother ship, we're official Goonies together." He tells me this like it's on a checklist of benchmark relationship milestones. "Together," he reiterates with a smile.

We snap pictures in front of the Goonies house and on the

beach in front of Haystack Rocks before we skip town. Then we coast into Seattle on a high from the silly day we've had. On the drive, I send some of the photos to Winnie and Cooper.

They call immediately. Winnie confirms that everything is going smoothly for the wedding and that I'm to continue having a great time. Cooper asks to speak with Ben about our Goonie adventure. Who knew that every man this age wants to be a Goonie? They laugh on the phone, reciting line after line. I'm pleased that they get along so well.

Much to our surprise—not—it's raining when we pull into our amazing hotel near Seattle's coastal trademark in the Pike Place epicenter.

This night is sort of a surprise to me. Ben did some looking around the other day on my laptop while I painted my toenails at the cabin. It had been such a long time, and I took extra care to do a good job, applying the polish as well as I did in my early twenties when all I'd been able to afford was Sally Hansen and ninety-nine-cent flip-flops.

I took pride in how good they looked. Ben even stopped his Seattle stalking to comment on how nice they were before he patted his lap for me to sit on it.

"Now, that I have everything lined out for Seattle. Come here. I want you to see this." It was a weather forecast for the Keys. Hot and sunny and perfect. I kissed his forehead and wrapped my arms around him. "This is the island we'll be on."

"Our own island?" We'd planned on getting a beach house or something like it, but a private island! That was just too much.

He told me that there would be island staff in the main house and there are also a few other bungalows. But they are off in their own secluded sides of the small landmass.

So you'll forgive my lack of excitement as we pull into Seattle and it's gloomy and rainy. But what did I expect?

Our first night is spent going down to the Ferris wheel that's near the ocean and just outside our hotel. It stops raining barely long enough for us to ride. I could have skipped it, but being tucked into Ben's side was a nice touch.

We eat at a wonderful seafood place not far from there and end up at the hotel bar before ten thirty.

"Are we getting old?" I laugh as I make fun of both of us for being a little more pooped after each leg of our trip. As wonderful as it is, the adventure is slowing us down little by little.

"No. We're just smarter," Ben wisely corrects.

"Okay? How does partying in the hotel bar in one of the best nightclub cities in the country qualify as smart?" I feel like I'm seventy and Einstein over here thinks it's great.

"Well we can drink all we like and crawl up to our room." He leans in and says to my ear, "And it will only take about five minutes for me to get inside of you instead of twenty-five or thirty if we'd gone anywhere else."

"Agent Ben, it sounds like you are trying to get me drunk." I pretend to be offended. "That doesn't sound like you at all. Where are your high morals tonight?"

He laughs. He's had more to drink tonight in this bar than he has the whole trip. Usually when we have drinks, it's a few beers, some wine, or a cocktail. Tonight, he's drinking bourbon on ice. And he's had about five.

"What morals? Agent Ben has weak morals. Trust me." His eyes are far away in thought now.

I've never seen him like this and it concerns me. But shit. Who doesn't have a bad drunk once in a while? I have them all the time. I respect his space and resign to letting him drink it out.

In the back of my mind, I wonder why I haven't gotten him drunk before. Maybe he'd clear up some of the mysteries that only every once in a while pop into my head.

What do they matter now though? What would they change? If I really wanted to know, I could have found out. Right? Obviously, knowing where he came from and why he went to D.C. that weekend are none of my business. If Ben wants me to know, he will tell me. It isn't like he doesn't speak his mind.

That's probably one of the things that make it so easy to trust him. He tells me things the way they are.

I excuse myself to go to the ladies', and when I'm on my way back to the side of the bar where we've taken up residence, I see a woman standing rather close to Ben.

My Ben.

It takes everything in my body not to sprint the straight shot to him and stake my claim. Not that we've ever labeled what any of this is, but it feels like something. Sure, we haven't swapped class rings or anything, but dammit, we're shirt buddies.

He's my shirt buddy, bitch.

I summon the calmness and mental clarity of a saint that I am not. When I walk up behind them, I hear her say, "I don't think she's that into you. I've been staring at you and waving and she doesn't seem to mind. Any woman that doesn't give a fuck if another woman is eye fucking her sexy man isn't that interested." Her voice is dripping with persuasion.

"You don't know what you're talking about," Ben says to her rather shortly.

"Why don't you ditch her and come up with me? Or I'll give you my extra key and you can stop by later?" Slut. It would have been more subtle for her to write "I'm a sure thing" on her hot pink dress.

Ben's voice has an edge to it now that's never been present when he's spoken to me. He snarls, "She couldn't see you. Lucky her. I'm not interested in anything you have to offer." He looks her straight in her cock-sucker and tells her to fuck off with a 'shoo-fly' hand.

"She better start paying attention. I hope she keeps you happy. Because if not, one of these days, someone's gonna be a lot luckier than her and me both."

She turns to leave and sees me. The tramp winks at me and slides her card onto the bar by his glass. Ben doesn't know I'm there since I'm behind him.

She walks straight past me, saying under her breath, "You need to keep your eyes on him."

I don't move, reeling from her gall. Ben knows I'm coming back soon, but I kind of want to see what he does to the card. My brain screams, *Get rid of it!* My heart prays for a sign that he meant exactly what he just said to her.

The bartender comes back to stand in front of him. Ben hands him the card and motions for him to pour four fingers instead of the two he's been ordering.

I feel relief, but I'm still worried about what is festering in his head.

I take my seat.

"Good, you're back. Let's go up to the room." He tips the al-most full tumbler of amber alcohol back and I finish my glass of wine. He pays for our drinks and buys a bottle to take up with us.

On the way upstairs, I feel a tension that I'm not used to from him. Forfeiting my pride, I ask, "Are you all right?" and squeeze his hand to get his attention.

The first time I ask, it doesn't make it past his ears.

"Ben, are you okay?" I say louder and lean around to look at him.

His eyes are glassed over and hazy. As someone who tries to hide their emotions, I can spot it when I see it. When someone is feeling as much pain as I see in his pitiful expression, it's a delicate situation and I walk lightly so as not to fortify his defenses with questions he doesn't want to answer.

He's drunk, but he's also somewhere else and unfortunately is-n't letting me go with him.

"I need a shower. Do you want to join me?" I smile as cheer-fully as I can, pretending I'm totally oblivious to the storm he's hosting internally.

"No. I'm just going to sit outside for a while." His eyes are still hollow, but he gently kisses my temple.

Ben goes directly outside, taking the bottle with him, and I fight my gut's instinct to follow and pry.

I shower and think over all the day's conversations. Nothing springs to mind. I can't think of anything that was tumultuous or even instigating much of a debate. We had a great time. It was right after we ate that his mood shifted.

I don't know what it is.

I dry off and lotion myself, trying to choose a path—talk to him or let him work it out on his own. I'm afraid of how it will feel if he doesn't tell me what's going on and what my mind will come up with if left to guessing.

Ben wouldn't let me be like this though. He would be there. Not prying, but giving me silent support. So that's what I decide to do.

I put the hotel robe on and go to him on the balcony. I curl up on his lap and wrap myself around him.

At first, he doesn't move to hold me, but I softly say, "I'm here. Whatever it is that's messing with you, let it go. I'm here." I kiss his neck and ear. "I meant what I said the other night. I want all of you, too."

Ben's arms embrace me and he buries his face in the crook of my neck. I only know he's crying when I feel the tears land on my arm and run down my elbow. He stays like that for a long while. Silent and fighting to hold on to his emotions.

"Shhh. Benny," I whisper and slowly rock us, trying to calm us both at this point. I'm almost crying myself. I'm a sympathy crier. Almost all the tears I've cried over the last ten years were because I saw other people crying first.

He speaks, slurring, "I'll fix it, Tatum. I have to fix it."

Whatever it is, I believe he will.

Today, we've done all the touristy things. We hit record shops and museums. He took me to see the market where they throw the stinky fish and we rode up the Space Needle to have lunch.

Ben's bad mood disappeared in his sleep. When he woke up, it was like it had never been there at all.

Since tonight is our last night before we fly out tomorrow afternoon to Florida, we're going out.

"I owe you a better night than last night. I'm sorry I drank so much," he apologizes for the third or fourth time, and he looks at me regretfully.

"Don't worry about it. And yes. You will take me out tonight. See what happens when we act old?" I bump his shoulder with mine as we walk back to the Four Seasons. "Besides, I have a dress that I haven't gotten to wear yet and I haven't seen you in a tie in, like, weeks. That's too long."

"Oh we'll do it up right then tonight. All you have to do is ask for what you want, remember?" His thumb runs over my knuckles, just how I like it, as we walk to the hotel.

"Oh that's right. Ben, please take me out tonight and free my pretty pucci print from its garment bag."

"What the hell is a poochy?" he asks, laughing outright. The way he says "poochy" is too funny not to laugh at. It does sort of sound a bit nasty.

"It's a fabulous fabric print. Good enough for you?" I smile and add, "I want to dance with you tonight."

"All you have to do is ask."

"Will you kiss me?"

Ben abruptly stops in the middle of the sidewalk and my feet leave the ground. He nails me with a deep one right there at the intersection of Union Street and First Avenue. When he finally plants me on my feet again, I'm a little less surefooted. Not quick to let go, he holds me around my waist and smiles down at me.

"What else will you do?" My wild eyes and pervy grin show him my true colors and hint to my sordid thoughts.

"Anything," he answers. "Now let's go clean me up for this

night out."

We shower together and I show him how to shave my legs. He does a great job, and I think I'll add that to his list of work duties when we return home. Shaving is considered a chore, right?

I'm buckling my pretty black gladiator heels when he comes out of the bathroom straightening his lapels. His hair is combed over neatly and he looks like he rules the world in that charcoal suit. No tie. Top button undone on his dress shirt. He's a king. His suit swagger exudes power. It's so fucking sexy that I contemplate scratching the whole night out and letting him fuck me against every surface in this place.

The concierge arranges for us a car and a table at an amazing restaurant that has live music and dancing. I have to hand it to Ben. For as short notice as this trip was, it's all come together like he'd planned it for months.

The Pier, the restaurant we go to, is lovely. Tables float across the back of a spacious room, and the dining area is perfectly distanced from the band to allow for conversation. Just past the white linen tables is a bar area with a dance floor. Each table has fresh hydrangeas, and the room smells like heaven.

Ben orders us a bottle of their offered red and approves of the taste he's given.

"I never understood that. What do you do if you don't like it? You think they just throw it away?" I wonder.

A smart-ass grin cracks across his lips. "I think they fill by-the-glass orders from those bottles." He chuckles quietly, unfolding his white napkin. "They'd have to be real bastards to waste it."

"Bastards," I confirm, wrinkling my nose.

The room is filled with couples and groups laughing and talking. The crowd is nicely dressed, and to say this place is classy would be an understatement. I bet there's a lady in the bathroom right this second waiting to give me a mint or a spritz of some stinky designer-impostor perfume.

My gaze wanders from table to table, playing my story game

by myself. At a table not far from ours, there are two pretty girls. They look to be in their younger twenties. I imagine that they are celebrating a job offer or a promotion.

I fabricate that the girl in the blue dress is in a committed relationship and her friend, the girl in the teal pencil skirt, is in love with blue-dress girl. She's prayed that her friend will dump the rich, big-dicked boyfriend and confess her mutual same-sex feelings.

Of course, I laugh to myself when I hit 'big-dicked' in my head and Ben busts me.

"Are you making up lies about strangers again?" he teases and runs his foot up my leg as he crosses his under the table.

"That's what I do. Are you ready to give it another shot? You have to get good at this. It's mandatory for my next boyfriend." I look to the sky as if reading a checklist written in the empty air in front of me. "Must play my game with me." I check it off. "Yup, it's on the list."

"Next boyfriend?" he croons.

"Yeah, the next boyfriend I have will play this exact game. It's a deal breaker."

"I guess your current boyfriend needs to get his act together then."

My heart leaps into my throat at hearing what he just said. I put a pin in it for now, but I can't help the overwhelming pride his self-titled position gives me.

Ben questions, looking around the vast room for a specimen, "The waiter?" He clears his throat like he's giving a speech. "He's thinking that he's only got three more hours until he can go home and look at porn on the Internet. He loves the job, but looking down into all this cleavage every night is giving him calluses and draining his bank account from purchasing so much extra tissue." Wrapping up, he shows me his perfectly straight teeth in the cheesiest grin.

"Ben, that's better!" He's either been practicing or just better under pressure. "Do the lady with the fur. Do her next."

This is when our server returns with hot rolls and our salads.

"Excuse me," I say to the stick-thin guy with a Freddie Mercury mustache. What a bad time for him to show up. When he walks away, Ben continues playing my ridiculous game.

"She's easy. She's wondering if she can still make brunch with Kiki and Trixy after her ass bleaching on Tuesday." He slaps his leg. Apparently that even surprised him. He can't help but cough his laughter into submission. Sweat beads on his forehead as he takes a sip of his wine.

"Yeah, that's it. See? It's fun." He makes me laugh, too. I'm aware of how juvenile it is. I know it's not nice to make fun of other people, but they'll never know and it's all just pretend. It makes me happy that he's playing along. And that he's kicking major fictional ass.

It makes me wonder if—or when—I go completely blind if he'll play the game for me. So I ask, following our trip rules.

"Ben, promise you'll play this when I can't see them anymore? You'll do it for me. Won't you?" I'm not trying to be sappy or darken the mood, but it would make me feel better to know.

He's the one who called himself my boyfriend.

"I'll do it. I promise." The green in his eyes dances. "I like you better outside of New York."

"That's sweet," I banter back sarcastically. "Any particular reason?"

"I don't know. You've just been different since we left. Different, but familiar. Just don't stop when we get back."

We shake on our deal. He'll give me random made-up play-by-plays of perfect strangers and I'll keep running my mouth. That's a win.

Ben and I eat the best steaks on this side of the world. The portions are just right. I'm utterly satisfied and not too full to get my dance on with my new boyfriend.

"Do you want to dance, Tatum?" My eyes keep drifting to the

dance floor that further fills with each new song the band performs. "You keep looking. Come on."

Together, we claim a place by the stage, and just like before, we melt into one solid being. Ben leads like he's been professionally trained.

"You're a great dancer," I say, complimenting him.

"My mother was a dancer. She taught me." He doesn't speak much of his parents, usually telling stories about his grandparents or his friend Keith. I think I would like all of them. Hungry for more information, I let him continue. "Her and my father used to dance all the time when I was a kid."

"That's nice. My parents danced a lot too, only they just stood there shaking their shoulders without moving their feet. You can't really choreograph moves to a Grateful Dead album."

He huffs, chortling. "They really are hippies, aren't they?"

My head nods a big yes. "Pot and all. They don't look as hippie-like in their older age as they did when we were kids, but you'll be able to tell. My mom's hair has never been colored and it's platinum silver. She's really pretty, and her skin looks better than mine. My dad had a beard the last time I saw him. He has glasses now, so that helps make him look more normal I think. You'll change your mind when you hear him talk though. It's a wonder that Cooper and I don't call everyone 'man' and 'dude' because he does."

"My parents smoked pot, too. I think." This is news. I always thought that we were the only kids with pothead parents.

"They did? I'm a little shocked," I confess.

"Not a lot, but I think they did every once in a while." He squints, remembering.

"Huh? That's a weird thing to have in common."

"It's kinda how I knew about the job," he says and stops there.

A revelation.

I try to keep my cool. He's about to let me know how he knew about the job opening. I've been dying to know for so long, but now I realize that it really doesn't matter. I hardly care anymore.

Still, curiosity blooms within me. "Oh? How's that?"

"I know someone who said that you had some sight issues and might be needing some help. And I have experience with that. Both my mother and father are blind."

"Both of them?" I stomp my feet and halt our dance. My hands grasp his biceps for balance. I look into his eyes. "Why didn't you say anything?"

"I thought it would make you mad. I don't know. I didn't think you'd like it. I didn't want you to close me off."

Ouch. He's probably right though. There is worry and insecurity in his eyes. He kisses my head tenderly, holding me tighter as we speak quietly face to face.

"Wow. Is that why you spent so much time with your grandparents?" I'm stunned. I knew that there had to be a reason that he always spoke of them going places and doing things that typically parents would do with their kids, but I never thought it would be this. I bet they did smoke pot.

"Yeah. My parents did what they could, or what they thought they could, but my Moo...grandma and grandpa did a lot," he explains quietly, setting us into motion again.

"That must have been an interesting house to grow up in. How did they manage? You said you have a brother right? Where was he?" I'm helpless to stop myself from firing so many questions.

"He was older and off to college by the time I was seven or eight. So he visited, but it was just me and them for the most part when I was a teenager."

"How are they doing now? Do they still live where you grew up?" On one hand, I'd like to meet them, but on the other hand, it sounds a little daunting.

"Yeah. Same house, in fact. My dad says that he can't learn his way around anywhere else now. They do pretty great actually." He kisses my head again, like he's trying to kiss away my rampant thoughts.

"I didn't see that coming." My body finally relaxes back into our rhythm. I lay my head on his shoulder and let him lead me around a little longer. "That's how you know so much about blind shit." I slap him on the arm.

"Blind shit. You're such a lady."

We dance for hours, and even though I have a whole new list of things I want to discover about Ben, we've made progress. He is trying just as hard as I am to build something lasting.

We're tired when we return to the room, and we lie facing each other, talking about the last few days and how much we are looking forward to the Keys.

Before falling asleep, I thank him for telling me about his parents. Something about the fact that two blind people had a good life makes me feel so much better and, I don't know...optimistic. Just knowing that some kind of normal will be possible if my sight leaves me in the dark is reassuring.

For the first time, I believe that Ben really can help me—and that I want him to.

CHAPTER
Twenty-Eight

SEX ON A DESERTED ISLAND is everything I imagined it would be. Sure, Ben and I aren't completely alone here, but it's easy to pretend.

The water is clear blue and the sand is powdery and white. I'm with a man who calls himself my boyfriend. Anywhere would look better with that knowledge, but as it happens, we are in paradise.

The bungalow Ben rents for us to stay in for the week is phenomenal. It's not a grand palace or anything like that. It is cozy and comfortable. We have a golf cart we can ride anywhere on—respectfully—and a few times, we pack a cooler and go exploring the trails that link the other cabins to ours. We never see any other residents though.

It's as if we're totally secluded in a real-life Jason Mraz video.

The little house has two bedrooms, a master suite on one side, and a smaller guest suite on the other. Even the rooms are far apart. The kitchen is economical and smaller than either of our own, but the refrigerator was stocked when we arrived, and we can call the main house for anything. Even full meals, if we want.

My favorite part of the house is the open veranda. The glass wall that faces the ocean opens up completely, giving the living room and the veranda a one-large-room feel. I love it.

We spent our first night sleeping on the queen-sized bed swing that hangs from the ceiling outside. Even though I know creepy crawly things are out there, I'm not nearly as scared of them in this postcard-like hideout. It's just too beautiful a place for evil to hide.

We sunbathe—both topless. Ben's skin turned dark brown the second his shirt came off and mine caught up a few cautious days later. He hasn't shaved since our last night in Seattle, so he's sporting a rustic almost-beard. I don't know if it's the sun that brings out the colors, but it is a lot redder than his dark blond hair.

We are drinking our weight in Corona. And we quickly grew tired of cutting up lime after lime, quitting on the beer garnish altogether by night two.

"We're on chapter five," Ben says as he looks for our last spot in the book he started reading to me the day before. "What do you remember before you took your second nap yesterday?" He pokes at me and I pretend like I'm going to roll away. He overpowers me and rolls me back, pulling me onto his stomach.

"Maybe you should just start over. You put me to sleep." His bare chest is irresistible and I kiss every place I can reach, lowering myself farther and farther down his body until I reach his swimming trunks.

Ben opens his book again and sets it on his chest, flipping the pages to find his spot. "Yeah, right here. Are you asleep yet?" He laughs at his own joke before I can. "Should I read out loud? I wouldn't want to wake you." His belly bounces with the laugh he gives himself. He's killing me.

"If you think now is the best time to read, do not let me stop you."

I kiss his hipbone and trail my tongue along the waistband of his shorts, stopping at the single button in the middle. I bite to release it and pull his zipper down with my teeth. I know what I'm doing to him because I feel a strong throb under my chin as I look up to see that his face is entirely hidden by the novel he's reading out loud—poorly.

I pull his shorts off with some help from him. That is, he lifts his ass off the mattress when the time is right. "Are you paying attention down there? This is getting good," he tries to say steadily but fails as he smoothes a hand through my hair.

I grab him with alternating hands, one always stroking up him. "Not interested. I'm busy. It's getting pretty good down here, too." Then, without warning him, I suck one of his balls into my mouth as carefully as I can and make a little humming sound with the back of my throat.

I hear, "Oh," and a hardback novel being shut and discarded to the side table.

His hands move to brush back the hair that falls haphazardly into my face on either side. I let the ball loose and lick him from base to tip, our eyes meeting around his now fully erect cock. I trace the vein that I've come to know very well. It laces up the bottom and wraps around to the left in a zigzag.

I open my mouth as wide as it goes and begin my slow descent on him. I take him all the way, feeling him tense and squirm with pleasure at the same time.

I seat and reseat him deep in my throat and lavish him with my mouth until I can tell he isn't going to last, his stomach muscles quivering with every swirl of my tongue. I bring my mouth off of him for only a second to lick my hand, making it wet enough for it to slip and slide over him with ease. While I work my hand and mouth on him, he makes the most erotic of groans and pants that are music to my ears.

"Oh, oh, baby. Tatum, I'm going to come. Ahh…" He stills one hand in my hair and the other one stretches above his head, gripping the rope that suspends the swinging bed we're lying on. His head goes back and he's lost.

He moves my head with his hand—not forcefully, but intensely enough that it's turning me on. It would be easy to slip a finger down my already naked body and lessen the desire I'm feeling, but instead I just stay the course. His body is so deserving of my rapt attention.

Five fingers thread through my blond hair and grip it at the nape of my neck as Ben's lean hips flex into me one last time. I hear the air leave his lungs when he fills my mouth with his hot come. I don't hesitate for a second to swallow and keep sucking until he gives me every last drop.

After a few minutes, Ben looks down, retracting his chin into his neck, and the position shapes his mouth into a pleased frown. He has thoroughly satisfied avocado-colored eyes.

"Get up here." He reaches for me. "You're mouth is criminal." I lay my head in the crook of his arm and he laces our fingers together, bringing them to his mouth for a kiss. Then he kisses my hair over and over. "You really do like books, you kinky little sprite."

"I told you. I have a weakness for a man and his book. Now, if your sight was worse—not that I'd wish it were—we could add some glasses to that pretty face of yours and blow the roof off of this motherfucker."

He shouts a laugh and kicks one leg up. "You're so eloquent," he says like he's serious and tickles my side.

We sleep outside that afternoon until past sunset. I wake when I feel a warm mouth on my breast. Then it's replaced with cool air. Tilting my head, I peer down to see. Sitting up while leaning over my body with one strong arm, he's playing with me.

I continue to watch his expression as he alternates between my breasts. His face exudes both wonder and entertainment. He has educated moves—first a wet lick and then a soft stream of air, working my nipples in unison.

"Whatcha doing down there, Benny?" I ask merrily.

An easy smile spreads across his lazy, tan face. The darker color of his skin makes his eyes infinitely brighter and so striking.

"Wasting time. Watching you. Being creepy. Take your pick," he answers idling between his teases.

"I'm hungry." Unashamed of my nakedness—since we've been mostly naked for two days—I stretch and move to sit up on my elbows.

"Me too. What are you going to cook for us, woman?" He

places a final kiss smack dab in the center of my cleavage.

"Woman? Nice touch." I push at him playfully. "I don't know. I'm not very good. How hungry are you?"

"Well, with what I want to do to you later, I'd say I'm going to need some sustenance. What can you cook?" He props himself on one elbow and looks at me curiously.

He almost appears hopeful, the poor guy. His expression reads that he still thinks that I've got at least one trick up my sleeve, and I'm about to break it to him that I don't.

If you want something microwaved, I'm your girl. If you need coffee, toast, ice cream, chips and salsa—from a jar—I am who you're looking for.

Looking at Ben right now, I can see overestimated expectations. It's time to let him down easy.

"I really can't cook. Like at all. Anything," I say disappointedly.

"Sure you can. You're just busy is all. When you have time and are hungry, what do you make? Like, what's your jam?"

"My *jam* is calling for Mexican or Chinese. I also am experienced with the 'let's have ice cream for dinner all week' *jam*. Seriously."

"Let's get you a jam then." He's up and pulling me with him. "What sounds good?" He's in the kitchen and opening all of the cabinets and the refrigerator in a flash.

"What is there?" I can see all of their contents, but my brain doesn't do quick meal assemblies. I don't work like that.

"What meat do you want?" He's standing between the stainless-steel doors of the side-by-side refrigerator, looking through its contents.

"Chicken."

"Yeah. Chicken." He searches for a moment. With triumph, he holds up a package of chicken breasts, victoriously proclaiming, "Got it!" Already I'm feeling better about this. He's found the meat. Now he can cook it.

But first. "Excuse me, Chef Boyardee? Do you plan on cooking in the buff? That seems a bit unsanitary. Bacteria and all. Want your shorts?" Regrettably, I think that I really shouldn't have said anything. I could watch him shuffle around in the kitchen naked every day for the rest of my life.

My concern lies in the singular thought that something tragic could happen to, well, his penis. I'm not much of a balls girl, so a mishap to them would be acutely unfortunate. But let's be very clear. It would be a crime against humanity to put his glorious penis in harm's way.

I won't stand for that kind of irresponsibility.

"Go put a shirt on and grab me those shorts," he bosses. Then he winks at me when I check his tone with my pulled face.

I look for probably thirty seconds before I locate the shorts on the floor next to the swing. You would think that since I put them there I'd be able to remember their whereabouts.

I didn't.

It is also rude to send a blind girl to find her sexy companion's pants. That feels a little like adding insult to injury.

He jumps into them, rights the zipper and button efficiently, and then assesses me. "No pants for you. From here on out, only my dirty t-shirts." He plants a quick peck on my neck before side-stepping me on the way to the sink. "Come here. Wash up."

I appraise them, thinking that I've done a myriad of things with these hands today and a good wash is probably warranted. I move next to him, sliding my hands into his soapy ones. His fingers move in and out of mine. He washes each of my fingers with a pair of his own, rubbing suds front and back. His large fingers clean my smaller ones surfacing a plume of affection within me.

I kiss his shoulder.

We rinse, and Ben rummages around, finding tools, pots, and pans. He hands me each one—for me to do what with, I don't have a clue.

"What vegetables?"

"I'd love a Caprese salad."

"Perfect."

He directs me and I participate, a willing student. As I listen to him instruct me step by step through each process, his voice trenches a permanent groove in my mind. His low tones and inflections wash over me and I listen with wide-open ears.

He tells me to smell everything and to watch the timer for the chicken while cutting up basil and tomatoes. In the end, it was so easy that I probably could have done it without much help.

I suppose just because you've never done something doesn't mean you should equate yourself to being bad at it. Or maybe he is just a good teacher.

He washes the dishes and I dry them, working in tandem, chatting about random things. I tell him about my matchmaking with little Devon and Cynthia. That earns a most delicious kiss as he says, "You are a romantic."

We take a walk along the beach and draw dirty stick people in the moonlit sand. Mine are the best because of the generous attention to detail I have when it comes to linear lovers.

We don't have our phones with us. No pictures are taken, but I won't soon forget the sight. At least I pray that these memories are more permanent than their likenesses, not fading out of my mind the same way the waves wash our pornographic scratches from the sand.

The next few days we spend actively doing things. Funny thing. Seeing through snorkeling goggles for a regular person is a lot like RP. It's not quite as hindering, but Ben finds it interesting that it is so similar when I tell him.

I watch him observing around us to see what he is missing, waving his hands out to his sides, testing how far he has to move them to see them when looking straight ahead.

He doesn't say a word about it. What would he have to say anyway? *This is frustrating? This isn't that bad?* Nothing would be the right thing, so I appreciate his unspoken opinions.

We jet around a cove with one of the island tenants on a small boat. Ben and I explore all the colorful fish and the shallow ocean bottom for hours, occasionally coming up and telling each other what we see and asking if the other noticed the same. We play in the water like children fascinated by everything around us.

"Ben, I have to pee," I say, bobbing next to him in the water.

"So go," he tells me, like it's the most natural thing in the world.

"For real? You'll see it. Gross." I look through the clear water and know just how obvious it will be.

"Just swim around and pee." The words he's saying sound so weird, but he doesn't look like he's kidding.

"It seems rude. Those fish live here." It just doesn't sit well with me, having spent hours admiring their beautiful habitat and then pissing all over it on my way out.

He confides quietly with one hand flanking his mouth like he's telling a secret, "I did it. I could do it again." He is kidding me. His smile is stubbornly trying to fight its way out as he squints and acts like he's concentrating. "Ahhhh…" he teases.

To hell with it. I take advantage of the diversion he's making and pee.

At first, it feels so wrong, and then it is incredible. I really had to go.

After we're back inside the boat, Ben says to Miguel, our guide, "Ms. Elliot went to the restroom in the water."

What a tattletale!

"I… Hey… I didn't know," I stutter through clenched teeth to the handsome asshole I am sleeping with. "You. Did. Too."

"Ha-haa!" Miguel hollers. "First timer!" When I face the tan Latin man steering us back to shore, he only winks and continues to laugh and shake his head.

"Mr. Harris, you're a dick."

"It's Benny."

I can't see his eyes through the mirrored aviators he's wearing, but I can see every white tooth in his smart-ass grin.

———•———

Our last night, so far, is bittersweet. We build a camp down by the water and have a fireside picnic. We eat fruit, which we never seem to grow tired of and mysteriously never run out of. We drink our last vacation Coronas and talk about all the things we've done over the last few weeks.

We take turns watching the stars while we roll around naked on the blanket, telling each other how good it feels as we worship each other's bodies.

I think we accidentally made love. I hate that term, but I don't know what else to call it. My body thanked him in every way that my words can't yet. My heart sought alternative means of communication to tell him just how much I am already his.

Curled up next to him while watching the fire, I ask, "What happens tomorrow when we go back to real life, Ben?" I want him to say the right thing, but I don't know what it is.

"What do you want to happen, baby?" He answers my question with his own and tightens his grip around my body like he's trying to attach me to him.

"I like this."

"And?"

"And," I sigh, trying to calm my nerves enough to speak the truth, "I'm nervous."

Ben puts his lips on my neck and talks with his mouth on my skin. "I think we just play it by ear. Tomorrow we go back to real life, but you'll be you. I'll still be me. We can still be us." I pray that the hope in his voice is right.

"What about your job? I can't pay you to do things for me. It doesn't feel right. It would feel like I'm paying you to be with me."

This time, he thinks a little longer before answering. "You don't have to pay me." What a simple solution.

"I have to pay you. It's your job."

"I don't need the money and I like helping you. Call it pro bo-no."

"Ben," I cry, even too whiny for my own liking. "I'm serious. This is a big deal. Should I start looking for another PA?" My voice rises right along with my anxiety.

"Hey, cool it. This is what we can do. Everything stays the same. I'll keep working. You can pay me or not pay me. I don't care. See how it goes. If it gets weird, we'll deal with it. Then, after your brother's wedding, I'll help you find a new assistant. How about that? We won't borrow trouble." He pets my hair and runs his hands up and down my arms.

"Okay. We won't borrow trouble. I like that. I'm paying you. Just tell me if it gets weird for you, too. Okay?" Really, I just don't want him feeling obligated.

That thought alone makes me cringe.

Minutes go by, and I think we're both in deep thought. I roll around to face him, needing to look at his face, when he quietly confesses, "I need you too, Tatum."

Those are the magic words. I don't know if I'll be able to make him happy, but I have to try. I know he's being honest.

"Thank you, Benny."

CHAPTER
Twenty-Nine

HOW LONG CAN the vacation blues last? I know I'm being a big baby, but I miss our time on the trip. Being with him constantly for that amount of time only made it so hard to let him go home when we returned.

We arrived in the city on a late flight, and instead of Ben going home, he stayed at my place. He was tired and so was I. I knew that, no matter what I said, he was going to see me home and help me upstairs with my luggage anyway.

We fell into my bed at about three in the morning and slept on top of the covers with all of our clothes on, four jean-covered legs knotting into a pathetic pile of flesh and denim on my welcoming mattress. Still not sure how we were going to find our footing in all of this, I fell asleep believing I would wake up and everything would be the same.

For the most part, it is.

The days when Ben worked for me gradually returned to almost normal. But since I wasn't working, he sort of just helped me as opposed to doing everything for me. We ran my errands together, did my shopping, and rescheduled all of the appointments and obligations I'd missed on our impromptu getaway.

Cooper was already out of town at a conference when we returned and Winnie left a few days later to Los Angeles to shoot a small part she had in an indie film written by one of our friends. Normally, I would have tagged along with her, visiting with old coworkers who had been sucked into California. Winnie took Tilly instead, which worked out great for her. Tilly is much more helpful than I could ever pretend to be.

It is awkward, at first, to wear our relationship around people who know Ben as my assistant. We ran into Wes at lunch one day and he just laughed, kissing me on the cheek when he left, saying, "You never fucking listen to me." Then, turning to Ben, he shook his hand and warned him, "Watch out for her. She's special."

Ben's only reply was that he wouldn't take his eyes off me. Then he squeezed my hand. Ben must have had the vacation blues, too.

Most days he spends hanging out with me, reading while I edit or write the few projects I'm committed to. He seems more and more distracted though.

The night I work up enough courage to ask him if this is working all right for him, I find him in my bed, naked, reading, and wearing thick, black lensless frames.

"What have we here?" I say, loving his timing. "My boyfriend will be furious if he knows you've tried to seduce me."

"I'm sure he will be," he answers nonchalantly, slowly licking his page-flipping finger and turning the ivory paper. Sexy bastard.

"I'll never leave him for you."

To this, he raises his questioning eyes above the dark frames to meet my gaze. "Never?"

"I don't expect so. He's too good in bed." I try to keep the joke out of my voice, and for the most part I succeed, choosing to cough instead of laugh.

"What if I'm better? How would you know unless we..." he trails off, laying the vintage hardback parted across his chest and running his hand down to his already hard cock.

He's fighting dirty.

I'm barely fighting at all.

He grips himself and tugs a little more forcefully than I would, the pressure of his thumb across the top of his shaft drawing the skin taut and towards the tip. My wittiness escapes me and I stare.

My legs squeeze together and I feel a familiar buzz amplifying and spreading over me. To be a participant or a bystander? It's so conflicting. I want to both touch him and stay away, to see how far he'll take this bad boy scenario.

"You need to know all of your options, and lucky for me, I'm one of them. How about you come here?" He nods for me to move closer with a sinful lick of his lips.

My slow steps quicken as I watch his serious face break into a quick smile and a wink, like he's telling me to play along. Then it resumes the obnoxious lover-man façade.

"I'll come over there, but I assure you—you'll be no Ben Harris." Instantly, his face drops and he flinches. He's a good little actor. I'm still playing reluctant, but I buy his mock hurt and cushion my jab with, "But he's not here, so you'll do."

I climb over to him, walking on my knees across the white comforter, and stop before reaching him. Ready for him to do his worst in the name of persuasion.

He's quickly up on his own bent legs, jostling me and tipping my balance on the ultra plush surface of my king-sized bed. Ben should have studied drama. His features are so determined that it's hard to not feel the powerful force of his steely appraisal.

While we're facing one another, one massive hand wraps around my neck and crushes my lips to his, his glasses crooking when our faces collide. His other hand latches on to my ass, palming my cheek and shaking it. He's never been like this with me.

"Tatum," he growls. "I'm going to fuck that name right out of your pretty little head."

My spine stiffens. Where is gentle Ben? Ha. Gentle Ben. I just thought of that. It doesn't matter though, because he isn't in my bed with me right now. I adore his usual playful worship of my body, but there is something in his tone that sinks into the marrow of my bones.

Fisting a handful of my hair, he resolutely tilts my head back far enough that I'm looking upside down at our image in the mirror behind us. He nips, licks, and bites his way around my neck and ears.

"I want you so fucking bad," he rages.

I can't tell if we are playing anymore, but he's acting so unlike himself that I just go with the notion that we are in a scene of sorts. "I want Ben Harris," I protest, finding just how wrapped up I, too, am in this game.

"God dammit, Tatum. Stop saying that." He keeps telling me to stop, but when I don't, he assaults my flesh with his mouth more vigorously.

I love it.

I'm helpless to end it and fuel the fire by insisting that I only want Ben Harris.

He's possessed. He rips at my shirt and robs me of my clothes, head strong and determined. I stay rooted to the spot on my bed, still on my knees before him.

I wink. He doesn't break character.

Confusion flashes through me. Did we stop playing?

"Benny?" I question in a whimper. I see a softening inside him after a long second, but his eyes stay in the trance I thought was fabricated by our game.

Sometimes you just have to fuck about it when there is nothing to say. Something inside of him is trying to claw out and I'll be his willing vehicle to unleash his fiery turmoil. I want to be this for him.

There is only one small tipoff that he's hesitant to proceed after I broke the moment, but I know he still wants it like this.

"Fuck me." The swear doesn't sound as confident as it should have, but I get my message across. "I want it. Fast and hard, Benny."

He moves his warm hand from under my ass to behind my knee, bringing it to wrap around his hip. Lifting me up so that my weight is on his leg, he leaves the other to dangle over the bed. He guides it to slide between his legs, aligning my wetness with his groin.

My hands clutch each other around his neck, and his stern warning of, "Hold on to me," isn't to be taken lightly. As he slides into me in a rush—fast and hard—I realize this angle comes with a promise of him deeper within me than he's been before. He plunges as far inside as possible, the position stretching my limits and bordering two famous friends, pleasure and pain.

I gasp from the sudden fullness.

"Can you take it, baby?" he asks as he stays fully immersed inside me, rocking forward only a little, testing my tolerance.

I don't know if I can, but I'll be damned if I'm not going to try. "I want all of it. Give me more," leaves my lips. I hope my mouth didn't just sign a check that my body can't cash.

His embrace gathers my weight in his arms, withdrawing from me just shy of entirely and coming back at me with a force I've never received. He pounds into me at a steady cadence and rhythmically drives my desire higher until I'm grinding my clitoris against his pelvic bone, the friction alerting every nerve in my being.

Every time I get close, he holds us still, teasing my persistent orgasm, ordering me to wait. "Don't worry, baby. You're going to come. Just not yet." Massaging my soaked core with his cock, he continues to roll his hips with punishing pressure, sending fire through my veins.

"I trust you, but I'm so close. Please," I beg. Losing all pride and shame, I give him all my control with the guarantee that he will deliver what I am so desperate for. "I'm yours. Please."

"Relax, baby. Do you feel this?" He rocks harder against me. "This is me. You're feeling *me*, Tatum. You can forget my name as long as you remember this. Remember how this love feels."

Love.

Without the strength to dissect his words, I focus only on the lust-fueled noise in my head. My need for release and our pleasure furiously readies every cell in my body to explode upon reaching zero on this backwards-ticking clock.

I pant my slow response. "Yes. I feel you. I feel you. Please." I hear my own desperation thick in my voice.

Keeping our bodies joined as they are, he lowers my back to the bed. He leans forward with me, straddling my leg and sinking to that deepest spot once again.

His index finger finds my clit and applies fast bursts of pressure until my head rolls side to side as my orgasm fights its way out.

I can't make a sound.

My mouth hangs open.

My eyes screw shut and I hold my breath.

I freeze as pure, unadulterated pleasure rockets through my whole body in waves. I hear Ben roar his release into the bed just seconds after mine blooms and feel him push into me like he's trying to climb inside.

He breaks apart from me rather too soon and lies spread out on my bed beside me, sweaty and panting.

"That was intense," I finally say to break the ice.

He rolls to me, looking me over, gauging my condition. "My God. Tatum, are you okay? I didn't mean to be so rough. I sort of lost myself there for a minute." If his concern alone could prevent the soreness that my vagina is guaranteed to feel tomorrow, then I'd mount him again right now.

"I'm okay, but the lady bits may think otherwise come tomorrow," I chuckle and turn to face him too. "Are you okay?" I have to know. I'm cool with role-playing and whatever, but I have a nagging feeling that there was a little bit of truth hidden in his performance. I just don't know what part.

He props his flushed face up on one hand to give me his full attention. "Yeah, why?"

"You just seemed angry or something. You're not angry though, are you? That was all just part of the whole fantasy. Wasn't it?" My inner voice screams to stop it at that.

"I'm not angry with you. Don't think that." He pulls me close and breathes a ragged breath in my hair. "I just have some things that I have to work out and they were on my mind. Baby, I won't ever be rough with you because I'm angry." He further wraps me up, drawing my legs in close. "I was in the moment and I got carried away."

I speak into his neck. "I believe you. It's just there's something inside me says that you're not telling me everything." I kiss him, hoping my honest words don't sting. "I'm here for you, Ben. You say you want all of me, but I want all of you too."

He waits an eternity to answer, which basically solidifies my theory that there is something. I don't know if it even has anything to do with us. I just don't know.

I find his hand and bring it between us up to my lips, raining kisses on it. Then I hug it close to my heart.

"You don't know what hearing that feels like, baby. It's the most precious gift I've ever received. I just need a little time. Besides, you know all the real parts."

I guess that has to be enough. For now.

CHAPTER
Thirty

"I BET YOU'RE EXHAUSTED, Molly," I say sympathetically when I call Winnie's sister to finalize everything for the bachelorette party that we're preparing for. Initially, she was going to orchestrate the whole night, but being majorly pregnant isn't really conducive to planning trips to the strip club and going to porn shops to buy dick supplies. So I've taken some of the weight off her shoulders and offered to do some of those things.

"I am. You know, I didn't think it would be this much work just carrying around a baby, but holy shit! It is. September cannot come soon enough." She confides in me that, since seeing her at the shower, she's gained another ten pounds. She claims that they all landed in her ass and that we'll have to make the aisle at the wedding a foot wider so that her butt can fit down it.

"Well, I've got all of this stuff under control. Don't worry about it," I reassure her.

"How is everything going with you? Your brother said you're dating your assistant. If you don't mind me asking, how in the hell does that work?" That's a good question. Sometimes it works like a dream and, like as of lately, sometimes it feels weird.

I glaze over the question. "It's working for us right now. We've talked and I'll probably get a new PA after the wedding."

"The wedding? Shit, Tatum, are you guys getting married!?"

What the... "Hell no! Winnie and Cooper's wedding, Molly! Shit. We just started dating a few weeks ago. Jesus. Who do you think I am?" my voice screeches.

"Right, sorry. Baby brain. Of course. It's going good though, I hope?" Molly and I have always gotten along. She's a more traditional version of Winnie. So I loved her immediately, but she could be so daft at times.

"We have a great time together." And when it isn't awkward because he's working for me and I'm not piecing parts of Ben's puzzle together, I've never been happier. But all that goes without saying.

"Good. Is he going with the guys to the bachelor party then?"

"He is. Cooper invited him when they were over for dinner a few nights ago. They get along really well. A lot better than..." And I shut that whole line of conversation down, continuing with, "Well, they get along. It's actually pretty funny watching them together. They're both such nerds." We laugh because it's true.

After talking with her and making a list, I make a few calls and sort out all the things she thought would be so stressful. It isn't like I have anything better to do.

I've rented a small theater, hired a bunch of male strippers, and planned for a bar service. It's better than going to three or four different places hoping for a good time. I don't like those odds. Not when I can plan a sure thing.

Who knew there are places you can call for this type of occasion and order a man in every flavor to come dance naked for you?

I love America.

When the day of the party arrives, Ben has Cooper pick him up at my place when Cooper drops Winnie off around two. They're going golfing and meeting up with the guys at the course before heading to some sleazy titty bar.

Winnie and I finalize some details for their big day, having spare time before Ray comes to get us.

With Ben off with Cooper, I finally have a little bit of time alone with my best friend. I really want to know what she thinks of the whole me-and-Ben thing. She'll be supportive regardless, but

I'm curious to know her take on it.

"Tatum, he's in love with you. I think you're in love with him. Don't worry about any of that other shit," she says flatly without any cushioning or fluff while rolling her eyes.

"But, Winnie, he's not telling me something. Isn't that, like, a huge red flag? I mean, he's perfect. He's attentive and sweet. He's funny and he keeps me on my toes. He's hot as fuck and eats pussy like it's the Last Supper, but I just have this feeling that, whatever it is, he isn't telling me because it's bad." Sounding like I've sucked a tank of helium, I finish, "What if it's bad, Winnie? What will I do?"

"That's your call, Tate. Is he worth it? Because if he is and you trust him, just let it go. It doesn't matter."

"You're right. I'm shit at this relationship shit. Shit." I face-palm myself. Obviously I'm overthinking everything.

Stress swearing is a legitimate condition. Just ask Dr. Meade. Last time I was in his office and he told me—again—that my condition was still progressing, I believe I said, "Well isn't that just fucking great. Fuck." It's hard for people to get used to it, but Winnie has heard way worse from me.

She tries to comfort my crazy mind by saying, "You'll get it. Just loosen up. Quit worrying about every little thing that could go wrong. For real. Just enjoy it." She kicks me under the table. "And since I'm not allowed to divulge any naughty talk about your glorious brother, I'll just say congrats on the oral. You deserve it."

We laugh and begin our night with a little pot that big Devon gifted her. Neither of us smokes anymore, but one summer between junior and senior year of college, we smoked enough weed to last us a lifetime.

We stand on my balcony puffing and passing the joint back and forth since we still have a lot of time before the party.

I say, holding my inhale, "This was a good idea." Then I exhale. Funny, you always have something to say with lungs full of smoke.

"Yeah." She sucks in. "Why'd we ever stop?"

It wasn't the jobs. Most everyone at my first job was blazed up for every one of their forty hours a week. "I don't know. Maybe the weed made us too lazy to find more weed," I answer as honestly as I can.

"Can you get marijuana for your sight?"

Why haven't I thought about that? "I don't know. I'll ask Dr. Meade next time I see him."

"Tell him... Tell him I need some too." She snorts and laughs her ass off.

"Yeah, I'll be all over that." I think about what that conversation would sound like and then laugh and laugh. He might go for it. If it could help. Then again, he probably would have already mentioned it. My dope hopes disappear.

I still plan on asking though. The squeaky wheel gets the grease, right?

Winnie and I get high. So high.

When Ray picks us up, I think he can smell it, because he reminds us that we're not allowed to smoke in the car. Not that we would, but I feel a little juvenile when I hear him say it. It's like being caught by your dad, only my dad would have just gotten in line for a hit.

The party is wonderful. Winnie is so greasy from the oily men rubbing on her all night. We do shots and dance with the entertainment. Molly even gets a lap dance, and she laughs so hard she pees. A few times actually.

The only men who are invited are Neil and Luis. For some reason, I thought that the big, beefy strippers would be put off by men being there, but they just play right along. Honestly, I think that Neil is more uncomfortable than they are. Luis hijacks more than one routine, getting up and trying to jump into their choreography without getting caught.

It's fabulous.

When I get home, I call Ben to tell him all about it. He doesn't answer, so I leave a message.

"I'm sure you're still out with my brother throwing dollars at boobies, but I just wanted to call and tell you I had a fun night." I stop, thinking about what else I want to say.

It's so easy to talk to voicemail sometimes. There's no inter-rupting. There aren't any sighs or buts. Only you.

"And I wanted to let you know that I got home. I missed you tonight. I'll talk to you tomorrow." I still don't hang up, my throat stuck on something else, feeling a little sad that he isn't here.

Then my cell lights up. I end his call and see a text from Cooper.

Cooper: You're boy is fun, but drunk. He's staying at my place.

Me: Thanks. Love you.

I'm glad that Cooper and Ben are getting along so well, but I didn't expect Ben to be the drunk one and Cooper to be taking care of him. At least not tonight.

"Tate, is it serious with Ben?" Cooper asks. He brought me breakfast and drops off the Jeep keys Ben left at their place this morning.

"I don't know," I answer honestly. "Why does everyone keep bringing this shit up? If you have something to say, then say it."

"Bitch," he says around a mouth of jelly doughnut. Weird how siblings get away with name-calling so easily. We've actually kind of mastered it over the years. He's called me a bitch so many times that it's almost my second name. He's my brother though. He loves me. He loves me enough to deserve the right to call me a bitch when I'm being one.

Them's the rules.

"Dick."

"Okay. Here it is." He wipes his mouth and looks me straight in the face. "I like the guy, Tatum. I do. How much do you like him?"

I must act like a real piece of work. Everyone insists that he's into me and they have no clue how I feel.

Whoa. I'm doing it again.

Was Kurt like this in the beginning? No.

I thought I was doing better. I thought that I'd progressed. Just goes to show you that, just because you think you're doing something, it doesn't mean you are. I guess.

"What are you talking about? I like him. A lot."

"You do? Then why do you seem so mechanical with him around us? I'm just trying to figure out what big brother talk I'm supposed to give you." Fuck. He's not taking it easy on me today.

"I like him. I mean...I care about him. Uhh... Where's my time machine? I want to undo this conversation." I start to pick up the trash to get away from him.

But he follows, turning me back around by the elbow. "So why do you act like that then?"

"You don't see what we're like in private, Cooper! Maybe I'm just not into public petting around my brother. Ever think about that?" I shout.

His face registers my point, but he knows better than to believe it. "It isn't about that. Are you worried about something? Is he good to you? I need something here." What a brother thing to assume.

Lowering my voice, I say, "Cooper, he's so, so, so good to me. He is. Maybe that's my problem. Maybe he's a little too good." I stand there looking down at my feet. "And here it is. I think it's just going to disappear like everything else. Maybe it's easy for me sometimes and almost impossible other times to even look at things, feel things, enjoy things. I might love him, Cooper. But what good does that do him? There are things he doesn't want to tell me, maybe because he doesn't trust me. I wouldn't trust me. I'm flighty and moody. I want him. I want him to leave. I need him. He could do better. Have more." I offer to keep rambling, but Cooper shakes his head indicating that it is enough.

Then I stand up, flinging around until I smack my hand against the counter. My knuckle gets the brunt of it. It's not bleeding, but I stick it in my mouth to better it somehow.

My fist is in the way, but it doesn't stop the rant I'm on. To hell with what Cooper wants to hear. "What if he gets sick of me, taking care of me, helping me? What if I don't have anything to offer him?"

His face is the epitome of compassion. "Love's like that, kid. It's a risky fucker. It's the ultimate best and worst thing." He pulls my smarting finger from my mouth, sets my hand at my side, and continues after some thought. "Only love can scare you this shitless. But would you want it any other way? That's where you're at, Tate. You're in love, but you're still fighting the fear. I hate to tell you, but you'll never win. First, it's a fear of them leaving or finding someone new. Then commitment sets in and washes you with worry for their safety. It doesn't end until the love does. So it's your call. You can end the worry, but you lose him too."

My arms furiously shoot up in the air. "You sell houses! What do you know?"

He grabs my arms again and calmly puts them back at my sides. "I know a lot about you, little sister. And believe it or not, I'm actually a pretty decent dude."

"You are." I hug my brother. "But you're still a dick."

CHAPTER
Thirty-One

A FEW OF US drive up to Martha's Vineyard a few days before the wedding. Winnie wants to oversee the preparation and I sincerely want to help. Since my talk with Cooper, I've been trying to be a little less neurotic—or moronic, is it?—about my relationship.

I'm going out of my way, trying to be affectionate with Ben around other people. Maybe Cooper was right. Maybe Ben needed reassurance just like anyone. I've also been sending him sweet text messages when we're away from each other. Well, my version of sweet.

Me: Send me a dick pic.

Me: I can hardly walk today.

Me: I'm thinking about you. I mean—you in glasses.

Things like that. Tatum's authentic romance. It's an acquired taste.

I think he likes it because he usually will send me a picture. He knows when I won't be able to walk the next day, so he knows that it's probably true. And he is forbidden to take the glasses home. Ever.

I think he might love me, too.

So it's the ride up north that I text him the following:

Me: When are you coming up here again? I already want you with me.

It isn't too long before I receive his reply.

Ben: I like that. I'll see you Friday.

Friday. Shit, it is only Wednesday evening. This is going to take forever.

Ben has become a regular visitor of my bed. He's spent more nights at my place than his own in the past weeks. I even stay there sometimes. It's peculiar being in his space, but I'm doing my best.

He left the bathroom light on for me that first night. So I thanked him generously. With my mouth.

We both slept very well.

It's Wednesday night and I can't sleep at all. Usually a good hotel bed does it for me. Even though it's a full size smaller than my king at home, it seems too big. I thrash restlessly and finally fall asleep watching the Home Shopping Network sometime around three o'clock.

I am not the most fun girl the next morning.

Flowers are arriving and being stored in large walk-in coolers, and the chefs prepare meals for us to taste for the rehearsal and reception. We reorganize the seating charts so many fucking times that I almost cry out of sheer annoyance. Who in the hell sits down at a reception after eating? It is a crock of shit, I tell you.

Sleep doesn't evade me tonight. I had Ben read me a few chapters in the crime novel he was into and I dozed right off, the inflection and steady tone of his voice like my very own sexy lullaby.

I have dreams about my own wedding. That's the most monumental part of the dream anyway. The rest is just some bullshit about Wes starting a game show. Which I will of course email to the Devons for them to recreate for next season.

It's finally Friday, I'm so relieved that I won't have to go much longer without seeing Ben.

What if I'd lost my sight while I was sleeping? That's the newest game I like to play with myself. It's called What Will Still Be Here Tomorrow?

My sight is fleeting, and I race to see and memorize everything lately. This wedding might be the last I watch. That makes me sad, but at the same time, I'm so thankful that I'll get the chance to see it.

The Hippies aren't staying at the same resort we are. Instead, they've opted for a spot at an actual vineyard owned by their friends that isn't too far. Winnie, Cooper, and I meet them when they arrive.

It is a beautiful day. The sun is out, and it's the perfect temperature—not too hot and not too breezy. This area received a lot of rain over the summer, so everything is still lush and colorful even into August.

"There's my girl!" my dad says as he bounds up to me, wearing khaki shorts and a misbuttoned shirt, with wide-open arms. "You look so pretty, Tater." He steps back to appraise me, his hands still on my shoulders. "Your hair is shorter, but it suits you," he says, placing a Dad kiss on my forehead. "And where's this bride?" He spins around, animatedly looking for Winnie.

"Hi, Mr. Elliot," Winnie greets and easily hugs him.

"Yo, I'm retired. It's Pat."

"Okay."

I say, "Hey, Pat. Where's my mom?" since I'm wondering if she's planning on joining us in the lot they've chosen to stay at for the weekend.

"She was sleeping when we pulled in. I just woke her up. She'll be out. Don't worry."

"Hi, Dad." Cooper begins to offer a handshake, and when Dad grimaces, he hugs him instead.

"Hi, son," my dad replies to Cooper before turning back to me. "I thought you were bringing your lover to the wedding, Tatum. Where's he at?"

"My lover? Uh. Gross. Ben, my boyfriend, is driving up later this afternoon. He had to be in Washington for work."

Why did I say that? Why?

Probably because I wanted someone else to ask the questions that I secretly needed the answers to.

Like clockwork, my dad asks, "What kind of work?" That's a good question, and coming from my very liberal father, he's more than curious what my *lover* would be doing there. "I thought the dude worked for you?"

"I think he's a spy on the side, Dad. It's all very mysterious. You don't want him to have to kill me, do you?"

"How exciting." A smile lights his eyes.

"My children!" Mom's silver head pops around the hippie-mobile and she literally skips in her sundress and signature cardigan into Cooper's arms. She kisses him all over the face. "My baby boy is getting married!" He no more than puts her down and she's embracing Winnie. "And to Gwendolyn! I love it. Sweetheart, you look fantastic. Are you excited?"

"Very!" Winnie tells her. They're still holding hands, swinging them in their shared anticipation. "I think everything is ready though. Thanks to Tate. She's helped so much."

"She has? How conventional of her." My mother comes to me, holds my face in her hands, and kisses me on the lips. She always does that. I've always felt weird kissing people on the lips. But as they've always been, my mother's lips are soft, and her smell envelops me. Lemons smell like her, I'm convinced.

"I have. It's been really fun."

"How's your sight, darling?" she says only to me. We don't talk a lot, but since this has been an ongoing thing since my teenage years, she knows that it isn't just magically going to right itself.

"Oh. It's fine. I'm feeling good." I wish I could tell her honestly how I feel, but I can't. I love my mother and my father, but it's always been Cooper who I rely on for anything emotional. It works for us.

They invite us in and we drink iced tea and chat about the events for both tonight and tomorrow. The two most easygoing people on the planet don't refuse any of Winnie's or Cooper's requests, which are few.

Grooms' parents don't really have much to do in a wedding, it turns out. Basically show up and have a good time.

My phone vibrates and it's Ben.

Ben: I'm here. Checking into my room.

Me: Your room? You mean my room?

We planned on sharing a room this weekend, but I don't dwell on it even though I left him a keycard at the front desk and they know who to expect.

Ben: I just went ahead and got one. Where are you?

Me: With The Hippies. Be there soon.

Ben: Room 55C.

I do everything I can to rush through the visit with our parents and get back to the hotel. I guess my urge to leave is noticeable, and Winnie saves me by telling them that she needs to head back to get ready.

Of course, we run into every Tom, Dick, and Harry we know when we get back. Wes is here, and most of our work friends are already occupying the lounge. Their laughter and commotion can be easily heard across the property, I'm sure.

Rehearsal isn't until four, and I have a few precious hours that I want to spend with Ben. Preferably naked—or something like it. I know it's only been a few short days since I last saw him, but I can't get to him fast enough.

His room is on the other side of the complex, not with our block. I navigate the long halls that only seem to get longer the faster I go.

Finally, 55C.

"Room service for Benny," I say through the door after only a light rap of my knuckles on it. I've never felt this much pull to one person in my life.

"I'm waiting for my girlfriend," he yells through the closed door. "Come back later."

"She, um, called. She's not coming. So you can let me in," I sing back in the same melody as he just used.

The door cracks open and only his eyeball shines through the space that the chain lock allows. "You are hot though." He meets me in the doorjamb, smooching my lips between the wood.

"Kiss me," I say, forfeiting the game to purchase a taste of him. I make kissing sounds, sucking the air between my lips.

He finds them with his and smacks one on me then licks them. "Back up, crazy. I'll let you in."

I shoot up. To open the door, he must first close it, and I don't need to be looking like I have a botched lip fill all weekend. My lips are spared, despite his rush to open up.

He opens the door, looking both ways like he's being sneaky. Bracing himself with one arm on the doorway, he urgently grabs me around the waist and pulls me inside.

"That was close. Someone could have seen us."

"I wouldn't care if they did. Come here." I'm hungry for one thing, and it's Ben. I frantically clutch at him like he's a soldier home from the war. My arms undecidedly roam from around his neck to his waist and then to his ass. Over and over.

"Someone missed me?" he asks, backing himself up to a wall and carrying me with him.

"I did miss you. Everyone else kisses like shit." I pepper kisses all over his face and neck.

"Well, stop kissing everyone. Just kiss me." He laughs, wrapping my legs more securely around him and blanketing my spread ass with both hands in support. I damn near eat the man alive.

"You smell so..." My brain fumbles. Adjective. Adjective! "Ben." I hold him tight and slow my assault. "I'm better near you."

"Oh, my sweet baby. I'm better near you too."

I watch as he wets his lips before he claims mine. I'm a closed-eyes kissing girl every time. But not this time. This one I want to see. As he deepens the kiss and moans into me, his brows knit together and he tightens his arms and chest around me. I've never witnessed such an expression.

On mute, his body said, "Mine.".

I close my eyes, deciding to feel it instead of merely watching.

I don't have to see anymore. I wanted to feel instead, and I can.

Maybe he is my lover.

That gross hippie was right. They always are.

It's all too soon that I have to leave for my room to get ready for the rehearsal. We're both sweaty and messed up so good that I don't want to leave. Ben keeps touching me and begging for one more time.

Before I consent, I leave for my own room for a shower and to change.

The rehearsal is limited to just the wedding party and parents. While Winnie goes through details with the officiant, Ben and our parents talk about our trip, and I decide to mess with Cooper a little.

"You know, if you're planning on being a pussy and crying, you might want to do it here. Get it out at rehearsal. You know?"

"You're probably right. Marrying Winnie assures me I'm never, *ever* fucking getting rid of you. Am I?"

We laugh.

He's right though. It will always be me and Winnie no matter what. I'm not too proud to say that they're both getting the very best.

We have an incredible night. My mom and dad chat Ben's ear off, telling him of their travels, and Ben's genuinely interested. He smiles at me every once in a while when he catches me looking at him.

After dinner, we karaoke in the hotel bar. Neil and Wes do "Rocket Man" and Winnie and I sign up for every Bon Jovi song on their list.

We drink and play late into the night.

CHAPTER
Thirty-Two

I WAKE UP THE MORNING of Cooper's wedding tangled in the most beautiful man's arms.

As I roll over to study his face, he stirs and says, "Good morning, baby," before pulling me in closer and trying to go back to sleep for a few more minutes.

"No. Wake up. Let's take a shower. I have to meet Winnie." I find my phone next to the bed and light it up to see the time. "It's already eight. Come on."

"What's in it for me?" His gravelly morning voice tempts me to misbehave. He's just too damn enticing with his disheveled fuck-me hair and his body that begs for my touch.

"I'll let you smack me around."

Ben lifts one eye open to gauge my face. "I'm listening."

"Well, I don't have much time. You're going to have to fuck me fast and har—" Before I have the word "hard" all the way out of my mouth, he has us off the bed and me over his shoulder, on the way to the bathroom.

He smacks my ass while waiting for the water to heat and doesn't set me down until we're in the stall.

"I hope you thought about walking down the aisle later before picking this fight. I'm going to make sure you're thinking about me with every step."

I love this kind of troublemaking. I hope he does fuck me fast and hard.

He soaps us both up quickly, squeezing the soap on his chest and puts two big globs on mine, dividing the gel on each breast. He washes me with one hand and himself with the other. I laugh the whole time.

"Are you going to help or just stand there?" he chuckles and gives me quick kiss, dipping his head under the water. He applies shampoo to our heads. I lift to wash my own and he does the same. "I like the way your boobies sway when you wash your hair," he confesses as he bends down and sucks a nipple into his mouth.

"Thanks. Your dick does that too." I peek at him with one soapy eye closed, but I have to see his face.

He pops back up with a silly grin. "It does?" Ben looks down as he gyrates his hips, swinging it around like a windmill, then rinses his hair. I laugh until my side splits and beg him to do it again.

When his hair is free of soap, he helps rinse mine, moving it around and scrubbing to feel when it's lather-free.

I kiss his wet chest.

"I love you."

Who said that? Shit! It was me.

The rinsing stops and there is no promise of repeat, with either the shampoo or my declaration. I don't know where it came from. I wasn't even thinking. It just fell out.

He doesn't say anything. I reach for the conditioner and squirt myself a handful. He just watches me with the most innocent of expressions. I rub the silky cream through my hair, root to tip, the tile becoming more and more fascinating.

Why did I have to say it like that?

"Ben?" I say just loud enough to hear over the running water. "I'm sorry."

"What? No." He sits down on the marble seat that's built into the wall. He pulls me by the ass to him. He head presses against my stomach. "Don't take it back."

"I wasn't thinking." I run my hand over his hair and over his forehead, looking into confused eyes.

"Did you mean it?"

If ever there was a loaded question. Here I am, having just told him that I love him, then I sloughed it off, and now he's asking if I'm a liar, too. The worst part of all is not knowing what he's thinking. How he feels.

I feel strength come from somewhere. Sometimes you don't get to pick when things happen. Life isn't a script or page we get to read from. Things aren't plotted out start to finish in a neat package. Sometimes your love slips out of your mouth when you're supposed to be having a quickie in the shower.

I choose to worry. I choose the fear. I want all of it. With him.

"Yes. I meant it." And I'm proud of it, too. I love Ben Harris and I want him to love me, too.

He doesn't say it, although I feel that it is there. I taste it in his kisses. No quickie in the shower for us.

Although, we do go back to bed. He worships my body and gently guides me to climax more than once with his talented mouth. Our sex is emotional and passionate. Ben studies me with pure adoration. When we're both coming at the beautiful end, I confess ten or a hundred more times that I love him.

I leave him lying in his bed, telling him once more as I walk out the door, "I love you, Benny."

I'm late getting to Winnie's room. It's a shit-show in there anyway. Luis is giving her a blow-out, and Molly is arguing with their mom about shoes.

Winnie looks stoic and unwavering. She appears to be only one who's calm.

"You look beautiful," I tell her in the mirror. I'm so thrilled that she's going to be my sister and even happier that my brother is getting the most perfect wife.

"So do you," she replies on a sweet smile.

I look at my feet and then I can't hold it in anymore. "I love him, Winnie."

"I know you do." She's not surprised at all. She looks more relieved than anything.

"I told him."

Winnie turns her head, abandoning our reflections to face me. "What did he say?" she asks quietly so no one will pay attention.

"He didn't say anything. And that's okay." It is empowering, the feeling of having everything out there. So much so that I believe and trust his heart, because I know I'm in it. He loves me even without saying it. I don't need his words to justify my own. It makes me stronger.

She watches my posture strengthen, my resolve set. I smile wide, even as an unwanted tear falls down my cheek. It isn't a sad tear—it is one of relief. Of happiness. My world just got bigger.

Winnie stands and embraces me like a real sister would and kisses me on the cheek, whispering in my ear, "I love you. And Ben does too. You're incredible."

When we pull apart, I wipe my tears and say, "I love you too. Let's go become sisters."

It seems that weddings make me a bit sappy.

———— • ————

The flowers are gorgeous. Every color surrounds the garden that Winnie and Cooper chose for the ceremony. Every chair is filled. Colorful hats adorn the female guests in the kindly setting August sun. The two acoustic guitarists play leisurely, both in sunglasses and tuxes—a combination that for some reason always looks so bad ass to me. Faces of friends and family litter the seats, and then it's my turn to walk.

I don't have the sore reminder of Ben cursing my steps, but I do think of him the whole way. He is sitting in the second row behind my parents with our friends from the show. I watched from the lane we were tucked in, sheltering the bride from curious eyes, as he talked and laughed with the people I adore.

When I walk past him, he makes kiss-lips and it distracts me momentarily.

I manage not to trip or fall over anything, and that in itself is a huge success. My brother meets me in the middle, kissing my cheek.

"I love you, Cooper."

"I know. I hear you love everyone," he whispers back to me as I step into my place. My eyes are wide with the realization that Winnie already told him about my profession to Ben. Typical.

Molly trails slowly, probably equally worried about tripping or falling as I am, but for totally different reasons. She looks so pretty, heaving her feet towards the altar with an extra thirty pounds.

Everyone stands for my luminescent friend. Seeing the bride come down the aisle is a frame-worthy moment. While everyone is looking at the bride, I look at my brother. Seeing her walk towards him on her father's arm, my brother laughs and wipes tears from his own eyes.

Winnie does the same.

They are both pussies. Happy-in-love pussies.

I am a pussy too and use the silk handkerchief, which Winnie's mother shoved into all our flowers—just in case.

They promise the usual things and one of their own—to never give up on their love. When they kiss, the crowd howls with delight. The kiss is storybook, but Winnie grabbing Cooper's ass is all them.

We dine outside under a massive tent with all four sides drawn up. They hung three chandeliers inside. The ambient light reflecting off the ceiling emanates a warm, romantic glow.

We eat first and are soon pulled in every direction for pictures. When all the ceremonious tasks are done, I go to Ben. He's with Molly's husband and a few of the other guys they went out with for Cooper's bachelor party.

He's sipping whiskey when I catch his eye. He excuses himself from his group and sets the lowball glass on the bar. He saunters my way, and like two magnets, we run into each other, neither of us stopping when we should.

He holds on to my arms, steadying me from our small collide. "You look so lovely."

"Thank you." I feel a little timid. I guess walking around with my heart on my sleeve can do that. But now I can relax and have fun with him. "I'm ready to dance with you."

"Aren't you worn out yet? You've been going all day." Concern laces in his voice.

"I am, but I'm having fun too." I step up on my toes to lightly kiss his lips. "I want a cocktail and then your ass on the floor."

"Let's get you a drink then." He grins and leads the way.

I practically chug my first glass of wine.

Ben and I mingle around for a little while. Cynthia and little Devon came for the night and are staying at the hotel. Sharing a room, I hear.

We finally make it to the wooden dance floor about an hour later. Wine glass in hand, I hang my arms over his shoulders and we sway to the cover band's version of Wonderful Tonight. It's cliché, but what isn't cliché about wedding reception music?

"I want to talk to you later," he says in my ear in a tone I'm all too familiar with, and I can only imagine that it's about what I said earlier.

"Alright. I'll have my personal assistant arrange it," I joke with a smile.

"Ha. Ha. I've been thinking about what you said."

I place a finger over his perfect lips. "I don't know what you're talking about."

The wine made me do it. He knows that there's more to what I'm saying, because he waits for me to continue.

I don't hold back, saying, "We're having such a good time. I want to the rest of the night to be easy. Okay? The only complications I'll accept involve getting out of this dress. You don't have to talk to me about anything later, Ben. We don't have to discuss it tonight. Please?"

I beg. "Can we please just do this tonight? Let's just be two normal *lovers* drinking and dancing at a fantastic reception. This may be the last one I see. Just put a pin in it and be here. With me. Right now."

He holds me tighter, and I take that as his agreement.

So 'lovers' is growing on me. Maybe it's genetic.

If Ben wanted me to tell him how I feel about things, he finally got it. Apparently, if you ever want to get something out of me, then take me to Martha's Vineyard.

He remains quiet as he leads us around the floor, caressing my back as we dance. His silence drives me mad, so I lean back to find his eyes.

"Is that okay, Ben? Whatever you think you need to tell me can wait until tomorrow. Let's have fun."

He looks conflicted, so I rub my thumb through his wrinkled brow.

"Tomorrow." I kiss him. I stroke my hand across his cheek, waiting for his answer.

He sighs, and I hear the burden weighing on him when he finally says, "Tomorrow." He squeezes his eye shut tight for a minute, nuzzling his face in my palm. When he reopens them, he takes my hand in his, kissing my wrist first, and says, "Let's have some fun, baby."

Whatever it is, he doesn't let it affect the rest of our night. We dance to almost every song. With the dance floor filled, we act like fools doing old dances from college and before.

Winnie and Cooper leave before most of us do. We hug and wish them a happy honeymoon. Ben and I close down the party.

We laugh through the halls on the way to Ben's room and make asses out of ourselves in the elevator when we get busted mid-kiss by an elderly couple.

They're cool though, telling us, "Have a good night. Just try to make it to your room first."

We laugh even harder, falling through his door.

Our energy levels drop rapidly as we hit his bed. We lie on our sides, having sex like tired spoons, and crash the minute we are done. We don't move an inch until morning.

CHAPTER
Thirty-Three

I LIE HERE SOMEWHERE between asleep and awake in bed with Ben, feeling warm and perfectly at peace. The rise and fall of his chest is hypnotic, and I stay as still as I can, not wanting to disturb him.

Our clothes are thrown all over the room like we ejected from them in an emergency last night. Which we sort of did. We were a little tipsy and drunk off of the fun and excitement brought on by the wedding.

It's probably midmorning, because the sun is coming around the side of the blackout-style curtains, strong and bright. I hear vacuuming in the hallway and carts being pushed past the door.

Looking around the room, I see a piece of paper slide under the door and presume it is the checkout sheet. I get up, thinking I'll take a shower and go get us some breakfast.

We made plans to ride back to the city together since the newlyweds are leaving straight from here for their honeymoon in St. Lucia.

First, I slip my legs free and gently unwrap Ben's big arm from around my body. Like I'm doing some sort of bed limbo, I slink my way out.

Stepping onto the carpet as quietly as I can, I make my way over to the bar, where my phone is. As I suspected, it is almost ten, and we are to be checked out by noon. I want to make sure my information is right, so I walk over to the folded paper that is lying on the carpet just inside the room.

When I read it, at first I think maybe I am still asleep and I'm just having a really fucked-up dream. I almost laugh out loud seeing that it reads Benjamin Meade.

I'm lost and sink to the rough floor, forgetting that I'm utterly nude.

Confusion drowns me.

Why does it say that?

How could the hotel make a mistake like this?

The only Meade I know is Dr. Evil, and Dr. Meade wasn't even invited. Besides that, his name is Mark. Mark Meade.

This has to be a weird coincidence.

Has my vision gone haywire and now I'm seeing things that aren't really here? It doesn't make any sense.

I stare at the paper—willing it to say something else, willing it to rewrite itself—for minutes before I finally register that Ben is saying my name.

"Tatum. What is that?" He hurriedly sits up.

In a voice that isn't my own, I answer. "It's a room receipt. Ben, it says Benjamin Meade on it. Why does it say Benjamin Meade on it?" My pulse quickens and a thin sweat breaks out over my hot skin. I'm so confused, but my gut tells me this isn't a freak accident

Finding courage to look at him, I see his head is hanging forward and he's methodically running both hands through his hair. From his reaction, I can predict I'm not going to like any of this.

"Just hold on. Please," he pleads.

"Why does it say this?!" I shout. "Just tell me it's a mistake. Tell me it's a big fucking mistake, Ben!"

As if my volume propels me into action, I'm on my feet again. I don't know what I'm looking for. My clothes? My shoes? A good enough reason to make this all a misunderstanding?

"Slow down. Please." He finds a pair of jeans and hops into them, slowly coming towards me at the same time, pulling them up the rest of the way with one hand, and reaching for me with the other.

I flinch back. How is his last name Meade?

"What did you do?" I petrify right there while staring at him. "Tell me! What did you do?!"

"Just calm down and let me explain, baby."

I don't know what part ignites the flash of red. It might be the "calm down." It might be the "baby." It's quite possibly the fact that I am somehow a huge fool.

"Don't. Don't," I say as he comes closer still. "Where are my clothes? I've got to go." I locate my dress and that's good enough. I just need my phone and my purse. It has my room key. "Don't," I say one more time as he makes another play in my direction.

"I didn't know how to tell you. I messed up. It just got out of hand." He's speaking so fast and following me around, ducking and swerving to land in my eye line.

"I. Said. Don't." I whisper so quietly that I'm not sure he even hears it. It takes every ounce of energy I can summon, as it's draining away so fast, just to hold back my angry tears. I have to leave. I have to get out of here before it all hits me for real.

"We thought it was best to tell you after the wedding. Please. We didn't want to hurt you." His usually calm and collected voice is broken and frantic.

So close to the door, now having my dress on and my things in my hand, I pause. Fuck my shoes. They'd take forever to put on anyway. Then one word registers in what he's just said.

We.

That one word kills my forward motion. It is a loaded bullet. Coincidentally, I know it will pierce me through the back.

Like anyone, I know the sound of my own voice. The woman's voice that leaves my lips isn't mine. She is ripping in half, her voice sounding of shredding hope and agony. In a sound so low, I ask, "You said 'we,' didn't you? Dammit, you said 'we.'" My tears pour hot on my cheeks and my face contorts. "Who are you?"

"Benjamin Meade. Please don't leave, Tatum. Please, let me talk to you. Let me explain. Let me apologize. Cooper thought—"

I clutch my stomach at the mention of my brother's name. This is all impossible.

"Cooper thought what?" I choke out.

"Turn around. Look at me."

Ben's voice is pleading, and my heart wants to look. I want to see if he looks like the Ben I know, but I can't.

"No. Are you Dr. Meade's son?" I can't make heads or tails. Dr. Meade isn't old enough to have a child our age, surely. Ben told me about his mother and father and his... "He's your brother, isn't he?"

"He is." From the closeness, I can sense that Ben is behind me. I can almost feel his hand touching my skin, but it isn't there. Only his shaky voice touches my ears.

"And he knew, too? Why?" I speak to the door.

"I don't know. I just wanted to talk to you that day. I didn't know you were hiring anyone."

"What were you doing in Washington?"

"Please stay." I hear the agony he feels, but I'm too numb to care.

"Answer me. Fuck. For once, just tell me!"

"I'm a doctor—a therapist. I work with injured vets. Well, I did, anyway."

"Is that why Dr. Meade, you brother—whatever—sent you?"

"He didn't send me, Tatum. He didn't even know I went to see you until later." His confession is quiet and measured.

My voice trembles as a more brutal betrayal surfaces in my heart. "And Cooper? When did he find out?"

"At his bachelor party. I told him everything."

Why didn't Ben tell me? Why didn't Cooper tell me?

I can't believe that my own brother didn't tell me the truth. Didn't warn me that I was being lied to. That I fell in love with a stranger.

"And?" I question, desperate for some logic.

"And he said that I had to tell you or he would. I told him I'd tell you after the wedding. I didn't want to ruin everything. Please believe me. I don't want to hurt you or mess everything up. I just... I fucked up, baby." I hear a sob choke him.

"Don't call me that!" I spit, hardened. I reach for the door, having heard enough. I want to go home. I want to crawl into a hole where no one will find me and disappear.

"You love me, Tatum. You have to let me fix this." Sorrow clings to his words.

I've never sounded colder than I do when I say, "I don't love you. I don't even know you. I wish I would have told you to leave that day. I wish I'd never met you."

"That's not true. You're just angry." I hear an agonized crack in his deep voice and it breaks my heart even more.

Opening the door, I walk out, but I can't resist looking at him. He's on the floor now, on one knee, arms slack at his sides. The eyes that I grew to cherish are hollow, red, and dim.

I dreamt of Ben on one knee, and the image of him smiling hopefully is shattered and replaced with the one in front of me, my precious memory burglarized.

He mouths, "Please," steadily over and over before his haunted eyes meet mine.

"You're fired." Then I laugh like a madwoman. "I'm sure you'll find something, Dr. Meade."

"I love you, Tatum," are the last four words I hear out of his mouth. Something about that both fills and drains my soul at the same time.

My shaky hands shut the door before I can change my mind. I'm not sure how they're capable, but my legs sprint me down the halls, and when I get to my room, I crawl into my bed.

I call the desk, pay for another night's stay, and instruct them to tell anyone who asks that I've left.

Not long after that, as I am lying there, staring out of focus at the ceiling, Ben's voice comes through my door. First, I think I'm hallucinating. My mind must be conjuring up the sound because I want to hear it so badly.

"I'm so sorry. You mean everything. I'll tell you everything, baby. Please just let me in."

I hold my breath, but only because I can't stop my heart from beating. I shut my eyes tight and will him away and for it all not to be true.

"Tatum, if you're in there, please... I know you're hurting. Let me make this right."

A member of the staff informs him that I've already checked out. Ben apologizes and says that he didn't know.

Then he's gone.

Another rush of misery and pain consumes me and I weep.

Though I only woke up an hour ago, it seems like I haven't slept in years. I don't turn the TV on. I don't shower. I don't eat.

I'm just here, replaying this morning and the last three months over and over. It was only three months.

I probably wasn't even in love with him.

It was probably just purely physical.

Why would he lie to me like that? Why would Dr. Meade let him? Why didn't my brother tell me?

My emotions alternate between seething mad and anguished. That's the truth of it. I'm so sad. I'm sad that I finally found someone who I thought saw me. The real me. And despite all my shit, I thought he wanted me anyway.

I am a blind fool—in more ways than one.

CHAPTER
Thirty-Four

I CAN'T GET IN TOUCH with Cooper and Winnie unless I call their resort, which I'm not about to do. So the day after yesterday's monumental mope at the hotel, I lick my wounds and call Ray.

That poor man drives all the way to Martha's Vineyard to pick me up.

He's a saint.

I sit in the back and stay pretty quiet for most of the ride home, wondering if he knew. Did everyone know except me?

I'm sure they all got together and talked about the poor girl who thought she was dating her personal assistant, when in reality she was dating a stupid motherfucking, lying, deceiving, pain-in-the-ass therapist. If it even was dating.

I consider moving. Maybe I'll go to L.A. Maybe I'll go back to The Keys, but as the thought of the island house comes to mind, my eyes burn. Fuck The Keys. Fuck all of Florida, too. Fuck the coastlines and both our oceans. Fuck Louisiana. Fuck California and the motherfucking Goonies. They all make my eyes burn.

The car ride sucks. I think Ray picked up on something being wrong at the very least, but he doesn't utter a word. When we're about ten miles outside of the city, he asks me if I need to go anywhere on the way home.

I quip, "Yeah, back in fucking time." He offers a tender, closed-lipped smile. The pitying kind.

My apartment's eerily quiet when I return. It's an added surprise to learn that I now hate this place, too. I sleep in the spare bedroom since it is the only place we neglected to make any memories or have sex.

Over the last few days, I basically move in here. There's a television and a bathroom of its own, so it isn't like I am put out. I order Mexican food from my landline and then unplug it, plugging it back in only to call one of those grocery-delivery services to bring me wine and ice cream. I love this city.

A week passes.

Phil buzzes, asking if I'm all right and telling me that Cooper called the desk to find out if I'd been home. Of course, Phil said that I had but he hadn't seen me. So he offered to check.

"Ms. Elliot, it's Phil," he says through the door, probably being paid by my prick brother or some shit like that.

"I know it's you, Phil. You just buzzed me from down-stairs and told me you were coming up. What do you need?" I ask with no inflection.

"May I come in?" His voice is too cheery, and it hurts my head.

"No."

"Are you all right? No one can get you on the telephone and they've called downstairs repeatedly."

I was afraid of that. "Sorry. Tell them I'm fine and to leave me alone."

"Cooper said he would be here tomorrow."

"Don't let him up. He's a dick."

"A dick, Ms. Elliot?" He clears his throat and regains his composure. "You've always gotten along well, I thought. Are you sure everything is all right?"

"Go away, Phil. I'll talk to them when I'm damn good and ready." It isn't his fault, and I feel a slightly bad for having put him in this awkward situation. But I'm not apologizing.

"You have flowers. I've brought them with me." He says it like it's supposed to cheer me up, but it does the opposite.

I suck my lip into my mouth, inhale, and then blow out a long stream of tormented air. "Are they from you?" Obviously, I know they're not.

"No. Of course not."

"Then I don't want them. Put them in the dumpster." Great. Now even dead foliage makes my eyes burn. Add it to the list.

"They're very pretty. Are you sure? What of the card?"

Poor Phil is only trying to do his job. I'm petulant and childish, but I can't find it in me to care enough to accept them. I don't want flowers or calls or visitors. I only want to be left alone.

Cooper buzzes from downstairs the next day, like Phil said he would. I answer. He pleads to come up and explain, but I'm not ready to talk about it and say, "Leave me alone."

"I love you, Tatum. Don't do this to yourself," he begs.

"I didn't do this to myself!" My voice rises louder than it has in over a week. "I didn't want this. I love you too, but not right now." He's dismissed, but it hurts me so to do it.

A few days later, it is Winnie downstairs. I don't know what hand she had in this, but those two idiots never kept secrets before. I'm sure she knew, too. When she rings up, that's the only thing I ask.

"Did you know?"

When she says yes, I ask her to leave.

Eventually, my worn and haggard body cleans itself, mostly just going through the motions, but it's an improvement. I rid my apartment of the empty ice cream containers and wine bottles.

I even turn my phone back on. There are hundreds of messages and texts. Many from my family and only one text from Ben. It takes me a few hours to finally read it after powering the device back up. It's short and simple.

Ben: I'm still Ben.

Then I cry again, reassuring myself that it'll be the last night of crying. That the next day, I'm leaving my apartment and getting on with things.

I'll call Neil. We'll find me another personal assistant and a new ophthalmologist. I'm going to go to work and start working on season openers for Just Kidding and try like hell not to feel the ache in my chest anymore.

Neil is more than happy to help me find another PA. He actually interviews everyone himself first and then lets me choose from three. Why didn't we do this before?

I don't bother calling Dr. Meade's office. Instead, I ask my new doctor, Dr. Meyer, to have his staff call for my records. Charlotte leaves me a few voicemails and asks me to call her back, also leaving Dr. Meade's personal cell phone number for me to call him. I never do.

I'm still a clean-break kind of girl. Some things don't ever change, and I'm a little glad to find one of them.

The Devons have been working in the office for a few weeks already. Devon and Cynthia are an official couple, approved by HR and everything. They're very cute and I hate it. My desk gets moved to the other wall that very day so that I don't have to face reception and watch their heartwarming antics.

Winnie returns to the office, bringing me chocolate and shoes. I let her in, having to know her side of the story before I'd decide if our long-term relationship can rebound. Secretly, I know deep down that I have to forgive her and Cooper eventually. However, up until then, I'm just not ready to hear any of it.

"Can I come in?" she asks timidly in my doorway on my third day back.

"Whatever." Yeah, not my most prolific moment. "Shut the door. Please."

"I like the new arrangement. It looks bigger in here." She noses around, feigning interest in the new furniture setup.

"Cut the crap, Gwendolyn. What did you know? And when did you know it?" Still not in the mood for lighthearted banter, I go straight to the point.

"Honestly, Tatum, I didn't know until our wedding night. After we—" I gag and that stops her before she says anything that will gross me out. She knows the rules. "Well, you know, we were talking about what you'd told me earlier about how you are in—" My hand flies up to indicate that there will be no talk of what I said. This was a bad idea. "Right. Anyway, we were talking about *that* and Cooper said that *he* had said *that* same thing to him about you and spilled his guts to him a few weeks ago." She sits down atop her favorite chair in front of my desk tentatively. "I was pretty pissed, Tate. Cooper told *him* that if *he* didn't tell you by the time we were back we were going to, but Be—" My shaking hand cuts through the air again, waving for her to halt once more. "Right. *He* said *he* was telling you after the wedding that night."

Considering that she didn't know much sooner than I did, I side with cutting her some slack. She didn't have a chance.

"Well, since you didn't have much time to tell me *and* it was your wedding day, you're off the hook."

She smiles before she thinks better of her timing and tames it down to a sympathetic grin. "What about Cooper? He's really worried and really, really sorry, Tatum. Will you please talk to him? He looks like shit." Winnie's plight is pretty convincing.

And I miss my brother.

"Alright, I'll call him," I relent.

"So how are you?" I can see the earnest concern in her pretty brown eyes.

"I'm fine." I brush some dust that isn't there off my desk and steel myself. "The season opener looks to be pretty badass. Wes will be in tomorrow and we can go over everything we have so far. The Devons shot a bunch of off-the-wall things over the summer. It's going to be a great season." All of that is true, and it's all I've got right now.

"That's good, but you didn't answer my question. How are you doing?" Winnie asks, pointing at me, giving me the 'tell me' best-friend eyes.

I look to the sky for some help or something, because I have to tell her. That bitch won't let up. I can already feel that all-too-common swell of emotion in my gut.

"Well, I lost my personal assistant, my boyfriend, and my ophthalmologist of over twelve years. What's left of my sight is tanking and my heart is broken." I have to stop and take a deep breath. I squeak out, "So, I've been better." My lip does that Goddamned twitchy thing that I know means the burning eyes are straight ahead and I try to stop, actively attempting to right my face.

Winnie walks around the desk and plops her big, beautiful ass on my lap, smoothing away my hair from my face. "Have you talked to him?"

"No. I don't want to," I pout against my will. Why did I let her in here?

"Don't you think that he could explain things?" Her voice is soft and soothing as she tries to comfort me.

I break a little, and I don't hide the tears from her, because I can't. "He lied to me, Winnie. He was a therapist. He was probably just trying to fix me, but he just broke me more. I feel so stupid. I thought I loved him, but I didn't even know him. How dumb is that?"

Only good friends will cry with you, and Winnie's the best. She's blubbering and reaching for the whole box of Kleenex, putting them on her lap, which is perched on top of mine.

"It all couldn't have been lies. He loves you too. I just know it. Tate, he told Cooper that he does."

"He didn't tell me." Then I correct, "Well, he told me once." I meet her mascara-messed eyes with mine. "When I left."

She makes a sympathetic O-face, squeezing my shoulders in a hug. "You poor thing."

"He was probably just saying it to get me to stay. I don't know." That's the part that always confuses me.

I shake my head to clear it. Blowing my nose, I kick Winnie off of me.

"I'm going to be fine. I have you guys." I hope that'll be

enough. "Besides, he only texted me once and I haven't heard from him."

"Cooper called him and left him a message. He didn't call back but sent a text the next day asking if you were okay." Her voice rises towards the end. Winnie's hopeful face is asking me what I think.

"Did my ass-hat brother text him back?"

She shakes her head. "He didn't know what to say."

When Winnie finally leaves my office, I send Cooper a message.

Me: You're a dick. I still love you though.

He replies quickly.

Cooper: I love you, too, Tater.

CHAPTER
Thirty-Five

COOPER AND I MAKE UP. He apologizes over and over, and frankly, I start feeling bad for him. He's my brother and I know that he didn't mean to hurt me. He even stood up for Ben, saying that I should have heard him out.

I put the kibosh on that conversation and compromise to only be his sister again if he doesn't bring it up anymore.

Just Kidding starts the season with amazing momentum and is bought into syndication. Reruns! That doesn't mean a lot to most, but to me it means that we did something right. The new shows are getting a lot of attention, and Winnie, Wes, and I even elect to hire a few new cast members.

A couple of weeks into the season, Winnie receives a movie offer and swears to keep her commitments to the show, but after Wes and I band together and promise to fire her if she doesn't take the offer, she finally accepts.

My little Winnie will be filming a movie this winter where she's the lead. It's a romantic comedy, so I'm not going to see it even if my stupid eyes still work. I still don't have the stomach to watch anything to do with fictionally happy people.

I've started seeing a Braille tutor, and I'm learning how to use a handy little device to type, should my sight fall away completely.

I'm taking care of business. And truthfully, I'm quite proud. I can either face this thing head-on or let it drag me under. It took a little while after Coop and Winnie's wedding for me to get back on track, but I'm actually feeling strong.

Still, the days have turned into weeks and then into months, but I haven't heard from him. Not once.

The only thing I have left is the damn letter. Phil pitched the flowers as instructed, but he didn't scrap the letter that had been tucked inside of them. Instead, he put it in my mailbox.

I knew it was from him, the handwriting it too familiar. I left it in mailbox, deciding that was a good place for it to stay.

I told my new assistant, Jenn, when she was hired to leave it in there when she brings my mail up, but yesterday she brought it up anyway. I found it on the counter.

We're supposed to get a massive storm, and I've told Jenn to cut out early. Everyone is making a huge deal out of it, but I just bought more wine and ice cream.

Sandy-schmandy. Hurricane Sandy will be yesterday's news by tomorrow.

The weather stations are predicting it to be the biggest hurricane to hit New York, maybe ever. But I'm a tough New Yorker and pretty much think that they're talking bullshit. I saw people at the store buying water and milk just like they did for Irene, insisting that the world was going to end.

Most of the schools are already canceled for tomorrow, and we told everyone to just stay home. It began raining this afternoon, and into the evening it is still coming down in sheets.

Cooper calls to see what my plan is and to know if I want to go there. I refuse, saying that I'm fine and not to worry. It's just a storm.

The more wine I drink, the more Ben's letter beckons to me from the kitchen.

Read me. Tick-tock. Drink. Repeat.

I finally break down and rip it open. I don't even bother sitting, choosing to stand and read it at the counter.

Tatum,

I wish I would have caught you before you left yesterday. I came by your room. It's killing me that I'm writing you all of this in a letter, but I'm at a loss for what to do.

My name is Benjamin Meade. Dr. Benjamin Meade—for the sake of clarity.

I know you don't remember the first day we met. You were leaving my brother's office. I'd met him in the city for lunch and you had an appointment with him after we returned. I know it wasn't right, but I eavesdropped on the whole thing. Something about you seized me. I couldn't help myself. I heard your voice laughing and I was so captivated. (I still am.)

My heart recognized yours even before we'd met, I think.

You were gone. Or I thought so, until you ran into me and knocked me down. Remember?

That was me. Ben Meade. I was still a student. You were so frantic and perfectly insane. You had on a blue dress and looked beautiful. I remember, you had on these funny underwear and were running late for an interview. You were a force I couldn't tear my eyes from.

We parted that day, and I wondered for the longest time where the funny girl was or what you were doing. What would have happened if I'd taken that cab with you or got your phone number.

That one encounter always stood out in my mind. You didn't know it then, and you wouldn't know it now if I weren't telling you, but just the thought of you helped me through a lot of rough times.

My best friend, Keith Harris, who I told you a little about, came back from Afghanistan that week you ran into me. Well, what was left of him did. I don't think he really ever came back to tell you the truth. He was broken and hurt far greater than the hospitals could mend.

I had gone to school to become a therapist, mostly to help people like my parents deal with life and help trauma patients recover.

But I couldn't help Keith. I was there for him as much as I could've been, but eventually he died of an overdose.

I left my residency and job and Washington. I came to New York to get away for a while and figure out things.

I was furious at myself. I couldn't help him and I was trained to. I let him down, and that was something I couldn't face.

Then, I heard your voice again. I was in my brother's office bringing by some papers for my apartment and you were there. I stayed in the back.

That was another mistake. I should have just gone up and said hello to you that day. I should have. I didn't. I heard my brother telling you about seeing a psychiatrist and how you didn't want to. I heard everything you talked about. And I agreed.

It was the wrong thing, but I looked up your address in their files after you left. I had to see you. Somehow get to know you.

It was totally coincidental that you were having interviews that day. I still don't know what drew me to your door. I didn't know what I'd say when you opened the door or if you would even be home. That part is a mystery to even me.

I'm sorry I didn't tell you. I wanted to so many times. In Seattle, when I was dealing with grief about Keith, I wanted to tell you then. There were other times too, almost every day. I should have told you that I was taking trips to Washington to help Keith's parents. He left a mess of everything. I feel responsible, like I have to clean it up. I owe them that much.

I'm sorry that I wasn't strong enough to be myself, to be the man you deserve. It was stupid. The irony of me telling you to open up isn't lost on me. I know how hard it was for you. Hell, it was so hard that I couldn't even do it.

I was lost, too. I'd lost my best friend when I should have been the one to help him. So, when I saw an opportunity to start over, even for just a little while, I took it.

Tatum, I love you. I've loved you for so long.

I should have told you. I wanted to tell you in the closet that night, but I just couldn't say those three words before I told you the truth.

I messed it all up. I should have come clean on day one or any of those times you tried to get me to. And I'm so sorry. I'm sorry I hurt you. I'm sorry I hurt us, because I think we're the real thing.

I'm sorry I didn't trust us enough to tell you sooner, but if I had to do it over and miss out on waking up with you in my arms or hearing you tell me you love me...I would do it again. Every second I spent with you made me better. You healed me.

There's nothing more that I want than to be the one you can lean on. The one you rely on. There's no one else I want to kiss or touch or laugh with. I'm in deeper than I ever dreamed. I don't know how to recover from this. I want you. I want us, for always.

I'm so in love with you.

Forgive me.

Your,

Benny

———————•———————

I've read it over and over for an hour. His words. The truth that I wanted to know all along. I've cried hundreds of tears and now my shirt is wet around the collar.

The ache from missing him in this moment is crippling. The thought of never seeing or talking to him again has been like a lead weight in my chest, ever present and growing every day.

I can pretend that it doesn't hurt in front of most people. I can even fool myself for small pieces of time.

Then, I see him in my kitchen cooking. My phone will ring and I'll pray that it's him. I sometimes look at myself in the mirror after a shower and gaze at the places he last touched, closing my eyes and trying like hell to feel him.

I crave him so badly that I almost don't care what he did or that he lied to me for so long.

After reading and rereading the note, I know that I have to call him. If that was the note from the flowers Phil brought up, like I know it is, then he wrote it over two months ago.

What if he's given up? Moved away? Changed his mind?

I look out the windows and all I can see is the rain pelting the streets below. The street lights shake and the gutters along the streets look like rivers. I wonder where he is.

I wish he were with me.

I want him with me.

I need him with me.

I need my phone! I have to talk to him. I love him.

When I pick up my phone to call his number, I only hesitate for a second out of fear. The kind of fear that Cooper told me about. The kind that means something. The kind of fear you only get from love.

I'm going to be strong. I'm going to tell him what I want. I have to try or I'll always wonder if I'm the one who made the biggest mistake of all.

I press the numbers in perfect sequence, like I dialed them yesterday, but the line is full of static and goes into this beeping bullshit. I try again. What the hell!?

I go to my home phone and dial his number from there, hoping that I can at least get a connection. Not knowing what I'm going to say if he answers, I run through the motion of his numbers for the third time in only seconds.

It finally rings, but only once before he answers. "Tatum?"

It's him. His voice. My Ben.

"Hi."

"Are you all right?" His end of the line sounds noisy and he's yelling into his cell. "Can't hear you!"

"Where are you?"

"I'm walking back to my place. Where are you?"

"I'm home." I can't wait any longer and shout a little, wanting him to hear me. "Ben, I miss you." My voice cracks.

"You do?" It's still so staticky.

"I do!" The line clears, but I still shout. "I miss you!"

He chuckles, and for the first time in weeks, I think there's blood pumping through my veins again. "I'll be there in ten minutes." He hangs up.

Our places aren't that far apart, but the storm is gaining strength. The flickering lights dim before going off few times and then they come back on. The mighty wind blows hard enough that it sounds like screeching against my windows.

The funny thing is that I can't move. I know that I should probably be getting candles ready or looking for my flashlights, but who am I kidding? I'm damn near blind and not too worried about the dark. I've been readying myself for it for a long time.

I buzz down to Phil and tell him that Ben is coming and to just let him up.

The minutes tick by endlessly. Ten. Fifteen. Twenty.

Like a child waiting for a parent to get home from work, I'm ready and open the door the second he knocks.

The very sight of him steals my breath away. Ben's here in the hall, drenched, water pouring off of him. He chases his breath and looks worn.

"I don't like storms," he reminds me.

"I know. Come in here." I show him in and go for towels. I remember that he has some clothes left behind and fetch them for him as well. "Here, get dry. You'll get sick."

His hair is a little longer than it was the last time I saw him and he's sporting a short beard. I want to touch it but control my hands. I don't know what to say or do.

I totally didn't think this through. What if he hasn't gotten over it? What if he is mad at me too since I just gave up and didn't let him explain?

The only way to know was to ask. No more hiding.

When he returns to the living room, he's drying his hair with a towel. He says, "I was looking for these," gesturing to the dry pajama pants and t-shirt he now wears. "I missed 'em." He's kind of smiling, and oh, how I've missed it.

"They were here. I should have called you." I start towards him.

"Tatum, I understand. What I did... It was..."

"Wrong," I finish for him.

His shoulders deflate some. "Yeah."

"So..." I say, shifting my weight back and forth from one foot to the other.

He looks shocked. "So? I didn't tell you my real name. That's a little bit bigger than *so*."

"I know, but... I just read your letter."

He looks to the table where it sits and to the counter where the ripped-open envelope lies.

"You just read it today?" His voice is relieved.

"Mmm hmmm. I just couldn't do it yet. It hurt too much." My shaking fucking lip.

Ben closes the space between us just as the lights go out. We face each other there in the dark.

"But then I just missed you and I wanted to know what it said."

He exhales his words like he's been holding them for weeks. "You missed me?"

"I just wasn't ready for the truth yet. I was scared to find out if everything you'd said to me was shit, you know?" I sobbed. "I just wanted it to be true so bad."

"It was, baby. I just messed up. It was us." His arms reach out to my arms and he shakes them a little like he's trying to get my attention. "Tatum, that was us. That was all us."

"It was?" I can't help but cry. Hot tears roll down my cheeks and neck in steady streams that lead right to my heart. "Do you really love me?"

"More every day. I thought if I just gave you some space you'd want to talk. When you didn't, I just kept waiting. Hoping." His voice quivers. "I want you."

"What do we do?" Such a simple question. I don't want to start over. I don't want to say goodbye. I just want to go back to where we already were.

The thunder claps and rattles the windows. I take his hand and move through my apartment with ease, knowing where everything is. Ben bumps along behind me as I pull him.

"We should get away from those windows." I walk us into the closet.

I don't know why, but it seems like the safest place, with no glass to shatter from the beating that the wind dishes out.

Kneeling down onto the floor, I drag him down with me. It feels a little like déjà vu. I'm in the same spot he found me in only a few months ago. Where he kissed me for the first time. Where I told him that I was all in.

"Remember what you said in here that night, Ben?" I ask, thinking back to my drunken pity party.

He brings a hand to my face and runs his fingers through my hair. "I remember."

"Then prove it. You said that you didn't want just part of me, that you wanted all of me and that you'd never stop." I climb over to his lap. "Please. Please don't stop."

"God knows, Tatum. I can't. I won't." His breaths rush out with his words.

I need him. My lips crush into his. I want him to be mine again.

To hell with what happened. He was who I needed. He is who I need.

Between our broken kisses, he declares, "I'm sorry, baby. I never meant to hurt you. I love you."

"I love you," I breathe heavily with every ounce of emotion I have back into his mouth.

He promises, "I'll fix it. I love you."

"Just trust me." It's funny coming from my mouth. I trust people, close people, but I never really thought about someone else trusting me before. "Please, I want all of you. I want the Ben who makes funny stories up about the strangers with me. I want the Ben who wears glasses because he knows I like looking at him in them and not because he needs them. I want the Ben who brings me schmear. Benny, I want the bad parts, too." Then my lips find his again, like I was thirsty for only him for months and I was just now getting a precious sip. "I want you."

"I'm yours, baby. Everything. No more secrets. No more lies. I swear, I'll tell you so much about me you'll change your mind and tell me to leave. Honest, you get everything." He thumbs away my tears and kisses my eyes tenderly. "No more crying."

We wait the storm out in my closet, talking and spilling our guts to one another. He holds me to him the whole time.

He tells me about how his brother almost kicked his ass when he learned about what he'd done. Picturing Dr. Meade as his brother is strange, but after I think on it awhile, I can see it.

I tell him about seeing my new doctors and the things I learned while we were apart. He listens closely as I tell him about Jenn, my new PA, and how she's pretty good but I've had better.

He's planning to finish his residency in NYC and getting rid of his place in D.C.

Late that night, we fall asleep in the middle of a hurricane in New York City. It is the best sleep I've had in a long time. Around five or six in the morning, I sense him picking me up and carrying me to my bed. He climbs in with me and we sleep some more.

It's like coming home.

It's not until a few hours later that I realize how bad the storm actually was. Upon getting up, I see outside and discover that the streets are a mess. Garbage and litter, boxes and junk thrown around all over. The awnings ripped off the building across the street from mine, and even some windows blown out down the block.

We don't leave my apartment all day.

CHAPTER
Thirty-Six

I MADE MY PEACE with Ben's brother, the evil Dr. Meade, and returned to his care. Ben moved into my apartment around Christmas. It was silly for him to have that great big place only blocks away, when we always stayed at my place anyway.

He didn't have a lot of stuff, and I made concessions to fit him in. I lost closet space but gained a personal shampooer. Even though we didn't lose that much time, we made up for every minute apart.

I think I benefited from the apartment merge more than he did. His books line my bookshelves, where tchotchkes and things were previously displayed. The hardbacks are an improvement to my apartment—just like Ben is to my life.

Ben continues to teach me how to cook, but kept it pretty basic after my chili disaster. He literally called his Moo-Moo to see if there was anything we could do to salvage it. She told him to put it in the trash. He said that we will try again, but he can make the chili from there on out.

We went to Ben's parents' house on Thanksgiving. It was strange seeing my ophthalmologist outside of his office, but it was also kind of nice. The familiarity was comfortable.

It's fascinating to watch Ben's parents. Gayle and Bill move effortlessly around their home, and it gives me a sense of peace. Both of them are smart, and they actually read a lot. They gave me a few book printed in Braille so I can practice.

When Gayle handed them to me, I was thankful that they couldn't see me blush. Ben's really ruined me on reading. We can never get very far—only a few pages at a time.

Cooper knocked up Winnie that winter on accident. His words, not mine. Winnie still did the movie since she wasn't showing and got a few pretty great award nominations for best comedic actress. She didn't win, but she was happy all the same.

Just Kidding lasted one more season. Then the Devons got their own show on a cable network and took Neil and Cynthia with them when they left for California. We still talk often, and it isn't uncommon for them to call when they're stuck on something they're working on, or arguing about.

Devon and Cynthia got married about a year after their move. You're welcome, Mr. and Mrs. Little Devon.

My sight dropped off a little more over those years but never left me completely blind. It's a struggle at times, but I'm also lucky.

Ben proposed to me one night while lying in bed. There was nothing showy about it. He said, "You're it for me, Tatum. Please be my wife. I love you." How could I say no to that? I wouldn't have anyway.

I was fortunate enough to see, with my own eyes, the tears that fell from Ben's on our wedding day as I walked down the aisle towards him—a precious gift I thank God for every day. He cried through the entire ceremony. He's a pussy like me.

Between you and me, it made me love him more.

I wore a killer custom-made gown from an upcoming designer Winnie had recommended. It was a mermaid-style strapless dress that my dad said made me look like a classic movie star. I wore my hair down since it had grown out some and had it styled in soft waves.

As he promised me in his personal vows to "give me all of himself, guard my heart like it was his own, and laugh at all my ridiculous jokes," he slipped a ring on my finger and made me

Mrs. Tatum Meade.

I'll proudly wear both—the name and the jewelry—for the rest of my life.

I remember meeting Ben on that first day. I mean, I didn't remember him when we met again, but I remember that day and the guy who tried to grab my ass on the street. I tease him and tell him that I knew the whole time, but he knows better.

Some days are more challenging than others, but I've found that with acceptance comes strength. With the support of everyone I know, I haven't lost an ounce of my independence.

I wake up every day cloaked in the love of a truly good man who adores me, and that means more to me than seeing the whole world. I see his love with my heart, not my eyes, and I don't have to memorize it, because it isn't going anywhere.

Sometimes a few things have to fade out to make room for better ones to fade in.

EPILOGUE

MY WIFE IS MANY THINGS. She's smart and as sharp as glass. She's forgiving. She's genuine. And she's the sexiest thing I'll never deserve. People gravitate towards her like they do to fireworks on the Fourth of July. And for the same reasons—they're both surprising, loud, and so beautiful.

It's hard to find a girl who stimulates your mind and wants to have sex with the lights on. So if you find one, keep her. There's never a dull moment.

I've learned so much about myself through my life with her. From our wedding day to the day our boy Harris was born, she's showed me how love can grow and amplify with every passing second. I'll never forget her first words to him when they put him on her chest.

"I see you, little guy. I get to see you," she whispered to him like a tired soldier, crying and battered from twenty-six hours of labor, but smiling anyway. "I'm your momma. This guy might say he's your daddy, but he has a bad time with names."

She's a brilliant mother. Tatum worried and fretted about not being able to care for him, but that woman could hear the slightest movement in his crib and was by his side in the blink of an eye. She's magnificent.

She also cussed every time he pooped for the first year, so it came as no surprise when his first sentence was, "Shit, Momma." Our sides hurt for days after that one.

She said that, since he was already funny when he first started talking, she'd have to work on her material. Harris stole her show.

They are so much alike. I have two forces of nature to yield to now on a daily basis. He throws wild fits when he can't get out what he wants or feels. That must be genetic. She laughs under her breath, but she knows how to talk him down from that three-year-old ledge he works himself out onto.

We're a happy family. I'm a lucky man. My wife loves me— this I know. She tells me all the time, and it's true.

The End

ACKNOWLEDGMENTS

Writing this book, my first book, has been an epic learning experience. Without the advice and support from the following, I wouldn't have made it through.

Thank you, readers. Lovers of romance, you own me now.

I'd like to thank the blogs and bloggers. Natalee and Kiki at Read This ~ Hear That, Kat at Momma Romance, Malory at Loverly's Book Blog, Bianca at Biblo Belles Book Blog, Autumn at The Book Trollop, Sandie and Book Boyfriends Reviewers, Mickey at I'm A Book Shark, Love N. Books, Brilliantly Novel, Words For Worms, Bookish Temptations, Turning The Pages, Natasha is a Book Junkie, Aestas Book Blogger, Ana's Attic Book Blog, Maryse's Book Blog and countless others. Some of you I'm close with and some I just loved. Reading your reviews and reviewing along side of you, as books over the past few years came out, was not only fun, but an education for writing my own. So, thank you.

I have to thank my amazing IRAC family, especially the OGs. You're advice, cheerleading and all around friendship means everything. I'm so lucky I was sprinting on Twitter one day. I'm equally thankful for Tumblr Inspirations. Our group is a game changer for me. Talented women, I love you.

Tessa Teevan, thank you for inviting Tatum and Ben into your wonderful publication, Incinerate. I'm forever grateful.

To the wonderful companies that literally made this book with me, thank you. Ari at Cover It! Designs my cover is beautiful and *is* Tatum and Ben. Mickey, at Mickey Reed Edits, you're kindness and hand-holding made this book what it is. And to Stacey Blake at Self Publishing Editing and Formatting Services, thank you.

Jennifer Beach, my beta and my friend. You're gentle nudges pushed me to the finish line and for that I'm forever grateful. Your blog, Back Off My Books, has been the flagship supporter of this novel and there isn't anything I can type here that would be enough. Thank you. Thank you. Thank you.

I want to thank my Mom and my sissy. Look! See what I can do.

I have to acknowledge my friends and family, that I love- the Mabies, Millers, Johnstons, Cates, Bevi, Fishers, Meyers, my fellow Kinderhookers, my biggest fans- the Goobie girls, my PDH & FA family, and my community. You believed in me, sometimes when I didn't. Better people in this world, I will not find.

Natalie, a.k.a Author N.A. Alcorn, my partner in crime. You've motivated me and cheered me on every single step of the way. Meeting you was a hinge in my life. I have no doubt that we'll be writing old lady smut someday, along side each other in a nursing home causing havoc galore. You're permanent, Natalie.

To my sweet husband. You're my everything. *Fifty-five cents, baby.* Let's go on tour.

ABOUT
the Author

M. Mabie lives in Illinois with her husband. She loves reading and writing romance, and she's an active member of the Indie Author Romance Chicks. She cares about politics but will not discuss them in public. She uses the same fork at every meal, watches Wayne's World while cleaning, and lets her dog sleep on her head. M. Mabie has never been accused of being tight lipped or shy. In fact, if you listen very closely, you can probably hear her flapping her gums.

You're encouraged to contact M. Mabie about her future works, as well as this one.

http://www.mmabie.com
http://www.facebook.com/AuthorMMabie
http://www.twitter.com/AuthorMMabie

CPSIA information can be obtained at www.ICGtesting.com
Printed in the USA
LVOW11s1632120216

474867LV00006B/568/P

9 781496 035158